1950: Much-decorated Col. L. B. "Chesty" Puller surveys a field of battle with the commander of the United Nations forces in Korea, Gen. Douglas MacArthur. General MacArthur would be relieved of command ten months later by President Truman. (Bettman Archive)

1951: Perhaps the most zany and popular show on television, *I Love Lucy*, starring Lucille Ball and Desi Arnaz, premiered on October 15, 1951. After seven full seasons, the show finished in 1958 as the highest-rated show of the decade. (Culver Pictures)

1952: The jubilant victors, Vice President Richard Nixon (left) and President Eisenhower, acknowledge the cheers that greeted them in Washington after their landslide victory. (Bettman Archive)

1952: "Do you want to go to the moon?" This question was just one famous phrase in the many spirited discussions between Ralph and Alice Kramden on *The Honeymooners*. The show's combination of humor and heart was embodied by its star, Jackie Gleason, ensuring the program's lasting popularity. (Bettman Archive)

1954: Posing with a few of his favorite bats, Willie Mays, the Player of the Year, leads the New York Giants to a sweep of the World Series. (Bettman Archive)

1955: Remember the twist? As the clean-cut master of ceremonies on the popular television program *American Bandstand*, Dick Clark demonstrated the latest dance moves to adoring teens and made young performers into stars. (Culver Pictures)

The American Chronicles by Robert Vaughan
Ask your bookseller for the books you have missed

THE AMERICAN CHRONICLES

VOLUME VII

COLD WAR

ROBERT VAUGHAN

BANTAM BOOKS

NEW YORK · TORONTO · LONDON · SYDNEY · AUCKLAND

COLD WAR

A Bantam Book / January 1995

ISBN 0-553-56077-8

Published simultaneously in the United States and Canada

Bantam Books are published by Bantam Books, a division of Bantam
Doubleday Dell Publishing Group, Inc. Its trademark, consisting of the
words "Bantam Books" and the portrayal of a rooster, is Registered in
U.S. Patent and Trademark Office and in other countries. Marca
Registrada. Bantam Books, 1540 Broadway, New York, New York
10036.

PRINTED IN THE UNITED STATES OF AMERICA

OPM   0 9 8 7 6 5 4 3 2 1

COLD WAR

CHAPTER ONE

Standing at the window of the Lambert Airport tower, looking out across the field through a pair of binoculars, an air traffic controller scrutinized the four-engine DC-6 in the traffic pattern for landing.

"He's turning onto final now," the controller said.

"You don't see any other traffic around, do you, Mr. Simpson?" an associate asked him.

"No," Henry Simpson replied.

"Good."

"*Uh, Lambert Tower, this is* Independence *on final,*" popped the voice of the DC-6's pilot over the loudspeaker. Normally a pilot's voice was heard only through the headset of the controller working that aircraft, but since all other traffic had been steered away to facilitate this particular landing, everyone in the tower could hear him.

1

"Roger, *Independence*. You are clear to land," Simpson said.

The pilot responded, acknowledging the call.

"His gear and flaps are down," Simpson advised the others.

"Mr. Simpson, we've had planes stacked up now for the better part of an hour. When can we bring them down?"

Simpson lowered his field glasses and looked around the control room. A half-dozen men, each in charge of a tier of airplanes, all now relegated to a holding pattern, were awaiting the landing of this one plane. "Anyone critical on fuel?" he asked.

There were no affirmative responses.

"If anyone gets that way, divert them to their alternates. Otherwise, tell them to be patient for just a few minutes longer. I'll reopen the field the moment *Independence* clears the runway."

"Yes, sir," the man who asked the question replied.

Simpson picked up a telephone and dialed a number. When it was answered he said simply, "Independence is on the ground."

In the headquarters building for World Air Transport, the secretary who took Henry Simpson's call hung up the phone, then walked across deep-pile, rose-colored carpeting to a closed door. Gold leaf on the frosted glass of the door announced:

WORLD AIR TRANSPORT
OFFICE OF THE PRESIDENT
WILLIAM CANFIELD

The secretary knocked lightly.

"Come in."

William Canfield was sitting at his desk. He was in shirtsleeves, though the jacket to his black suit was hanging on a rack just behind him. To the left of his desk was a large brown-leather sofa, where Willie's wife, Liesl, was sitting. Tina, their three-year-old daughter, was lying on the sofa with her head in Liesl's lap.

Liesl was also dressed in black, and though she was composed now, it was obvious that she had been crying, because her eyes were red and puffy.

"Mr. Canfield, the plane has landed," the secretary said.

"Thank you, Norma," Willie answered. "Notify the driver and the police escort, would you please?"

"Yes, sir, at once."

Willie stood up and slipped on his jacket.

"Are you all right?" Liesl asked.

Willie looked over at his wife and smiled. "Yes, I'm fine. How about you?"

"I'm all right," Liesl replied. Her speech retained a trace of an accent that revealed her German origin. "It's just that when I think of your poor mother, how she is going to have to carry on alone now . . . I worry for her."

"Well, she'll miss Dad, sure enough, but she's always been a very independent, very self-reliant person. She'll be okay, believe me." He held his hand out toward Liesl. "The police want us already in the car when it goes out to meet the plane."

"Very well," Liesl answered. She persuaded her daughter to sit up. "Come, Tina. It is time for us to go."

Yellow sawhorses marked SLPD TRAFFIC BARRICADE blocked the street at Market and Eleventh. The St. Louis Police Department had cordoned off a wide area around Christ Church Cathedral and wasn't letting the through traffic get any closer than two blocks away. When the big black Lincoln, which was escorted front, back, and both sides by motorcycle policemen, arrived at the barricade, one of the traffic cops quickly pulled it aside to let the entourage pass. Once the cars were through, the barrier was replaced.

A couple of telephone repairmen on the scene had watched the police turn away traffic, but neither of them had been curious enough to ask what was going on. As the Lincoln limousine drove by, one of the men stared at the small man with the rimless glasses riding in the backseat.

"Hey, Marty, son of a bitch! You know who that was? That was Truman!" he said, turning to his colleague. "I swear that was President Truman."

"Truman? Oh, yeah! Of course!" Marty replied, the light dawning.

"What do you mean, 'of course'? What are you talking about? What is Harry Truman doing in St. Louis?"

"Didn't you read the papers yesterday? I'll bet you anything Truman's here for the funeral."

"Who died?"

"Jeez, Tony, are you living under a rock or something? Bob Canfield died. You know, the guy who founded Canfield-Puritex."

"You don't say. Hell, I thought he died a long time ago. I mean, Canfield-Puritex . . . that's been going on forever, hasn't it? How old was he, anyway? Eighty? Ninety?"

"According to the paper, he was sixty-nine."

"Sixty-nine? Get outta here! Sixty-nine? That's all? I sure thought he was a lot older. I mean, what with all the money he had and everything. Just how much do you think he was worth, anyway?"

"Well, according to the newspaper," Marty said, referring again to his unimpeachable source of information, "Canfield-Puritex is one of the ten wealthiest corporations in America, and Bob Canfield was the majority stockholder. I wouldn't be surprised if he wasn't worth a hundred million dollars or more."

Tony whistled. "All that money, just from selling Corn Toasties and Dog Vittles!"

"You *have* been living under a rock," Marty scoffed. "Nobody gets that rich from a single enterprise anymore. The Canfields branched out years ago from breakfast cereal and animal feed. They've got canned and frozen vegetables and meats and candies, too. According to the article, they also own land all over the country . . . farmland down in the southern part of the state and timberland up in Oregon or Washington or some such place. And paper mills, too. Hell, Tony, every time you wipe your ass on Feathersoft toilet paper, you're putting money in Canfield's pocket. And don't forget, they also own World Air Transport."

"You know, it's kind of funny when you stop to think about it," Tony said.

"What is?"

"Well, here Bob Canfield had all that money and all, but he's lying in his coffin with empty pockets. It just goes to show you that when you come right down to it, everyone's really equal."

Marty chuckled. "Well, that's the good old U.S.A. for you. Every last one of us has an equal chance to make a hundred million—so hand me that multimeter, will you? 'Cause if we don't get this job done, the telephone company'll fire us, and we'll never make our *first* million."

Connie Canfield was waiting in one of the many small rooms at the back of the cathedral. She was alone, which was as she wanted it, though a number of well-meaning people had offered to sit with her so that she wouldn't have to be by herself. What they didn't realize was that she wasn't really alone—nor was she really there. Transported by the power of her mind, she was reliving a sweet moment from nearly fifty years earlier.

Connie was walking down the hill from the commuter station toward Statue Circle in the quadrangle—the quad, as it was known to all—of Jefferson College. It was 1904, and Jefferson was still an all-male school and several years away from being designated a university. The few females on campus were, like Connie, visitors from Mary Lindenwood College in St. Charles.

Reaching the Statue Circle, she smiled at the four young men lounging beneath the great bronze Rodin statue of Henry Spengeman, the founder of the school. The youths, Bob Canfield, J.P. Winthrop, Terry Perkins, and

David Gelbman, were seniors and, as upperclassmen, were permitted inside Statue Circle. That these four were ensconced on the pedestal itself inferred that their status was above other seniors'. Unlike the rest of the area inside Statue Circle, the pedestal wasn't reserved by tradition but had been staked out at the beginning of the school year by these four, who, by dint of their popularity, social position, athletic ability, and academic achievement, had established themselves as the crème de la crème of the senior class. They called themselves the Quad Quad, and Bob Canfield was the leader of the group.

"I'm sorry I couldn't come to the meet," Connie told them, referring to the intercollegiate track meet held earlier in the day. "But I had an exam in English Lit. How did the Quad Quad do?"

"Bob took the laurels in his event, while David came in second," J.P. answered. "Terry was second in the one hundred, and I was third."

Connie looked at Bob, her heart bursting with pride and love. "Oh, wonderful! I do wish I could have come,"

"I do wish I could have come."

"What?" a startled Connie asked. Looking toward the doorway, she saw that Demaris Hunter had entered the room and uttered the very words she herself had just been thinking. "Oh, hello, Demaris. I'm sorry, I didn't hear what you said."

The actress walked over to the settee. "I said, I was shooting a movie in Europe when the ceremony was held at Jefferson, inaugurating the Canfield School of Business. But I do wish I could have come. Under the circumstances now, I feel it was particularly rude of me to let the filming come first."

"Oh, don't be silly, Demaris. Bob was a huge fan of yours, and he understood perfectly why you couldn't come. Besides, you sent such a lovely gift for the foyer of the building." Connie gave a small, wistful laugh. "And, as I recall, Bob said he would rather have the gift anyway."

Demaris laughed, too. "That sounds like Bob. I can

just hear him saying something like that." She leaned down to embrace Connie. "Oh, Connie, if I can do anything, be of any help whatever . . ."

"Thank you, but John and Willie seem to have everything under control. It was sweet of you to come, though. It's wonderful to think of Bob having so many friends."

"The President of the United States, Governor Adlai Stevenson, Charles Wilson, Edsel Ford, Nelson Rockefeller, the head of the Petzold Media Group, the head of Tannenhower Brewery . . ." Demaris said, ticking off the names on her fingers. She gave a low whistle. "I'll say this, your husband had some pretty impressive friends."

"You included," Connie said. "You are such a dear for being here."

"There's no way I *wouldn't* be here," Demaris replied. "I was supposed to leave for Korea this morning but I told the USO to get someone else; I couldn't make it."

"Have you been to Korea before?"

"Yes, I went last Christmas with Bob Hope, so I don't feel that I'm letting people down. It's a messy little war, Connie, not at all like the last one where everyone knew what they were fighting for. I do hope we can get this one over with soon."

"Who will take your place?"

"Marcella Mills."

"Marcella Mills? I'm sure the boys will appreciate her."

Demaris smiled. "She does raise a few temperatures. Did you hear what Joan Crawford said about her?"

"No, what?"

"She said that Marcella wears clothes in a way that makes everyone a student of anatomy."

Connie chuckled. "Miss Crawford does have a way with words."

"Grandmother?" a new voice said.

Connie looked toward the door and saw her sixteen-year-old grandson, Morgan—the older child of her older child.

"Yes, dear?"

"They're about ready to start now. Dad asked me to come get you."

"Oh, thank you," Connie said, standing. She walked over to the doorway and took Morgan's arm.

"I'd better get back in there as well," Demaris said. "Please, remember: If there's anything I can do for you, just let me know."

"You're very sweet," Connie said. "Thank you for offering, but I'll be all right."

With her arm through Morgan's, Connie went back into the cathedral chancel. The church was packed with people and banked high with bouquets, wreaths, and sprays of flowers. Bob's casket sat on a catafalque in the transept. In keeping with Episcopal tradition, the casket was closed, and Connie was thankful for that. She didn't want to see her husband's face in death; all she had to do to see him alive was close her eyes . . . and she wanted to keep it that way.

Connie was well aware that everyone was looking at her as Morgan escorted her to the family pew, where her two sons, John and Willie, waited with their own families. Morgan's sister, fifteen-year-old Alicia, was having a particularly difficult time. But then, she always had been her grandfather's favorite.

Connie passed by President Truman's pew, and when he nodded almost imperceptibly to her, she nodded back. Governor Stevenson, who had recently been selected as the Democratic candidate for president, looked down awkwardly.

When Connie reached her seat, she put her arm around her granddaughter and pulled the young girl to her. Alicia silently sobbed on her grandmother's shoulder.

Faith, Alicia's mother, a tear-soaked handkerchief clutched in her right hand, reached over with her left hand and touched Connie lightly on the arm. Connie squeezed her daughter-in-law's hand for a moment, then looked at the front of the church.

The Jefferson University choir began singing the school song, "Golden Leaves on Jefferson Ground." The blend of rich voices resonated through the cathedral as if the music were coming from a host of angels. After the school anthem, the choir sang a hymn.

> "Eternal Father, strong to save,
> Whose arm hath bound the restless wave,
> Who bidd'st the mighty ocean deep
> Its own appointed limits keep:
> O hear us when we cry to thee
> For those in peril on the sea."

Though known as "The U.S. Navy Hymn," it was also one of the hymns from the Episcopal Hymnal and was Bob's favorite. After an earlier heart attack had reminded him all too forcefully of his mortality, Bob had talked with Connie about funeral arrangements, requesting her to have the hymn sung at his funeral. Since then Connie had been unable to listen to it without choking up. Today was no exception.

The last note of the song reverberated through the great stone hall of the Gothic cathedral. Several seconds of silence followed.

Someone coughed.

Out in the narthex a door closed.

A plane passed overhead, the engine drone finding its way inside.

The priest moved to the pulpit and looked out over the crowd of mourners, almost as if he were counting the house. Then he began to read:

" 'I am the resurrection and the life, saith the Lord. He that believeth in me, though he were dead, yet shall he live; and whosoever liveth and believeth in me shall never die.' "

He read several more passages, then delivered a homily. When finished, he nodded at the pew where six young college students, all wearing white carnations in their lapels, sat. They were the pallbearers, composed of past and present members of the Most Exalted Order of the Quad Quad of Jefferson University. Dutifully they stood and took their positions on each side of the coffin and bore Bob Canfield out of the gloom of the church into the daylight.

Willie watched Harry Truman take a sip of his coffee and then put the cup back in the saucer. The President's glasses reflected the sun, and for a moment Willie couldn't see his eyes. Then Truman shifted his head slightly, and Willie could see the eyes plainly. They were bright, clear, and sparkling with good humor. Willie couldn't help but wonder how, with all the adverse press the President had been getting, Truman was able to maintain that humor.

"I am a reader," Truman was saying. "Always have been, always will be. Someone used an adage about reading in an article once, and I thought it made a pretty good quote: 'All readers aren't leaders, but all leaders must be readers.' Pretty good philosophy, don't you think?" he asked the Canfield brothers.

"Yes, Mr. President, it is," John replied.

"That's the kind of sage wisdom you might find in Mr. Franklin's *Poor Richard's Almanac*." Truman took another swallow of his coffee. "Mostly I read history," he continued. "I consider myself somewhat of an historian— something John probably remembers from his days working in the White House."

"I do remember, Mr. President. You have an excellent grasp of history," John said.

Truman smiled. "I appreciate the compliment, but I'm not by any means an academic historian. I am what you might call a popular historian."

"What's the difference?" Willie asked.

"Well, I can give you what I consider to be the difference. An academic historian is expert in one field of history—say, the effect of the Industrial Revolution on the English public education system. And if you were to ask such an august gentleman a question about the Industrial Revolution and the English public education system, why, I'm certain he would be able to tell you anything you want to know . . . and quite a few things you don't care to know," he added with a laugh. He held up his finger. "But ask him a question about Civil War battles fought in the state of Missouri, and he wouldn't have the foggiest idea. Now, a popular historian would be able to tell you a little about the Industrial Revolution and a little about Civil War battles fought in Missouri and perhaps throw in a small discourse on the Napoleonic campaigns as well. A popular historian's interests are much more eclectic than those of the academic historian. And speaking as a popular historian—and, if I may add immodestly, as someone who has had some small effect on history—I predict that when the American chronicles of this century are written, your father, Robert Canfield, will be regarded as one of the most influential men of our time."

"That is very kind of you, Mr. President," Willie said. "But you must know that Dad spent his entire life working in the private sector."

"That's exactly my point," Truman replied. "Men like your father—and like Henry Ford, Harvey Firestone, J.P. Morgan, and John D. Rockefeller—are the men whose ambition, energy, and dedication have made, and continue to make, our nation what it is. What would free enterprise and democracy be without men like these? Such men are the architects of our civilization. Politicians and military leaders merely support the system that men like your father have built for us."

"He would be very honored to know that you think so, Mr. Truman," Willie said. "It's going to be hard to carry on without him."

"You do have a big pair of shoes to fill, gentlemen," Truman said. He smiled. "But I can't think of anyone better able to fill them than you two."

John smiled sadly. "You'll notice, Mr. President, that it will take the both of us to fill one pair of shoes."

"Well, I didn't say it would be easy. I just said I was certain you could do it. How are your enterprises going, by the way? There are no unpleasant surprises in store for the economy, are there? Is business doing well?"

"Yes, sir," John said. "I am pleased to report that Canfield-Puritex is doing exceptionally well."

"As is World Air Transport," Willie added. "We now have landing agreements in fifteen countries."

"What about that new jet airliner the British are flying?" Truman asked. "What is it called? The Comet? Are American carriers going to be hurt by that?"

"Well, sir, there's no denying that we'll feel the effects of it," Willie admitted. "But the Comet is terribly expensive to operate—and BOAC doesn't have that many of them yet." He smiled. "Despite what it says in their ads, jets aren't making all other forms of transport obsolete."

"How long in your opinion, Willie, before we have jet airliners?"

"I'd say we're at least eight to ten years away before engine technology is developed to make jet airliners profitable."

"Yes," Truman said, "that's what I've been told by others as well. You know, there are those in Congress who want to establish an official government airline, like BOAC. They say we will have to have jet airliners right away to compete with the rest of the world. And, as you pointed out, since jet airliners cannot yet turn a profit, private enterprise wouldn't be able to bring this about. Only a national airline could afford something like that. What do you think of such a plan?"

"Mr. President, that would be a terrible mistake," Willie replied. "It would be the ruin of private airlines. We have to operate in the black. We couldn't compete with an airline that didn't care whether it was successful or not. Why, such a thing would have just the opposite effect of what Congress is looking for. It would set America's airline operations back by ten years or more."

Truman smiled. "That is exactly what I said to them. And I told them that if they tried to pass something like a national airline, I would veto it. You'll be happy to know that they quit talking about it."

"Good."

"Of course, pretty soon it won't be my problem anymore. It'll be the problem of the new president."

"I wish you were running again," John said.

"I considered it," Truman said. He took off his glasses and polished them as he smiled at John and Willie. "And contrary to what my critics think, I would have won again, just as I did in '48." He put the glasses back on, fitting them very carefully over each ear. "But I've had enough politics to last one lifetime. I'm ready to go back home to Independence, where I will follow the news in the papers and on radio and television, just like any other concerned citizen. My only regret . . ." He let the sentence hang.

"What is your only regret, sir?" John asked quietly.

"My only regret is that I am leaving Korea for the next president to handle. I would give just about anything to settle that business."

"The Communists are offering nothing in the peace talks?"

"Peace talks?" Truman scoffed. "Those sons of bitches are treating it like we're meeting in Versailles, not Panmunjom. They aren't there to talk peace, they're there to dictate terms. Well, by God, they won't dicate them to me. And I'll tell you the truth of the matter, they won't dictate to the next president either, no matter who he is—be he Democrat or Republican."

"I don't mind telling you, Mr. President," Willie said, "I'm just as glad I'm not a part of this war. And my hat is off to those who are."

"We owe them more than a tip of the hat," Truman said. "A lot more. This isn't like the last war. Then we had bond rallies, bands, and waving flags at every corner. In this war our boys are nearly forgotten, yet they're fighting as cruel an enemy and as difficult a war as any we've fought in our history. Yes, sir, Willie, we owe them a great deal more than a tip of the hat."

CHAPTER
TWO

The "follow me" jeep led the big four-engine transport off the taxiway and onto the perforated steel planking apron of the parking area. There a ground guide stood, beckoning with batons held high to direct the pilot to the proper place.

Inside the airplane the USO troupe, tired from the long flight from the States, collected their hand baggage and prepared to deplane. Marcella Mills, who had managed to comb her hair and put on makeup even while the plane descended into Kimp'o through turbulent air, sat quietly now, looking through the window across the two oil-smeared engine nacelles at her first sight of Korea.

The airfield was a beehive of activity, from taxiing aircraft to racing fuel trucks to scurrying jeeps. On the other side of the chain-link fence that surrounded the airfield were several low buildings. Some were permanent,

14

though many more were temporary Quonset huts that had been erected to support the increased endeavors for conducting a war. Beyond the buildings sat a low mountain range, blue-green with lush vegetation.

The four engines were shut down, and the sudden silence, after hours of roar, seemed almost jarring. A portable stairway with MILITARY AIR TRANSPORT SERVICE painted on the side was pushed up to the door, and the young serviceman who had acted as their flight steward during the transoceanic flight twisted the door handle, then swung the door open. An Air Force captain stepped on board.

"Ladies and gentlemen," he said, "I am Captain Bollinger. On behalf of the United Nations Command, I welcome you to Korea. Please follow me to the reception room, where we will clear customs for you, then make arrangements for your stay in the beautiful 'Land of the Morning Calm.'"

Marcella was the last one to leave the plane, and when she stepped out onto the upper platform of the boarding stairs, the soldiers and airmen gathered on the tarmac below began whistling and shouting.

"Marcella! Marcella! Give us a wave, Marcella!"

She smiled broadly, then waved. "Hello, boys," she said in the breathy voice that had become her trademark. She threw one hip toward them. "I just know we're going to have lots of fun here."

"I'm in love!" one of the men shouted.

"Will you marry me, Marcella?"

"Don't listen to him, he's already married."

"Have you ever heard of a divorce? Marry me, Marcella!"

Several of the men had cameras, and Marcella posed for them, moving a hip or leg provocatively.

"Okay, men, that's enough," Captain Bollinger said. "We have to get these people through customs."

*　　*　　*

On the opposite side of the field from where the USO plane had just landed, a jeep bounced and clanked across the steel planking.

"Hey, Sarge, did you see in *Stars and Stripes* who's comin' here to entertain the troops?" the driver, Airman Third Turner, asked.

"Yeah, I seen it," Sergeant Bates replied.

"Marcella Mills," Turner said, as if Bates hadn't answered him.

"I said I knew."

"Marcella Mills is the sexiest woman in Hollywood . . . in America . . . in the world, even. Oh, my, wouldn't you like to be on a mountaintop with her, with a cold piece of pie and a hot piece of ass?"

"Turner, you're as full of shit as a Christmas turkey," Bates snorted.

"What? You don't think she's sexy?"

"I don't waste my time thinkin' about it one way or another. Somebody like that—hell, she might as well be on Mars or somethin' as far as people like you and me're concerned. We live in two totally different worlds."

"Yeah, well, she can come to my world any time she wants," Turner said. He turned off the perforated planking and started across the field. A billowing cloud of red dust roiled up from behind the jeep.

"Get back up on the PSP," Bates ordered.

"What for?" Turner asked. He pointed over the hood of the jeep. "We're just goin' to that Quonset hut over there, for chrissake. Jesus, if you make me drive on the PSP, we're goin' to have to go all the way around the friggin' field."

"I don't care if we have to go all the way around Korea," Bates said. "This dust is murder on the aircraft engines."

"There ain't even any planes parked around here," Turner complained.

"Get back up on the goddamn PSP!"

"All right, all right," Turner muttered, turning around to go back to the steel planking that made up the runways, parking aprons, and service roads of the airfield.

"You're so damned peculiar about all these planes. You'd think every last one of 'em belonged to you."

"They do belong to me," Bates said easily. "They're on the ground a hell of a lot more than they're in the air. And when they're on the ground, they're my responsibility."

"You ain't responsible for every plane in the whole friggin' Air Force."

"How do you know? I learned a long time ago that you never know when one of 'em might be assigned to you," Bates declared. "So it's best to take care of 'em all."

"Whatever you say. You're the sergeant. I'm just a lowly airman, tryin' to make a livin'." Turner was quiet for a moment, then asked, "Say, Sarge, you know anythin' about this guy we're pickin' up?"

"Nothin' except he just arrived this mornin' and he's a captain."

"He's supposed to be some real hotshot pilot, didja know that?"

"They're *all* hotshot pilots," Bates said. "They think all they have to do is strap a plane to their ass and fly. Most of 'em never give a second thought to what it takes to keep the damn things in the air."

"Yeah, but this guy really is a hotshot," Turner insisted. "I was talkin' to Airman DuPont over in Personnel, and he told me this guy was an ace in the last war. He shot down thirteen German planes."

"That a fact? Who was he with?"

"I don't know. DuPont didn't say."

"There's Incoming Officer Personnel over there."

"I know where it is. I'm the one come down to get them two new lieutenants last week, remember?"

"Yeah, after you stopped at the beer garden for a brew," Bates reminded him.

Captain Travis Jackson stepped out of the arriving officers' shack and looked out over the airfield. He stood out from the others because while almost everyone else was wearing fatigues, Travis was wearing his tropical worsteds, complete with jacket and tie. Travis Jackson also stood out from the others because of the color of his skin.

He had arrived in Korea just past dawn that morning, hot, tired, and grimy after two days' flying aboard a military air transport flight. The first thing he had done was shower, using the converted wing tank that served the officers in that capacity. After the shower he had changed into the TWs. He had kept them fresh by not packing them in his duffel, carrying them instead in a hang-up garment bag. Remembering now how carefully Quinisha had hung the uniform for him on the day he left gave him a twinge of homesickness.

"I've got it all wrapped in tissue paper," Quinisha told him. "That way when you take it off the hanger, it'll look as good as it does now. My mama taught me about wrapping things in tissue paper."

"I wish I could wrap you and Andy in tissue paper and take you with me," Travis responded.

Quinisha smiled wistfully at him. "Baby, don't think I haven't been thinking about that. I don't know how I'm going to make it with you gone." Almost immediately the smile faded, and tears spilled down her cheeks.

"Here, now," Travis said, wiping her tears with the tips of his fingers. "What's all this crying about?"

"I don't want you going off to Korea. It would be different if it was something like the last war, when everyone cared. But, Travis, nobody cares about this war. Most people had never even heard of Korea before this started."

"Quinisha, the Air Force has been good to us," Travis countered.

"I know, I know," Quinisha acknowledged.

"And we can't take just the good and walk away from the bad, now, can we? If the Air Force wants me to go to Korea, then I'm going, and we won't make any fuss over it."

Quinisha leaned into Travis, and he wrapped his arms around her. They stood like that for a long moment;

then they looked over at little Andrew, who was crawling around in the corner, playing with a piece of packing material.

"He'll be walking and talking by the time I get back," Travis said.

"I know."

"All I can say is, you better make damn sure he learns to say 'daddy.'"

Quinisha smiled through her tears. "Honey, I promise you, that will be the first word he learns."

That conversation had taken place less than ninety-six hours before, but already it seemed to Travis that he had been gone weeks, maybe even months or years. Dressed in those same lovingly packed TWs, he now stood outside the Incoming Officer Personnel shack, waiting for ground transportation to his squadron. Three rows of ribbons, including the Distinguished Flying Cross, made a bright splash of color above his left breast pocket. Silver wings were above the ribbons, and, because the sun was very bright today, he had added a pair of mirrored sunglasses to his ensemble.

A B-26B took off, both engines roaring as it sucked its gear up into its belly. Travis watched it, envious of its crew because they were flying but not envious of their plane. The B-26 was a holdover from the last war; Travis was here to fly the Air Force's newest and fastest Saberjets. He had trained for it, and he was ready for it.

"Excuse me, sir. You Cap'n Jackson?"

Travis turned to the speaker, a big, sandy-haired sergeant first class. "Yes. Are you my transportation?"

"Yes, sir, I reckon I am," the sergeant said, saluting. "That is, me and Airman Turner are. My name is Sergeant Bates. Where's your gear, Cap'n? I'll send Turner after it."

"Over there," Travis said, pointing to his duffel and AWOL bags that lay against the fence.

Turner got the two bags and put them in the back of the jeep. Bates climbed in beside them, giving up the passenger seat for Travis. Turner put the jeep in gear, and they drove off, the PSP clanking underneath the wheels.

Three prop-driven fighters, also holdovers from the last war, roared by less than one hundred feet over their heads, then pulled up on the far side of the airfield. Their silver wings flashed in the sun.

"F-51 Mustangs. Do we have many of those left over here?" Travis asked.

"We've got some," Bates replied. "And the Aussies and the slopes have some."

"Slopes?"

"Koreans."

The jeep turned off the main road, then went down a smaller road that led behind a long line of F-86 Saberjets. Yellow bands were painted around the wing tips, the vertical stabilizer, and just behind the bubble canopy. Several of the aircraft were being worked on. Some had their engine cowlings open and the inspection panels removed, while others had mechanics sitting on top of them or crawling around underneath.

"This is it, sir, the Eight Hundred First Fighter Squadron, our home away from home."

"We've got the F model, I see," Travis said, examining the planes closely.

"Yes, sir. We just got 'em in about six weeks ago. Still workin' a few bugs out of 'em, but I think they're goin' to do just fine. You checked out in Saberjets?"

"I was instructing in them back in the States."

"Well, sir, then I reckon they'll have you operational real quick. Though seein' as you're goin' to be our XO, I don't know how much flyin' you'll be doin'."

Surprised by the sergeant's statement, Travis twisted around in his seat to look at Bates. "Where did you get the idea I was going to be the executive officer?"

"Why, from Colonel Kirby, our CO."

"My orders didn't say anything about me being the XO."

"No, sir, I reckon not. Fact is, the Table of Organization and Equipment calls for a major, but we don't have none, and you'll be the senior captain."

"Surely we've got some reservist with earlier dates of rank."

"Yes, sir, I reckon we do have one or two with earlier DORs. But you're a regular officer, and the old man likes to use regulars whenever he can."

"Damn," Travis said.

"You don't want to be the XO?"

"Who would want that job, Sergeant? XOs get all the responsibility and none of the authority. If the officers and men have a bitch, they take it to the XO. If the old man is pissed off because something doesn't suit him, he takes it out on his exec."

Sergeant Bates chuckled. "I guess you have seen how it works before."

"How long have you been in the squadron, Sergeant?"

"I come over with it, sir."

"You know all the officers?"

"Most of 'em, yes, sir. There's maybe a few of the reserves I don't know that well."

"Do you know them well enough to know who I'm going to have trouble with?"

"Trouble, sir? What kind of trouble?"

Travis gave Bates a sardonic smile. "Come on, Sergeant, you weren't born yesterday. This isn't a good suntan I'm wearing."

"Oh, yes, sir," Bates said, grinning. "Yes, sir, I see what you mean. But I don't think you're goin' to have a problem. I mean, we've already got a couple of colored pilots in the squadron. And Mr. Pounder, the supply officer, is colored."

"What about Lieutenant Willis?" Airman Turner put in. "He wears that rebel flag on his helmet and all."

"Who is that?" Travis asked.

"Nobody, Cap'n," Sergeant Bates quickly interjected. "Turner was just talkin' out of turn, that's all."

Travis studied Bates's face for a moment, then said, "Never mind. It's probably just as well I don't know. That way I'll start out treating everyone the same."

"Yes, sir, that's what I was thinkin'," Bates said.

Four planes with open canopies sat in front of the long line of jets. All four aircraft were manned, and the pilots were sitting in their seats, reading. Their helmets were resting on the front of the canopy opening, and one of them sported a big rebel flag.

"Why are those airplanes parked out there like that?"

"That's the hotbox, sir. If we get a quick call for help, those are the fellas who are up."

"Lieutenant Willis is one of them, I see."

"Yes, sir," Bates replied in a surprised tone. "How do you know that? Do you know him from somewhere?"

Travis pointed at the helmet decorated with a Confederate flag. "Isn't that his flight helmet? Or are there several painted like that?"

"Oh, I see. No sir, there's only one. Listen, Cap'n, I don't want you to get the wrong idea about Lieutenant Willis. He's a good officer and a damned fine pilot. I mean, I wouldn't want you to make a judgment on him just 'cause he's from the South."

"Believe me, Sergeant, I don't hate everyone from the South," Travis replied. "If I did, I'd have a hard time with my own family. I'm from Mississippi."

"Yes, sir. I didn't mean to imply that you would. I just didn't want you to pay any attention to what Turner said, that's all."

"I will reserve judgment," Travis promised.

Turner stopped the jeep in front of a Quonset hut. "Here we are, sir. Squadron headquarters. The old man is inside."

Like all the other buildings in the squadron compound, this one was surrounded by a waist-high barrier of sandbags. A barrel of sand sat out front, with a sign on it ordering CLEAR ALL WEAPONS HERE BEFORE ENTERING BUILDING!

"Me and Turner got to get back to work," Bates said. "We'll drop your gear off over at the officers' hooch for you."

"Thanks," Travis replied, stepping out of the jeep.

He paused briefly, then entered the orderly room, where he was greeted by the staccato tapping of someone typing at a desk in the far corner. A sergeant stood up as Travis approached his desk.

"Yes, sir. Something I can do for you?"

"I'm Captain Jackson," Travis said, handing over his orders. "I'm reporting in."

"*You're* Captain Jackson?" the sergeant asked, looking at the orders,

"Yes. Why? Were you expecting someone else?"

"No, sir," the sergeant said. "That is . . . No, sir."

"Captain Jackson?" A tall, thin, nearly bald lieutenant colonel stepped out of his office. "I thought I heard you out here."

"Captain Travis Jackson, reporting for duty, sir," Travis said, saluting.

"Bill Kirby," the colonel said, returning Travis's salute, then sticking out his hand. "I'm the CO of this motley group. Come on in. Coffee?"

"Thank you, yes, sir."

"Airman, two coffees, mine black and . . ." He looked at Travis.

"Black, sir."

"Both of them black."

Travis followed Kirby into his office. Kirby indicated the chair across the desk, and Travis sat down. As the senior officer settled himself in his own chair, Travis examined the things on the wall behind the colonel. A manning chart was tacked up immediately behind Kirby. Just to the right of it was a photograph of a Bell X-1 rocketplane; standing in front of the plane, smiling and holding a helmet was Kirby.

Noticing Travis looking at the picture, Kirby said, "That's me, all right."

"What's it like?" Travis asked.

Kirby grinned. "It's the most fantastic thing in the world. Like riding on a bullet. I had her up to eight hundred ten miles per hour at sixty thousand feet. Of course, the new rocket-plane by Douglas has already gone over a thousand miles per hour and better than seventy-five thousand feet high, so what I did was tame. Still . . ." He sighed. "Well, enough of that. Let's get down to the business at hand. Captain, I plan to make you my XO. You have no objections, I hope?"

"Colonel Kirby, of course I'll serve wherever you put me. But if I had my choice, I wouldn't be the executive officer."

"Why not? It's the number two position in the entire squadron. I'd think an ambitious young officer like you would jump at the chance."

"Yes, sir. But I understand you have a few reserves who have senior DORs. I'm thinking about those fellows, that's all."

Kirby studied Travis; then, inexplicably, he laughed loudly. "That's bullshit, Captain, and you know it. But then, Jimmy Overstreet said I'd have to keep my eye on you. He told me you would say any kind of bullshit you could think of to get away from a desk and into a cockpit."

"You've spoken to Colonel Overstreet about me, sir?"

"Damn right, I have. If I'm going to consider putting a colored officer as my second-in-command, I want to be damn sure he can handle the job. Otherwise it'll be nothing but trouble. And Jimmy Overstreet said you could handle it even if you were orange." Kirby laughed. "And he also said you would hate it. He tells me you're the best flyer he ever knew."

"Colonel Overstreet may be a bit prejudiced. In my behalf," Travis added quickly.

"Hell, yes, I'm sure he is. He told me how you saved his ass during the last war, how you single-handedly jumped three Germans who were stalking his crippled B-17."

"I had the element of surprise on my side," Travis explained. "I knocked the first one down before they even knew I was around and the second one before he could recover. The third one got away. I just took advantage of the situation, that's all."

"Hell, that's what a fighter pilot is *supposed* to do. You're supposed to take advantage of the situation," Kirby said. "Now, what's the real reason you don't want to be the XO? Are you afraid you won't get enough flying time?"

"Yes, sir, that's part of it," Travis admitted.

"Well, don't worry about that. We are undermanned

and overworked here. You'll fly missions, Captain, as many as anyone in the squadron—maybe more. Then in your spare time, when everyone else is sleeping, you'll take care of the paperwork in your office. Unless that's too much work for you."

"No, sir, I can handle that all right," Travis said. "But it's been my observation that far too often XOs wind up being responsible for everything that goes wrong, while not having the authority to make things right."

"Well, you can put your mind at rest on that, Captain," Kirby said. "I believe in the old military axiom, 'You can delegate authority, but not responsibility.' Whatever you are in charge of, Captain Jackson, you'll have the authority to deal with it. You have my full backing. And if something goes wrong, it's my ass on the line, not yours." He smiled. "Now will you take the job?"

Travis laughed. "If you put it that way, Colonel, there's no way I can turn it down."

"Good, good," Kirby said, standing up quickly and coming around his desk to shake Travis's hand.

A knock sounded on the door, and an airman stuck his head in.

"We have an alert, Colonel. Some B-29's are on their way to bomb Konan, and radar has picked up bogeys coming south of the Yalu."

"Who's in the lead slot in the hotbox?"

"Lieutenant Willis, sir."

"Willis? Good, good. Scramble them."

"We have a lieutenant leading a mission?" Travis asked.

"Yes, well, not just any lieutenant. We have Lieutenant Willis," Kirby said. "The truth is, I'd as soon have him there as anyone in the squadron, captains included."

"He's that good an officer?"

Kirby snickered. "Good officer? Hell, Captain, if we weren't fighting a war, I probably would've put him in jail months ago. He's a *terrible* officer, the damnedest handful I've ever come across. But he's one red-hot pilot." He laughed again. "He's going to shit a brick when he finds out the new XO is colored, I'll tell you that."

"He's prejudiced against Negroes?"

"Hell, yes—Negroes, Orientals, Jews, Mexicans, Irish, Yankees, Californians, and people who are left-handed. He is particularly prejudiced against people he feels are less competent than he is, and since he feels that *everyone* is less competent than he is, that sort of leaves him alone against the world."

Travis eyed the colonel. "I can see right now that Lieutenant Willis is going to make my stay interesting."

The object of Travis's conversation, First Lieutenant Train Willis, was, at that very moment, flying at 25,000 feet on a heading of 025 degrees at a true airspeed of 385 knots. Train, whose unusual first name came from his mother's side of the family, was searching the sky in front of him, having been vectored to this position by target acquisition radar. At first he thought radar must have made a mistake; then he saw them: two small swept-wing aircraft ahead and below his flight.

"Tallyho, the yellow peril," Train said into his headset. "Radar was right. Two MIG-15's heading straight for an intercept course with our B-29's. Do you have them, Mad Dog Flight?"

"*Roger, Mad Dog Leader, we see them,*" Train's number two replied.

"*Mad Dog Leader, I don't think they see us,*" another pilot suggested.

"I think you're right," Train answered.

The Americans had the advantage because they were about three thousand feet higher and a mile behind the MIGs.

"Mad Dog Flight, maintain relative position. I'm going to drop down and check them out."

"*Roger, Mad Dog Leader,*" number two answered. The other two responded by clicking their mike buttons twice.

Train put his Saberjet into a slight dive, increasing his closing speed as he came upon the two MIGs. Suddenly getting an idea, he rolled his plane into the inverted position and, flying upside down, eased his plane forward, just over the top of the MIG in trail. While still inverted, he drew closer, until the curve of his canopy was no more than ten feet above the curve of the MIG's canopy. Train looked down at the MIG.

"Hey, Gook, look up here," he called—though as he was transmitting on the American frequency, the Chinese pilot wouldn't have heard him. But the MIG pilot certainly sensed him, and he looked up.

Behind the MIG pilot's goggles, Train could see his eyes grow wide with surprise, then fear. Train laughed loudly and rolled his plane back upright. The MIG and his wingman tried to run, and that was their mistake, for they flew right into Train's optimum line of fire. He opened up on the wingman with .50 caliber machine-gun fire and .40-millimeter rapid-fire cannon. Pieces began coming off the Chinese plane; suddenly it exploded. Train couldn't avoid flying through the smoke and debris, though fortunately his plane suffered no damage.

The second MIG took advantage of the explosion of his wingman to do a wingover and beat a retreat back north. Train and his group chased him, but the MIG crossed the Yalu before they could catch him.

"Damn!" Train shouted in impotent fury. "One of these days that river isn't going to stop me!" Reluctantly he called off the pursuit. "All right, Mad Dog Flight, let's do a one eighty the hell out of here and go find our big friends."

Travis had changed into fatigues and was taking a walking tour of the flight line when the four Saberjets returned. He watched them land and followed them as they turned off the active taxiway and started for the revetments. It was very hot, and because the clear Plexiglas of the canopies created a greenhouse effect, making it even hotter in the cockpit, the pilots opened their canopies.

As the four jets were coming down the taxiway behind the revetments, Travis was shocked to see the pilot in the lead airplane suddenly stand up in his seat. He raised his arms over his head, clenching his hands together as if he were a boxer who had just won a championship fight.

"Look at Lieutenant Willis," one of the mechanics said, a grin splitting his oil-smeared face.

"Ain't he a card, though?" another added, laughing.

The plane was still traveling at a pretty good clip, and Train, standing on the seat, had no control over it. It veered off the taxiway, heading straight for a fuel truck.

"Oh, shit! He's going to hit that truck!" someone yelled.

Realizing what was happening, Train dropped back down into his seat to try to regain control. But he wasn't quick enough, and he struck a large portable generator with such force that the jet's wing tip was ripped off.

After the generator, the plane struck a big wheel-mounted fire extinguisher. The top of the fire extinguisher came off, and foam spurted from the canister onto the PSP. The airplane barreled through the foaming extinguisher straight for the fuel truck that was at that moment pumping fuel into another plane. The truck driver, seeing the impending collision, started running; the lineman pumping the fuel slid off the wing and ran as well.

At the last possible minute Train managed to regain control of the airplane, and he diverted it, avoiding a collision. The men on the flight line who had witnessed the near disaster cheered with relief.

Train taxied the aircraft into its assigned revetment, following the signals given by the ground guide. When the plane was in its proper position, the guide moved his hand across his throat, the signal to the pilot to cut the engine, and the hissing, whistling sound of the jet engine stilled. Though the engine was off, undulating heat waves shimmered up from the aircraft's tailpipe. The crew chief of Train's plane moved the egress ladder into position so that the pilot could climb down.

Travis walked out to the airplane and examined the damage done by the two ground collisions. Not only was the wing tip damaged, there was a crease traveling nearly halfway down the wing toward the wing root. Travis was certain that the spar, too, had been damaged, which meant that this airplane would require, at the least, a new wing.

"Somethin' I can help you with, mister?" Train asked in an insolent tone as he sauntered toward Travis.

"That was a damn-fool thing you just did, Lieutenant," Travis snapped.

Train, eyeing Travis's captain's bars, stopped. "Yes, sir, well, I'm sorry about that, but you see, I was celebratin' my fourth MIG. One more and I'll be an ace."

"If you're as stupid in the air as you are on the ground, you'll wind up a notch on some MIG jockey's belt."

"Yes, sir. Well, if it'll make you feel better, I'll be extra careful tomorrow," Train said sarcastically.

"There isn't going to be a tomorrow for you, Lieutenant."

"There isn't going to be a tomorrow for me? Now, just what the hell is that supposed to mean?"

"I mean you're grounded."

"Grounded? Who the hell says so?"

"I say so, Lieutenant. Captain Travis Jackson, Safety Officer, Accident Officer, and Executive Officer."

"Executive Officer?"

"That's right, Lieutenant. Do you have a problem with that?"

Lieutenant Willis glared at Travis for a long moment. "No, sir, I don't have a problem with that," he finally replied, though his expression said just the opposite. "But Colonel Kirby may have a problem with your grounding me when we're short of pilots."

"If you want to appeal to Colonel Kirby, be my guest," Travis said, stepping aside and extending his hand toward the squadron headquarters building.

Train looked at the building, then back at Travis. "No, sir. You're the XO. I have no call to go over your head. How long will I be grounded?"

"Until after the accident board meets and gives their evaluation," Travis replied.

"Yes, sir. Well, I guess they'll be needin' an accident report then, won't they? I'd better go fill one out," Train said, his tone caustic. Putting on his flight helmet, he turned and walked away.

Knowing that normally pilots would wear their soft hat and carry the flight helmet while on the ground because the flight helmet wasn't particularly comfortable, Travis was certain that Willis was wearing the rebel-flag-painted helmet just for his benefit. He watched the angry young lieutenant's rigid back as he stalked away.

Several airmen had gathered close enough to have overheard the conversation between the two of them, including the other three pilots of Mad Dog flight. When they saw Willis walk away, they, too, left.

"Cap'n Jackson, I'm curious," Sergeant Bates called from where he stood at the wing tip of Willis's airplane, surveying the damage. "When you was a kid, did you ever take a stick and hit a hornets' nest?"

"Not that I can recall. Why, Sergeant? Do you think I've done that now?"

Bates glanced at Willis's retreating back, then back at Travis. "Could be, Cap'n. Could be."

Word of Travis's arrival—and of his almost immediate run-in and grounding of Lieutenant Willis—spread quickly. That night at dinner in the Officers' Mess, Travis found himself sitting alone. He might have been able to explain it away by his being new and the other officers' preferring to eat with their friends. But the table where Willis was eating had nearly double its usual capacity, with extra chairs having been brought over and crammed around it. When the two young Negro lieutenants also went to another table, Travis knew that his isolation was deliberately exclusionary.

"Mind if I join you, Cap'n?"

The speaker was a gray-haired warrant officer, easily in his midfifties. He was also black.

"You sure you want to?" Travis asked, holding his

hand out by way of invitation. "Everyone else seems to be giving me the cold shoulder."

The warrant officer chuckled. "Yes, sir, well, if you get too cold, I can always give you an extra blanket. I'm Julius Pounder, the supply officer."

"That's good to know. Tell me, Mr. Pounder, which is it? Am I that unpopular, or is Lieutenant Willis that popular?"

"Well, Lieutenant Willis is a popular fella, all right," Pounder said. "About the most popular fella in the squadron."

"Real hotshot pilot, huh?"

"I guess so. But bein' a supply officer, I don't really know much 'bout how good a pilot he is," Pounder said. "Course, he was popular to begin with, bein' as he was an All-American football player."

"All-American football?" Travis said in surprise. He looked over at Willis, then snapped his fingers. "My God, you don't mean Choo Choo Willis? That's Choo Choo Willis, who played quarterback for Ole Miss?"

"Yes, sir, Train 'Choo Choo' Willis. That's him all right." Pounder laughed. "I thought 'Train' was part of 'Choo Choo,' till I found out that was his real name. That was his mama's maiden name."

"Choo Choo Willis . . . Well, I'll be damned. I once saw a picture of him on the cover of a magazine." Travis remembered the picture, obviously posed, of a young man, his arm cocked as if ready to throw a pass, his steely eyes studying potential pass receivers downfield.

"Yes, sir, I expect he was on the cover of lots of magazines," Pounder said.

"Okay, Chief, so he's a popular man," Travis said. "What I can't understand is why *those* two are such fans of his." Travis nodded toward the black lieutenants.

"You mean Lieutenant Ware and Lieutenant Mack? Ah, don't be too hard on 'em, Cap'n," Pounder said. "They're good boys, both of 'em. They're just tryin' to fit in, that's all. You can see how it'd be if they was to come over here and sit with you tonight. They'll come around in a day or two, and so will most of the others."

"What about you?" Travis asked. "Aren't you afraid you won't fit in?"

"Cap'n, I come in this man's Air Force—when it was this man's Army—back in 1926. I figured then that if I kept my nose clean and didn't piss off any of the white boys who mattered, I would someday make sergeant. Well, I did better than that. I was appointed to warrant officer junior grade. Now I'm a chief warrant officer, and that's as high as a warrant can go. I got my rank. I don't need to fit in."

Travis chuckled. "I see what you mean, Chief. I suppose there's something to be said for being at the top of your field."

A sudden burst of laughter from the Willis table prompted Travis and Pounder to look over.

"Cap'n, you don't look like the kind of man who'd back down on nothin'," Pounder said. "Don't you back down on this."

"I don't plan to," Travis replied. "Why do you say that? Are you anxious to see our young football hero taken down a notch or two?"

"No, sir," Pounder said, surprising Travis with his answer. "It ain't that at all. The truth is, Lieutenant Willis is a good man who maybe needs to be reined in just a bit. I think this could be good for him."

Travis smiled. "So, you, too, have come under his spell."

"Yes, sir, I expect so, but not like you think. You see, I know somethin' about Lieutenant Willis that nobody else knows."

"What is it?" Travis asked, curious. "Can you tell me?"

"I'm not supposed to. But I'm goin' to tell you anyway, 'cause I think maybe it would be good for you to know. It happened two months ago, when Airman Collins forgot and left a special tool chest out on the flight line overnight. When he thought of it the next morning, he ran out to check for it, but it was too late; the tool chest was gone. Do you have any idea how much a special tool chest costs?"

"Some idea, yes," Travis replied.

"One hundred seventy-eight dollars," Pounder said, not to be denied the emphasis of his story. "That's a lot of money for an airman first."

"That's a lot of money for *anybody*."

"Yes, sir. Well, a report-of-survey was made, and it came up that Collins was liable for the money. One hundred seventy-eight dollars. I was told to draw up the papers that would take the money from Collins's pay. But Lieutenant Willis heard about it, and he came in to see me. 'Chief,' he says, 'I want you to take this money and pay off the report-of-survey so that Collins ain't stuck with it.' And he gave me the money. In cash."

"That was generous of him, all right," Travis said. "It sure must've made him high in Collins's book."

"Well, no, sir," Pounder said. "That's just it. You see, he made me promise not to tell Collins—not to tell anybody. Till this day, Collins has no idea where that money came from, and neither does anyone else . . . except, now, you."

"Willis must think Collins is a pretty valuable man to have work for him."

"Yes, sir, well, that's another thing. You see, Collins doesn't work for Willis. Collins is in the special details section."

"That *is* rather remarkable . . . and commendable," Travis said. "Especially as Willis didn't want anyone to know."

"Yes, sir, and here's somethin' else remarkable about it. You know how Willis wears that helmet of his with the rebel flag and all, but he did all this for Collins. And Collins is colored."

Travis stared hard at Pounder. "I'll be damned," he finally said softly. He got up and took his cup over to the coffee maker. As he poured himself another cup of the black, steaming brew, he glanced over at Willis's table and saw the lieutenant looking at him. When their eyes met, Willis smiled slightly and held his cup up in salute. Travis, whose cup was now full, did the same.

UIJONBU, KOREA

The stage for the USO show had been built by the engineer batallion, whose members reserved the best seats for themselves. Though it was located a safe distance away from the actual fighting, there was always the possibility of snipers, or even a raid conducted by a suicide squad, so several infantrymen were posted at security points around the show area, while an entire company of military police kept watch closer in.

The two song-and-dance men who shared the bill with Marcella Mills were received warmly by the soldiers and airmen. Their jokes and comedy routines garnered a lot of good, appreciative belly laughs and applause. But the audience's nearly fanatical enthusiasm was reserved for Marcella. The men started screaming, yelling, whistling, and stomping their feet from the moment she came on stage.

"Hello, fellas!" she said.

"Hello, Marcella!" the men yelled back as one.

"I am so happy to be here to perform for you boys."

"Not as happy as we are!" someone yelled, and everyone laughed.

"Did any of you see the last picture I did? It was called *Panama Fever*. There was a song in that picture called 'Hot in Panama.' I'd like to sing it for you now."

Panama Fever was a torrid musical in which Marcella played the role of "gentleman's escort"—movie euphemism for prostitute—and several scenes in the picture had her, in the words of one critic, "absolutely naked, for all that she was covered by a slip."

One particularly steamy scene in which Marcella's nipples were clearly visible under the clingy silk slip was cut from the movie before it could be shown, but the resultant publicity helped propel the movie to a box-office smash. The song "Hot in Panama" was another bone of contention among those who found the movie a bit too risqué. On the surface the lyrics were perfectly innocent, but the way Marcella sang the song made almost every word a double entendre.

Marcella grabbed the microphone with her left hand, threw her left hip out toward the audience, put her right hand under her mane of golden-blond hair, then, with half-closed eyes and through pouting lips, began to sing breathily:

> "Ooooh, I'm hot,
> Ooooh, I'm hot,
> Oooh, I'm hot in Panama
> The temperature's so high
> That I'm about to fry
> Here in Pa . . . Pa . . . Panama."

By the time she finished her number, the GIs were nearly berserk from screaming and whistling at her.

"Thank you, boys," she said. "If everyone over here is as sweet to me as you have been, it's going to be a wonderful trip."

"Don't go anywhere else, Marcella!" someone shouted. "Stay here with us!"

"Oh, but I've got to go. Don't you think the other boys over here should get to see the show?"

"Fuck the others!" someone shouted, and there was some nervous laughter.

"No, stay here and fuck us!" another shouted. This time the laughter was uninhibited, and the lust rippling through the audience was almost palpable.

The commander of the Military Police, whose job was not only security, but also to maintain order, suddenly was fearful for Marcella's safety. He directed his troops onto the stage.

"*Boo!*" someone yelled, and his catcall was joined by a chorus of others. The MP captain leapt onto the stage and took the microphone.

"Men, if you don't stand at ease, we will be forced to stop the show. Remember, you are American fighting men. You are not a mob."

"Hey, look!" somebody shouted. "Marcella ain't got on no panties!"

Bedlam broke out all over again, and the MP captain

had no choice but to end the show. With much blowing of
whistles and pushing and shoving, the audience was finally dispersed. Meanwhile, Marcella and the others were
put in the back of a military ambulance and whisked
away.

The next day the commanding general of the United
States Armed Forces in Korea issued an order that can-
celed the remaining tour of the Marcella Mills USO show
due to its "disruptive influence upon order and military
discipline." Marcella and all the members of her troupe
were immediately put on a MATS C-54 for the return
flight to the United States.

Reading about the show and its aftermath in *Stars
and Stripes*, Travis Jackson turned to Colonel Kirby, who
was sharing a table with him in the Officers' Mess, and
said dryly, "Certainly nothing like that would have happened here, now, would it have, sir?"

Kirby eyed Travis. "Oh, no, Captain. Absolutely not.
Our men are far too well-disciplined to create a ruckus."
He shot a meaningful glance at Train Willis, who was
seated at a nearby table, then muttered, "Far too well-
disciplined . . ."

CHAPTER
THREE

OCTOBER 1952, FROM *EVENTS MAGAZINE*:

RICHARD NIXON'S SPEECH
WELL RECEIVED

Favorable reaction is still coming in on Senator Richard M. Nixon's speech, delivered on a nationwide television hookup last month, in which he declared that he had done nothing wrong.

Senator Nixon, the Republican nominee for vice president, was accused of misusing political contributions, specifically an $18,000 election fund. The senator declared that the fund had been used as it was intended: for traveling expenses, the printing of speeches, long-distance telephone calls, and other legitimate purposes.

Senator Nixon declared also that his wife, Pat, did not own a mink coat, but that she did own a very respectable Republican cloth coat. He also said that his daughters had received one gift that he did not intend to return—a "little cocker spaniel dog" that his six-year-old daughter Tricia has named Checkers.

MARCELLA MILLS APOLOGIZES TO DEPARTMENT OF DEFENSE

Hollywood star and sex goddess Marcella Mills issued a written statement apologizing to the Department of Defense for "any disruption I might have caused in the efforts of our fighting men in Korea."

Miss Mills was ushered out of Korea last month after doing only one show of a scheduled ten-show tour. She caused a near riot with her very sexy rendition of "Hot in Panama"; then things got completely out of hand when Corporal James Anderson of Gebo, Wyoming, pointed out to his fellow soldiers that Miss Mills was not wearing underwear.

Miss Mills insists that she *was* wearing underwear and sent Corporal Anderson an autographed pair of "the panties I was wearing that day." Corporal Anderson, while expressing pleasure at receiving the unique autograph, stands by his initial observation.

UNDERSTANDING YOUR TEENAGER

Parents of the modern teenager are complaining that they can no longer understand the language their children speak. "It isn't English," one exasperated father said. "Nor is it any other civilized language known to man. I'm at my wit's end trying to comprehend it."

As a service to its readers, *Events* herewith provides a glossary of terms in use by the "hip" teen of the fifties:

BREAD: money.

COOL: a desirable accolade. If your teenager thinks you are cool, you are doing well.

DIG: understand something. Do you "dig" it?

DDT: an insult, meaning "drop dead twice."

DRAG: This has two meanings. One refers to anything or anybody who is "uncool." When referring to cars, however, it means a short, quick race, starting from a standstill to test the car's acceleration.

PASSION PIT: a drive-in movie.

GROUNDED: placed on restriction, such as "house arrest" by one's parents.

WHEELS: a car; preferably one's own, not the family car.

BOMB: a "hot rod" or "souped-up" car.

RAKING: lowering the front end of the car.

CHOPPING: lowering the roof of the car.

MILL: the car's engine.

DUAL CARBS: two carburetors.

DUAL STACKS: two exhaust pipes.

EISENHOWER VOWS TO GO TO KOREA

In a speech delivered in Detroit, General Dwight David Eisenhower, Republican candidate for president, vowed to go to Korea if elected.

"It is no longer acceptable for the American people to have to wait for peace," Ike said, referring to the stalled peace talks. By going to Korea, he stated, he would learn how best to serve the American people by bringing the war to an early and honorable conclusion.

JOHN CANFIELD NAMED HEAD OF CANFIELD FOUNDATION

John Canfield, 45, has been named head of the Canfield Foundation, a philanthropic organization established by his father, the late Robert Canfield, the founder of the Canfield-Puritex Company who died at his home in St. Louis two months ago of a heart attack.

The Canfield Foundation has been very active in the support of colleges and universities, in particular, Jefferson University in St. Louis, where the

Canfield School of Business is located. According to John Canfield, all programs currently in effect will stay in effect.

Robert Canfield amassed his fortune (estimated at $350 million) through interests in agriculture, food processing, lumber, and paper. The Canfield family is also the majority stockholder in World Air Transport, the nation's third largest airline.

In 1907 the senior Canfield joined with J.P. Morgan and other financiers to help avert a bank and stock market collapse that would have plunged the country into a depression. Speaking at Mr. Canfield's funeral, President Harry S Truman said, "He was more 'do' than 'talk.' He was one of this century's, and America's, greatest men. We could do with a few more just like him."

1952, A YEAR OF LITERATURE

Perhaps never in our country's history have so many wonderful works of literature been produced in one year.

From John Steinbeck there is *East of Eden;* from Herman Wouk, *The Caine Mutiny.* Flannery O'Connor has given us *Wise Blood,* Thomas Costain, *The Silver Chalice.* Ernest Hemingway has written *The Old Man and the Sea,* perhaps his best work since *The Sun Also Rises.* And just when everyone thought Eric Twainbough was finished after his last two disastrous efforts—*Tea on the Veranda* and *Trespass of the Damned*—he confounds his critics and delights his fans with *The Challenge.*

The Challenge is, as of this writing, number one on all the best-seller lists—no small accomplishment, given the quantity and quality of this season's offerings.

Twainbough lives on the island of Bimini with his second wife, the former Shaylin McKay. *Events* readers will remember Miss McKay's wartime reporting for this magazine. Though no longer on our staff, Miss McKay continues to be a contributing editor and has just accepted an assignment to go to Korea for a series of frontline reports.

BIMINI

Eric Twainbough stood on the rear deck of his house and watched the palm trees on the beach bow before the wind. Though not quite a hurricane, the storm had all the looks of one, with heavy squall lines, strong winds, and thick clouds. Down at the waterfront those boats that could be pulled out of the water had been. The others were tied fore and aft with double lines and, when possible, covered with canvas.

"You're going to catch a cold," Shaylin said, coming out onto the deck. She was carrying two cups of coffee, and she handed one to Eric.

"Nonsense. It's seventy degrees," Eric replied.

"I don't care. You're getting soaked, and in the rain and the wind you'll get cold enough."

"I like the cold. Don't forget, I once wintered in the wilds of Alaska."

"You were a young pup then, not an old dog," Shaylin teased.

"Oh, so I'm an old dog, am I?"

She smiled affectionately. "Yes, but you're *my* old dog."

Shaylin came up beside him, and he put his arm around her as the two of them looked out over the frenzied sea. In her forties now, Shaylin admitted to using a rinse to keep her hair red. Eric was sixty-two, and his hair and beard were more white than gray. He was a big man, with broad shoulders, a deep chest, and a substantial girth.

"Are you going to work anymore today?" Shaylin asked.

"No," Eric replied, sipping his coffee. "I don't think so."

"You seem to be having trouble with this book."

"No, I'm not," Eric said defensively. He took another swallow. "Well, maybe I am, a little."

"What seems to be the problem?"

"*The Challenge.*"

"*The Challenge?* I don't understand. That was a wonderful book. The critics loved it; it's selling well. How can that be a problem?"

"That's just it. They took me over the coals pretty well for *Tea on the Veranda* and *Trespass of the Damned*. When I was writing *The Challenge* I felt like I had nothing to lose. In fact, I was looking forward to coming off the floor again, so to speak. I knew it was a good book. I knew it would sell well, and I knew the critics would like it. It was as if I had a wonderful secret. But with this book . . ."

Shaylin spoke quickly to break the sudden silence. "I thought you told me this was a good book—your best book."

Eric snickered. "Come on, Shaylin, you're a writer, too. You know how it is. Everything you write is the best thing you've ever written at the time you're writing it. It has to be that way. You can't go half speed. If you do, nothing you ever write will be worth a damn. It's only after you've finished the work that you can review it with some degree of objectivity."

"You said you knew that *The Challenge* was good. Was that the same thing you're saying now? That you knew it was good just because you were working on it?"

Eric took another swallow of coffee, mulling over his answer. "Well, now, there you have caught me in the inconsistencies of my trade," he finally said. "No, it wasn't exactly like all the other books—good just because I was working on it. It was good because I knew it was really good."

"And this book?"

"I don't know," Eric admitted. "I think it's good. I hope it's good. But what if the critics are just waiting for the chance to chop me off at the knees again? They like nothing better than to come at you when you're on top."

"To hell with the critics," Shaylin said. "If you're satisfied and the publisher is satisfied and, most importantly, your readers are satisfied, what difference does it make what the critics think? In fact, you know what I'll do for you?"

"What's that?"

"I'll pesonally visit every critic who matters and tell him to kiss my Irish ass."

Eric guffawed. "You'd do that for me, would you? Ha! Tart that you are, you'd like nothing better!"

Shaylin gave him a sly smile. "Well, Eric, my love, I didn't say I wouldn't enjoy it. I just said I would do it."

"I wish you weren't going."

"To see the critics? Okay, if you don't want me to go, I won't."

"You know damn well that's not what I mean. I wish you weren't going to Korea."

"Eric, we talked about this. I asked you if I should go, and you said you thought it would be a good opportunity for me."

"It's not like we need the money."

"It isn't for the money, Eric; you know that."

"Yeah, I know. But I ask you, who do you have to prove yourself to? Certainly not me—I know you're a good writer. And not to your readers. And I wouldn't think you have to prove anything to yourself, either."

"I'm not doing it to prove anything." Shaylin sighed. "Look, if you don't want me to go, I'll write New York tomorrow and tell them that I can't make it."

"You'd do that for me?"

"Of course I would."

Eric chuckled. "Damn you."

"What?"

"You know damn well that if you tell me you won't go if I don't want you to, I'm going to give in."

Shaylin laughed. "You've discovered all my secrets, haven't you?"

"Go ahead, go to Korea."

"You're sure?"

"Yeah, I'm sure. Maybe if I had a little peace and

quiet around here for a while, I could get something written."

"Oh? So now *I'm* the distraction, am I?"

"If so, you're the best damned distraction I've ever had," Eric said.

"You tease about it," Shaylin said. "But maybe you *will* be able to work better while I'm gone. And, since I'll only be gone for about six weeks, you won't really have time to start missing me."

"I'll miss you," Eric said simply.

She touched his cheek. "I'll miss you, too."

"Keep your head down over there."

"Don't you worry any about that. You were with me during both the Spanish Revolution and World War Two. You know what a coward I am when there's shooting going on."

"Yeah," Eric agreed. "But I won't be with you this time. Unless you want to wait until I finish this book. Then we could both go."

"I thought you said you didn't want to go this time. You said you'd catch the next war."

He chuckled. "I did say that, didn't I? Well, I covered the Russian Revolution, World War One, the Spanish American War, and World War Two. . . . I guess I've earned a break."

"Anyhow, if I waited until you finished your book, this war might be over. Ike says if he's elected, he'll go to Korea and end it."

"Yeah, he did promise that. What do you think, Shaylin? Will he be elected?"

"I like Ike," Shaylin quipped. "Of course, it's kinda hard not to like him," she added. "Just think, Eric, do you realize that if he's elected, you and I will actually know the president of the United States? I mean know him *personally*?"

"That's pretty heady stuff for a young cowboy from Wyoming," Eric said, grinning.

"Speaking of cowboys, I wonder if Ike still reads paperback Western novels," Shaylin mused.

"I'm sure he does. Western readers are very loyal people." Eric sighed. "I wish my readers were that loyal."

The wind, which had been steadily increasing in velocity, suddenly blew a large piece of corrugated tin across the sand. It wrapped itself around a dancing palm tree for a moment, then worked itself loose and skittered on. Concurrent with the increased wind was a heavier rain, and now Eric and Shaylin were getting drenched.

"You still want to stand out here?" Shaylin said. "Because if you do, I'll stay with you. But we probably look like a couple of damn fools."

"All right, you win," Eric said, conceding to the elements. "Let's go inside, cover up, and listen to the rain."

KOREA, TWO WEEKS LATER

Shaylin's tent was, like the others, squat and mottled green, spread along the side of a lonely hilltop near the village of Tongduchon. When she arrived in Korea, she had asked permission to go as far forward as they would be willing to let her go, and Tongduchon was it.

There was no war here, but there was plenty of evidence of war. It was the site of a Mobile Army Surgical Hospital, better known as a MASH unit, and every day casualties were brought back from the front—some by ambulance, some by jeep, and some, if their wounds were critical enough, by helicopter. Augmenting the human destruction, less than one hundred yards from her tent lay the wreckage of a Marine Corsair.

On her first day in camp Shaylin had decided to examine the wreckage and walked across the compound to the site. Someone who had seen the crash had said that the Corsair came down low to strafe the hill just beyond. It spewed out rockets and machine-gun fire; then, when the pilot tried to pull out of his strafing pass, the airplane wobbled once and crashed. No one knew what made it wobble; as far as anyone could tell, it hadn't been hit by ground fire.

The dark-blue metal of the airplane was so twisted

and torn that the only way Shaylin had been able to tell it had been a plane was because she had been told so. However, a stenciled line of print on one of the mangled pieces of metal, clearly visible in the wreckage, said: CUT HERE FOR RESCUE. But there had been no rescue. The pilot had been killed in the crash.

The two weeks at the MASH unit passed uneventfully. There were a couple of radios in the compound area, and on days when the weather was good, they could pick up American broadcasts from Japan. The American deejay, transmitting from his comfortable office over in Tokyo, was apparently extremely taken with a new record by Kay Starr, "Wheel of Fortune," for he played the song so many times that Shaylin knew it word for word after just one day. Even when she wasn't hearing it over the radio, she was hearing it in her mind. She decided she had to get out of the camp, one way or another, or she would go crazy.

She put in a request to go all the way up to the MLR, or main line of resistance, as the front was being called in this war. But so far the request hadn't been granted. It hadn't been denied, either, so she still maintained some hope that permission would eventually be granted. However, one of the doctors, himself a colonel, told Shaylin he had overheard the big brass talking about her. The reason they had made no decision yet was because they didn't want to. If they told her she couldn't go forward, they would be abridging the freedom of the press. On the other hand, if they told her she *could* go forward, and then she happened to get seriously hurt or even killed, they'd have a lot of explaining to do. For the brass it was clearly a no-win situation.

Fed up with their indecision, Shaylin decided to take matters into her own hands. Overhearing that one of the ambulances would be starting back toward the MLR, Shaylin threw her few belongings into her duffel bag, then hurried to the outskirts of the camp, where she knew the ambulance driver wouldn't have the chance to check on her story. Flagging him down, she told him that she had been cleared to go to the front if she could get her own transportation. The driver was a private who never questioned anything if it was told to him authoritatively, and Shaylin was a past master at speaking authoritatively.

The ride was harrowing. A peaceful stretch of road would suddenly turn into an obstacle course, and the ambulance driver had to swerve and dodge exploding shells, some all too close for comfort. Occasionally they passed burned-out convoys—from both sides—some still smoldering.

Finally they reached the MLR, a series of loosely connected foxholes on the top of a hill. Shaylin hopped out of the ambulance and found a hole occupied by one soldier, who was facing away from her.

"Hi," she said in a friendly voice. "Got room in your hole for one more?"

The soldier turned around, his eyes wide with shock. "You're a woman!" he said.

Shaylin laughed. "I was the last time I checked." She pulled out the top of her shirt and looked down. "Yep, I still am," she joked.

"But . . . what are you doing up here?"

"I'm a woman, but I'm also a reporter," Shaylin explained. "I'm up here to write about what's going on. That is, if you don't mind sharing your foxhole with me."

"No, ma'am. Uh, that is, yes, ma'am, I'd be glad to share my hole with you." The soldier quickly moved some things around. "Let me make some room for you."

"Don't bother," Shaylin said, dropping into the pit. "I won't take up much space." She took her canteen from her belt and took a drink of water; then, screwing the cap back on, she looked out over the valley below the hill. "Are they down there?"

"Yes, ma'am," the soldier said. "We figure there's maybe two companies of infantry."

Shaylin looked around the top of the hill. "What do we have here?"

"One platoon. But we have the hill. It's hard as hell

to drive someone off a hill. I know. We had to take this one."

Shaylin got out her small notebook. "What's your name, soldier?"

"Prosser, ma'am. Private First Class Kenny Prosser. I'm eighteen years old, and I'm from Clarksville, Georgia."

"Kenny, you don't have to call me 'ma'am' every time you speak to me."

"Yes, ma'am."

"What in the blue blazes of hell are you doing up here?" a loud, angry voice suddenly demanded. Shaylin turned and saw a lieutenant coming toward her. He was bending low, carrying a carbine in his left hand.

"I'm doing my job," Shaylin said. She smiled and stuck out her hand. "I'm Shaylin McKay."

"I don't give a damn if you're Bess Truman!" the lieutenant snapped. "You've got no business being up here."

"I have permission," Shaylin said.

"From whom?"

"From General Ridgeway."

Shaylin did have permission from General Ridgeway to be in Korea and to "operate in as far forward an area as is reasonable in order to accomplish the mission." By her interpretation, this area met that criteria.

"We'll just see about that," the lieutenant said. "RTO!"

"Yes, sir," the radio operator answered.

"Get me Six."

"Yes, sir," the radio operator said. Then, speaking into his handset, he said, "Vexation Six, Vexation Six, this is Vexation Three, over."

Suddenly, and without warning, there was a flash of light, followed by a loud explosion and a column of smoke and dust. When it cleared away, the radio operator was lying on his back in a pool of blood, his head turned to one side and his eyes open but unseeing. The hand holding the receiver and the arm to which it was attached were separated from the body. The radio was no more than pieces of twisted metal and shattered tubes.

"*Incoming!*" someone screamed, though the warning was hardly necessary.

"Get in your holes and stay down!" the lieutenant yelled, racing for his own hole. "They'll be coming up after this!"

The Chinese did not come, but they continued to bombard the hilltop with mortar and artillery fire. Then the sun went down, and it grew dark.

Shortly after dark came a loud screeching sound.

"What's that?" Shaylin asked.

"A loudspeaker," Kenny answered. "They're about to play some music for us."

"Music?"

"If you can call it that."

Almost immediately Shaylin understood what Kenny meant as she was forced to endure the most god-awful cacophony she had ever heard. The Chinese loudspeaker was already into the second song before Shaylin realized, with a start, that she recognized it. The Chinese were playing American songs with their own atonally keyed string and reed instruments. Shaylin thought it sounded like a concert emanating from hell.

After a half-dozen songs a man began to speak. His voice was heavily accented but easily understandable, like the silken Oriental voices of character actors in movies.

"*Good evening, American troops. Here is the news that your officers do not want you to hear. All along the front our glorious forces have met and defeated the best you can send against us. We are undaunted by your wealth. We are undaunted by your weapons. We are undaunted by your American arrogance.*"

"Yeah? Well, fuck you, you undaunted son of a bitch!" a GI yelled, and nervous laughter rippled up and down the line.

"*We are peace-loving peoples who came to Korea only to defend our national borders. We did not start this war. If the Americans will go home and leave us in peace, we will also leave Korea.*

"Think about it, my friends. You have it in your power to end the war now. All you have to do is leave your weapons and come over to our side. We will feed you, clothe you, and protect you. Come now, before it is too late!"

"Suck my dick, asshole!" another GI shouted.

"Sorry 'bout the language, ma'am," Kenny quickly told Shaylin. "The other guys probably don't know there's a lady present."

"Honey, I've heard it all before," Shaylin said. She laughed. "Matter of fact, I've *said* it all before." She looked at Kenny, his features barely discernible in the ambient light of the moon. She could very easily be his mother.

"Are you scared?" Kenny asked.

"Yes."

"I am too," the youth admitted. "But you don't need to be worryin' none 'bout bein' scared. Lieutenant Brewster says everyone's scared. He says them that ain't scared ain't got good sense."

"If that's all it takes, you're looking at someone with a lot of sense," Shaylin quipped.

The screeching from the loudspeaker stopped. There were several moments of silence; then a green rocket arced through the night sky.

"What was that?" Shaylin asked.

"I don't know exactly."

All at once the night erupted with dozens of bugle calls—though not the bugle calls one heard in the movies, when the cavalry launched a charge. It strained the imagination to even refer to them as bugle calls. They sounded like nothing more than a bunch of discordant notes, and that might have been their purpose. Never had Shaylin heard anything so jarring, so soul shattering . . . so frightening.

The bugle calls were followed by clanging cymbals and loud screams and screeching.

Suddenly there were a half-dozen pops high in the air, and flares, launched by American artillery, floated down on parachutes. The flares painted the entire valley in a harsh white light. And in that wavering light Shaylin could see hundreds of Chinese moving across the valley and up the hill. She rose to get a better look.

"Get your ass down, you stupid shit!" someone bellowed from one of the other foxholes, and Shaylin immediately ducked back down.

"Sorry," she mumbled quietly.

"Yes, ma'am. Well, he didn't have no business cussin' at you like that, but he was right. You'd best stay down. We're in for bloody hell for the next little bit, I expect."

The whole valley exploded with gunfire. The Chinese fired burp guns, rifles, carbines, mortars, and recoilless rifles. The Americans answered with heavy machine-gun fire and massive artillery barrages. One by one the flares went out, but the valley continued to be lighted by white phosphorous explosions and a fiery crisscross of tracer ammunition. The tracer rounds from the Chinese weapons were green; from the American weapons, orange. Although there were many, many more Chinese soldiers down in the valley than there were American soldiers on the hill, Shaylin was gratified to see that in the intensity of firing, there seemed to be as many orange tracer rounds as there were green. The Americans were more than holding their own.

The whole scene had an incredible, rather bizarre beauty to it, and Shaylin found herself caught up in the mesmerizing effect of the graceful flight of the tracer rounds. Often they would hit the ground or rocks, then ricochet, creating an ancillary line of fire. Sometimes Shaylin followed the trajectory until the tracers burned out in the air, presumably then becoming blackened missiles of death, racing dangerously through the sky under the cloak of darkness. Furthermore, the bursting phosphorous shells beyond the line of hills on the other side of the valley lit up the sky as if there were an early sunrise.

The attack broke up after about ten minutes. As Kenny had said, it was hard to attack a heavily defended hill, and the strength of the American firepower drove the Chinese back. For nearly an hour after the attack, American artillery continued to launch flares over the battlefield. Shaylin studied the valley floor, expecting to see it littered with hundreds of bodies. To her surprise she wasn't sure she saw any.

"I'm amazed," she said.

"What's that, ma'am?"

"I don't see any bodies out there. How could the Chinese have come through such a ferocious barrage without anyone being killed?"

"Oh, there was some killed," Kenny said. "Some of 'em down in the valley you can't see, even with the flares. Tomorrow, in the sunlight, you'll see them. Some of 'em the Chinese took back with 'em. But the ones up here, you'll see 'em real good."

"Up here? Up where?"

"On the hill, ma'am," Kenny said. "The ones that made it this far."

Shaylin felt her skin crawl. "I didn't know any of them made it this far."

"Yes, ma'am, lots of 'em did," Kenny said. "Fact is, I got a couple myself. I'll show you with the next flare."

As if on cue, another barrage of flares erupted. When they did, Kenny pointed to the gnarled stump of a tree about ten yards in front of their hole. "There's one," he said easily.

Shaylin gasped. The Chinese solder lay facedown, his arms extended over his head and his rifle lying in the dirt in front of him. She had had no idea he was there, yet he was so close she could almost reach out of the hole and touch his rifle.

"Oh, my God!" she whispered. "I didn't know anyone had gotten that close."

"Yes, ma'am. Truth is, the other one's even closer. He's right over here."

Shaylin moved to Kenny's side of the hole and looked out. A body lay no more than five feet away. This one hadn't even been carrying a rifle. Instead, a potato-masher-type grenade lay in front of him.

"I reckon he was goin' to drop that grenade on us," Kenny said. "But, as you can see, the spoon is still attached, so he never even got the pin pulled."

"Well," Shaylin said, sinking down to the bottom of the hole, feeling as though the wind had been knocked out of her, "I wanted to be up front."

"Yes, ma'am, but I expect the lieutenant will be sendin' you back tomorrow."

Shaylin laughed nervously. "You want to know something, Kenny? I won't fight him."

K-14 AIR BASE

Lieutenant Train Willis, wearing a clean, freshly pressed uniform, presented himself to the operations officer at squadron headquarters. As he stood in front of Captain Mitchell's desk, he could see into the XO's office through the partly open door. Captain Travis Jackson was seated at his desk, working on some papers. A feeling of anger came over Train, directed at the black executive officer.

Train had been grounded now for fourteen days. For fourteen days, while he fumed, he had pulled such disagreeable duties as inventory officer, vector control officer, officer in charge of posting all flight and technical manuals, and FOD officer. The latter required that he drive up and down the runways in a jeep, looking for foreign objects that could be sucked into and damage the engines. Thirty minutes ago he was told to report to the commanding officer to receive the results of the accident investigation board.

Captain Mitchell looked up at Train. "The old man is expecting you. Go on in."

"Thanks."

Train stood in front of Colonel Kirby's door. He gave his boots a last-minute polish, rubbing their toes against the back of his trouser legs. Out of the corner of his eye he caught Captain Jackson looking at him. He looked back defiantly, then knocked on the CO's door.

"Come in, Willis," came the colonel's voice.

Train stepped into the office and walked over to

Kirby's desk. He stopped two paces in front of the desk and saluted sharply.

"Sir, Lieutenant Train Willis, reporting to the commanding officer as directed."

Colonel Kirby returned Train's salute.

"Stand at ease, Lieutenant," he said.

Train felt the uneasiness growing in the pit of his stomach. "Stand at ease" did not mean "at ease." Had he been put at ease, he could expect good news as a result of the accident investigation. "Stand at ease" was a position of only slightly relaxed attention, generally reserved for when someone was going to get a chewing out.

Train shifted to the "stand at ease" position, his feet spread to the width of his shoulders, his hands clasped behind his back, his eyes straight ahead.

Colonel Kirby picked up a folder that Train could see was the accident investigation file. Kirby looked at it for a long, silent moment, then sighed and put it down.

"When are you going to learn that you are not Choo Choo Willis, throwing touchdown passes and boffing the cheerleaders?" Kirby asked.

"I beg your pardon, sir?"

Kirby read from the folder. "Thanks to you, Lieutenant, we have a damaged generator, a mangled portable fire extinguisher, and the complete scrapping of one wing assembly, which comes to a grand total of eleven thousand, six hundred and eighteen dollars and thirty-one cents. What do you have to say about that?"

"Well, sir, I could handle the thirty-one cents pretty easily," Train quipped.

"Can you? *Can you, Lieutenant?*" Colonel Kirby shouted at the top of his voice, at the same time standing up and slamming his hand down on the desktop.

Train winced. "I'm sorry, Colonel. I was just trying to make a joke."

"This is no joking matter, Lieutenant."

"No, sir," Train said humbly. "I see that it isn't."

"What in God's name were you thinking, climbing up on the seat like that?"

"Colonel, I . . ." Train stopped and sighed. "I have no excuse, sir."

"Don't give me that standard 'I have no excuse' bull-shit." Kirby sat back down. "At ease, Lieutenant."

"Thank you, sir." Train felt some hope returning.

"Willis, I want you to tell me, in your own words, what was on your mind when you did such a damn fool thing."

"I was thinking of the men on the flight line, sir."

"What do you mean? You were showing off for them?"

"No, sir," Train answered. "I mean, well, yes, sir, I guess I was," he amended. "But not the way you think. You see, the boys on the flight line do all the work and get none of the fun. You know how it is for them, Colonel. It's always too hot or too cold or sometimes the supply system is so screwed up, they have to make do with nothing, and yet they keep the planes flying. I just thought that by my celebrating getting the MIG like that, I mean in front of them, it would be like it was their MIG, too. I was sort of including them in the glory. I know it doesn't make sense, but that's what I was thinking."

Kirby shook his head slowly. "The hell of it is, I suppose it does make sense in some convoluted way. It makes sense—but it was a stupid, stupid thing to do."

"Yes, sir, I know that now."

"The board found you totally culpable."

"Yes, sir. I don't see where they had any other choice."

"The board recommended that you be found"—Kirby picked up the file and quoted from it—"negligent and incompetent."

Train let out a short gasp.

"Do you know what that means, Willis?"

"Not exactly, sir, but I'm sure it isn't good."

"No, it isn't good. It isn't good at all. For a finding of negligent and incompetent you could be permanently grounded. You could even be cashiered out of the Air Force."

"Yes, sir," Train said quietly. There was nothing else

he could say. "I'm sure Captain Jackson has his reasons for it, him being a colored officer and me being from the South."

Kirby held up his hand. "Now, just hold it right there, Lieutenant, before you let your alligator mouth write a check your hummingbird ass can't cash."

"Yes, sir."

"For your information, Captain Jackson, as the reviewing officer, submitted a different recommendation. He recommended that you be found 'careless and imprudent,' which as you know is a far lesser charge."

"That was very good of the captain, sir."

Kirby dropped the folder onto his desktop. "You're damned right, it was very good of him. In fact, if I had been the reviewing officer, I would've gone with the board's recommendation, and I tried to talk Travis into going along with it as well. But when I gave him this assignment, I also gave him the authority that goes with it, so if 'careless and imprudent' is what he wants, I'm going to back him up."

Train couldn't hold back a smile. "Yes, *sir!*" he said.

"Now, about the eleven thousand dollars' worth of damage . . ."

The smile left Train's face as he waited for the other shoe to drop.

"I'm going to report-of-survey the damage," Kirby continued. "I can't expect any of my officers to have to come up with that kind of money."

"Thank you, sir!" Train said with a huge sigh of relief.

Kirby pointed a stern finger at Train. "But, mister, let me tell you this: If you get out of line in this outfit one more time—just one more time—I'll have you up before a court-martial board so quick you won't know whether to shit or wind your watch."

"Yes, sir. I understand, sir," Train said.

"Now, report to Captain Jackson. He's taking you up for an evaluation flight this afternoon. If you handle yourself to his satisfaction, you're back on flying status."

"Yes, sir!" Train said, coming to attention and saluting. "Thank you, sir!"

Kirby almost offhandedly returned the salute.

The flight line was the only place in Korea where one wasn't constantly assailed by the smells of manure, fish, and rotting vegetation. That was because the flight line constantly smelled of fuel, oil, and hot jet exhaust. Some might have found the smell unpleasant, but to Train it was as sweet as perfume, and he was damn glad to be back.

He put his helmet on the wing of his plane and began the walk-around inspection. He felt someone approach, and when he looked around, he saw that Captain Jackson was with him, watching his every move.

"Captain, you aren't going to watch me make the preflight, are you?"

"Why not? That's part of your mission, isn't it?"

"Yes, sir, but I haven't had anyone observe my preflight since I was in primary."

"Perhaps it's time you *did* have someone observe."

Train sighed. "Yes, sir," he said. He squatted down under the wing and depressed the strainers to drain off the water that had, through condensation, accumulated in the fuel tanks. "By the way, sir, I want to thank you for recommending a lighter finding."

"I thought about going along with the board," Travis replied. "But from everything I've been able to determine, you have the makings of a good flyer. And, as you yourself pointed out to me, we are undermanned. Just don't make me sorry."

"No, sir, I'll try not to." Train finished his walkaround, then took his helmet off the wing. He saw that Travis was looking at the rebel flag. Clearing his throat, he asked, "Does the flag bother you, sir?"

"As a reminder of a time of oppression and slavery, it isn't one of my favorite symbols."

Train shifted uncomfortably. "No, sir, I guess it wouldn't be. But despite what you might think, I don't wear it for those reasons. This flag is also the symbol of my university football team. I wear it for Ole Miss, not for Marse Robert."

"And why do you think the University of Mississippi

chose that flag as their symbol, Lieutenant? Remember, it *is* a segregated university."

"I don't make the rules, Captain."

"But you did attend school there."

"Yes, sir, I did. And I make no apology for it. Ole Miss is a fine school, and I'm proud to have gone there."

Travis gave a brief shake of his head. "I doubt that this is something we can settle between us." He turned toward his own plane. "Air-to-air frequency will be one twenty-two point nine. Come up to flight push as soon as we leave departure control."

"Yes, sir," Train said. "By the way, where are we going?"

"Do you know the railroad tunnel at Hill three two six?"

"Yes, sir."

"We're going to take it out," Travis said matter-of-factly.

Train laughed.

"What's so funny, Lieutenant?"

"The way you said 'We're going to take it out' as if we were just going to the store for groceries or something."

"You don't think we will?"

"Have you been there before, Captain?"

"No, but I've examined the strike photos from previous missions. To take it out all you'd need to do is put a few bombs right into the mouth of the tunnel. No one has done that yet."

"No, sir, no one has," Train agreed. "Captain, one of those previous missions was mine. Would you like me to explain just why no one has put a few bombs into the mouth?"

"Please do."

"If you examined the strike photos carefully, you saw that the tunnel is at the end of a long draw. To get your bombs into the mouth of the tunnel, you have to actually go down into that draw. It's a very narrow draw, Captain, with no more than ten feet of clearance off either wing tip. And to make matters worse, the draw makes

about a forty-five-degree turn just before you reach the
tunnel."

"Well," Travis said, smiling, "then that should make
quite a formidable challenge for a couple of hotshot pilots
like you and me, shouldn't it, Lieutenant?"

Train knew then that the challenge Travis Jackson
was talking about was between the two of them. He had
just thrown down the gauntlet. It was up to Train to pick
it up. Train stared at Travis for a long moment, then
smiled wryly.

"I'm game if you are, Captain."

Moments later the two Saberjets were streaking
north. Train hadn't realized how much he missed flying
until now. Here, high in the thin atmosphere, he could
experience the sense of freedom of "slipping the surly
bonds of earth." They were going fast—so fast that the
roaring scream of his engine was behind him, and he was
aware only of the soft whisper of air past his canopy and a
rush of the squelch in his earphones.

Below was the jagged, twisting, convoluted landscape of Korea. The mountains were bare and ugly, and
Train knew that in their folds and at their summits strug-
gles of life and death took place daily between human
beings who were fighting this war on the most elemental
level. He knew, also, that a bit farther north lay the railroad tunnel of Hill 326. The number meant that the hill
was 326 meters high. All hills were designated on military
maps by their altitude.

The hill probably had a real name, Train thought.
One of those totally unpronounceable Korean names that
when translated to English would mean something like "I
love you and I hope you love me, but if you don't, I want
you to take a long hike across this mountain without shoes
so that your feet blister."

Train laughed at his name for the hill. It really wasn't
that funny, but it felt good to relieve the tension—and the
tension was beginning to build up. This was not going to
be an easy mission. If, as Captain Jackson said, they really

were going to take out the tunnel . . . Well, they were in for a hell of a time.

"*Two, are you on this push?*" Travis Jackson's voice popped over the squelch.

"Roger, One," Train replied, keying his mike. "I'm with you."

"*There's the hill.*"

Train looked up and saw the hill. He had been so preoccupied that he hadn't even noticed it.

"Roger the hill."

"*I'll make the first run,*" the captain said. "*You fly high cover and keep an eye open for any MIG who might want to sneak up on us. After I come out, you can make your run.*"

"Roger," Train said.

Train put his jet into a wide orbit as Travis started down toward the draw. Train watched him go down, down, down, until—from this angle—he thought the Saberjet was going to slam into the ground and erupt into a rose of flame. Finally he saw the Saberjet level out far below, then skim along the railroad tracks, so close to them that Train was convinced that if Jackson lowered his gear, he'd be driving.

Every gun on both sides of the draw opened up on the speeding Saberjet. The tracer rounds flew back and forth across the narrow valley so thick that Train was reminded of one of those crystal-ball paperweights that, when inverted, started a miniature snowstorm. Jackson's plane could have been inside one of those little crystal balls. Except those little snowstorms were peaceful, charming scenes. This one was deadly. And the situation was even more alarming yet when Train factored in the calculation that he was actually seeing only one-fifth of what was being sent up, for between every tracer round there were four other rounds not marked by tracers.

Suddenly the end of the draw exploded in a large, fiery ball, and for a moment Train thought his captain had gone down. He searched frantically for the tiny silver jet, then, with a sigh of relief, saw it in a twisting climb away from the draw.

"You okay, One?"

"Affirmative," came the calm response.

"I lost sight of you for a while; I thought you were gone."

"It was pretty tight," Travis admitted.

"Yeah, I guess so. Well, now that they're all stirred up, I guess I'll go down and give 'em a whack."

"You don't have to."

"Say again?"

"Fly cover. I'll go back."

"Negative," Train said. "I'm going down."

"Okay, if you want to. I'll fly cover for you."

Train flipped his airplane over, then dropped out of the sky, finally pulling out of his dive just before the entrance into the draw. He was already lower than he had been on the last mission he'd flown against the tunnel, but he knew that Travis Jackson had gone much, much lower, and he was determined to match him. Train took a deep breath, held it, then pushed his Saberjet on down into the draw itself. Now on each side of his canopy he could see the jagged edges of the cliffs sliding by in a blur.

Even if there were no Communist gunners at all, Train would have had only a fifty-fifty chance of flying through the draw without crashing into the rocks on one side or the other. But there *were* gunners, and they were firing with everything they had so that the sky around him was crisscrossed with speeding balls of fire and erupting puffs of smoke—all aimed at him.

Just ahead, the valley made a sharp turn to the left, and Train stood on his left wing to stay on course. Then he saw the tunnel and the smoke coming out of the mouth from Jackson's run. Amazingly, it looked as if Captain Jackson had done exactly what he'd said he was going to do: He had put his bombs right into the tunnel.

Train waited until the last minute, and then he toggled off his own bombs. Aided by the rapid weight reduction, he was able to pop up and out of the valley, using the same twisting, climbing tactic his flight leader had used before him. The G-force pulled against him as he climbed out, and he could feel his face distort under the pressure.

Then, when he rolled out at the top, there was a momentary and nauseating sense of weightlessness.

"Good job, Two," he heard Travis say. *"Now hang around up here while I go down for a look-see."*

"You're going down again?"

"Roger," Travis replied, and Train saw him peel off for a second pass.

The gunners were angrier and readier this time. It didn't seem possible, but from Train's perspective it looked like the firing was even more intense.

"What the fuck are you doing, you dumb nigger? Are you trying to show up the white man?" Train muttered, though as he didn't key his mike, the words went nowhere. "You're going to get your black ass killed, that's what you're going to do."

Incredibly, Captain Jackson's Saberjet emerged from the other end of the valley, still apparently unscathed. He came back up to Train's altitude.

"Okay, Two, let's start back."

"Roger," Train answered. "One, what did the target look like?"

"We got it," Travis said easily. *"You want to take a look for yourself?"*

Train knew that Jackson was baiting him, but there was no way he could walk away from the challenge. "Yeah, sure," he said casually. "Why the hell not?"

Peeling out of formation, Train dropped down for one more pass through the valley. Incredibly, the firing was much less severe than it had been the first time; perhaps the gunners had expended most of their ammunition. When he passed over the mouth of the tunnel, or more accurately what *had* been the mouth of the tunnel, he saw that the bombing runs had been extremely successful. There was so much rubble over the railroad that it looked as if half the mountain had been brought down. No supplies would be coming this way for a while.

"What do you think?" Travis asked when Train rejoined him after a few moments.

"You were right. We took it out."

ONE WEEK LATER

Train followed the young, dark-haired, sloe-eyed girl down a twisting alley of the little village that was just outside the main gate of the airfield. The streets of the "ville," as the GIs called it, teemed with humanity: vendors pushing their carts, young boys shilling for the vendors and pimping for the whores, and the whores themselves—from prepubescent girls to withered old women—plying their vocation. The market pool for all these services was the off-duty American soldiers and airmen who wandered around the ville with their pockets full of military payment certificates, looking for whatever diversion they could find from the rigors of duty in Korea.

The alley Train found himself in reeked, like the rest of the ville, with various unpleasant smells—urine, rotting fish and cabbage, and the manure used to fertilize the nearby rice fields.

The girl abruptly stopped and turned to smile at Train, then pointed to a door that was so small, Train would have to bend double to pass through.

"Your friends have *takusan* party in there," she said.

Train started to go in, but the girl held up her hand to stop him.

"No!" she said. "First, I catchee you shoes!"

"Oh, yeah, I forgot. No shoes inside," Train said. He took off his shoes and handed them to her, and she added them to the numerous pairs lined up neatly just outside the door. Giving his socks a quick tug to get them back in place, Train then slipped through the sliding door.

The room, which was about twenty feet by forty feet, was devoid of furniture. About ten officers and an equal number of very pretty Korean women sat cross-legged on the floor around a large tablecloth arrayed with various aromatic, colorful foods.

A long handmade banner tacked on the far wall showed a Chinese MIG going down in flames. Behind the MIG was a Saberjet. The torso of the pilot of the Saberjet, drawn in cartoon style, was sticking out of the cockpit, its size way out of proportion to the rest of the plane. The pilot was obviously meant to be Train Willis, because he was wearing a flight helmet decorated with a rebel flag. The cartoon Train was holding up his hand with all five fingers extended; words in a drawn balloon over his head read, "And number five bites the dust!"

As soon as Train stepped inside, someone started to sing, "For he's a jolly good fellow!"

Other voices took up the song.

> "For he's a jolly good fellow,
> For he's a jolly good f-e-l-l-o-w,
> Which nobody can deny."

The off-key rendition ended on a peal of laughter. Lieutenant Terrance W. Balfour, a southerner like his colleague, handed a glass to Train and said, "Have a drink, Choo Choo! This is Mokely's Whiskey"—his southern drawl turned silky as he emulated the tones of a radio announcer—" 'the preferred whiskey of ninety-one members of the Korean Parliament.' " Everyone laughed at the quotation from the billboard that stood just outside the main gate of K-14 Air Base, touting the drink, in English, as the drink of choice of most Korean parliamentarians. But rather than enhancing the desirability of the whiskey, the billboard made it the butt of many American jokes.

"Yeah, they drink it all right," somebody said. "When they can't get furniture polish."

There was more laughter, and then one of the officers proposed a toast.

"To Lieutenant Train Choo Choo Willis, for getting his fifth MIG. Only he would've gotten it a long time ago if our shade XO hadn't grounded him."

"Hear, hear," someone else concurred, and everyone took a drink.

"I was beginnin' to think he was never goin' to let you fly again," Balfour said.

Train laughed. "I was beginnin' to think that, too."

"Then he goes and adds insult to injury by finally lettin' you fly again, then goin' along as your wingmate to observe your techniques. Ha! I'll bet that was a laugh."

Balfour shook his head. "I'll tell you one thing, if he'd been my wingmate, I'd've given him plenty of room."

"Why, Terry?" Train asked.

"Why? Well, hell, why do you think? He's a nigger aviator, isn't he? And I learned a long time ago that if there's one thing you want to stay away from, it's a nigger aviator."

"You can't say that about all of 'em, Terry," one of the other pilots said. "Lieutenants Ware and Mack aren't bad. Hell, I've flown with both of 'em. Neither of 'em's any more of a doofus than any other second lieutenant."

"Ware and Mack are different," Balfour insisted, "because they came up after the flight schools were integrated, so they got their trainin' from white instructors. They say Jackson learned to fly at that nigger flight school they had somewhere down in Alabama during the war."

"Tuskegee," someone supplied.

"Yeah, Tuskegee. Can you imagine what their trainin' must've been like?" Sniggering, Balfour imitated the voice of Kingfish on Amos and Andy. "Now, lookee heah, gemp'muns, dis heah be one of dem dere airyplanes. Buts before you flies it, you gots to learn to put on your goggles."

He made circles with his thumbs and index fingers and held them to his eyes. "Now," he said, "I be's a nigger aviator."

Everyone laughed, including Train.

"Is that our colored captain or what?" Balfour asked.

"Not exactly," Train said.

"Not exactly? Hell, he went to Tuskegee, didn't he?"

"As far as I know, he did. But if so, I have to be the first one to admit that he learned somethin'."

"What did he learn?"

"Have you ever seen him fly?" Train asked. "I mean, *really* fly?"

"I've flown a couple of missions that he's led," Balfour replied. "At least we all managed to be goin' in approximately the same direction at the same time."

The others laughed again.

"No," Train said, waving his hand. "I mean really

gut-wrenchin', turnin' the airplane inside out, maximum-G, minimum-clearance kind of flyin'. Have you ever seen him do that?"

"No."

"Well, I have," Train said. "Captain Jackson is no hero of mine, but you sure as hell won't catch me sayin' he's not good at what he does. The fact is, he is damn good, and that's one of the problems I have. Seems to me like there's nothin' more arrogant than a colored man who is good and knows he's good."

"Like Jackie Robinson," someone said.

"Or Don Newcombe."

"Or Joe Louis."

"Joe Louis isn't arrogant."

"No, and he's not the best, either," someone suggested. "Rocky Marciano's the best."

Train said, "I don't know about baseball or boxin', but I do know about flying. And Captain Travis Jackson is the best flier I've ever seen."

"Train, are you saying he's better than you?"

"Yeah, he is," Train confessed. "I don't like to admit it, but on my best day I couldn't match him."

"I'll be damned," Balfour said, sounding awed by the prospect.

Train smiled. "Which is all the more reason why I don't like the wiseassed son of a bitch!"

"Let's drink to that!" Balfour suggested, and the pilots all hoisted their glasses.

NEAR TONGDUCHON

Shaylin had been thoroughly chastised when she returned to her tent on the hill at Tongduchon, and the colonel in charge was ready to send her back immediately to the States. Two things stopped him. One was Shaylin's assurance that she wouldn't try to sneak forward again—she had been so terrified by the experience that she had no desire to repeat it. The other was Shaylin's story.

Following procedure, it was submitted to the division

PIO for clearance, and the public information officer was so impressed with the story that he made a thermafax copy for the general. The general passed it around to several of his colonels, telling them that this kind of feature might possibly rouse the American public from their apathy toward the war in Korea. As a result, everyone was ordered to give Shaylin VIP treatment.

Shaylin didn't realize that her article had been passed around to so many people, so when she went to the colonel to request permission to go along on one of the security patrols, she was prepared for him to give her a hard time.

She stated her proposal, adding quickly, "Not one of the patrols that go forward. Just a routine surveillance patrol."

These patrols did little more than check on the integrity of telephone wires—land lines, they were called—between friendly elements. They rarely encountered a foe, doing so only if they happened to run across an enemy patrol probing the American lines.

To Shaylin's surprise, she didn't need a convincing argument. The colonel agreed to let her go.

"As a matter of fact, a patrol is just about to head out," he told her.

She hurried out of the colonel's tent before he could change his mind.

There were six on the patrol, seven counting Shaylin. A sergeant was in charge; he went first, while his second-in-charge, a corporal, brought up the rear. One man on the patrol carried a Browning automatic rifle, the others carried M-1 rifles. Shaylin carried nothing but a canteen.

The patrol was more physically demanding than Shaylin thought it would be. Moving at a pace slightly faster than a comfortable walk, they trekked across built-up dikes through the rice paddies and along narrow, winding roads that saw a lot more water buffalo traffic than motor vehicle traffic. They climbed up mountain trails so steep that Shaylin could sometimes touch the ground just by putting out her hand. They passed through tiny villages where dozens of children rushed out to greet them; noticing that one of the soldiers was a woman, the excitement rose to a fever pitch.

There were some rewards. Reaching the summit of one of the hills, they stopped for a few minutes' rest, and Shaylin could enjoy a sweeping vista of the country known as "The Land of the Morning Calm."

"Miss, don't get too far away," the sergeant said, as Shaylin walked toward the edge for a better view.

"I won't," she promised. She started out on an overhanging precipice when she felt something snap underfoot, as if she had just stepped on and broken a twig. She had just time enough to look down in curiosity to see what it was, when there was a blinding flash of light, then a searing heat . . . then nothing.

CHAPTER FOUR

OCTOBER 23, 1952, FROM "TRAILMARKERS,"
EVENTS MAGAZINE:

SHAYLIN MCKAY AWARD ESTABLISHED

Kendra Petzold, chairman of the board of the Petzold Media Group, announced that an award has been established in the name of the late Shaylin McKay. Miss McKay, who was married to novelist Eric Twainbough, was killed by a land mine last month while doing a series of articles on the war in Korea for *Events*.

"Shaylin McKay established a standard of excellence to which all women in journalism should aspire," Mrs. Petzold said when making the announcment. "Therefore, from this day forth, the Petzold Foundation will endeavor to annually recognize the woman journalist who most lives up to that ideal, by awarding her the 'Shaylin.'"

Mrs. Petzold pointed out that the award is in

addition to the Petzold Prize, for which both men and women are eligible. She also noted that the Shaylin is not limited to women writing for the Petzold Media Group, but will be awarded to deserving women regardless of their professional affiliation.

GREAT BRITAIN TESTS ITS FIRST
ATOMIC BOMB

Great Britain, though the United States' strongest ally, has been excluded since the war from American bomb secrets by the MacMahon Act. That act is now a moot point, as the United Kingdom detonated its own atomic bomb off northwest Australia, aboard a British naval ship. Now there are three members of the nuclear club —the most exclusive club in the world—the U.S., the U.S.S.R., and the U.K.

Scientists around the world are urging that further nuclear testing be stopped lest the proliferation of atomic weapons grow unchecked. Such proliferation, they warn, could "turn the world into a nuclear wasteland."

ST. LOUIS GRAYS BASEBALL TEAM SOLD;
TO BE RELOCATED TO BALTIMORE

Hamilton Twainbough, president of the St. Louis Grays baseball team, announced that the team was being sold to a consortium in Baltimore.

"It was a very difficult decision," Mr. Twainbough stated. "St. Louis is a wonderful baseball town, and nowhere in America are the fans as enthusiastic as they are here."

Mr. Twainbough did not go into all the reasons as to why Tannenhower Brewery sold the Grays, but it is widely known that there has been dissatisfaction in some quarters over the fact that for many years now, the Grays have not fielded a winning team. By contrast, the other St. Louis team, the Cardinals, have been consistent contenders. Hamilton Twainbough alluded to that when he stated, with a smile, "Now, like so many other St. Louisians, I, too, will become a Cardinals fan."

Part of the deal includes the selling of Sportsman's Park to the Cardinals. Though owned by the Grays, both teams have used Sportsman's Park as their home field, carefully organizing their schedules to accommodate that arrangement.

The St. Louis Grays, affectionately known by their avid fans as "the Graybies," won the American League title in 1944, only to lose the World Series to the Cardinals in the "Trolley Car Series." They also enjoyed a brief period of competitiveness during the late twenties when Lenny "Swampwater" Puckett was their leading pitcher. Mr. Puckett, who until last year was "The Voice of the Grays," is now reportedly negotiating to do the television commentary for selected baseball games to be broadcast by the NBC television network.

FRANKIE LAINE PERFORMS AT THE LONDON PALLADIUM

Frankie Laine, best known for his bellowing voice and loud songs ("My Heart Knows What the Wild Goose Knows") performed in London to sell-out crowds for two weeks. One American music critic, also somewhat of a wag, is reported to have said, "Good. I hope they like him so much that they keep him over there."

SIKESTON, MISSOURI

When Buck Campbell opened his eyes, he had no idea where he was. He had played a show last night, he knew that. He could remember the music, the bar, and the cigarette smoke. He could also remember a girl . . . and a fight. But Buck wasn't sure whether he'd participated in the fight or merely watched it.

He got out of bed and reached for his battered Stetson, then, naked except for the hat, walked to the window to look out over the field behind the motel cabin. A cold, steady rain was falling, and water stood in muddy troughs between the rows of knee-high cotton plants.

A rusting, wheelless '36 Plymouth sat on blocks in the motel's backyard. Its yawning hood exposed the cavity where the engine had been. A rabbit was huddled under the right front fender, water dripping from its long, dangling ears.

"I tell you the truth there, Brer Rabbit," Buck rumbled, "you look just about as miserable as I feel."

He felt an urgent need for a drink and looked around the room. A whiskey bottle lay on its side on the dresser, empty and useless. An open can of Tannenhower beer sat on the bedside table, the brand easily identifiable by the closed-wing eagle clutching the crossbar of the T in its talons. Hefting the can, Buck determined it was about half full. The top was covered with cigarette ash.

He held the can up in the wet, gray light and, looking down through the two triangular holes punched in the lid, saw a soggy cigarette butt floating around inside. He shook the can, and the smell of stale beer and wet tobacco wafted up to his nose.

"Ah, what the hell," he shrugged. "Might as well get my cigarette and my beer at the same time." He raised the can and drank the warm, flat beer, using his lips and teeth to hold back the cigarette butt.

Behind him the door opened, and the motel maid came in to make the bed. Not noticing Buck standing near the window, she went about her business, humming "Brighten the Corner, Where You Are."

"Howdy, ma'am," Buck said, turning and saluting her with his can of beer. "Would you be kind enough to tell me where I am?"

The maid took one look at the naked man in the cowboy hat, screamed, then ran from the room.

"What the hell, lady!" Buck called to her. "Was it somethin' I said?"

Shrugging again, Buck returned to the window, the

rain, and the old, rusting Plymouth. The rabbit was gone, and a dog was sniffing around the car.

"You son of a bitch," Buck growled at the dog. "What the hell'd you run the rabbit off for? All he wanted was to get outta the rain."

"Mornin', Buck."

Buck turned away from the window to find Frankie Porter, his lead guitarist, standing in the doorway. Frankie was decked out in a silk shirt of bright yellow—a color echoed by the piping on his brown pants—a red kerchief around his neck, and pointed-toed, high-heeled cowboy boots. His belt buckle was a huge silver horseshoe.

"Hi, Frankie," Buck said. "Come on in."

"What's wrong with the maid? Did you try to attack her or somethin'? I passed her outside, screamin' like she'd been raped."

"You know, I don't know what the hell did get into her," Buck replied, raising the beer can to his lips for another drink. "All I did was say good mornin' and ask where I was." He burped.

"Where'd you find a beer this mornin'?" Frankie asked. "I thought we drunk 'em all last night."

"I saved one," Buck said, setting down the now-empty can. "Say, have you figured out where we are yet?"

Frankie laughed. "Hell, yes, I know where we are. I didn't get *that* drunk last night."

"Yeah, well, the thing is, I didn't know where we were *before* I got drunk."

"This here is Sikeston, Missouri, and we're in the El Camino Motel," Frankie said.

"How long we goin' to be here?"

"Two more nights. Then we go over to Poplar Bluff."

A knock sounded at the door.

"Come in," Buck called.

When the door opened, two women stepped inside. One was the maid who had been in Buck's room a few minutes earlier, and the other was Pearline Poindexter. Buck realized he knew her name as soon as he saw her, but he didn't know why he knew her. Then he remembered that Mrs. Poindexter ("You fellas can just call me

Pearline," she had told them yesterday, when they checked in) and her husband, Corey, were the owners of the motel. How could he remember that, he wondered, and not know where he was?

"Do you see what I told you, Mrs. Poindexter?" the maid gasped, turning her back in embarrassment. "I came in here to make up the room, and there he was, naked as a jaybird, just the way you see him now. I'm an honest workin' woman, Mrs. Poindexter . . . I ought not to have to put up with somethin' like that."

Unlike the maid, Pearline, who was a very attractive, midfortyish woman, did not turn away. Instead, she stood there, unabashedly staring at Buck's nakedness as a small smile played across her lips.

"Of course you shouldn't have to put up with it," she said.

"Pearline, I'm just real sorry if I upset your maid. Lord knows, I sure didn't mean to," Buck said. He spoke quietly and politely, but his voice was rumbling and deep. Someone once said that he spoke and sang like a train letting off steam.

"That's quite all right," Pearline replied.

"All right?" the maid gasped. "But he's naked, Mrs. Poindexter. He doesn't have any clothes on."

"I can see that, Ima Jean," Pearline replied. She studied Buck. "But he *is* in his room, after all. It's not as if he was out running around in the parking lot. Why don't you just go and take care of one of the other cabins and leave Mr. Campbell in peace? I'm sure you'll get the opportunity to make up his cabin later."

"Yeah, listen, Ima Jean, I'm about to go to breakfast, anyway," Buck said. "You could come back in a few minutes, and I'll be out of your hair."

"You're going to breakfast?" Pearline asked, laughing.

Buck looked at her quizzically. "Yeah." He glanced at his guitarist. "What about you, Frankie? You had breakfast?"

Frankie chuckled. "And lunch."

"No shit? What time *is* it?"

"Four-thirty."

"In the afternoon?"

"Yes, in the afternoon."

"Well, I'll be go to hell. What do you think of that? It'll be time to do our show before you know it. Pearline, I sure hope you and Mr. Poindexter are plannin' on catchin' the show tonight."

"Mr. Poindexter had to go to Memphis today," Pearline replied. "He won't be back until tomorrow. Late tomorrow," she added pointedly. "But I'll be there. I wouldn't miss it for anything."

"I'll do a song just for you," Buck said.

Pearline started to leave, but she stopped at the door and turned around. "I do hope you manage to get dressed before you sing, you naughty boy," she said, wagging a finger back and forth, playfully chastising him.

"Oh, uh, yes, ma'am. I suppose I'd better get dressed at that," Buck said, tipping his hat. "I'll see you tonight."

"Well, I certainly hope you don't see as much of me as I've just seen of you," Pearline teased.

"Why not? It might be fun. I mean, what with your husband bein' gone and all."

Pearline laughed nervously. "You are a naughty, naughty boy."

"Damn!" Frankie said after Pearline left. "I thought she was goin' to jump your bones right here in front of me."

"Ah, she's a sweet kid," Buck said.

"Kid? She's forty-five if she's a day. Hell, she's got ten to twelve years on you."

Buck grinned. "What's a few years 'tween friends?"

The sign in front of the roadhouse read:

TONIGHT!
BUCK CAMPBELL AND THE DRIFTING COWBOYS!
FIFTY CENTS COVER CHARGE!

The band reached the stage by going through the kitchen and its accompanying smell of hamburger grease and fried onions. A very thin old man, wearing a white apron and a white cook's cap, scurried back and forth along the big industrial range, flipping over hamburger patties with his spatula.

"You know, them hamburgers don't smell half bad," Lucky Jennings said. "Sure wish we had time to grab us a bite before we went on."

"You've had all day," Buck said.

"Yeah, well, I just didn't think of it before now."

Johnny Patterson leaned down to look through the serving hole between the kitchen and the waitresses' station. "Look at 'em out there," he said. "Ain't they a fine-lookin' bunch?"

"Come on," Buck said. "Let's get set up."

The stage was a small, unpainted pine platform at one end of the bar between the kitchen and the dining room. When the crowd saw the band come onto the stage, they started getting restless.

"Hey you! Fuzz face!" someone from the audience yelled.

Buck looked over his shoulder at the crowd and saw a big man sitting at a table near the front. The man had turned his chair away from the table, where a pile of crushed beer cans tottered. Sitting with his legs spread wide, facing the stage, he was wearing coveralls and a red-and-blue St. Louis Cardinals baseball cap. "Yeah, I'm talkin' to you," he said, noticing Buck was looking at him. "You better play real good tonight. I had to pay half-a-dollar extra just to get in here. If you ain't good, I'm goin' to have to whip your scrawny little ass."

"Think you can handle him, Buck?" Frankie asked quietly.

Buck looked back at the big man. "Ah, he's no problem."

"No problem? Hell, look at the son of a bitch! He's twice as big as you."

"I can handle him, though," Buck replied. "Shit, I could be out the back door before he even reached the stage," he added, and the other band members laughed.

It took them a couple of minutes to get set up, tuned up, and ready for their first song.

"Hey! Play 'I'm Walkin' the Floor over You,' " somebody shouted.

"No, no, let's hear that one by Hank Williams. 'Ramblin' Man.' "

"Why don't you let 'im play some of his own songs?" another suggested. "I was here last night. He's pretty good."

"Thanks," Buck called to the man. "If it's all right with you folks, I'll just do a mix. Some of my songs and a few covers."

"Well, quit talkin' about it and start doin' it!" someone shouted.

Buck turned to the others in the band and gave the downbeat. "A one, a two, a one, two, three . . ."

He ripped into his first song as if he were challenging the crowd to find fault with it and sang as if there were thousands cheering him instead of just under a hundred. The men who had taunted him now sat quietly, listening to the rasp of his voice, caught up in the power and sweep of his music.

But the women were most affected by Buck Campbell. Pearline and the waitresses and the women customers at the tables and the bar were rapt. Their eyes shone and their lips parted as they listened. It was as if Buck's music were some sort of magic sexual charm, more seductive than sweet words or good looks.

The music wasn't traditional country; nor was it Western. There were a lot of chord changes, and Buck sang against a strong rhythm that seemed to move into the very pulse of the listeners.

His lyrics were also different. He didn't sing about the usual country themes of "cheatin', hurtin', and cryin' "; rather, his unusual rhymes and rhythm patterns told stories of experience, such as a lifetime of love in a single meeting.

> "A pine that lives a thousand years
> Is sadder than a cactus flower,

"'Cause the cactus blooms for just an hour,
And leaves without remorse or tears.'"

Buck interspersed his original songs with those of artists such as Hank Williams, Hank Snow, and Roy Acuff. When the show was finished, the crowd stood and cheered. No one cheered any louder or more enthusiastically than the big man in coveralls who had threatened to "whip Buck's scrawny little ass" if the show failed to entertain him.

Finally the applause ended, and the crowd filed out, still talking about the show or, in many cases, singing or humming one of the songs. The waitresses began cleaning off the tables and resetting the chairs, while the band put away their instruments.

"I thought you all played real pretty tonight," Pearline said, approaching them.

"Thanks," Buck replied, turning around to look at her. She was wearing a simple black dress with a low-scooped neck. She was leaning against a post, one hip thrust out. Whether the pose was calculated or not, Buck didn't know, but it accented her curves. Her forehead had a patina of sweat, and a curl of hair stuck to it. She pushed it back, then licked her lips.

She spoke to the entire group, but she looked directly at Buck when she asked, "Are you boys hungry? 'Cause if you are, I asked Homer to fry you up some hamburgers and french fries."

"Hey, that sounds great!" Lucky Jennings said. "I been hungry all night!"

"You was born hungry and you had a relapse," Johnny said, and Frankie and Buck laughed.

"That's real kind of you, Pearline," Buck said. "We appreciate that."

"Yes," Pearline said. She pushed her hair back again, then took a deep breath. "Actually, I thought maybe while the rest of the band was eatin', I have a few, uh, ideas I'd like to discuss about tomorrow night's show with you. Maybe you wouldn't mind comin' back to my apartment and talkin' it over with me?"

The open hunger in Pearline's eyes had become almost palpable.

Buck smiled. "I can't think of anything I'd rather do. Frankie, will you see to it that my guitar gets back to my room? I think Pearline and I might have a lot to talk about."

"Sure thing, Buck. I'll take care of it," Frankie promised.

The office to the motel was in a corner of the living room of the Poindexter house. It was unmanned now because the "No Vacancy" light had been turned on. As soon as Pearline and Buck stepped inside, she turned the OPEN/CLOSED sign around to CLOSED. Then she locked the door.

"Sometime even with the 'No Vacancy' sign on, folks'll stop by and ask for a cabin," she explained. "It's got to where if a body wants any privacy at all, they've got to lock the door."

"I imagine it could get real hectic livin' in a motel all the time," Buck said.

"Oh, honey, you have no idea," Pearline said. "The stories I could tell." She stretched, putting her arms over her head and again thrusting her hip out to one side. She had a very good shape and she knew it, and she took advantage of the stretch to show it off. "Oh, look at me," she said, putting her hands on her waist. "I'm gettin' as fat as a sow. I'm just goin' to have to start exercisin' more."

"Pearline, you're not fat at all," Buck said. He walked over to her and put his hands on either side of her waist. "Lookee here, I can just about make my fingers touch."

She thrust her pelvis against Buck. Feeling him react with an erection, she smiled up at him. "Did I do that to you?"

"I reckon you did."

"You know, I really ought to watch myself," she said. "Folks are goin' to say I'm nothin' but an older woman tryin' to interest a younger man."

"Honey, you're young enough to get me interested,

and I'm old enough to get the job done," Buck said, pulling her tight against him, then bending down to kiss her.

"You knew this was what I was wantin' you to come back here for, didn't you?" Pearline said after the kiss.

"I was hopin' it was," Buck replied.

"Really? You were wantin' to do it too? I mean I wouldn't want to think it was just me."

Buck chuckled. "No, darlin'. I'm wantin' to just as much as you."

Pearline crossed her arms in front of her, grabbed the hem of her dress, and pulled it over her head. She then unfastened her bra and stepped out of her panties. Her body was smooth, her breasts full. The soft growth of hair at the junction of her legs was so light that in the shadowy room it was barely visible.

"So you're wantin' to as much as me, huh? Well, honey," Pearline said, standing there naked, "you're in Missouri now. And you know what we say in Missouri, don't you?"

"What's that, darlin'?" Buck asked.

"Show me." Pearline turned and walked back into the bedroom.

Buck followed, wriggling out of his clothes as he went. "Well, now, that's just what I aim to do," he said.

They lay in silence, their sweat-coated bodies bathed in the eerie glow given off by the pink and green neon tubes that outlined the squat motel office building.

"You are quite a man, you know that?" Pearline asked, breaking the stillness.

"Thank you, darlin'. And you're a sweet kid," Buck replied.

"I don't know what you've got there," she continued, "but whatever it is, if you could bottle it and sell it, you'd make a million dollars."

Buck raised up on one elbow and looked down at her. "What are you talkin' about?"

"I'm talkin' about sex, honey, pure and simple."

Buck chuckled. "There are already folks who sell it. They call 'em whores—whether they be men or women."

"No, no, you don't understand," Pearline replied. "I'm not talking about selling, uh, what we just did. I'm talking about sex appeal. You got it in a big way, honey, and it don't have nothin' to do with your looks, 'cause the truth is, I've seen lots of men better lookin' 'n you."

"Gee, thanks."

"No, I'm serious," Pearline insisted. "It's not somethin' I can put my finger on. It's your singin', I guess. But then, I don't understand that, either, 'cause if it was just pretty singin', why, Frank Sinatra, Bing Crosby, Tony Bennett, Nat King Cole, all of 'em sing prettier'n you."

"Well, if I'm not very good lookin', and I can't sing as pretty as any of them fellas, what am I doin' here? Why aren't you with one of *them*?" Buck bantered.

"Because being good lookin' and singin' pretty isn't what it's all about, Buck Campbell. The truth is, you are the sexiest man I have ever been around in my entire life. And it isn't just me. I was lookin' at all the other women there tonight, and there wasn't one of 'em—not a one, not even the young married women who were there with their husbands—who wasn't thinkin' the same thing I was. You were affectin' 'em just like you was me, and that's what I meant when I said you should be bottlin' it and sellin' it."

"I appreciate the nice words, darlin', but I think you're lettin' your imagination run away with you," Buck said.

"Not me," Pearline replied, grinning. "It's the other women who were there tonight who are lettin' their imaginations run wild." She laughed. "I'll bet there's more than a few husbands takin' advantage of amorous wives tonight, not knowin' what got 'em so excited. Their wives are lyin' in bed with their husbands, imaginin' that he's you." She reached up to grab Buck. "Only I don't have to imagine, do I? My husband is in Memphis, and I've got you—the *real* you."

Buck laughed. "Then do you mind if I ask a question?"

"No, go ahead."

"If you find me so all-fired sexy, why are we wastin' all this time talkin'?"

"Oh, my. You mean to tell me you think you might be interested in doing it again?"

Buck's laugh was raunchy. "Hell, honey, I'm a performer. Anytime I get a chance for an encore, I just naturally gotta do it."

NOVEMBER 1952, SIKESTON, MISSOURI

Fifteen-year-old Bobby Parker stood leaning against the side of a stake-bed truck at the Saturday morning sale barn, taking in the crowd. The auction barn was less than a half mile from Bobby's house, and he liked to walk over and peruse the action, listening to the auctioneers calling for bids in their singsong voices.

Earlier he had watched a sale of heifers and bulls inside the sale barn. But since today's temperature was very pleasant, he wandered outside to see what was going on in the flea auctions being held from the trunks of cars and the backs of pickup trucks. Though most of the real business at the sale barn went on inside, where the farmers bought and sold livestock and farm machinery, the flea auctions also did a brisk business—more often among the farmers' wives who, like their husbands, were also looking for bargains.

Actually, Bobby enjoyed the flea auctions even more than the stock auctions, for they were of a small enough scale that even he could participate.

"Here's a nice big platter, ladies and gentlemen," one of the flea auctioneers said, standing on the back of his pickup truck and displaying a serving platter.

"That'll hold a lot of fried chicken," a woman called from the crowd.

"Depression chicken you mean!" a man chimed in. "It'll be rabbit, not chicken, we'll be eatin' 'round here. In case you forgot already, we just had us a Republican elected president. Hoover was the last Republican president—and I 'spect you all remember what happened then."

"Better listen to the man, ladies and gentlemen," the auctioneer said without missing a beat. "If you menfolk go out and bring in a rabbit for your wife to cook, she's goin' to want to have a place to put it, and this platter will do it for you."

"Fifteen cents," somebody called.

"Fifteen cents? Come on, boys, the Depression hasn't started yet. Ol' Ike hasn't even been sworn in."

"Twenty cents."

"Twentytwentytwenty, I got twentytwentytwenty, lookin' for twenty-five, fivefivefivefive, who'll give me five, twentytwenty twenty, give me fivefivefive, who'll give me five—"

"Twenty-five!" a man called.

"Twenty-five, now thirty, now thirty, now thirty-thirtythirty. Who'll give me thirtythirtythirty? I've got twenty-fivetwenty-fivetwenty-five; who'll give me thirty, thirtythirtythirty—"

"Thirty," Bobby shouted. He didn't particularly want the platter, though he did have thirty cents, and he would give it to his mother if he bought it. What he actually wanted to do was see the bidding move along and to know that he had powered its movement. But the bid stayed where it was for the longest time, and Bobby thought that he had, in fact, bought the platter and was feeling a bit anxious about it when, to his relief, someone upped his bid.

Bobby wandered away from the flea auction. His attention was caught by the sound of a car engine being revved, and the loudness of the muffler—or lack of one— told him that it had to be Eddie Malone's car. Eddie's father owned the sale barn, and he was one of the reasons Bobby came down on Saturday mornings to hang around.

Following the sound, Bobby found Eddie by the raised hood of his car, leaning over the fender and working on the dual carburetors, making the engine race by actuating the throttle connecting rod with his hand. The engine would roar, then pop and snap as the RPMs came

back down. That was called "cooking off," and the more
an engine would "cook," the "cooler" it was.

"Hi, Eddie, what're you doin'?"

"It's been runnin' a little rough," Eddie explained,
racing the engine a couple more times. Then he straightened up and slammed the hood. "I think I got it now."

Eddie's car was a black '39 Ford coupe V-8. All the
chrome had been removed from the hood, and it had been
leaded and smoothed over. Eddie kept the car clean and
waxed all the time, and it glistened in the sun.

At seventeen, he was two years older than Bobby,
though the two boys were about the same size. Eddie
smiled and wiped the back of his hand across his face,
leaving a black smear. "So, what do you want to do?" he
asked. "Stay here and watch the farmers buy pigs or go
for a ride?"

"Where we goin'?" Bobby asked.

"I thought we might run over to Charleston and have
a look around."

"Charleston? The speed run?"

"Not yet. I'm not ready yet. When I'm ready, you'll
know—and so will Brad Lewis." Eddie laughed. "He'll
really know when he has to fork over the fifty bucks."

"Boy, I don't know if I'd've made that bet," Bobby
said. "Do you really think you can go from here to
Charleston in ten minutes?"

"Does a bear shit in the woods?" Eddie answered.
"Hell, yes, I can do it in ten minutes. It's only thirteen
miles."

"Yeah, but you have to go through Miner Switch and
Bertrand," Bobby reminded him. "And the road has about
forty turns."

"It only has four right-angle turns."

"Yeah, but it's full of curves. There aren't but about
two or three places where you can pass. If you get behind
some slowpoke, you'll never get around him."

Eddie laughed. "That depends on whether or not
you're a chickenshit. Come on, I'll show you."

The two boys got into the low-slung car with a slamming of doors.

"Check out the new tach," Eddie said, pointing to the newly installed tachometer. He revved the engine a couple of times, and the tach needle swung over. "Ain't that somethin'?"

"I'm goin' to get me a car just like this someday," Bobby said, though he knew, and he knew that Eddie knew, that it was just wishful thinking.

"You don't want a car like this," Eddie said.

"Are you crazy? Sure I do!"

"Hey, man, if you had your own car, who would I get to ride copilot? I gotta have somebody watch the instruments and keep track of time for me when I make the speed run, don't I?"

Bobby's heart leapt in excitement. "You mean you're goin' to let me make the speed run with you?"

"Sure. That is, if you want to."

"Do I ever!"

"Then let's take a practice run," Eddie suggested.

He grabbed the floor-mounted gearshift lever that, because of his modification, was only about half as high as it was originally, and dropped the car into first gear. He drove slowly through the parking lot, but the moment he pulled out onto Malone Highway, he pushed the accelerator to the floor, causing the back wheels to spin and squeal and the tires to smoke. Just as he intended, everyone in the parking lot looked out toward the highway to see what was going on.

"Whooeee! Lay down the rubber!" Bobby shouted.

"Now check this out!" Eddie called over the noise of the engine. With a quick, snapping motion he popped the lever into second gear, getting a chirping sound from his wheels. By the time he shifted into high, he was already doing forty-five.

"Watch it, Eddie, there's a cop!" Bobby warned,

"Where? I don't see no cop," Eddie said, though he immediately downshifted and put on his brakes.

"There he is, up there."

The police car was sitting behind a billboard so that only the front part of it could be seen. But that was all that was needed to identify the car because the chrome-

covered red light/siren was mounted on the left front
fender, and Bobby had seen it glinting in the sun.

"Yeah, I see him now. Wave at the nice man, Bobby,"
Eddie snickered.

With broad grins on their faces, Bobby and Eddie
waved at the policeman as they drove by.

"Shit! That was Harold Wallace!" Eddie said, referring to Sikeston's chief of police. "Think he wouldn't like
to run my ass in?"

"Well, just drive slow until we get out of town,"
Bobby said.

"I'm tryin' to. The problem is, it's hard to hold this
baby down."

They drove on through town, past the Malone The-
ater, where the matinee today was *The Quiet Man* with
John Wayne. They passed the shoe factory, the City Pig
Café, the Studebaker garage, the Homestead Hotel, the
Cotton Oil Mill, the airport, and the Bulldog Drive-in,
staying below the speed limit all the while.

Bobby looked over at the Bulldog, knowing it was too
early for anyone to be there but hoping someone was who
might see him. The Bulldog was the hangout for everyone
in town, though very few kids under sixteen went there.
He could hardly wait until he had a driver's license so he
could drive himself out here, maybe with a carful of
friends, for a Coke.

As soon as they crossed St. John's Bayou, Eddie
spoke. "Check out the back window, and look all around.
See any cops?"

Bobby did as instructed. "No," he finally said.

"Hold on!" Eddie shouted, dropping the car into second and accelerating rapidly.

Bobby watched the RPM and the speedometer needles climb. Eddie didn't shift into third until he was doing
better than fifty. Then he continued to accelerate.

"Call out my speed!" Eddie yelled.

"Sixty! . . . Seventy! . . . Eighty!" Bobby shouted,
his voice rising higher with each plateau.

They swept up behind a car and then around it without even slowing down.

"Did you see him?" Eddie whooped. "I thought we were going to suck him up our exhaust."

"Ninety!" Bobby shouted, and now he felt fear creeping in with excitement. "Ninety-five!"

The engine was roaring, and the scenery flashed by with dizzying speed.

"Oh, shit!" Eddie cried, and Bobby, whose eyes had been glued to the speedometer, looked up to see a car coming right toward them.

The driver of the car, a new '53 light-green Mercury, seriously underestimating the oncoming Eddie's speed, had pulled out to pass the car ahead of him, and now he was stuck out in the left lane with nowhere to go.

Bobby felt his heart in his throat as he sat watching the car come closer, its massive silver grille flashing brilliantly in the sun. Even though the combined closing speeds of the two cars was around 150 miles per hour, it seemed to Bobby as if everything was moving in slow motion, and he examined, almost leisurely, the emblem above the grille of the oncoming car. He knew that in the next thirty seconds he was going to die, and there wasn't a damn thing he could do about it.

It was the driver of the car that was being passed who saved them all. He pulled way over onto the shoulder, giving the Mercury room to get back. The three cars passed simultaneously—so close together that there wouldn't have been room for a person to stand between them—with a tremendous blast of air, but no contact. It was over in the blink of an eye.

"*Son of a bitch!*" Eddie bellowed. "Did you see that son of a bitch? Tryin' to pass like that? The son of a bitch nearly killed us!"

"Yeah," Bobby said weakly. He thought, but did not say, that driving ninety-five miles per hour on a twisting two-lane road hadn't helped matters.

There wasn't another incident like the near-miss with the Mercury, but there was an anxious moment when Eddie passed a large trailer truck as they were approaching a curve. Reaching Bertrand, he slowed down to thirty-five, pounding on the wheel in frustration as he crawled through the town.

"It'll be our luck for some farmer to come into town with a truckload of pig shit or something," Eddie groused. "I hate farmers."

"You hate farmers? How can you hate farmers? That's how your dad makes a living—by selling to farmers."

"I don't hate their *money*," Eddie said. "I just hate *them*. Hey, check out the babes up there."

Three teenaged girls were standing on the corner just ahead. Bobby rolled the window almost all the way down, then put his arm around the glass. He pressed the arm against the window, hoping to make it look as if his biceps were bulging.

"Downshift," he said.

Eddie downshifted, and the exhaust roared. He let up on the accelerator as they came even with the three girls, and the engine snapped as it cooked down.

Bobby looked at the three, concentrating on the one he thought was the youngest. He smiled and nodded his head toward her, and, embarrassed, the girl laughed and looked down. As they passed, Bobby checked in the outside mirror and saw that the three were talking to each other and laughing.

"Did you see her?" Bobby asked. "She wants me, man! She *wants* me!"

"You want me to go back?" Eddie asked.

"No," Bobby said quickly, afraid that he really would. "We don't have time. We're making a practice run to Charleston, remember?"

"Yeah, but it's only practice," Eddie said. "If we could pick up a couple of girls, we can forget about the practice."

"There are three of them back there."

"So? One of 'em's going to have to be disappointed, that's all."

"No, no, that's all right," Bobby said, feeling his armpits starting to sweat. "Let's keep goin'."

To his relief, Eddie did.

As soon as they passed the city limits sign for Bertrand, Eddie accelerated again. There were two more right-angle turns, then a fairly straight shot on into Charleston. They were doing a little over eighty when they passed the city limits sign for Charleston.

"Whew, I'm glad we didn't pass any highway patrol," Bobby said.

"What if we had? Except inside city limits there's no speed limit in Missouri," Eddie said. "He couldn't have done anything to us."

"I guess not," Bobby said. He knew that Eddie was right, there was no speed limit in Missouri, but the highway patrol could stop a driver if his driving wasn't "reasonable and proper." Bobby doubted that over ninety miles per hour on a back road could by any stretch of the imagination be considered reasonable and proper.

"How long did it take?" Eddie asked.

"What?"

"The run from Sikeston. How long did it take?"

"I . . . I don't know," Bobby said. "I didn't look at my watch."

Eddie hit the dashboard angrily. "Goddammit, Bobby, why the hell do you think I brought you along? You were supposed to keep the time!"

"You didn't tell me to."

"Hell, I didn't think I had to," Eddie snapped. Then, because it was clear that Bobby's feelings were hurt, he smiled. "Ah, it doesn't matter. This was just a practice run anyway. But I'll bet we beat ten minutes."

"I know we did," Bobby said. "It was no more than nine minutes, I'm sure."

"Plus, we slowed down to flirt with those girls," Eddie reminded him.

"Yeah. When it comes to the real thing, we'll do it easily."

"Well, we'll find out tonight."

"*Tonight?*"

"Yeah. You can come, can't you?"

"Yeah, sure," Bobby said with more certainty than he felt. "I just didn't know it was tonight, that's all."

"What say we cruise around for a bit, then get on back to Sikeston?"

"Yeah," Bobby said. "If we're going to make the run tonight, I have some things I need to do."

What he had to do especially was convince his mother and father to let him go out tonight.

"Go? Go where?" Alice Parker asked.

Bobby shrugged. "Just out with the guys. You know, ridin' around."

"Riding around? You won't be at somebody's house?"

"Well, maybe some," Bobby said. "But we'll probably go out to the Bulldog."

"Aren't you a little young for that?"

"Mother, lots of kids my age go to the Bulldog," Bobby said. "Some of them even drive."

"Drive? At fifteen? Who would let their kids drive at fifteen?"

"You just don't understand," Bobby muttered. "Kids like Billy Murchison, Harold Aufdenberg, Jerry Calhoun, and Travis and Troy Raggins drive all the time. And they're my same age."

"They're in your same class; they aren't your same age."

"Well, they're not sixteen yet," Bobby said. "Anyway, I'm not asking to drive. Eddie Malone is going to pick me up. I just want to go, that's all. Please?"

"Oh, I suppose so," Alice acquiesced. "But for heaven's sake be careful. And tell Eddie to watch his driving."

"Don't worry about Eddie, Mother. He's the best driver I've ever met," Bobby said.

"I'm sure your father would be happy to hear you say that," Alice said dryly.

"Well, sure, Dad's better," Bobby agreed. "But he's a truck driver. I'm talking about just drivin' cars."

"What about me?" thirteen-year-old Harry piped up. "Can I go, too?"

"No, you can't go," Bobby said.

"Mother, make him take me, too."

"Aw, Mother, you aren't going to make me take my little brother, are you?" Bobby complained. "That would ruin everything."

"It wouldn't hurt you to take him."

"Yeah," Harry said, grinning. "It wouldn't hurt you to take me."

"Yes, it would. It would ruin everything. Nobody wants little brothers hangin' around. Besides, there probably wouldn't be room for you."

"Oh, I hadn't thought of that. Bobby's right," Alice said. "There probably wouldn't be room for you."

"So what am I going to do?" Harry asked. "Stay home and babysit with Freddie?"

"If you want to, you can go over to Elmer and Helen's with us tonight," Alice said.

"What are you goin' to do over there?"

"We're going to eat supper, then watch television."

"Yeah. And don't forget Mary Helen is over there. She's in love with you," Bobby teased.

"She is not."

"She is, too; she told me so."

"Mother!" Harry complained.

"Stop teasing your brother, Bobby."

"I'm not teasin' him, Mother. Mary Helen is madly in love with him."

Alice's face tightened. "Bobby, do you want to go out tonight or not?"

"Yes."

"Then stop teasing your brother."

"All right."

Harry smirked, and when he was sure Alice wasn't watching, he gave Bobby the finger.

"Mother?" Bobby said.

"What?"

Bobby saw the look of panic on Harry's face at the thought of being tattled on. That look was victory enough, so Bobby smiled smugly and said, "Just if Sid Caesar does anything really funny tonight, I want you to remember it, so you can tell me."

"Oh, I'm not very good at that," Alice said. "You'll have to let your brother do that."

"I'll bet he's funnier tonight than he's ever been," Harry said, pouting. "And I'm not going to tell you shit."

"Harry!" Alice gasped.

"What'd I say?" Harry said. "I didn't say anything. I said I'm not goin' to tell you *it*."

"That's right, Mother. That's what I heard him say," Bobby said.

"Well, it didn't sound like it."

"But that's what I said," Harry insisted.

"Well, be more careful with your pronunciation next time."

"I will," Harry promised, looking at Bobby with an expression of thanks. Bobby returned the look with one that said Harry owed him . . . and sometime soon he'd collect.

Later that night, when Eddie and Bobby pulled into a parking slot at the Bulldog, Les Paul and Mary Ford's "How High the Moon" was playing on the jukebox inside and being piped over the loudspeakers outside. All over the parking lot, car doors were opening and slamming as groups of kids moved from car to car, carrying their Cokes and an occasional hamburger or order of french fries with them.

Clearly the most popular boys were those wearing the red-and-black school jackets imprinted with a block letter S. The sleeves of the football players' jackets were festooned with felt footballs, numerals, and honors, signifying their status as members of a football team that hadn't lost a game since 1947. Their female counterparts were all members of the Red Peppers, a pep squad more like a sorority than an ordinary pep squad.

A carhop came to the window of Eddie's Ford.

"What'll you have?"

"Cherry Coke and an order of fries," Eddie said.

"Ditto," Bobby said with a casual wave of his finger.

"Hey, Eddie! You'd better not eat anything," Brad

Lewis called from one of the other cars. "You don't want anything to slow you down, do you?"

"Lewis, don't you worry none about me slowin' down," Eddie called back. "You just have your money where your mouth is."

"I got my money, wiseass," Brad replied, holding up the money. "What about you?"

"Right here," Eddie said, pulling a fifty-dollar .bill from his billfold.

"Are you goin' to do it or just talk about it?" someone said with a snigger.

By now the two boys' bantering had drawn a small crowd around the rivals' cars. Some supported Eddie, some supported Brad, but most, clearly, were just there for the excitement of the event.

"Why don't you two guys have a race?" someone asked, a suggestion greeted enthusiastically by everyone present.

"That'd be fine with me," Eddie said. He looked at the car Brad was driving. It was his parents' '51 Chevrolet. "But I doubt if he can get that lead sled over sixty."

"We didn't say anything about a race," Brad replied. "You bet that you can go from here to Charleston in under ten minutes, and I said that I had fifty dollars that says you couldn't. Now, are you going to do it? Or do you want to back out?"

"I'm ready when you are," Eddie said.

"I'm ready now."

"Okay, get in."

The smile left Brad's face. "Get in? What do you mean, get in?"

"Aren't you goin' with me?"

"Hell, no, I'm not going with you! You think I'm crazy?"

"I'm going with him," Bobby said.

"Then *you're* crazy."

"At least he isn't a chickenshit, Brad," somebody cackled, and there were several concurring remarks.

"You have to hold the stopwatch," Eddie said. "If you

don't go with me, how am I goin' to prove to you that I won the bet?"

"I don't know," Brad said. "Maybe you could call here when you get there."

Eddie shook his head. "No, that won't do."

"Why not?"

"What if it takes me two or three minutes to get the operator? By the time I get her and she puts the call through, it might be four or five minutes. You'd never believe I got there in time."

"I know a way we could do it," Billy Murchison put in. He smiled. "For ten percent of the pot."

"Foolproof?" Brad asked.

"Foolproof," Billy promised.

"I'm game if he is," Brad said.

"All right," Eddie agreed. "How can we do it?"

"Simple," Billy said. "Who's betting he won't make it?"

Half a dozen kids raised their hands, and Billy picked one of the boys.

"Who's betting that he *will* make it?"

This question elicited about the same number of responders, and Billy chose one of the boys from that group.

"All right," Billy said. "You two guys go with Aufdenberg over to Charleston now. I have two keys to my tool chest; I'll give Aufdenberg one of them. Eddie, just before you leave I'll start the stopwatch, put it in the tool chest, and lock the box. When you get there, Aufdenberg will unlock the box, stop the watch, and all of you can look at it. That way we'll know how long it took."

"Yeah!" someone said. "Yeah, that's a good idea."

"Okay with you?" Billy asked.

"Yeah, it's fine with me," Eddie said.

"All right by me," Brad agreed.

"Wait," Bobby said. "If you're going to do it that way, you should add thirty seconds."

"Thirty seconds?" Brad complained. "Hell, no. The bet was ten minutes. Exactly."

"Yeah, but it'll probably take thirty seconds to set the

watch, put it in and lock it, then take it out at the other end."

"Bullshit. It's not going to take any thirty seconds," Brad said.

"No, but he's right, it'll take a little time," Billy admitted. "How about twenty seconds? Eddie wins the bet if it's under ten minutes and twenty seconds."

"Yeah, Brad, that's fair," one of the others said, and, reluctantly, Brad agreed.

"Okay. You guys get on over there," Billy ordered. "We'll give you about a half hour to get there and get ready, and then we'll start."

"I'm going, too," someone else said.

"Yeah, me, too," another put in; soon more than half the cars in the Bulldog parking lot had driven away.

For the next twenty minutes people hung around Eddie's car, speculating as to whether or not he'd make it. Several asked to see his "mill," and Eddie obligingly opened his hood to show off the engine.

"Dual carbs, the cylinders are bored, and I have three-quarter race cams," Eddie explained.

"Are you really going to ride with him?" Sue Ann French asked Bobby as she sidled up to him. Sue Ann sat beside Bobby in Algebra and was one of the prettiest girls in the class.

"Yes."

"Why? Isn't that dangerous?"

"Not really," Bobby said, enjoying the attention. "Eddie's a good driver. Besides, one of the reasons I'm goin' is for safety."

"For safety? What do you mean?"

"We're going to be runnin' between ninety and a hundred the whole way. That means Eddie is goin' to have to keep his eyes glued to the highway. So while he's watchin' outside, I'll be watchin' inside."

"Inside?"

"The instruments," Bobby explained. "I'll be readin' off his speed, the RPMs, engine temperature, that sort of thing."

"Wow," Sue Ann said, and her eyes sparkled in what

Bobby hoped was admiration. She wore her blond hair in the style of Veronica Lake, and she reached up to brush a fall of it away from her face. "Aren't you just a little frightened?"

"Nope. Like I said, Eddie's a real good driver, and I'll be providin' him with all the information he needs so he can keep his attention on the road. When you have a team that works well together like Eddie and me, it's not really all that dangerous."

"You make it sound like you're just going to the store or something."

"Oh, no, it's more dangerous than that," Bobby said quickly, fearing his glory was in danger of abating. "A lot more dangerous. I just meant that we're takin' every precaution we can to eliminate as much of the danger as possible, that's all."

"I'll keep my fingers crossed for you."

"Thanks a lot," Bobby said, flattered by Sue Ann's attention. "Uh, listen, would you like to go out with me sometime? Maybe tomorrow we could go to a movie."

"You mean your parents let you drive?" Sue Ann asked.

"Uh, no," Bobby admitted. "But I can get someone to drop us off at the movies."

"Well, I'd like to," Sue Ann said diffidently. "But I think I'd better stay home and wash my hair."

"Okay. I just thought I'd ask," Bobby mumbled, deflated by the answer.

It was nearing the time to leave, and Eddie moved his car to the edge of the road. Everyone followed him, carrying their soft drinks, french fries, and hamburgers.

"Put the watch in the box and hand it through the window to Bobby," Eddie told Billy. "Then get out of my way."

He raced the engine several times as they sat there waiting for the final seconds, making certain that the Charleston group had had plenty of time to get there.

"Get ready!" Billy said, holding the watch over the toolbox.

Eddie raced the engine again.

Billy pushed the button, put the stopwatch in the box, closed the lid, and snapped the padlock. He thrust the box through the window to Bobby. "Go!" he yelled.

"Go!" Bobby shouted to Eddie, taking the box. For one panic-stricken moment he nearly dropped it back outside the window, but he managed to grab it just as Eddie peeled out onto the highway, gravel thrown from his spinning wheels.

Eddie was doing sixty by the time they reached the Sikeston Drive-In Theater—and that was their first problem. It was the last weekend of the season for the drive-in, which was showing a double-feature Western, and cars were slowing down to turn in from both directions. Eddie had to brake hard to keep from hitting one of the turning cars.

"Shit!" he screamed. "Get the hell out of my way, grandpa!"

Impatiently, Eddie swung around the car, then pushed the accelerator all the way to the floor.

"Eighty . . . ninety . . . one hundred! We're doin' one hundred miles per hour!" Bobby shouted.

They were going so fast it almost seemed as if they were catching up with their headlight beams. Objects would appear briefly on the side of the road, illuminated by the light, then disappear rapidly into the darkness beside and behind them.

They reached the turn into Bertrand in just over four minutes. Eddie took the turn at better than fifty, with all four wheels screaming in protest. A quarter of a mile later he took the second turn, which brought him out just in front of Bertrand High School, dark now on a Saturday night.

"I'm goin' to try and sneak through here at about fifty," Eddie said. "So keep an eye open for their cop."

"There he is, up there," Bobby said, pointing to a black and white '49 Ford. He laughed. "Looks like he's in that café, probably having a cup of coffee."

Eddie slowed to thirty as they passed the small restaurant. Bobby could see the policeman inside, sitting at the counter, his back to the window. As soon as they were past the café, Eddie accelerated to fifty, and by the time they were at the edge of town, he was doing seventy.

"Five miles to go!" Eddie exclaimed. "How much time do we have left?"

"Just under four minutes, I think," Bobby said, checking his own watch.

"We'll make it."

Within moments Eddie was up to one hundred again. They came up behind a trailer truck, and as they approached it, Bobby felt his mouth go dry. It was one of his father's trucks. What was it doing here? Then he remembered that Beans Lloyd, who drove for his father, would be making a trip to New Orleans tomorrow. Beans lived in Charleston and was no doubt bringing the truck home to get an early start the next day.

Eddie pulled out to pass the truck, only to be greeted by the blinding lights of an oncoming car. Behind the lights of the first car were more lights, more behind that, and more behind that. Four cars were coming, and there was no way to get around the truck until all four had passed. Eddie had to slow down to forty-five.

"*Damn, damn, damn, damn!*" Eddie screamed, pounding in frustrated rage on the steering wheel.

"It's not fair," Bobby said. "We nearly made it."

"Nearly made it, my ass!" Eddie said. "We're goin' to make it! Hold on!"

He suddenly whipped the car off the road onto the shoulder.

"Eddie, you aren't going to pass him on the right?" Bobby shouted.

"The hell I'm not," Eddie replied, and by now the car was halfway up the right side of the trailer.

Just ahead, Bobby could see a couple of mounted reflectors marking the entrance to a farmer's driveway. He braced his hands on the dashboard as the car, doing better than fifty, crossed the driveway. The driveway was slightly elevated so that when the car hit it, all four wheels left the ground. When it came back down, Bobby bounced up from the seat and banged his head painfully against the roof.

"*Shit!*" he yelped.

By now they were even with the front of the truck. Just ahead of them was another obstacle, this time a farm-to-market road that passed over a culvert. If they hit the culvert the way they'd hit the driveway, they'd wreck the car.

The culvert drew closer alarmingly fast. Bobby braced himself for the impact, speculating on how much of his body would be cut by flying glass—or worse. At the last minute Eddie whipped back onto the road just in front of the truck. Bobby heard the truck's air brakes come on, then heard the angry blast of the truck's air horn. He shut his eyes and breathed a quick prayer—first a plea, then thanks—as he realized they'd made it.

"There they are!" Eddie shouted. "Just on the other side of the city limits sign. See 'em?"

His heart still pounding, Bobby looked ahead. A half-dozen cars were sitting in the parking lot of an implement dealer, closed for the weekend.

Honking his horn, Eddie slid into the parking lot with his wheels throwing gravel. "Where's Aufdenberg and that damned key?" he yelled.

"There he is," Bobby said, pointing as Aufdenberg and several others came running toward the car.

At that moment the truck they had just passed came by. Beans came down hard on the air horn, and Bobby prayed that he wouldn't stop, for if he did and saw him, then told his dad about what had happened, Bobby wouldn't get out of the house again for a month or more.

"Hurry, hurry!" Eddie hollered.

Aufdenberg began fumbling with the key.

"Goddammit, you're all thumbs! Can't you open a damn lock?"

"There, I got it," Aufdenberg said. He took off the padlock, then opened the box and removed the watch. "Okay, I stopped it. Open the door so I can see it."

Bobby opened the door so that the light came on. Aufdenberg looked at the watch.

"Nine minutes and fifty-three seconds." He grinned. "Hell, you didn't even need the extra twenty seconds."

CHAPTER
FIVE

SPRING 1953, NORTH KOREA

Train Choo Choo Willis felt the hit as he came off the target near Samdung. There wasn't that much to it, he thought, no more than hitting rough air at near VNE— velocity not to exceed. He did, however, feel a momentary panic as he thought of all the aircraft he had watched blow up in midair, and he held his breath and felt his stomach roil as he waited for the explosion. When, after a couple of seconds, his airplane *didn't* explode, he breathed easier.

"Whooee!" came Lieutenant Terry Balfour's voice over the radio. *"That was one hot mama down there."*

"Highpockets Flight, this is Highpockets Leader. Did everyone make it through?" Train asked.

"Highpockets Leader, this is Four. We all got through."

"We've got secondaries down there!" Balfour abruptly radioed. *"Look at that son of a bitch go up!"*

Train twisted around to look down at the target below and behind them. As Balfour had pointed out, several secondary explosions were taking place, evidence that the intelligence they had received was correct. This had been a major ammunition storage depot.

"Let's head back to the shed," Train told the others, and the four-plane flight did a wide one-hundred-eighty-degree turn to the south.

"*Highpockets Leader, this is Two. Are you all right?*" Balfour asked, moments later.

"Affirmative. Why do you ask?"

"*You're spewin' out somethin',*" Balfour said. "*Don't know what it is, but you're losin' it pretty fast.*"

Train checked his panel, then groaned. "Uh-oh, here it is," he said.

"*What is it?*"

"Fuel. I'm below a hundred pounds."

"*Do you have enough to get over the mountains?*" Balfour asked.

"I don't know."

"*Why don't you try to get as high as you can before fuel exhaustion? Maybe you can glide far enough,*" Balfour suggested.

Train chuckled dryly. "You remember what they used to tell us about the F-86? It's proof positive that even a brick will fly if you provide it with enough power."

"*Yeah, well, you don't have any choice, do you?*"

"I don't know. If I start across and see I'm not goin' to make it . . . Well, I'd rather try and set it down somewhere, preferably while I still have power."

"*Set 'er down? Choo Choo, I don't have to remind you that we're still in North Korea, do I?*"

"Yeah, well, I didn't think that was Arkansas down there," Train replied.

"*Hell, give it a try,*" Balfour said. "*If you don't make it across, you can always bail out.*"

"Negative. I like my chances better with a controlled crash landing than a parachute jump in the mountains."

"*Okay, it's your funeral,*" Balfour said.

Train chuckled again. "Nice choice of words."

"Sorry."

"Oh, shit!"

"What is it?" Balfour asked anxiously.

"I'm afraid the issue has just been settled for us. I've lost my engine."

"Can you get a restart?"

"On what? The fuel's down to zero."

"You want to eject?"

"Negative. I still think I'd rather ride it down. I don't think I'd be as easy to target as I would floatin' down in a parachute."

"All right. Want help with the pre-crash-landin' checklist?"

"Yeah, thanks."

"External stores, jettisoned," Balfour said, reading from the checklist.

Train hit the toggle switches to release the last four bombs he was carrying. They tumbled down from their wing mounts, then exploded like fiery rose blossoms in the rice field behind him.

"Check," he said.

"Booster pumps off."

"Check."

"Fuel off."

"Check."

"Speed boards deployed."

"Check."

"Flaps down."

"Check."

"Trim tab, nose down."

"Check."

"Gear . . . You want it up or down?"

Train saw a narrow, twisting road in front of him and considered trying to set down there. For that he would want his gear down. Then he discarded that notion and decided to opt for a rice field adjacent to the road. For that he preferred to land on his belly.

"Gear up," he replied.

"All right, gear up," Balfour said. *"Main buss off, secondary buss on."*

"Check."

"Seat belt and shoulder harness tight."

Train drew the harness in as tight as he could get it. "Check," he said.

"Blow the canopy."

Train pulled the canopy jettison lever, and the plastic bubble popped away from the plane. That action was followed immediately by a blast of wind coming through the cockpit.

"What's your airspeed?"

"One-forty," Train replied.

"Don't let it get too low."

"Right."

"You're headin' for the rice field? Your approach looks pretty good," Balfour said.

"Terry, have you guys got enough fuel to make an area pass after I'm down?" Train asked. "I'd like you to take a look, and if you see any unfriendlies, brush 'em away for me."

"You don't worry about that, Choo Choo. If we see anyone, we'll cut 'em down like they were Notre Dame linebackers," Balfour said. *"By the way, there's an irrigation ditch runnin' alongside the rice field there. Do you see it?"*

"Yeah, I see it."

"That might be a good place to go as soon as you get out of the plane. You've got your pistol with you, don't you?"

"Fat lot of good that does me. I couldn't hit a bull in the ass from three paces with this thing."

Balfour forced a laugh. *"Well, hopefully you won't have to defend yourself against any bull's asses. Okay, brace yourself; you're about there. Good luck, ol' buddy!"*

Train skimmed low over the rice paddy, holding the Saberjet off the ground for as long as it would fly, keeping it as level as he could, letting the airspeed bleed away until, finally, it dropped below stalling speed. He hit flat, bounced once, then hit again. The plane began to slew sideways, and even though the gear was still retracted, he instinctively kicked rudder and brakes to correct the skid.

Of course his action had absolutely no effect on the velocity or direction of skid. He saw that he was headed straight for a large dike at the other end of the paddy, so he braced himself for the impact.

The plane slammed hard into the dike, breaking one wing off at the root. Train was thrown forward, and though the harness kept him from hitting the instrument panel, his arms flew up and he hit himself in the mouth with his own fist. His mouth filled with blood, and he realized that he had knocked out a tooth.

Balfour's plane roared by just overhead, so low that Train could feel the turbulence from its passing. Balfour pulled up a half-mile away, and the sun flashed brightly on his craft's silver wings.

God, Train thought, as he spit out blood and the broken tooth, *God, that's beautiful.* Never had the thought of flying seemed so magnificent to him as at this very moment, on the ground in a broken plane, watching Balfour's airplane fly by overhead.

Train smelled shorted wires; then smoke began to curl up around him. He knew that though the usable fuel on board had been exhausted, there'd still be some trapped in the lines. In addition there was hydraulic fluid and oil, both of which could burn, and there were at least a thousand to fifteen hundred .50 caliber rounds and five hundred or so .40-millimeter cannon rounds still on board. He had to get out fast!

He started to unhook the seat belt and shoulder harness, only to discover a very sharp pain in his right wrist. He knew then that the same blow that knocked out his tooth had also broken his wrist. He momentarily panicked, fearing he might not be able to get out, but finally, using his left hand, he was able to operate the quick-release mechanism. Now, in addition to the thick smoke, he could also hear and see flames. He stood up, put his foot on the edge of the cockpit, then jumped to the ground and ran from the plane as fast as he could. He reached the narrow irrigation ditch just as the fire reached the ammunition chutes. The rounds began cooking off, snapping and popping as if the plane were a giant

popcorn popper. Tracer rounds spewed out, sending up
sparks like the "Golden Fountain" fireworks displays Train
could remember from Fourth of July celebrations of his
youth.

Terry Balfour flashed by again, and Train stood up in
the ditch to wave at him. Terry wagged his wings, and
then he and the other three planes made a circle around
the entire perimeter. After two such wide circles, apparently neither of which revealed any enemy soldiers, all
three F-86's flew by low overhead. The pilots all wagged
their planes' wings in one last good-bye before they
climbed up to altitude for the trip back. Train knew that
the three would be critically into their reserves by the
time they reached K-14 and would probably have to de-
clare a fuel emergency when they landed. He prayed
they'd make it back all right.

The thunder of their engines grew quieter and quieter until he could no longer hear them. Then he could no
longer see them. He was alone on the ground in North
Korea, it was silent, and he was afraid.

Travis Jackson, now a major, was in his office, working on fuel consumption reports, when Lieutenant Terry
Balfour came in.

"Sorry for bargin' in, Major," Balfour said. "But this
is an emergency."

"What is it, Lieutenant?"

"It's Choo Choo Willis, sir. He's down."

"Down? Do you think he's alive?"

"Yes, sir, I know he is. Or at least he was when we
left him. We flew over him, and he was standin' up, wavin'
at us. He's in a hell of a spot, Major Jackson, and we've
got to get him out of there."

"Where is he?" Travis stepped over to the large map
on the wall.

"Right here," Balfour said, pointing to the map. "Just
north of Hill Eighteen-thirty."

"In the plains or the mountains?"

"In the plains. He set down in a rice paddy."

"What about Air Rescue?"

Balfour shook his head. "No good, sir; they won't go."

Travis looked around in surprise. "What do you mean, they won't go?"

"They said they've only got one chopper up right now, and they won't risk it by sendin' it that far."

"The hell they won't," Travis growled, walking back to his desk and picking up the phone. He gave the crank an angry twist.

"Turtle Switch," the operator said.

"Turtle Switch, get me Long Arm." Travis covered the mouthpiece and looked up at Balfour. "Who'd you talk to?"

"Some chickenshit arrogant bastard named Grisham. Captain Grisham," Balfour said.

"Long Arm; Sergeant Davis speaking, sir," a voice answered over the phone.

"This is Major Jackson. I want to talk to Captain Grisham."

"Yes, sir, right away, sir."

There was a moment's pause, then, *"This is Captain Grisham."*

"Captain Grisham, this is Major Jackson. I have a pilot down in hostile territory, and I want a rescue mission mounted immediately."

"Sorry, Major, no can do," Grisham said as matter-of-factly as if he were a store clerk telling a customer he was out of a particular brand of soap.

"What do you mean, no can do?"

"I mean just that, Major," Grisham said. *"We only have three H-19's. Two of them are down for parts and will be for at least three days. Until one of those is back up, I've made the decision not to commit the third to any mission north of the thirty-eighth parallel."*

"You've made the decision?"

"Yes, sir, I made the decision. After all, that is my prerogative, Major. I am the commander."

"Goddammit, Grisham, this war is being fought

north of the thirty-eighth," Travis exploded. "And I've got a good man down up there."

"Yes, well, they're all good men, aren't they, Major? Sorry, I wish I could help you. I really do. But if I make exceptions to the rule, then what's the sense in making the rule?"

"That's my question exactly, Captain. What's the sense in making the rule?" Travis demanded angrily. He slammed the phone down and looked over at Balfour. "What about the Army or the Navy?" he asked.

Balfour shook his head. "No good, sir. I've tried 'em both. The closest Navy facility is too far away to do us any good, and the Army has a maximum effort under way with a one-hundred-percent commitment of all their helicopters. Actually, they're willin' to let us have one, but there's no way they could get it in position to go before nightfall. And the way I look at it, if we don't get him out of there before it gets dark, we may not get him out at all."

"Do you think he was injured in the crash landing?" Travis asked.

"I don't know, sir. His airplane looked pretty banged up. But Choo Choo's a tough bird. And like I said, he was standin' there wavin' at us when we flew by."

Travis crossed to the window and looked out over the busy airfield, taking in the activity. Two Saberjets were taking off out on the airstrip, a huge C-124 was being unloaded, and an F-51 Mustang with its engine cowl off was being worked on by a mechanic who was standing on the deck of a big yellow maintenance stand.

Behind the F-51 sat a row of four L-19's, single-engine, high-wing Cessnas not too dissimilar from the light airplanes Cessna manufactured for the civilian market. The small two-seaters were used by forward air observers, spotters who called in artillery or air strikes. Travis stroked his chin as he assessed them.

"Tell me about the area where he's down," he said. "What's it like?"

"It's near the mountains," Balfour replied. "He's in a big rice paddy with an irrigation ditch alongside. That's where I last saw him. Standin' in the ditch."

"Any roads?"

"Yes, sir, a narrow, twistin' dirt road. I think he even thought about puttin' down on the road, but you'd hardly be able to put a Piper Cub down there, let alone a Saberjet. He changed his mind."

"Could you get an L-19 down on that road?" Travis asked, looking back toward Balfour.

"An L-19?" Balfour's eyes narrowed in thought. "I don't know," he finally said. "Yes, sir, I think someone who really knew how to handle a light plane could get it down. Whether he could get it down without damagin' it so he could get it back up again might be a different story."

"Do you think it's impossible or just damned difficult?" Travis asked.

Balfour smiled. "Damned difficult. Major, I see what you're gettin' at, and it might work. The question is, will you be able to talk one of the spotter pilots into givin' it a try? Air rescue isn't a part of their mission, you know, and there's no way you could order someone to try this."

"I don't intend to order anyone, Lieutenant. I intend to go myself."

"You? I beg your pardon, Major, but there's a helluva lot of difference between flyin' one of those puddle-jumpers and a jet."

Travis smiled. "I know. I've dusted crops in a Stearman and in a Super-Cub. Both of them have similar flight characteristics to the L-19. It's been a while, Lieutenant, but I figure I'll get the feel of it on the way up."

"Yes, sir," Balfour said. "Major, with your permission, I'm goin' to lay on an F-86 for myself. You'll need an escort."

"Thanks. I'll be glad to have you along. You'd better give me about an hour's head start, though. Otherwise you'll run out of fuel trying to loiter with me."

Flying north at fifteen hundred feet, cruising at approximately one hundred ten miles per hour, Travis looked over the short, flat nose of the engine and through the spinning arc of the propeller at the gently rolling blue-green hills of Korea's northern mountain range. The rice paddies and vegetable fields spread a patchwork quilt beneath him, interspersed with small clusters of houses, some with roofs of tin, others with roofs of thatch, all built around an enclosed atrium that, despite its fancy name, was no more than a dirt courtyard. The enclosed courtyard was as much a part of the family living space as any room in the house, and cooking, eating, communal bathing, and a half-dozen other activities took place there.

The flight was slow, almost leisurely, as if there were no sense of urgency to the mission. After several years of flying powerful jets at high speed, Travis had almost forgotten how pleasant flying a small airplane could be. He promised himself that when he returned to the States, if there was any way he could swing it, he would buy a small airplane—maybe a Cessna 170 or a Cub Super-Cruiser or a Bellanca. He could almost picture this as one of those airplanes, and he could visualize Quinisha and little Andrew flying with him.

He smiled. Lord, now, wouldn't he cause a few eyebrows to lift if he were to land at the airport in Jackson, Mississippi, to visit Quinisha's parents? Uppity black folks stepping out of a private airplane? It would be worth it, he thought, just to see the expressions on everyone's faces.

Suddenly, balls of fire were flashing by in front of his windscreen. Twisting around in his seat, Travis saw two MIG-15's bearing down on him, flames winking from their noses and wings.

He was flying a plane with a top speed of just over a hundred miles per hour, being pursued by planes with top speeds of six hundred. There was no way he could fly faster, so he decided to make slowness his ally. He chopped the throttle, dropped the flaps, and hauled back on the stick. The little L-19's airspeed fell to sixty miles per hour, and both MIGs overshot him. While they were trying to turn around, Travis dropped way down to hug the tops of the mountains.

"Birddog, this is Highpockets. Where are you?" the radio said, breaking into Travis's concentration.

"I'm down on the deck," Travis replied. Looking around, he spotted a Saberjet coming fast. "I'm at your eleven o'clock, low."

"Roger, I've got you," Balfour confirmed.

"Highpockets, we have company," Travis said. "Two bandits at your four o'clock. Do you see them?"

"I see four at my two o'clock."

"Damn!" Travis said. "They've got help."

"Start back, Birddog. I'll give you cover," Balfour offered.

"Negative. We came after Willis, and we're going to get him," Travis said. "You do what you can to keep them busy. I'll try and sneak by."

"Roger. Oh, and Birddog, for what it's worth, I want you to know that I consider it a hell of an honor to be on this or any mission with you."

Travis Jackson and Train Willis had long ago put aside their animosity and replaced it with respect for each other's flying ability. At first the respect was begrudging, though now it was more freely given. Lieutenant Terry Balfour, on the other hand, had been one of the last hold-outs. He was always stiffly respectful while subtly letting it be known that it was Travis's rank and not the man he respected. Travis was surprised, then, not only by the warm sincerity of Balfour's words but by the unexpected joy he experienced in hearing them.

"Thanks, Terry," he said.

Train Willis had been on the ground for nearly four hours. He had found a hollowed-out place in the side of the ditch where he could sit and be out of sight from the casual passersby. At first he had feared that his crashed plane would lead someone to him, but that didn't seem to be the case. Several people had come to look at the plane, but they all left without initiating a search. Initially Train had wondered why; then he assumed that they figured he had bailed out and was somewhere else, perhaps even rescued by now, and the plane was all that was left. The plane, then, was more a curiosity than a beacon.

He had spent the first hour trying to get his bearings and wondering what his best move would be. Should he stay there and hope for rescue? Or should he try to make his way back south? He knew that he was about one hundred miles north of the northernmost American main line of resistance. It would be a long hike through enemy territory to the MLR, but if he moved only at night, he could probably avoid the Chinese and the North Koreans, and he could make it in three nights.

He made his decision: If nobody came for him by nightfall, he'd start on his way.

He sat in the ditch, assessing his injuries. The broken tooth had finally stopped bleeding, though his mouth was still very sore. What was hurting most was his wrist. He tried holding it very still, but despite his best efforts he couldn't keep from moving it, and each move, no matter how small, brought excruciating pain. If only he had something he could use for a splint.

Train thought of the compression bandage that he and every soldier and aviator carried in a small kit on their belt. It was for covering a bleeding wound, but he didn't have a bleeding wound. Maybe he could make it work on his broken wrist.

Taking it out, he wrapped it several different ways, but none of them helped. Then he got the idea of using the barrel of his forty-five automatic pistol as a splint, so he pulled the gun from his holster, lay it alongside his wrist, and wrapped the bandage around it. Using his teeth —made painful because of the broken tooth—and his left hand, he finally secured the bandage. He felt somewhat foolish with his pistol tied to his wrist, but it did bring him some relief. Settling himself back against the side of the ditch, he resumed his wait.

Now that he was still again, he could hear voices from somewhere nearby. The first few times he had heard people around his downed plane, he had peeked over the side of the ditch. The Korean curiosity seekers had all been civilians. After that he had quit sneaking looks, reasoning that each time he did so, he increased the risk of exposing himself. He no longer even gave it a second thought when he heard them.

He looked at his watch. He had been on the ground for four hours. No, four hours and seventeen minutes, he corrected himself. It would be dark in another three hours. If nobody came for him by then, he'd leave.

He felt sleepy and wondered if he should try to get some shut-eye. On one hand, he would need it if he was going to travel all night. On the other hand, what if Air Rescue came for him and he didn't hear them because he was asleep?

No, surely he wouldn't sleep right through a rescue attempt. If anyone came for him he'd hear the engine noise. Especially if it was a helicopter. Those damn things popped to beat all hell. Train closed his eyes. Maybe a nap . . . just a little one . . .

"*Mi guk! Mi guk! Idi wah! Bali, bali!*"

Train's eyes flew open, and he looked up at the top of the bank of the ditch. There, looking back down at him, were a Korean soldier and a civilian. The soldier was very young, probably still in his teens. The civilian was an old man, and Train recognized him as one of those who had come earlier in the day to look at his plane. When Train had sneaked up to have a peek, the civilian must have spotted him and was now turning him in. Train wondered whether it was out of patriotism or for a reward—or maybe both.

Not that it mattered.

"*Mi guk!*" the young soldier repeated.

Train knew that meant "American."

"*Idi wah! Bali, bali!*"

He could understand that command as well. It meant: "Come here quickly."

After that the teenaged soldier spouted off a long string of words, none of which were intelligible to Train. When the youth didn't get the desired response, he raised his rifle to his shoulder and aimed.

"Hold it, hold it!" Train said, getting up. "I know you said come here, but I don't understand all that other shit."

The soldier spoke again, then motioned with his rifle, and, in response, Train climbed up the side of the bank. Once on top he looked around to see if there was anyone else around. There wasn't.

"You . . . come . . . with . . . me," the Korean said with difficulty.

"Damn, why didn't you tell me you could speak English instead of making me have to listen to all of your gobbledy-gook shittin' Korean?" Train muttered.

"You come with me," the Korean said again, as laboriously as before, and Train realized that the kid was probably mouthing phonetically just about all the English he knew—no doubt taught to him by his officers for just such an occasion.

There were six MIGs against one Saberjet and one L-19 Birddog. On the face of it the two Americans were at a severe disadvantage, but, in fact, shooting them down proved difficult for the Chinese pilots. The MIGs first concentrated on the small, high-wing spotter plane, a seemingly easy kill. That proved deceptive. The pilot of the little unarmed plane proved to be a man of extraordinary skill who managed to twist and turn the plane in ways that seemed aerodynamically impossible. At one point the Chinese pilots would have almost sworn that he was backing up.

With the MIGs concentrating on the unarmed plane, Terry Balfour had an unopposed approach on his first run. One MIG exploded under his cannon fusillade; another caught fire, and its pilot ejected. Two of the MIGs broke off their attack against Travis and turned toward Balfour. He started running, and they followed him, taking two more away from attacking Travis.

But the Koreans must have decided that since spotter planes were most often used to adjust artillery fire, it was the more valuable of the two targets, because the two who were chasing Balfour broke off their pursuit and started back. That gave Balfour the opportunity he needed. Turning, he gave chase to them, shooting one of them up so badly that the craft had to limp back to the north with the other one flying escort for him. When Balfour returned to the fray, he found Travis still avoiding the remaining two MIGs by the skill of his flying. Balfour opened fire from a long range, and the two MIGs, the last of their number, quit the battle and turned north themselves. The little L-19 had a few holes in the wings and the fuselage, but none were threatening to the structural integrity of the aircraft. The mission could continue.

"Good job, Terry," Travis said.

"Yes, sir, well, you didn't do so bad yourself," Balfour radioed. *"I'm going on ahead now to make sure everything's all right."*

"I'm coming balls to the wall behind you," Travis replied.

"Balls to the wall, my ass. I could walk faster than you're going," Balfour joked.

"I'm pedaling as fast as I can," Travis retorted, chuckling.

Balfour laughed. *"I'll see you there,"* he said, flying off and leaving the little airplane churning through the air behind him.

Standing facing his two captors, Train saw the F-86 coming through a notch in the mountains behind them, so the North Koreans were oblivious of its presence. The aircraft grew larger and larger, coming so fast that it was approaching ahead of its own sound. The pilot pulled up sharply, trailing a slender stream of smoke. At that moment the sound of his screaming engine arrived, a thunderous avalanche that reached down into the very guts, causing every molecule of the body to tingle in harmonic response.

The Koreans, unaware of the plane until the sudden burst of thunder, let out shouts of surprise and fear. They turned quickly to see the jet climbing up from its low-altitude, high-speed approach.

"Hey, how about that?" Train shouted, laughing and pointing at the plane. "You see that? That's my buddies comin' after me! So if you know what's good for you, you'll get your asses the hell outta here!"

The young soldier began shaking in terror, and Train, seeking to take advantage of it, pointed north with his unbandaged left hand.

"Go!" he said.

But the young soldier raised his rifle with trembling hands to his shoulder and aimed directly at Train, flipping off the safety.

"No!" Train shouted. "Don't do it!"

Suddenly Train remembered his own pistol, covered by the bandage on his right wrist. Incredibly, it seemed the Korean hadn't noticed it. Train put his left hand to his wrist and slipped his finger around the trigger, then pointed his hand at the young soldier.

The youth still didn't realize that Train represented any danger to him. He was sweating profusely now, frightened by the jet, trying to decide whether he should shoot his prisoner.

Train knew that he couldn't chance that the young soldier would decide in his favor. He pulled the trigger, and the pistol went off, firing through the fold of the bandage.

The bullet hit the young soldier in the throat. He dropped his rifle and reached up with both hands. Blood gushed through his fingers, and he pulled them away from the wound and looked at them in surprise. Then he looked at Train through eyes wide in pain and shock, as if wondering where the shot had come from.

"You dumb son of a bitch!" Train shouted. "I told you to leave! All the hell you had to do was get the hell out of here! I didn't want to shoot you! I didn't want to shoot you!"

He had already killed several men during this war. But this was the first time he had ever looked directly into the face of one of them as he died. And one so young.

The old civilian, seeing what had happened, turned and ran. Train ripped the bandage away from the pistol so he could control it better, then took a long, careful aim. Then he sighed and lowered the gun. The Korean was unarmed and running away. He represented no immediate danger. The old man reached a fallen bicycle, climbed on, and began to pedal furiously.

The jet made another pass and wagged its wings. Train waved back, laughing loudly. That was when he saw the L-19 coming through the same notch in the mountain that the F-86 had.

"Hey!" he shouted out loud. "Hey, what are you doing here? Where's the helicopter? How the hell are you goin' to get me outta here without a helicopter?"

As if answering his question, the L-19 turned toward the road, then lined up for a landing. Train saw the flaps extended, and he heard the engine bark and pop as the power was cut back.

"Are you crazy?" he shouted. "You won't be able to get that thing down and back up again!"

Despite Train's warnings, which of course the L-19 pilot couldn't hear, the plane continued on final landing approach.

"Birddog, you'd better expedite," Terry Balfour said over the radio. *"I just saw three truckloads of slopes coming down the road."*

"Can you help me out with them?"

"I'll do what I can," Balfour replied, rolling his plane around into a shallow attack dive toward the curve in the far end of the road.

Train saw the Saberjet begin what was obviously a strafing run, then heard the guns open up. Looking around, he saw what the jet pilot had seen: three truckloads of soldiers coming at full speed toward him. And they were already as close as the landing L-19!

The third truck in the convoy suddenly exploded, sending up a big fireball, followed by a greasy column of smoke.

"Yeah, yeah!" Train shouted. "That's good! Only you

should've done it to the first truck. The *first* truck, you idiot! That would've stopped the other two!"

The jet had to go a long way out before it could rack around into a tight one-hundred-eighty-degree turn and come back for a second strafing run. He started firing from a long way off, much too far to be effective, but Train understood that it was a desperation move designed to keep the approaching soldiers off guard. As it turned out, it wasn't totally ineffective after all, because Train saw a couple of soldiers fall, while others jumped from the backs of the still-moving trucks and began running.

The L-19 was on the ground now and rolling fast toward Train. He ran out to the road to meet it. The small two-seater skidded to a stop, its engine racing, and it pivoted around in the road, facing the same direction it had just landed from. The door opened, and an arm reached out, urging Train to come faster. The hand and the face shouting at him were black.

"Major Jackson! Is that you?" Train yelled as he approached the plane. "Damn, I've never been gladder to see anyone in my life!"

"Get in, Choo Choo," Travis shouted, using Train's nickname for the first time. "We don't have time for chitchat."

"Let's go!" Train replied, putting his knee on the floor and reaching in with his right hand to grab hold of the passenger seat back.

Even though Train wasn't fully inside, Travis opened the engine to full throttle, and the plane started racing back down the road. He raised the tail wheel just as Train pulled himself aboard, and he got airborne just as Train dropped into the small canvas seat.

A spray of bullets whacked through the aluminum skin on the left side of the aircraft, then through the open right door. A pink spray spattered the windshield.

"Pull it up! Pull it up!" Train shouted, loud enough to be heard over the engine and propeller noise.

By now they were just inches above the rice paddy, having already run out of road. When Travis didn't respond, Train grabbed the stick between his legs and pulled it back himself, recovering from the shallow dive. He felt absolutely no counterpressure on the control stick.

DELTA, MISSISSIPPI

Quinisha Jackson took the basket of wet clothes out into the backyard. She had a clothes dryer that she used when the weather was bad, though she preferred letting the clothes dry in the sun because she thought it made them smell fresher. Besides, though she wouldn't admit it to anyone, she felt somewhat self-conscious about using the dryer when so many of her neighbors didn't have one. In fact, very few of them even had automatic washing machines, having to depend on wringers and washtubs.

"Andrew, don't you get dirt in that basket of clothes, now, you hear me?" she said, scolding the small boy who was running toward the basket as fast as he could go.

"Cookie, cookie," Andrew said.

"You just let Mama get finished here; then we'll go in and eat lunch. And I'll read Daddy's letter to you. I've already read it once, but it's good enough to read again."

The letter from Travis had come that morning, informing her that she was now married to a major.

I'm still a long way from being a general, "but I'm a long way from being a second lieutenant, too. I'll be glad when this war is over and I can come home to you and Andrew, but I don't mind admitting that it's been good for my career. If it lasts long enough—and the way the peace talks are going it looks like it's going to last awhile—I'm sure to make lieutenant colonel and maybe even full colonel. Wouldn't that be something? And believe it or not, the other officers, with a few exceptions, now accept me without question. Captain Willis, the officer I had trouble with in the beginning, has actually turned out to be a pretty good man. I wouldn't go so far as to say we're friends or anything like that, but I wouldn't mind serving with him again somewhere. That isn't likely, though, because he has his heart set on playing professional football, and he works out all the time to stay in shape. If I know him, he'll probably make it.

Quinisha was happy that Travis had made major and happy that he was getting along with the other officers. But she wasn't at all happy about prolonging the war so that he could make colonel. If she could choose between his being a lieutenant and home with her or a major and over there, she'd take the lieutenant.

Quinisha heard a car stop out front, and she walked around the side of the house to see who it was. She was surprised to see that it was an Air Force car.

"Now, what's an Air Force car doing here?" she asked aloud. Then she smiled. "Come on, Andrew. Let's go see what they want. I bet they've come to tell us about your daddy being promoted to major." She took off the apron she was wearing and touched her hair as she started toward them. She was glad she had just made a pitcher of iced tea; it was a warm day, and they would probably welcome a glass.

Two Air Force officers, one a colonel and the other a first lieutenant, got out of the car. Stump Pollard also got out. What was Stump doing here? Quinisha wondered. Stump was the retired chief of police of Delta and an old friend of the Jackson family. Travis had once told her that when he was a child, Stump was the one person who had kept him from hating all white people. Until Stump, Travis said, he had thought that all white people were evil. But Stump had treated him and everyone else, black or white, fairly and with respect. He certainly had been particularly helpful to Quinisha since she returned to Delta to wait for Travis to complete his tour of duty in Korea.

"Chief Pollard," she said, smiling and respectfully calling him by his old title, "what a pleasant surprise. Would you gentlemen like some iced tea? I just got a letter from Travis and I'll—" Quinisha stopped. Something in the expressions of the three men, especially Stump's, made her blood run cold. She put her hand to her mouth and took a half step back. "No," she said, the word a choked whisper.

"Quinisha, I—" Stump began, but she held her hand out toward him and shook her head.

"No," she moaned. "No, I don't want to hear it."

"Why don't you go inside and sit down?" Stump suggested. He reached for her, but she angrily twisted away from him.

"No," she said, louder this time. "I . . . I just got a letter from him. He's been promoted to major. It's in the house. I'll show it to you."

"Mrs. Jackson," the colonel said, "it is with regret that the United States Air Force must inform you that your husband, Major Travis Jackson, was killed in action yesterday."

"No! My God, no!" Quinisha screamed, and she put both hands to her face and began sobbing.

Stump put his arms around her, and though she resisted at first, she finally let him hold her to him, and she sobbed uncontrollably into his chest.

"I . . . I hope it's some comfort to you, ma'am," the colonel continued, "to know that Major Jackson gave his life saving one of his men. For that heroic action he has been recommended for the Medal of Honor. I'm sure you know that that's the highest accolade our country can bestow on one of its fighting men. You can be very proud of that."

"Comfort? Pride?" Quinisha cried. "I don't want comfort, pride, or medals. I want my husband!"

"Yes, ma'am," the colonel said. "Mrs. Jackson, you have our heartfelt sympathy."

Andrew, crying now, wrapped his arms around his mother's leg. Quinisha reached down to pick him up, then walked over to sit down on the front porch. She rocked the boy back and forth, crying softly.

"If there is anything we can do . . . anybody we can call for you . . ." the colonel suggested.

"Colonel, thank you," Stump said. "Why don't you

and the lieutenant go now? I'll stay here with Mrs. Jackson."

"But shouldn't she have some of her own people here with her?" the colonel asked.

Stump turned and looked hard at the man. "I *am* her people."

CHAPTER SIX

APRIL 1954, FROM ''TRAILMARKERS,''
EVENTS MAGAZINE:

MCCARTHY BLASTED ON TELEVISION BY EDWARD R. MURROW

Senator Joseph R. McCarthy, whose current dispute with the United States Army is being followed by television viewers nationwide, came under attack from a different source last week. CBS television commentator Edward R. Murrow said in a broadcast that McCarthy has been using "half-truths and distortions" and has succeeded only in "confusing the public about the internal and external threats of Communism."

The telecast of Murrow's remarks has garnered an unexpected and unprecedented amount of favorable public reaction, indicating that Senator McCarthy's base of power and support is not as great as was previously thought.

Many pundits believe that the McCarthy era may be ending with the Army hearings, and Murrow's telecast is merely hammering the final nails in the coffin. The hearings, chaired by Senator Karl Mundt, have taken their toll on McCarthy, and Joseph Welch, special counsel for the Army, has more than held his own with the bombastic Wisconsin senator's bellows.

The specific charge the Army has made against McCarthy and his chief counsel, Roy Cohn, is that Cohn made threats against the Army in an attempt to gain preferential treatment for G. David Schine. Schine, an Army private, was formerly an investigator for the McCarthy subcommittee. McCarthy has countered by charging that the Army was attempting to blackmail him into dropping his investigation of Communists in the military.

VIETMINH CONTINUE HEAVY ATTACKS ON DIEN BIEN PHU

A military spokesman for the French admitted that the situation of the French troops surrounded in the fortress of Dien Bien Phu is critical.

French casualties continue to mount as the Communist guerrillas tighten the noose and increase artillery attacks. The French had hoped to be able to lure the Vietminh out into a set-piece battle where they could be defeated by superior firepower and aerial strikes. However, bad weather has prevented the French from resupplying their troops, so the superiority in firepower as well as numbers now favors the Vietminh. Such air strikes as the French have been able to mount have been, for the most part, sporadic and ineffective.

President Dwight Eisenhower, responding to a question as to whether American troops would be committed to help the French, refused to rule out that possibility. However, critics of the idea of American intervention point out that with the war in Korea over less than a year, public support for any further American military involvement—such as an adventure in Vietnam—would be lukewarm, and the U.S. should avoid sending troops into Southeast Asia.

A spokesman for the administration warned the Communists against playing American public opinion for their own benefit. "There is legitimate discussion as to which is the right thing to do. That is part of the democratic process. However, should it become necessary to commit troops to Vietnam, there is no doubt but that all Americans will unite behind their government, just as they did during World War II."

HYDROGEN BOMB TEST PRODUCES
MOST POWERFUL BLAST
IN HUMAN HISTORY

Scientists are unsure of just how powerful the H-bomb was that was exploded at a secret test site in the Marshall Islands recently because the power of the blast was greater than the ability of their recording instruments to measure it. The blast sent radioactive debris far beyond the safety zone that had been set and is said to have totally obliterated the small atoll on which it was detonated. The bomb is at least a thousand times more powerful than the one dropped on Hiroshima.

The success of the test was no doubt a surprise to many of the scientists who insisted that an H-bomb was not possible. Robert Oppenheimer, the "Father of the Atomic Bomb," was one of those who doubted the possibility of the H-bomb and who lobbied against any efforts toward its development. Oppenheimer was recently dismissed from the Atomic Commission and his security clearance withdrawn because of "known friendships with members and former members of the Communist Party" as well as "a general lack of enthusiasm for the improvement of America's defense system." In addition to his oft-stated belief that such a bomb could not be developed, Oppenheimer was also against the bomb for what he termed "moral" reasons.

In a related story, Dr. W.W. "Dub" Wilkerson, also one of the developers of the atomic bomb, has been called to Washington to face questioning about an article he wrote for last month's *Scientific Essayist* magazine. In his article, Dr. Wilkerson suggested that the development of the hydrogen bomb is a crime against humanity on the same magnitude as the Holocaust. Such a bomb, Dr. Wilkerson's article stated, "could kill as many people in one blast as all of Hitler's gas chambers did during the entire war. Do we really want to be a part of such a monstrous thing?"

Dr. Wilkerson is a professor of physics at Jefferson University in St. Louis and is no longer active in weapons development. According to a spokesman for Jefferson, the university will stand by Dr. Wilkerson's right of expression and free speech.

DEMARIS HUNTER TO HOST A TELEVISION VARIETY SHOW

Actress Demaris Hunter announced that she has come to an agreement with NBC to host *The Demaris Hunter Show*.

"Some consideration was given to having a weekly anthology series, each drama starring Miss Hunter," a network executive said. "However, we felt that it would be too difficult to find enough video plays of sufficient quality for a star of Miss Hunter's magnitude. Using the variety format, on the other hand, affords the opportunity for comedy skits and thus takes advantage of Miss Hunter's wonderful comedic talent. In addition, she will act as hostess for other acts, such as singers, comedians, dancers, and even an occasional dramatic piece."

NBC acknowledged that they were being innovative by having a variety show hosted by a woman, but they pointed out that singer Dinah Shore's musical show has long enjoyed a terrific level of success, proving that the public will watch a program hosted by a woman if it is of high enough quality.

CHOO CHOO WILLIS LEAVES STEELERS, SIGNS WITH NEW YORK FOOTBALL GIANTS

Train "Choo Choo" Willis, who reported to the Steeler training camp last year directly from his service in Korea with the U.S. Air Force, has been traded by the Pittsburgh Steelers to the New York Football Giants.

Mr. Willis started six games for the Steelers and passed for an impressive 1500 yards, but he was injured in a game against the Chicago Cardinals and finished the season on the bench. When asked about his injury, Mr. Willis replied, "I've never been healthier. I'm ready to play, and I'm looking forward to helping New York take the title next season."

In order to get Choo Choo Willis, New York traded two linebackers and a draft choice to Pittsburgh.

In an unrelated item, Mr. Willis will be a guest in the White House for a special ceremony this week, when President Eisenhower will award the Medal of Honor posthumously to the widow of Major Travis Jackson. Major Jackson, a colored Air Force major, was killed when he landed a small plane behind enemy lines to rescue Mr. Willis, then an Air Force captain.

WASHINGTON, D.C.

"More coffee, Professor Wilkerson?" Faith Canfield asked, getting up from the table.

"Yes, thank you," Dub answered.

"I'd like some, too, if you don't mind," John Canfield said to his wife.

Faith smiled. "I know you do, darling. That's why I didn't even bother to ask you."

The three were having breakfast in the Canfield suite at the Willard Hotel.

Dub looked over at John as Faith poured the coffee for him. "You know, John, I am so embarrassed about all this," he said. "The last thing I wanted to do was make trouble for the university."

"You haven't made trouble for Jefferson."

"Yes, I'm afraid I have. If I'm found—" Dub paused. "What would be the right word for the result of a Senate hearing? Guilty? If I am found guilty, and the university refuses to dismiss me, they'll lose a great deal of money. Federal support, research grants, ROTC programs . . . everything."

"The government wouldn't do all that," John insisted.

"I wish I could be as confident as you," Dub said, shaking his head. "But I'm afraid they will. The government can do anything they want to do."

John reached across the table and squeezed Dub's hand. "If they withhold funds, they withhold funds." He smiled. "But don't worry about it. Whatever funding the government takes away from the university as a result of this, I will personally make up."

"That's very generous of you, John, and I know you mean it. But it's more than money. It's not like it was in the old days. Then the university was truly independent —not only in finances, but in policy and administration. Today all colleges and universities, public and private, are caught up in a federal-and-state-administered network of money and red tape. Even if you did make up the funds the federal government withheld, there would be other sanctions. Doors to cooperative research programs with other universities would be shut. There would no longer be an exchange of information. And to make certain everyone gets the message, other universities will face the same sanctions if they have anything at all to do with us. That would extend to all aspects of university life—fraternities and sororities, sports. . . . Why, can you imagine JU without its football or basketball team? Students would leave in droves, and the doors would eventually close. No, John, if this hearing goes against me, I will have no choice but to resign."

"That would be giving in," Faith said.

"Yes, it would. But I see no alternative."

John poured some milk on his Canfield-Puritex Corn Toasties. His spoon poised to dip into the crisp little flakes, he looked across at Dub. "Well, then, we'll just have to convince the Senate Hearing Committee not to find you guilty. We came here to give you our support, and that's exactly what we intend to do."

"You mean you'll be attending my hearings?"

"You bet." John smiled at his wife. "Faith and I both. Though from what I understand, occasionally they'll be discussing top-secret information, at which times attendance will be restricted to the committee members, the defendant, and his counsel."

Dub smiled wanly. "It's so ironic. Some of the information they'll be discussing is so secret that I don't even know about it. I haven't had anything to do with the development of nuclear weapons since my work with the Manhattan Project during the war." He sighed. "I should've kept my mouth shut—or rather, my pen still. I should never have written that article for the *Scientific Essayist.*"

"Professor, you violated no law in writing your opinion on the morality of developing something as awesome as a hydrogen bomb," John said. "My lawyers have gone over that article word by word, and they assure me that there is no violation of military or state secrets, and there are no seditious or even libelous statements. You had every legal, ethical, and moral right to express your opinions."

"So did Oppenheimer."

"It was different with Oppenheimer," John rejoined. "He admitted to having close personal contacts with Communists in the past. You have nothing like that to contend with."

"No, I don't," Dub said. He smiled. "All I can say is, I'm glad McCarthy isn't heading the committee investigating me."

"McCarthy has his own neck to worry about now. The hearings aren't exactly going his way."

"I read in the newspaper that in addition to the radio, TV, and newsreel coverage, two thousand people a day are attending McCarthy's hearings," Faith said.

"Is that right? Well, today we'll be a part of that two thousand," John said, smiling. "Your father told me earlier that he got passes for all of us."

"Oh, how fascinating!" Faith said. She grinned. "It's been quite a while since my father was in the Senate. It's good to see that the 'old-boy network' is still functioning."

"Yes," John said. "Though I'm afraid the old-boy network is being strained to its limit with this McCarthy thing. If there was ever a United States senator who tested the boundaries of peer forbearance and patience, it's 'Tail-gunner Joe.'"

"Tail-gunner Joe," Dub said derisively. He clucked his tongue and shook his head. "What was his claim? That he fired more rounds than any other aerial gunner during the war?"

"Yes, and do you know the basis of that claim?" Faith scoffed. "My father checked into it. McCarthy never was a real tail gunner. He just got into the backseat of an airplane one day and shot a bunch of bullets into the trees."

"He's a disgrace to all the young men who really were tail gunners," Dub said. "I hope he gets his comeuppance. But can I actually sit in on the McCarthy hearings? I mean, my own hearing is scheduled for today, too."

"As a matter of fact, you're to be in the same caucus

room. Your hearing will convene just after the McCarthy hearings adjourn," John said. "So, not only can we attend the McCarthy hearings, we *should* attend them, just to make certain that we're on time."

When John, Faith, and Dub entered the caucus room later that morning, they found it ablaze with light and crowded with TV cameras. Though Senator Joseph Mc-Carthy was now one of the litigants, he was smiling and bustling around the room as if this were yet another hearing of which he was in charge. When Chairman Mundt called the proceedings to order, however, it became obvious that McCarthy was *not* in charge. He took his seat at one end of the long, elliptical table, apart from the seven senators sitting in hearing. McCarthy, his black-stubbled, heavy jowls spread in a wolfish grin, sat separated from his peers and his base of power. He stared across the table at his adversaries, Secretary of the Army Robert Stevens and Special Counsel Joe Welch.

John, Faith, and Dub settled into their seats in the front row as the hearings began.

"When we adjourned yesterday, Mr. Secretary," Chairman Mundt said to Army Secretary Stevens, "you were testifying. Would you like to continue?"

"Yes, Mr. Chairman, thank you," Secretary Stevens said. "What I had in mind was to try to convey to the committee, in probably rather tired language—"

"Yes, yes," McCarthy interrupted, sighing loudly and leaning back in his chair with his arms folded across his chest. He glared menacingly at the secretary.

Secretary Stevens, obviously flustered by McCarthy's rude interjection, cleared his throat, then continued his testimony.

"Uh, convey to the committee the idea that in carrying out this job and always resolving doubts in favor of the American people, that at the same time we ought not to be unfair or work hardships on individuals unnecessarily."

"Oh, yes, that's a fine sentiment, Mr. Secretary. A

fine sentiment indeed," McCarthy said, sarcasam dripping from every word.

Counsel for the Army Welch leaned over to say something to Stevens.

"Mr. Welch, please," McCarthy said. "I think the secretary is intelligent enough to give this simple testimony without your whispering in his ear. Can't we have one unfettered exchange?" McCarthy hunched forward and pointed across the table at Welch. "If you're going to sit there and mollycoddle him through every bit of dialogue, we're never going to get through this. The American people are not going to be served, and Communists and their fellow travelers everywhere are going to be laughing up their sleeves at the inability of our government to do one simple thing—and that is root out Communism wherever it might be found."

"Mr. Chairman, the senator is determined to find Communists behind every pillar and post, and if they aren't there, he is perfectly willing to put them there," Welch said.

"Mr. Welch," Roy Cohn, McCarthy's counsel, spoke up, "it is a known fact that the United States Army, whom you currently represent, is riddled with Communists at all levels, and Fort Monmouth, which is the focal point of these hearings, is no exception."

"Are you trying to convince the American people that the Army—their Army—is riddled with Communists?" Welch asked.

"Yes, Mr. Welch, that is exactly what I am saying," Cohn replied smugly.

"Well, Mr. Cohn, when you find that there are Communists and possible spies in a place like Fort Monmouth, I think you should inform the FBI. I don't want the sun to go down while they are still in there. Will you not, Mr. Cohn, before the sun goes down, give those names to the FBI?"

McCarthy fumed and glared at Welch.

Cohn cleared his throat. "Mr. John Edgar Hoover and his men know a lot better than I how to go about such things. I do not propose to tell the FBI how to run its shop."

"All I am suggesting, sir, is that we just nudge them a little."

The gallery laughed, and Cohn adjusted his collar.

McCarthy's scowl deepened. "Point of order," he grumbled.

"Do you want these spies and Communists to remain anonymous?" Welch asked.

"Surely we want them out as fast as possible, sir," Cohn said.

"Point of order," McCarthy said again.

"Well, then, may I add my small voice, sir, and ask that whenever you know about a subversive or a Communist or a spy, you would tell the FBI? And, please, hurry."

"Mr. Chairman!" McCarthy called. "I rise to a point of order."

"Senator, may I suggest that we abandon this line of dialogue and return to the testimony of Secretary Stevens?" Mundt said.

"Point of order!" McCarthy said sharply.

"Just a minute, Senator," Mundt replied impatiently.

"No, Mr. Chairman, I will not wait a minute. This very vicious smear must be answered now," McCarthy insisted. "Point of order!"

Senator Mundt sighed and put his hand to his forehead. He was clearly uncomfortable with his role, no doubt thinking that if he could, he would snap his fingers and make the entire proceedings go away.

"Very well, Senator, what is your point of order?"

McCarthy stood up. "I am glad we are on television, Mr. Chairman, Senators." Again, he pointed across the table to Welch. "I think that millions of people will now be able to see just how low a man can sink. I repeat, I think they can see how low an alleged man can sink, when someone like the Special Counsel for the United States Army belittles the principles of freedom-loving Americans everywhere."

"The chair believes that is not a point of order."

"It is a request of the chair."

"It is not a point of order."

"I think this is a matter of personal privilege."

Mundt sighed. "Very well. A point of personal privilege."

"Thank you, Mr. Chairman," McCarthy replied. "I want to respond personally to the special counsel. I have some information I feel must be shared with this committee and with the American people. I think we should tell Mr. Welch that he has in his law firm a young man named Fisher who has been for a number of years a member of an organization named as the legal bulwark of the Communist Party."

Welch looked at McCarthy with an obvious expression of shock and dismay.

"Mr. Welch, I just felt I had a duty to respond to your urgent request that before sundown, when we know of anyone serving the Communist cause, we let the agency know. I have been rather bored with your phony requests to Mr. Cohn here that he personally get every Communist out of government before sundown when you have one in your very office, sir."

Welch rested his head on his hands for a long moment, and there was absolute silence in the chambers. As was evident by their expressions, every senator on the committee and most of the gallery believed McCarthy had gone too far. He had just attacked someone who had nothing at all to do with the hearings or this case.

McCarthy, with a sneer and a jerk of his head, sat back down. Finally, Welch looked up and and raised his left hand, not to point, but merely to emphasize his statement. He spoke in a low, quiet, almost pained voice.

"Until this moment, Senator, I think I never really gauged your cruelty or your recklessness. Fred Fisher is starting what looks to be a brilliant career with us. Little did I dream you could be so reckless and so cruel as to do an injury to that lad. I fear he shall always bear this scar needlessly inflicted by you."

McCarthy opened his mouth to speak, but Welch prevailed.

"Let us not assassinate this lad further, Senator. You

have done enough. Have you no sense of decency, sir, at long last? Have you left no sense of decency?"

John, Faith, and Dub sat in the caucus room after the Army-McCarthy hearings had adjourned. The room seemed quite dark now that the television lights had been extinguished. But though gone, the looming presence of the lights and the cameras still dominated the now-empty room.

John looked at his watch. "I would've thought the committee hearing your case would be here by now."

Just then the big carved door opened. Turning to see who was entering, Faith smiled. Her father, former Senator Champ Dawson, was walking toward them.

"Hi, Dad," she said when he reached them. She shrugged. "Nobody has shown up yet. We don't know what's going on."

Champ smiled. "I do."

"What's happening?" John asked. "Why the delay?"

"The committee caucused just a few minutes ago out in the cloakroom." Champ chuckled. "It just so happens that four of them will be up for reelection this year, and they've decided that public opinion has made a dramatic swing against McCarthy and his whole witch-hunt philosophy—"

"Which is exactly what they themselves are doing," John interrupted.

"You mean which is what they were *going* to do," Champ corrected. "They've called the whole thing off. It seems those four senators have decided that having 'witch-hunt' on their records isn't the best way to face an electorate."

"You mean I don't have to go before a hearing?" Dub asked.

Champ shook his head. "You're off the hook, and the university is off the hook."

"Well, I'm not ready to let the U.S. Senate off the hook," Faith said. "I think they should apologize to Professor Wilkerson for bringing all this up in the first place."

"No, no, I don't want an apology," Dub said quickly. "I don't want anything except to go back to my classroom."

"But they owe you," Faith insisted.

John laughed. "Wow, talk about your woman scorned —and you weren't even scorned. No, Dub is right. The best thing to do now is just get out of here. Don't you agree, Champ?"

"Yes, there's no sense in tweaking the beard now."

"Especially after all the work you did for us to get the thing dropped," John added.

"What makes you think I had anything to do with it?" Champ asked.

John laughed. "You forget, Senator, you are not only my father-in-law, I also used to work for you. I know the famous 'Dawson Persuasion,' and you can't convince me that it's no longer effective just because you're no longer a member of the Senate. I'm sure you had a few words of wisdom for the committee."

"Well, now that you mention it, I guess I did point out to the four who were going to have to go back and face their constituents this year that, on balance, they may have more to lose than to gain by pushing this," Champ admitted. "Maybe they just saw the light."

Dub stuck his hand out to Champ. "It's easy enough to see why they saw the light. You turned it on for them. Thank you, Senator. From the bottom of my heart, thank you."

THE OVAL OFFICE ANTEROOM, THE WHITE HOUSE

Quinisha Jackson was wearing a dark-blue dress, a matching veiled hat, and white cotton gloves. She was sitting in a big leather chair, holding Andrew on her lap. The boy was dressed in a miniature Air Force uniform, complete with silver wings and the gold oak leaves of a major.

Stump Pollard sat to Quinisha's right, Train Willis to

her left. There had been a flurry of activity when they arrived because they had to pass through a crowd of White House tourists, and many of them, recognizing Choo Choo Willis, had asked for his autograph.

Now it was very quiet, with only the four of them and the appointment secretary in the room. The telephone on the woman's desk rang quietly, and she picked it up, spoke a few words, then hung up. She looked over at the group and smiled.

"That was the press office," she said. "The photographers and reporters are on their way over. It'll be just a few minutes longer."

"Thank you," Quinisha replied.

After several moments of silence Train cleared his throat. "Mrs. Jackson, there's somethin' I've been wantin' to say to you."

"Yes?"

"I, uh, don't know if the major ever mentioned me in any of his letters or not, but in the early days after he arrived—well, we had a few, uh, differences."

"Yes, he mentioned you, Mr. Willis," Quinisha said.

"Yes, ma'am. Well, for what it's worth I want you to know that from the very beginning he had my respect. He was the best pilot and one of the finest officers I ever met. He always kept his cool, he was fair, and he was dependable. Toward the end, though, even before he gave up his life to save mine, he had more than my respect. He had my admiration. I wish I had told him that I wanted to give him my friendship as well. And my bein' here with you to watch the President award the Medal of Honor is the proudest moment of my life. Though I must confess my pride is tempered by a deep sadness, because I know that I'm responsible for—"

"No, Mr. Willis, you are not responsible," Quinisha interjected, putting her hand on his arm. "Travis chose the Air Force. He was happy to serve, happy to be in Korea, and happy to be a flier. I know in my heart that he was happy when he drew his last breath. And don't worry about not telling him you wanted to be his friend. You were his friend and he was yours. After all, 'Greater love hath no man than this: that he lay down his life for a friend.'"

Train squeezed Quinisha's hand. Looking at their different skin tones, he realized that at another time in his life he would have been appalled—furious, even—that a colored woman would have the temerity to touch him. He quickly looked away.

Andrew stared at him, his big brown eyes wide, then said, "Mama, that man is crying." He pointed at Train. "Why is he crying?"

"Hush, child," Quinisha said softly, bending down to kiss Andrew on the cheek. "He is crying because he is a good man."

The door to the Oval Office opened then, and an Air Force colonel stuck his head out. "Mrs. Jackson, would you and your guests please come in?" The colonel caught his secretary's eye. "When the press arrives, hold them here until we call for them."

"Yes, sir," she replied.

Quinisha, Andrew, Stump, and Train stepped into the Oval Office. Besides the colonel there was an Air Force general, three men in civilian clothes, and President Dwight D. Eisenhower. Eisenhower walked around from behind his desk, his famous smile and blue eyes welcoming. He held out his hand to Quinisha.

"Mrs. Jackson, how good it is to see you. And you too, Andrew," he added, bending over to shake Andrew's hand.

"Mr. President, this is my very good friend Stump Pollard," Quinisha said.

"Stump?" President Eisenhower said.

"It's a name I picked up when I played football in college, Mr. President," Stump explained. "Many years ago."

"Sounds like a pretty good name for a football player," the President said. He looked at Train. "And speaking of football players, Mr. Willis, your name I know. I read about you being traded to the Giants. How do you feel about that?"

"I'm looking forward to it, Mr. President," Train said.

"I think the Giants have a legitimate shot at the title next year."

"I don't know. Cleveland looks pretty good," Eisenhower said. He paused, then shifted gears. "You're one of the men who recommended Major Jackson for the medal, isn't that correct?"

"Yes, sir. Lieutenant Balfour and I made the initial recommendation."

"I've never read a more deserving citation. Flying behind the lines in a small airplane, landing in the midst of enemy fire . . . It's truly the stuff of heroism. The other recommending officer was Lieutenant Balfour, you said?"

"Yes, sir, Terry Balfour. I wish he could be here with us too, but he was killed shortly after when he was shot down."

Eisenhower shook his head. "The price young men must pay for old men's follies," he said somberly. "The top priority of my entire presidency shall be to defuse the tension that exists in the world today so that fine young men like Major Jackson and Lieutenant Balfour will be able to watch their children grow to adulthood."

Eisenhower looked at Andrew with eyes that Quinisha felt showed the most profound sadness she had ever seen. He was taking the death of Travis and Lieutenant Balfour and every other young man who had died in the war as personally as if they had been his own children. In that moment of insight Quinisha realized that they *were*, indeed, his children.

The President sighed, then looked at the colonel. "Has the press arrived?"

"I'm sure they have, Mr. President."

"Then call them in, and let's give this lovely lady the medal her husband paid so dearly for."

CHAPTER

SEVEN

DEMARIS HUNTER TO BE IN SIKESTON
FOR COTTON CARNIVAL PARADE

The Henry Meldrum Post of the American Legion announced today that motion picture star Demaris Hunter will be their special guest for the Cotton Carnival Parade to be held in Sikeston tomorrow.

The Hollywood producer Sam Goldwyn is said to have once remarked, "Producers don't make stars. God makes stars, and the public recognizes His handiwork." Demaris Hunter is one of those stars. Millions of appreciative fans have flocked to her films in the past, and soon many more millions will see her on television as hostess

139

of *The Demaris Hunter Show,* a weekly variety program.

A first-magnitude star of Hollywood, Demaris Hunter is Missouri's own, having been born and reared in St. Louis. The onetime Goddess of Love and Beauty of the St. Louis Veiled Prophet Festival will judge the Miss Sikeston beauty pageant to be held this evening. Tomorrow morning she will ride in the parade marshal's car, and then she will judge the Miss Cotton Carnival contest to be held tomorrow night after the football game. The city of Sikeston is indeed honored to have Miss Hunter visit our town.

Late that Friday afternoon Demaris flew down from St. Louis in a small private plane, landing in Sikeston just after dusk. She was met at the airport by some of the parade officials, then taken out to the country club for dinner. After dinner she gave a short speech, explaining that though she had been in Hollywood for almost thirty years now, she was at heart still a Missourian. She then went on to talk about the television show she would be hosting, which was set to begin in just three more weeks and for which she was currently on a nationwide promotion tour.

"The competition is going to be stiff," she told her audience. "I will be going up against the likes of Ed Sullivan, Milton Berle, and Sid Caesar."

"Well, if it's a beauty contest, Miss Hunter, you'll win hands down," someone shouted, and everyone laughed.

Demaris spent a couple of hours mingling with the dinner guests, and then her hosts took her down to the Cotton Carnival grounds, where a special platform had been erected to stage the two beauty pageants.

The judging of that night's contest—for Miss Sikeston—went smoothly, and the girl chosen as winner told Demaris what a thrill it was to be selected by a famous movie star.

After more mingling and handshakes and smiles and answering dozens of questions (*"The best screen kisser?*

Oh, Clark Gable. The best off-screen kisser? Now, you don't really expect a lady to tell you something like that, do you? The most exciting new star? Watch James Dean. I believe he's going to be something very special."), Demaris was taken to the Dunn Hotel.

"We don't call it the Presidential Suite, Miss Hunter, but President Truman did stay in this very suite once," she was told when she was shown to her room.

"It's quite lovely," Demaris replied graciously. "I'm sure I'll be very comfortable here."

She had had a long, busy day, so once she was in bed, it was mere moments before she was asleep. But about two in the morning she was awakened by sounds from the next room.

"Ohhh!" a woman's voice moaned loudly. "Oh, my, yes, it's wonderful! It's wonderful!"

A rhythmic creaking of bedsprings accompanied the staccato squeals the woman was making.

When Demaris realized what had awakened her, she was first embarrassed, then engrossed. Though she was ashamed of herself, she couldn't stop herself from listening.

"Oh," the woman moaned again. And then the "ohs" turned to little screams of pleasure as the thrashing grew more and more frenzied.

Demaris kicked the covers off as she began to perspire. She was mortified by her reaction, but unable to control it.

Finally the man and the woman moaned in unison, a long, loud moan; then their cries and the sounds of the straining bed stopped. For several minutes there was total silence.

Demaris just lay there, so aware of her body that she could almost feel the blood moving in her veins. She tingled all over, from the soles of her feet to the top of her scalp. She thought about the couple's absolute silence, and for one irrational moment she was afraid she'd been caught eavesdropping.

Then she heard the bed creak again, followed a moment later by the sound of water running. After that the couple began talking, and their voices were as clear as if they were in the same room with her.

"Thanks a lot for droppin' by, sweetheart," the man's low, rumbling voice said.

"Are you kiddin'? I should thank you!" the woman replied. "You were good, honey. Real good. It's been a long time since anyone made me feel like that."

"Yeah? Well, I always think it's better when both people enjoy it," the man said.

"So, listen, what're you doin' tomorrow?" the woman asked. "I mean, is there somewhere I could call you? Could we get together or somethin'?"

"I'm sorry, darlin', but I'm goin' to be tied up all day tomorrow, and then I reckon we'll be pullin' out of here tomrrow night. We've got a show to do down in Tupelo."

"Too bad," the woman said. "But it's probably just as well. You know what they say. When you play with fire too much, you can get your fingers burned."

"You afraid I'm goin' to burn your fingers?" the man asked with a chuckle.

The woman giggled softly. "Honey, you're so hot you're burnin' me all over." She sighed. "I guess I'd better get goin'. Marv is on the night shift at the shoe factory, and he'll be gettin' home in another hour or so. If I'm not there, I'm goin' to have a lot of explainin' to do."

"Listen, you be careful now, you hear?" the man said.

"I will. Good night, honey."

"Good night. That Marv's a lucky man. You're a sweet kid."

Demaris heard the door close, realizing as she lay there that she had a strange, empty feeling that she couldn't explain. Finally she sighed and sat up, then walked over to the window and pulled the curtains to look outside.

Her room fronted Malone Avenue, and directly across the street was Legion Park, where the Cotton Carnival had been set up. Over in the corner of the park were a number of small house trailers, mobile homes for the carnies and roustabouts. The trailers, like the rides and booths, were dark now. The stage where Demaris had judged the Miss Sikeston contest was empty and as dark as the rest of the grounds.

A car door slammed, followed by the sound of an engine starting. Headlights stabbed into the night, and Demaris watched a white Studebaker pull away from the curb in front of the hotel. She couldn't see the driver and hadn't seen the driver get into the car, but she had a feeling that it was the woman who'd been in the room next door.

The Studebaker, going east on Malone, met a big trailer truck coming west. Both truck and car dimmed their headlight beams. Demaris wondered about the truck driver. How far he had come? How far was he going? Had he ever seen any of her movies? What would he think if he knew that, right now, she was just above him, looking down at him as he drove by?

As the truck drew even with her, the driver flipped a cigarette out, and a small shower of orange sparks burst along the pavement for a brief moment. The truck rumbled on by, and Demaris watched the red and orange running lights until it was out of sight. Finally, with a sigh, she let the curtain fall back and returned to her bed. She could hear a soft snoring through the wall; the man next door, whoever he was, had gone to sleep. She turned over, fluffed up her pillows, and managed to do the same thing.

Leading off the Cotton Carnival parade were the fire trucks, glistening red paint and highly polished chrome shining brilliantly in the morning sun. Their clanging brass bells and flashing lights alerted the thousands of parade watchers lining the route that the festivities were about to begin, and the onlookers cheered lustily.

The fire trucks were followed by a couple of police cars, then by a shiny black Cadillac convertible with red-leather seats. The side of the convertible had a sign reading: DEMARIS HUNTER, HONORED GUEST. Demaris was sitting in the back seat, holding a bouquet of long-

stemmed red roses, waving at the crowd. Most were seeing her in person for the first time and wanted to determine if she really was as beautiful as she appeared in
movies and on TV.

"She has to be over fifty, doesn't she? Hell, she's
been in the movies since I was a kid," one man asked
another.

"Yeah, she's over fifty all right, but I saw her gettin'
into the car a while ago. Let me tell you, she's still one
fine-looking woman."

The car carrying Demaris was followed by the
Charleston High School band, resplendently outfitted in
blue-and-white uniforms. Charleston's band was followed
by the band from Chaffee High School, and Chaffee was
followed by the Poplar Bluff band. There were twenty-
eight high school bands in all, brought up by the Sikeston
High School band, dressed in red and black.

Once under way, the bands all competed with each
other so that only those parade watchers immediately
alongside an individual band could actually make out the
music being played. To everyone else along the route the
numerous bands and their separate marching songs came
across only as a discordant cacophony of sound, under-
scored by the thump of bass drums and the clash of cymbals.

Interspersing the bands were other parade elements,
including other convertibles. Each of these cars displayed
one of the Cotton Carnival Queen candidates, beautiful
young high school girls perched identically on the top of
the cars' backseats, with their voluminous dresses spread
out over the trunks. They were more than just candidates;
each had already been selected beauty queen of her
hometown. Tonight Demaris Hunter would crown one of
them Miss Cotton Carnival.

In addition to bands and beauty queens, the parade
featured mechanical cotton pickers, combines, tractors,
trucks, and new cars—because more than anything else,
this parade was a celebration of the commercial spirit of
the thriving Bootheel community of Sikeston. The cars,
on loan from Sikeston's car dealers, were brand-new 1955

editions, and for many the Cotton Carnival parade was the first opportunity to see the new models. Each year they were as eagerly awaited as the floats, and the amount of applause a car generated was an early mark of what the car's success would be for that year. The clear winner the year before had been the Oldsmobile Holiday 88.

Bobby Parker's mother let him out of the "family boat"—a green-and-yellow version of that selfsame 1954 Oldsmobile Holiday 88—in front of the high school gym. This was as close as she could get him to the assembly area, which was fine with Bobby, who had no desire to be seen being brought to the parade by his mother.

He left the French horn case in the car, tucked the horn under his arm, then hurried up the street, passing the other high school bands standing in position, waiting for their turn to join the parade already in progress.

"You better run!" someone from the Cape Girardeau band shouted as Bobby passed him.

"You ain't goin' to make it!" shouted a member of the Caruthersville band in their assembly area.

"I'd sure hate to be in your shoes!" a Malden trombone player teased.

The entire trumpet section of the Kennett band played a special razzberry for him as he passed them, and his face was burning with embarrassment by the time he reached the staging area for his own band.

"Bobby, where's your lyre?" Billy Murchison asked.

"I forgot it."

"You're going to be in some deep shit if Mr. Collins sees you. You remember what he said during sixth hour yesterday."

"I don't need music anyway. We're playin' marches, and all the French horn does is play the offbeat. The bass drum goes boom, and I go toot. Boom, toot, boom, toot, boom toot, toot," he demonstrated. "That'll cover every march in the book."

"Yeah, well, just don't let Mr. Collins see you, is all I can say," Murchison said.

Judy Boyce, the drum majorette, blew her whistle, and the members of the band moved out into Tanner

Street to form up and wait their turn. It was hot, and the sun beat down hard on the red coats and black trousers. More than one bandsman removed a hat to wipe sweat away.

"Last one," Harold Aufdenberg said. Aufdenberg was the right guide, and Bobby was standing next to him.

"Last one what?"

"We're seniors. This is our last Cotton Carnival parade."

"Yeah," Bobby said. "Yeah, that's right, isn't it?" He found the thought of this being the last Cotton Carnival parade he'd ever march in a little sad, but he didn't mention it because he didn't want anyone to know he felt that way. He looked around at several other seniors to see if he could tell by the expressions on their faces whether they, too, were just a little sad.

"Did you go to the Miss Sikeston contest last night?" Sue Ann French asked. She played the clarinet and marched just behind Bobby.

"No, I didn't get to. Who won?"

"Barbara Grant."

"Yeah, I thought she'd win. Just like I think you'll win next year."

"What makes you say that?"

"I just think you will," Bobby said. "I mean, if being pretty counts for anything. You're the prettiest girl in the junior class."

"Thanks," Sue Ann said, smiling.

Bobby cleared his throat. "Say, uh, Sue Ann, would you like to, uh, go to the movies with me tomorrow afternoon?"

"Oh, I can't," she said lightly. "I have to wash my hair."

"Oh, uh, yeah. Okay, maybe some other time," he said, though this was at least the fourth time he had asked her out, and she had turned him down every time with the same excuse. *No wonder her hair was so pretty*, Bobby thought. *She must wash it more than anyone else in the world.*

Just before they started, Mr. Collins, who would be

marching along with the band, looked back over the group. "We'll start out with 'King Cotton March,' then 'Washington Post,' then 'The Thunderer,' then back to 'King Cotton March,' 'Washington Post,' and 'The Thunderer' again. And if we need more, we'll start the cycle all over again. Does everyone understand? Parker, where's your lyre?"

"Where's my what?" Bobby asked, playing for time.

"Your music holder. Where is it?"

Bobby felt someone slide a lyre into his hand, and he held it up to show Mr. Collins. "Oh, I've got it right here, Mr. Collins."

"Where's the music?"

"Music?" Bobby replied. "I didn't know anythin' about music. I just heard you say bring the lyre."

"Parker, what good is your lyre without the music?" Mr. Collins asked in an exasperated voice.

"I don't know, Mr. Collins. You know, I was thinkin' that, too. I was wonderin' why you'd tell us to bring the lyre but not tell us to bring the music."

Everybody laughed. Collins just shook his head in resignation, then looked ahead, waiting for the signal from the parade director to move out.

Finally it was time to get under way, and the drum line picked up the cadence.

Judy held the baton up, blew the whistle, then brought the baton down. The band moved out playing the "King Cotton March." Some of the bands had drum majors instead of majorettes, and some of the bands with majorettes had them dressed in a military-type uniform with long pants. Judy Boyce, however, wore the same sort of costume as the twirlers, so that her long, shapely legs were bare. Bobby was glad. From his marching position he had a very good view not only of Judy but of Linda Murbach, the head twirler, as well. He liked to watch their prancing legs under the very short skirts. Once he had mentioned that to Murchison, and Murchison accused him of being "a dirty old man at seventeen." Then Murchison admitted that he enjoyed it as well.

Somewhere along the parade route Bobby's mother,

father, and youngest brother began yelling and waving at
him. Bobby stared straight ahead, embarrassed by their
demonstrativeness and sure that everyone was secretly
laughing at him—though during the course of the parade
most of the other members of the band had been, or
would be, subjected to the same embarrassment. At least
Harry, Bobby's middle brother, hadn't added to it. A
sophomore, too old to watch the parade with the rest of
the family, Harry would be off with a group of his own
friends and was probably already over at the carnival
grounds, not even watching the parade.

After marching for what seemed an eternity under
the sweltering sun, the parade broke up, and Bobby and
his friends immediately went to look at the new cars on
display. There were a couple that Bobby especially liked,
the two-door hardtop Ford Victoria and the two-door
hardtop Chevrolet Bel Air. The Ford was aquamarine and
white, the Chevy gray and pink.

"Which one do you like best?" Murchison asked.

"I don't know. I like them both," Bobby said.
"Maybe the Ford."

"Yeah, but the Chevy has a hotter mill. Their new
V-8 is the best engine goin' right now."

"Who says?"

"Everybody says. Besides, look at it. Don't you like
the lines?"

"Yeah, it's cool-lookin', all right."

"Hey, you guys, check out the sound," one of
Bobby's fellow band members—a drummer named Bert
—said.

"What sound?"

After the parade, a series of fifteen-minute concerts
were provided by the individual bands, of which the
Sikeston band would be last—a fact they bemoaned since
it meant remaining in uniform all day. In between each
band, some professional group—usually a country band—
would perform, and their music would be played over the
loudspeakers throughout the carnival grounds so that no

matter where anyone was they would be blasted by the music.

"The music," Bert said insistently. "Listen to it."

"I don't dig hillbilly shit."

"Yeah, me neither, but I don't think that's hillbilly."

"Sure, it's hillbilly. That's all they ever do."

"No, wait," one of the others said. "Bert's right. Listen to it. That's not hillbilly . . . or at least not any kind of hillbilly I've ever heard. What do you say we cut out of here and catch some of it?"

Buck Campbell had started his set with "You Are My Sunshine," typical country-music fare. Then he did Hank Williams's "Hey, Good Lookin'," also country. During both numbers the carnival crowd continued to mill around the grounds. No one stopped at the stage to listen.

"Hey, Buck, they're not exactly runnin' over each other to get here, are they?" Buck's band mate Frankie Porter noted.

Buck took a drink from a paper cup, then wiped the back of his hand across his mouth. "Yeah, well, who can blame 'em with this shit we're playin'?"

"We ain't got no choice," Frankie replied. "The fella that hired us said we was to play only traditional hillbilly songs."

"Okay, so we'll just start our own tradition," Buck suggested. "How 'bout 'Cactus Flower'?"

When Buck started playing his own music, most of the fairgoers were all over the lot checking out the entertainment the carnival had to offer, such as Dunk the Colored Boy, Loop the Duck, Fool the Weight Guesser, Bumper Cars, Tilt-a-Whirl, and Flying Swings. Gradually, though, as they heard the music, they drifted toward the stage to see what was going on. The most enthusiastic of the fans seemed to be the teenagers.

The audience grew and was brightened by the different-colored uniforms of all the bands. The swelling crowd spilled back from the stage into the midway, blocking off some of the attractions so that customers couldn't reach them—though so many were gathering now to hear the music that the other attractions were beginning to suffer anyway. The Test Your Strength/Ring the Bell, a favorite of the football players, was completely deserted. The Flying Swings—also an exclusive domain of the high school crowd, being considered too dangerous for the very young and too foolish for the old—was equally devoid of patrons, and its operator closed it down entirely. The Bumper Cars did only half its normal business, and the Tilt-a-Whirl shut down. Only the Ferris wheel continued to operate—and only because the young people who rode it assured others that the view of the stage from the top of the wheel was better than from the back of the crowd.

Buck Campbell ended his set with one of his own songs, "Rockin' Rollin' Heart."

"My rockin' rollin' heart is keepin' us apart.
What am I to do? I'm so in love with you.
But you don't care if I live or die.
You don't care if I laugh or cry.
I want nothing but this, to be smothered by your kiss,
And your love."

The song had a lilting melody and a staccato rhythm that spoke directly to the teenagers, and when the set was finished and it was time for the next high school band, everyone groaned in protest, including the band about to play.

Demaris Hunter wasn't expected back on the carnival grounds until it was time to crown Miss Cotton Carnival, so she spent the afternoon in her room, going over a script for her first TV show. Though she had an excellent view of the carnival grounds from her window, she hadn't planned to look out. She did, however, raise the window for some air, and that was when she heard the music. At first she thought it was country music, and she groaned inwardly; that was the one kind of music she couldn't stand. But after a few songs the music seemed to change, and she found herself listening to it. The applause grew louder with each number until by the sixth song it was thunderous. Curious, Demaris put the script aside and walked over to the window to have a look.

She was amazed at what she saw. The stage was surrounded by carnivalgoers of all ages. Everyone, especially the teenagers, was enjoying the singer's music, but the reaction of the females in the audience was what fascinated Demaris most. High school girls with freshly scrubbed faces and virginal souls were expressing—there were no other words for it—pure sexual ecstasy as they listened and swayed in time with the music. Demaris might have passed off the reaction as youthful extreme were she not seeing the same expression on the faces of more mature women as well.

She hadn't seen anyone exude as much raw sexual magnetism as this singer since Frank Sinatra during the war. Girls and young women screamed and reached up to try to touch him.

Why? Demaris wondered. This singer, whoever he was, didn't have the pure, sweet, golden voice of a Sinatra or a Crosby. His voice was rumbling, almost gravelly, like someone whispering in the middle of the night.

Whispering in the middle of the night! My God, this was the man she'd heard in the room next to hers the night before!

Demaris knew at that moment that she had to have him on her show.

DECEMBER 1954, OREGON

Eric Twainbough brought the two peanut-butter-and-jelly sandwiches he was having for lunch into the living room of the small cabin on the McKenzie River, then settled back in his chair to watch the basketball game between the University of San Francisco Dons and the Jefferson University Bears. The announcer was breathless in his description of the game:

"This is the game of the season, folks—perhaps the game of the decade. Big Bill Russell and the Dons are putting their twenty-two-game winning streak on the line against Artemus Booker and the Bears. The Bears have a fourteen-game winning streak of their own, not having lost since the NIT finals last year. There is time-out on the clock with six minutes to go in the game. Just three minutes ago San Francisco had a sixteen-point lead, but that's been cut to six points by the brilliant play of Artemus Booker, who has hit his last five attempts."

The buzzer sounded.

"Play is back in now, and the Dons have the ball. They're slowing the pace down, working the ball for the opportunity to feed it to Bill Russell, but Booker is on Russell like glue. Oh, my, there's a loose ball, and the Bears have it! Booker's on a fast break; there's the alley-oop pass to him! Score! The lead is cut to four, and the Dons want a time-out!"

"All right, Artemus!" Eric shouted to the TV set. "Hey, Loomis, look down here. Can you believe that grandson of yours?"

Eric felt a special affinity for the grandchild of Loomis Booker, a man he considered his surrogate father. In 1904, when he was a fourteen-year-old working on a Wyoming cattle ranch—he had made his way there after being orphaned two years before in Montana—Eric had hopped a freight train to visit the St. Louis World's Fair. After surviving a series of misadventures during the long journey, Eric saw his goal in sight. But just before his train arrived in St. Louis, he was discovered by a railroad detective, beaten, and thrown from the boxcar. Loomis Booker, then working as a janitor and handyman for what was still Jefferson College, found Eric alongside the track, more dead than alive, and nursed him back to health.

Taking in Eric, Loomis had given the youth much more than first aid; he also gave him love, support, and an education. Loomis Booker was himself a self-educated man. His enterprise was eventually recognized by Jefferson University, and he was awarded a doctoral degree, becoming by many years the first Negro to graduate from that institution.

Jefferson University remained segregated until 1951, lowering the color barrier three years before the Supreme Court decision that made school segregation illegal. Now the university was fully integrated, and one of Loomis's grandsons was not only a student there, he was J.U.'s star basketball player—one of the premiere basketball players in the country.

The cat pawed at Eric's ankle.

"Not now, Plaidcat," Eric protested. "Can't you see I'm watching this game?"

Plaidcat meowed and jumped into Eric's lap. Eric stroked him, trying to keep him quiet, but the cat continued to meow.

"All right, all right, I'll open a can of food for you," he said, getting up from the chair but keeping his eyes on the TV set.

The basket by Russell is good, and he was fouled, so there is a chance for a three-point play.

"Miss it," Eric said as he pulled a can opener from the drawer and opened a can of Puritex cat food.

Free throw is no good. Russell gets his own rebound, up good, and fouled!

"Damn!" Eric said, spooning the food out for the cat, who began eating even before Eric was finished.

The free throw was good.

Damn! Eric shouted. "Russell just made five points in about five seconds. Wake up, Bears! You can't stand around on the court with your thumbs up your asses and expect to win!"

The Bears didn't heed Eric's wake-up call. Only Artemus continued to play well—so well, in fact, that at the conclusion of the game he was selected as the Canfield-Puritex Player of the Game, even though Jefferson lost by a score of 89 to 86.

With a sigh of disgust, Eric turned off the TV, then walked out to his back porch to look at the wild-running river.

He had stayed on in Bimini for nearly a year after

Shaylin died, but it had been too hard for him there. She was such a presence in that house that he could almost see her, and once or twice he even spoke to her before he realized he was talking to a shadow. He completed the book he had been working on when she was killed, *The Edge of Infinity*, then closed up the house and moved away.

At first he tried to live in New York, but he didn't like it. Then he decided to cross America by car, figuring that if he came upon any place that appealed to him, he'd settle there. He rented an apartment in St. Louis for a while because his son and daughter-in-law, Hamilton and Amy, and granddaughter, Paige, lived there. But even that couldn't keep him, so one day he packed up and moved on, thinking perhaps to return to his western roots.

He went all the way to Oregon, settling on the Mc-Kenzie River in the shadow of the Three Sisters Mountains. Here was the majestic Cascade Range with lush, green, towering trees and tumbling white water so clean and pure that it tested healthier than the most scientifically treated city water. It was so beautiful that Eric, writing his publisher about it, said that "if God ever made a place any prettier than the McKenzie River, he kept it for Himself."

A stray calico cat had wandered onto his place the first week Eric moved in. He had adopted the cat, which he called Plaidcat, and that was his only company.

The Edge of Infinity had done very well, making the best-seller lists of *The New York Times* and *Publishers Weekly* and being critically acclaimed as well. As a result, colleges that had for the most part turned their backs on him were now welcoming him again, and he had more invitations to speak than he could handle.

"Mr. Twainbough? Are you Mr. Twainbough?"

Eric was startled by the voice, for he had been so involved in watching the river that he had neither seen nor heard anyone arrive. Looking around, he saw a young man wearing the uniform of a Western Union messenger standing on the top step of the porch.

"Yes," Eric said. "I'm Eric Twainbough."

"I have a telegram for you, Mr. Twainbough. Sign here, please," the youth said, stepping onto the porch.

Eric signed the form on the clipboard, then handed it back, rummaging in his pants pocket for some change for a tip. The boy thanked him, then scampered down the stairs to his motorcycle. Eric briefly watched the vehicle as it took off, amazed that something as loud as a motorcycle had been so completely drowned out by the clamorous rushing river. Hardly any wonder he had been startled by the youth.

Curious as to who would send him a telegram, Eric tore open the yellow envelope and took out the message. It was from his publisher:

WHY DON'T YOU GET A TELEPHONE LIKE EVERYONE ELSE WHO LIVES IN THE TWENTIETH CENTURY STOP HAVE JUST BEEN INFORMED THAT *THE EDGE OF INFINITY* HAS BEEN AWARDED NOBEL PRIZE STOP WILL YOU GO TO STOCKHOLM TO ACCEPT THE AWARD STOP

STOCKHOLM, SWEDEN

The first thing Eric Twainbough discovered upon his arrival was that he was not the only recipient of the Nobel Prize for Literature. For the first time it was to be a shared award; Ernest Hemingway had also won it for *The Old Man and the Sea.* But Hemingway had sent word that he wouldn't be able to come to Stockholm; therefore, Eric had the ceremonial part of the award all to himself.

He got out of the taxi in front of the Grand Hotel, then, as the bellman loaded his bags onto a cart, turned to look across the Strommen Canal at the Royal Palace.

Although the sun was shining brightly and there was no snow on the ground nor ice in the canal, it was cold, and puffs of steam came from the doorman's nose and mouth as he stood in front of the hotel, greeting arrivals. The doorman was wearing a long military coat that looked very much like the dress coat for the uniform of the Czarist Russian officers.

For a moment Eric had a strong memory of his time in Russia just prior to the Russian Revolution, and he thought of Katya, the Russian princess he had been in love with.

He wondered why after so many years of not thinking about her that thought had suddenly surfaced, then realized that it was probably a combination of things: the cold, crisp, clear weather like St. Petersburg's; the stately, almost Czarist-style buildings; and, of course, the doorman in his White Russian officer's coat.

"Mr. Twainbough," a tall, thin, blond-haired man said, smiling as he approached with his hand extended, "I am Oleg Svensen. I will be your personal guide while you are in Stockholm. Please, allow me to welcome you to Sweden."

"Thank you," Eric said. He nodded toward the front of the hotel. "Do I need to check in at the front desk?"

"No, everything is taken care of. If you'll just come with me, sir, I'll take you directly to your suite, where you can freshen up from your flight and get ready for the news conference."

"News conference?" Eric asked as they stepped into the elevator.

"Yes. Seven please," Svensen said to the elevator operator. Then, continuing his conversation with Eric, "It will be held at nineteen hundred hours this evening. There will be many representatives of the world's press here to meet all the Nobel Prize winners."

Eric stroked his beard. "I've already given about a dozen news conferences. I was hoping they might slow down a bit."

"Oh, heavens no, sir, they are just starting. In fact, I fear you will be in the spotlight for this entire week. You see, the Nobel Prize Commission feels it is very important to be accommodating to the press."

Eric smiled. "Well, I have nothing against the working press. After all, I used to be a member myself. I'll make your conference, Mr. Svensen, bright-eyed and bushy-tailed."

"I beg your pardon, sir?"

"I'll be there."

"Oh, very good, sir."

The elevator stopped, and the doors were opened. Svensen led the way down the hall to suite 712, then let himself into the room with a key, which he then handed to Eric. Walking over to the large windows, he opened the curtains, then pointed with pride to the scenery outside. "As you can see, this room affords a lovely view of the Riddarholm Church, the Strombron Bridge, and the Royal Opera House. I hope you are satisfied with your accomodations."

"Yes, thank you, it's quite nice," Eric said.

The luggage arrived.

"Do you wish the porters to unpack for you?"

"Uh, no, no thanks," Eric said. "I'll take care of it." He reached for his pocket, but Svensen extended his hand to stop him.

"The gratuities are all taken care of by the Nobel Prize Committee," he said. "Please, we want only for you to enjoy your visit with us."

"Thanks. So far I haven't seen anything not to enjoy."

"Oh, I nearly forgot," Svensen said, taking an envelope from his inside jacket pocket. "A lady asked me to give this to you."

"Thanks," Eric said, taking the envelope.

"If there is anything I can do for you, anything you need, please don't hesitate to call me. You are my sole responsibility for the entire time you are here," Svensen said just before he left the room.

Eric sat in one of the big, overstuffed chairs near the window and looked at the envelope. There was something very familiar about the writing. He tore open the envelope.

Eric,

First, allow me to extend my most sincere congratulations to you for winning the Nobel Prize for literature. I am very pleased but not surprised, except I would have thought the Nobel Prize

Committee would have recognized your work long before now.

I am in Stockholm on business. My room number is 511. Perhaps we could get together for a drink?

Fondly,
Tanner

Eric picked up the telephone, and when the desk answered, he asked to be connected to room 511.

"Hello?" a woman's voice answered.

"Are you staying out of the night fog?" Eric asked.

The question was in reference to the way they had met more than thirty years earlier. Tanner Tannenhower, then a recent graduate of Jefferson University, was taking the "grand tour" of Europe—considered a rite of passage for wealthy young graduates in the 1920's.

Eric, then one of the many expatriate writers living in Paris, had seen Tanner across a crowded, smoke-filled dance club. He had seen, also, that when she left the club, she was followed by an unsavory-looking character. On a hunch, Eric had followed them both, and though he nearly lost them in the thick fog, he caught up with them in time to save her from a dangerous situation.

That chance meeting led to a whirlwind romance and then marriage. The marriage lasted for about ten years, and when it broke up, it wasn't because they had fallen out of love but because Eric's writing had led him in one direction and Tanner's obligation to her family business— she had inherited the Tannenhower Brewing Company— led her in another. For a while they tried to maintain the marriage even though separated, but it didn't work, and finally they were divorced, each going on to marry again. Tanner's second husband, Mitchell Morrison, had been chief of operations for the Tannenhower Brewery. He died a year before Shaylin was killed.

Answering Eric's question, Tanner laughed a deep, throaty laugh. "If I do, will you come charging in on your white horse to save me like you did the last time?"

"Was that a white horse I was riding?"

Tanner laughed again. "I do believe it was. Oh, Eric, I am so proud of you . . . I can't begin to express just how much. And, of course, Ham is popping his buttons."

"I am very pleased to have been selected," Eric said. "Though I must say I'm a little surprised. And, don't forget, I'm having to share this with Hem."

"How is Ernest? I haven't seen him in years."

"I went fishing with him once this summer. He's still feeling some effects from that double airplane crash. He's all right, I guess, but he's not the same Hemingway we knew in Paris. He told the Nobel Prize Committee that he was too busy working to come get his award, but the truth is, I don't think he's physically up to it."

"That's too bad," Tanner said, and they both fell silent. After a few moments she asked, "Will you be eating dinner tonight? Or is your body clock still messed up from the trip over?"

"My body clock is still messed up, but I will be eating dinner."

"Then how about joining me? My room at eight?" Tanner offered.

"I'll see you then."

"More wine?" Eric asked, picking up the crystal decanter.

"Yes, thank you," Tanner replied. "So tell me, how do you like Oregon?"

"It's very beautiful out there. I even like the fact that I don't have a phone in my house, though I guess that is selfish of me."

"Yes, it is," Tanner said. "If I wanted to call you, I wouldn't be able to."

"Why would you ever want to call me?"

"No reason in particular. But we do have a few things in common—like our son, our daughter-in-law, and our granddaughter."

Eric grinned. "That's true."

"You know, it's too bad it didn't work out for you when you were in St. Louis."

"The whole time I was there, I felt as if I was visiting," Eric said. "I mean, it was nice to be able to see Ham and Amy and Paige." He chuckled. "By the way, I'm glad to see our grandchild gets her looks from you. She's a beautiful girl."

"She is beautiful, isn't she?" Tanner said.

"What are you doing in Stockholm?"

"We've bought an interest in a brewery here. I came over to take a look at it."

"I thought Ham was handling all that now. I thought you had retired."

"I have. But Ham figured I would enjoy the trip. And because it coincided with the Nobel Prize awards, I agreed with him." Tanner reached across the table and placed her hand on Eric's. "I feel a sort of proprietary interest in your writing, ever since I sat on that sofa in your garret thirty years ago, reading your first manuscript. I knew then that you were really something."

"Ahh," Eric said, waving his hand. "I just did that to get you in bed. Didn't you know that?"

Tanner smiled. "As I recall, I didn't run away."

"Damn, woman, you look as pretty now as you did then. How the hell can you do that? How old are you now?"

"Eric, don't you know you should never ask a lady her age?"

"Not even one you've been married to?"

"*Especially* not one you've been married to."

"You don't look a day over thirty, but I know that can't be."

"All right, if you must know, I'm fifty-two."

"A pup, a mere pup," Eric said. "I'm sixty-four."

"And a hansdome sixty-four you are," Tanner said. She ran a perfectly manicured finger around the gold rim of her wineglass. "So, what's next for you? What are you working on now?"

"I'm not working on anything at the moment."

"You should."

Eric laughed. "You sound like my publisher."

"I just remember how miserable you used to get

when you weren't working on something. What was it you called it? A sublime despondency? Do you still get that way?"

"I have my days," Eric admitted. He leaned back in his chair and stroked his thick gray beard. "The truth is, I still miss Shaylin, and I'm having a difficult time getting myself to work."

"Shaylin was very good for you," Tanner said.

"What about Morrison? Don't you miss him?"

"Mitch was a wonderful man," Tanner said. "He was very good with the company, and we got along splendidly."

"Sounds like a résumé."

"How dreadful! I didn't mean it to," Tanner said, flustered by his remark. "The answer to your question is, yes. Yes, I do miss him. I'm very glad he came along when he did. We had a wonderful marriage."

"I'm sorry," Eric said. "I didn't mean to imply otherwise. It was a thoughtless comment, and the moment I said it, I wished I could have called it back. Listen, why don't we drop all this old-times talk and think about the present. You're going to be here through the ceremony?"

"Yes, I told you, I wouldn't miss it for the world."

"Then let's spend some time together, getting reacquainted," Eric suggested. "I don't know how much free time I'll have, what with press conferences and so forth. But what time I do have, I would like to spend with you —if you're agreeable."

Tanner smiled. "I think that would be very nice."

CHAPTER EIGHT

Walking across the expansive lobby, Buck Campbell stopped at the enormous burled-wood reception desk flanked by red velvet ropes and put his guitar case by his feet. He stood there for a minute, waiting to be acknowledged by the young woman seated behind the desk. She never looked up from the magazine she was reading.

"Excuse me, ma'am," Buck finally said. "I'm here for *The Demaris Hunter Show*?"

"You're much too early," the receptionist said, finally raising her head. "We won't begin issuing passes for another three hours."

"I have to have a pass?"

"Yes, of course you have to have a pass," she rejoined in a don't-these-rubes-know-anything voice. "No one can go anywhere beyond this point without a pass."

"Oh. Well, is there someplace I could wait?"

"You're going to wait here for three hours?"

Buck smiled. "Darlin', what you don't understand is I've been waitin' for this for ten years."

The receptionist sighed. "All right, I suppose you can wait over there." She pointed to the far wall. "That's where the line will form."

Buck didn't quite follow her logic, but he touched the brim of his hat and said, "Thank you kindly." Leaving the guitar by the desk, he walked over to the wall and sat down on the floor, leaning back and pulling his legs up, then wrapping his arms around his knees as he watched the comings and goings in Radio City Music Hall.

Buck had been sitting there for nearly an hour and a half when a young man in a page's uniform stepped out of one of the elevators, shot a glance at the country singer, then walked over to the desk.

"Who's that?" the page asked the receptionist, pointing at Buck.

"A real big fan of Demaris Hunter's," she answered. "He's been waiting here for over an hour now, just so he'll be first in line to see the show."

"He *must* be quite a fan," the page said.

Listening to their conversation, Buck suddenly felt a bit foolish for not having been clearer about who he was. "Ma'am, excuse me," he said, "but I'm not here to see the show. I'm s'posed to be *on* the show."

The page and the receptionist both sniggered.

"*On* the show?" the girl said in a snide voice.

"Yes, ma'am. Leastwise, that's what Miss Hunter told me when she asked me to come."

A queasy look suddenly came over the page's face. "What's your name?" he asked.

"Campbell. Buck Campbell."

"*Oh, my God!*" the page shouted. "They're going crazy up there looking for him. They've got three people calling every hotel in New York to see if he's checked in."

"I haven't checked into any hotel yet," Buck said. "I thought I'd come here first."

"Becky, ring Mr. Keefer's office for me," the page said, picking up the phone. A second later he spoke into the phone. "Mr. Keefer, this is Larry Blackman. I'm an

NBC page. You can stop looking for Buck Campbell. He's down here in the lobby. Yes, sir, the lobby." Larry laughed. "Can you believe it, Mr. Keefer? He's been waiting in line for a ticket." The page's face sobered instantly. "Yes, sir! I'll bring him up right away, sir!"

He hung up the phone, then looked over at Buck. "Mr. Campbell, you want to come with me, sir?"

Buck stood up and walked over to the front of the reception desk, then picked up his battered guitar case. Holding it up and displaying it to the two NBC workers, he grinned. "Guess I'll be needin' this, won't I? Well, I thank you for callin' upstairs and checkin' for me, son," he said to the page. "I was gettin' a bit uncomfortable sittin' on the floor like that."

"Mr. Campbell," Demaris Hunter said, smiling in greeting when Buck entered the studio a few minutes later. "It's good to see you. Did you have a good trip up?"

"Pretty good," Buck said. "Had a speck of rough weather over Ohio, but it smoothed out some after that."

"Yes, flying can sometimes be very frightening. Was it your first flight?" Demaris asked.

Buck smiled. "Not exactly, ma'am. I was a waist gunner on a B-17 durin' the war. 'Course, the B-17 isn't as comfortable as the Connie."

"You were a waist gunner? I once did a show in England for the men who flew in the bombers."

"Yes ma'am, I seen it." Buck grinned. "That's somethin', ain't it? I mean, there I was, just one of the screamin' bunch out there in the audience, lookin' up at you on the stage. And now here I am, goin' to be doin' a show with you."

Demaris laughed. "Yes, it is something." A very thin man with watery-blue eyes walked over to join them. Demaris smiled at him. "Hello, Bruce. We found our guest, as you can see. Mr. Campbell, this is Bruce Wilson, our assistant director. He'll show you your dressing room, where you can change into your costume for the show."

"My costume?" Buck said. He looked down at his

denim trousers and red western-cut shirt. "I reckon I'll be wearin' this."

"Oh, no, Mr. Campbell, that will never do," the AD said, tsk-tsking.

"Well, it's got to do." Buck smiled. "See, I made it up here from Memphis, but my suitcase didn't. I checked with the airline, but as far as they know, it could be in Los Angeles by now."

"How much time do we have?" Demaris said.

"One hour and twenty-seven minutes," Bruce replied.

"Damn!" Demaris groaned. "I wanted to rehearse a short skit with you, Mr. Campbell, but we don't have enough time. Well, I guess we'll just have to skip the skit. I'll just introduce you and let you sing. Bruce, you take him somewhere and buy him an outfit for the show."

"Oh, that will be loads of fun," Bruce replied dryly. "Come along, cowboy."

Buck was about to explain that he wasn't actually a cowboy and in fact hadn't been on a horse more than two or three times in his whole life when he realized that the explanation was completely unnecessary.

Buck's cracked, well-worn boots sank into the deep-pile carpeting of the swanky men's shop. The shop, with its ornate gilt trim around ivory-colored walls, indirect lighting, and soft music with no apparent source, didn't sit well with Buck, and he stopped dead in his tracks.

"What the hell is this place?" he growled.

"The Manhattan Range Shop," Bruce replied. "They specialize in western clothing. All the right people buy their clothes here."

"We buyin' clothes for you or me?"

"Why, for you, dear man, for you. You heard what Demaris said."

"Let me tell you, pardner, unless I see somethin' more'n what they got hanging here on the racks, I'm not interested."

"Trust me," Bruce insisted.

A tall, rail-thin young man appeared from some-where back in the shop. "May I help you?" he asked in a sweet, friendly voice.

Buck's eyes widened as he took in the young man's outfit. He was wearing fire-engine-red boots, shiny black trousers with white piping along the pockets, and a red-satin cowboy shirt. Buck shook his head, then wandered over to look at some of the clothes stuck back in shelves along the wall.

"Hello, David," Bruce said, turning to face the employee.

"Bruce, how are you?" David gushed. "I haven't seen you since—well, since Lord knows when."

"It was Emil's 'Yellow Brick Road' party, don't you remember?"

"Oh, yes, how could I ever forget *that* party?" David said, and he and Bruce laughed, clearly sharing a private joke. "And who is this rugged-looking gentleman?"

"This is Buck Campbell. He's a guest on Demaris's show tonight."

"Oh, well, I shall certainly be watching," David said.

"And," Bruce continued, "we want something that will make him not quite as . . . rugged . . . as he appears now."

"More's the pity," David replied, sighing. "I think there's a certain charm to his ruggedness, don't you?"

"Yes, I quite agree. But there's no need for him to be *common* rugged, is there? I mean, can't we make him *polished* rugged?"

"Polished rugged." David laughed. "Oh, Bruce, you are quite the astute fellow." He pulled a cloth tape measure from his pocket and walked over to take Buck's measurements.

Buck frowned and narrowed his eyes as David measured his waist, neck, and arms. But when the salesman suddenly bent down to get his inseam length, Buck jumped.

"What the hell you plannin' on doin' down there?" he snapped.

"Oh, dear me, you are the jumpy one, aren't you?" David said, smiling wryly.

"Mr. Campbell, he's just measuring the length of your pant leg," Bruce explained.

"You could ask me before you start grabbin' at my crotch."

"Now, why in heaven's name would I want to ask when it's ever so much more fun just to grab?" David quipped. He and Bruce laughed, despite Buck's glare. "Okay, I think I have all the measurements I need," he said, standing back up. "You just wait here, Mr. Campbell. I'll be right back."

"Listen," Buck said to Bruce after David was gone, "can't we just check at the airlines again? Maybe my luggage is here by now. I've got some nice things to wear. Hell, I been in this business for ten years now; I know you got to have stage outfits."

"Really?" Bruce said. "Where have you been playing?"

"Hell, all over the place. Missouri, Tennessee, Arkansas, Kentucky, Mississippi, Louisiana, Texas. You name any beer joint, honky-tonk, or dive between Nashville and Dallas and I've been there."

"Yes, well, wouldn't you like to get out of honky-tonks?"

"Why? Honky-tonk people are my kind of people."

David returned then, carrying a dark-coffee-colored satin cowboy shirt with cocoa-brown fringe down the sleeves and across the chest. In his other hand was a pair of coffee-colored pants, with the same cocoa-brown fringe down the legs.

"Now, this certainly refines our friend without detracting from that attractive ruggedness, don't you think?" he asked, holding out the ensemble. "Matches all the way up and down." He smiled broadly. "Shall we try it on?"

"We ain't tryin' that on," Buck insisted, stabbing a finger at the clothes.

"Mr. Campbell, be reasonable!" Bruce pleaded. He looked at his watch. "Do you realize in just over an hour you'll be going out live to forty million Americans? We must get you properly dressed!"

"Yeah? Well, far as I'm concerned, there ain't nothin' proper about *that*!"

"Then what *would* you be interested in?"

Buck walked over to the shelves. He pulled out a pair of new jeans in his size, then a bright orange shirt, then a tan jacket. He shoved them at David. "Drop those in a bag," he ordered.

"Mr. Campbell, you can't wear that," Bruce protested.

"Why not?"

"You're a showman, Mr. Campbell," Bruce said. "You do know that you can't wear the same thing while performing that you would wear on the street. You must have something that will catch the audience's attention."

"I've got a bright orange shirt," Buck pointed out. "The audience'd have to be blind not to notice that."

"They *are* blind, Mr. Campbell. At least, color-blind," Bruce said. "You're on television, for chrissake. There *is* no color."

"Oh," Buck said softly. He stroked his chin. "Yeah, I forgot."

"Mr. Campbell, if I may make a suggestion?" David offered.

"It damn well better beat your last one."

"Yes, well, I didn't know that I was dealing with someone with a mind of his own," David said smoothly. "So many of my customers come in here and turn everything over to me. They have no personality, and they want me to create one for them with the clothes I sell. I can see that you are different."

"I sure as hell hope so."

"Perhaps you could keep the jeans and the orange shirt but replace the tan jacket with this." He took a fringed buckskin jacket from a hanger and held it out to Buck. "You see," he continued, "the fringe, the oversized patch pockets, and the epaulets give the jacket texture. Color is unimportant then. And the three items together would make a most attractive outfit."

"Try it on, Mr. Campbell, please?" Bruce begged. "We've only got fifty-two minutes."

"If you like it, you can wear it out of the store," David suggested. "It would save you time getting ready for the show. You can use one of the dressing rooms back there."

Buck sighed, then grabbed the clothes and walked in the direction David pointed. "All I can say," he shouted over his shoulder, "is that the damn dressin' room better have a lock on the door!"

"Ladies and gentlemen of the audience, please remain quiet and in your seats. We now have less than five minutes until air time," a disembodied voice instructed over the studio's PA system. The house lights went down, and the stage lights came up. Huge cameras were moved through the shadows, and camera operators and stagehands darted back and forth, leaping adroitly over the coils and bundles of cable as they made ready for the live, coast-to-coast broadcast.

In the control room the atmosphere was very tense as everyone readied themselves for the show. The "on-line" monitor, which displayed what NBC was telecasting at that precise moment, showed Dinah Shore smiling and looking at the camera as the credits rolled over her picture.

"*See . . . the . . . U.S.A. in your Chev-ro-let, America is asking you to call . . .*" Dinah sang. Then she kissed her fingers and flung the kiss toward the camera. "*Uhhmmm-wah!*"

Her face left the screen, replaced by a picture of a Chevrolet rolling down the highway.

"*The Dinah Shore Show has been brought to you by Chevrolet and your Chevrolet dealers coast to coast,*" the voice-over said. "*Stay tuned now for The Demaris Hunter Show.*"

"Stand by," the studio director said.

The picture of the Chevrolet was replaced by an animated xylophone and, as the hammer struck the three notes, the letters NBC appeared.

"Cue the dancing Old Gold packages," the director said. "Camera on packages, coming up . . . *now.*"

The on-line monitor showed two oversized cigarette packages, one Old Gold Regular, the other Old Gold Kings, dancing across the stage. Long, shapely female legs extended from the bottom of the packages, and alluring arms protruded from either side. The left hand of each package held a lit cigarette.

"Cue announcer . . . *now.*"

"Old Gold Regulars and Old Gold Kings—for a treat instead of a treatment—bring you The Demaris Hunter Show!" a golden-voiced announcer said.

"Theme music," the director said.

The orchestra began playing "The St. Louis Blues."

"Miss Hunter's guests tonight are Cliff Arquette!"

The audience applauded.

"The Notre Dame Glee Club!"

More applause.

"George Jessel!"

More applause.

"Marcella Mills!"

Thunderous applause.

"And Buck Campbell."

The audience continued to applaud, though by now the applause was for the show itself since no one had ever heard of Buck Campbell.

"And now here she is, ladies and gentlemen, our favorite movie star . . . Demaris Hunter!"

The music came back up as Demaris swept out onto the stage and did a pirouette, then a curtsy to the audience.

"Brighten the pink gel," the director said. "Kill the shadows under her eyes . . . make her look twenty-five. Ah, great, great, guys. You are all geniuses. She'll love you for it."

"Good evening," Demaris said, "and welcome to my show. Tonight we have . . ."

"Demaris! Demaris!" an off-camera voice shouted, interrupting Demaris's introduction.

"Cliff Arquette!" Demaris said brightly.

The applause signs came on, and the audience dutifully responded.

"What are you doing out here?" Arquette asked.

"What am I doing? Well, I'm introducing my show, that's what I'm doing."

"Good for you. You always have such wonderful shows." Arquette held up a piece of paper. "But before you do that, I've got a letter here from Mama. Would you mind if I read it to your audience?"

"A letter from your mama? Of course you can read it, Cliff. Your mama writes such fascinating letters, and she has such a grasp of reality."

The audience, all of whom had heard Cliff Arquette's nonsensical letters from his mama before, laughed at Demaris's remarks.

"'Dear Sonny,'" Arquette started. Then he stopped and looked over at Demaris. "Grasp of reality, you say," he mumbled. The audience laughed again, and Arquette returned to reading his letter.

Backstage, waiting in the Green Room, Buck sat on a sofa with his hands locked behind his head as he looked over at the Notre Dame Glee Club members. The young men were adjusting each other's ties and straightening jackets, preparatory to their number, which was due right after Cliff Arquette finished. In addition to the glee club, the room was filled with a dozen or more dancers who were incidental to the show and the two dancing cigarette packages. Buck shifted his gaze to the TV monitor, which showed Cliff Arquette bantering with Demaris Hunter. Larry, the page who had brought Buck up from the lobby, was now in charge of the coffee and refreshments. He walked over to Buck and asked, "How's it going?"

"Fine," Buck replied. "Say, I thought George Jessel and Marcella Mills were going to be on the show tonight."

"They are."

Buck looked around the room. "Well, where are they?"

Larry laughed. "Really, Mr. Campbell, you didn't expect them to crowd into the Green Room, did you? They are stars. Marcella Mills, George Jessel, and Cliff Arquette each have their own dressing rooms. The Green Room is just for extras."

"Oh," Buck said, his ego abruptly punctured. "Well, listen, how much longer before I go on?"

Larry looked at the clipboard he was carrying, then at the clock on the wall. "Thirty-seven minutes," he said.

Buck stood up. "Good. That'll give me time to eat one or two of them sweet rolls there. I didn't get a chance to have supper, and those look pretty good."

"You . . . you're actually going to eat one?" Larry asked in an astonished voice.

"Well, yeah I'm goin' to eat one," Buck replied. "Two, in fact, 'less there's a limit of one per person."

Larry laughed. "No, no. There's no limit. Eat all you want. It's just that, well, no one ever eats anything."

"Why not?" Buck asked, taking a bite of one of the sweet rolls. "They're pretty good."

"They're all too nervous, I guess," Larry explained. "Tell you the truth, in all the time I've been working here, I never saw a guest eat anything in the Green Room. The food's put out for every show, but they're always too nervous."

"Well, that's a hell of a waste," Buck said.

Larry grinned. "Not really. Us pages generally have it all consumed by the time the show is over." He peered at Buck. "Aren't *you* nervous?"

"No," Buck replied easily. "Can't say as I am. What's there to be nervous about?"

"You're kidding me. Do you mean to tell me you aren't in the least bit nervous?"

"Not at all." Buck finished the first pastry and started on a second. "Should I be?"

Larry looked incredulous. "Mr. Campbell, in a few minutes, you'll be singing before forty million people! Don't you realize that?"

"Well, goddamn, son, I'm not goin' to have to sing for 'em one at a time, am I?" Buck replied. "I mean when you're singing, whether it's for one person or forty million, the work's just the same."

"I . . . I guess so," Larry said, clearly amazed at Buck's equanimity.

"Listen, I'm just goin' to close my eyes over here and relax a bit, if you don't mind," Buck said. "You'll tell me when it's time, won't you?

"Yes, sir, I'll tell you," Larry promised. "That's my job."

"And you're damn good at it, too," Buck said. He walked back to the chair he'd been sitting in, slumped down in it, and dropped his hat down over his eyes. Within moments he was snoring.

Immediately after the conclusion of *The Demaris Hunter Show*, the NBC switchboard was lit up like the Rockefeller Center Christmas tree, and the operators were fielding dozens of calls.

"His name was Buck Campbell. Yes, tonight was his television debut. No, I don't think he has any records available yet, though I'm sure that will change soon. Sorry, we have no firm announcement as to when you'll be able to see him again on Miss Hunter's show, though plans are being made. Yes, thank you for calling NBC Television," one harried operator said, repeating the same speech for what seemed like the thousandth time.

Next to her another operator was responding to another caller. "Yes, we are very pleased with the way it went tonight. We've been getting calls from all over about Mr. Campbell. Thank you for calling."

"Campbell. C-A-M-P-B-E-L-L," a third operator was intoning patiently. "Yes, I'm sure any mail sent here would be forwarded to him."

*   *   *

When Julian Keefer knocked on the door to Demaris Hunter's dressing room, it was answered by the young black woman who was Demaris's personal dresser.

"Is she decent, Evie?" Julian asked.

"Hell, no, I'm not decent!" Demaris called from the back of the room. "It's no fun being decent, you should know that. But come in anyway."

Julian stepped into the room, then looked toward the dressing table. Demaris was sitting in front of the mirror in bra and panties, taking off her makeup.

"Demaris, you aren't even dressed," Julian gasped, averting his eyes.

"Oh, for heaven's sake, Julian. Time was when a healthy, red-blooded man enjoyed a free peek. I haven't let myself go that much, have I?"

In fact, at fifty-three Demaris was still a beautiful woman with smooth, firm skin and very few signs of advancing middle age. But she enjoyed teasing her producer, who had a reputation of being somewhat prudish.

"You are a lovely woman," Julian said, holding his hand over his eyes. "But it isn't proper for me to be in here while you are in such a state of . . . undress."

"I'll put something on," Demaris said, laughing. Her maid handed her a pink flowered-silk dressing gown, and she slipped into it. "There," she said. "You can take your hand down now. I'm decent."

"Thank you," Julian breathed. "That's much better."

"How do you think the show went?"

"That's what I wanted to talk to you about. The show was wonderful, but we seem to have generated some sort of phenomenon."

"Buck Campbell?"

"Yes. Someone has told you already?"

"Told me what?"

"About the reaction we're getting."

"No."

"Our switchboard has been ringing nonstop since the moment the show went off the air, and Western Union has delivered five hundred telegrams—with word that there are many more on the way."

"I'm not surprised."

"I am. I'm absolutely flabbergasted," Julian admitted. "I have to tell you that halfway through his first number I was certain we had made a terrible mistake in having him on the show. What *is* it, Demaris?"

"I'm not sure I can explain it," Demaris said. "But I realized it the first time I saw him, which is why I wanted him on. There's something about him—something visceral—that can't be explained. If we're smart, Julian, we'll get him to come back. Fast."

Julian grinned. "Even though I don't understand what so many obviously see in him, I'm not entirely dumb. I've already signed him for three more shows."

Demaris stood up and hugged her producer. "Good boy, Julian. You're watching out for my best interests."

He chuckled. "Not just yours, darling."

Buck Campbell propped himself up on his elbow and read the glowing-green clock dial on the nightstand. One-thirty. He had been in bed for an hour and a half, tossing and turning, unable to sleep. He knew that it wasn't just the excitement of the show keeping him awake. When he was on the road, his shows never even ended until long after midnight, and most of the time he didn't wind down until around four or five. He usually crawled into bed just as the sun was coming up. Trying to go to bed at midnight was as foreign to him as sleeping until two in the afternoon was to most other people.

He thought about the show—again. He had been paid $3,500 for his appearance tonight and had agreed to do three more shows for a total of $12,000. Fifteen thousand five-hundred dollars was more than half of what he had made so far in his entire career. For nearly ten years he'd been playing beer joints and honky-tonks, eating greasy hamburgers and driving from dawn to dark to get to his next engagement. Now that might all be coming to an end. Another couple of appearances on television like tonight's and he might actually get a recording contract. If he could sell a few records, he could get by on fewer road shows. That is, if he could put together another band. The band had come apart in December when the lead guitar got a job with Hank Snow. The other members of the band, marginal musicians at best who realized they could never hope to be more than sidemen, took more conventional jobs.

Unable to stop the flood of thoughts and get to sleep, Buck sighed, got out of bed, and padded over to the window to look at the city skyline. A lot of lights were still on, but most of the windows of most of the buildings were dark.

"Shit," Buck grumbled aloud. "Has everyone in this damn town gone to bed? I thought New York City was an all-night kind of place. Who the hell goes to bed by one-thirty anyway? Hell, most of the time I'm just gettin' started at one-thirty."

He thought about taking a walk until he found something open. Maybe a few beers would relax him, and then he could come back and try again to go to sleep. Maybe there'd be a bar right here in the hotel. He picked up the phone and called the front desk.

"Desk," a lethargic male voice answered.

"Is there anything open in this place?" Buck asked in a low, rumbling voice.

"I beg your pardon?"

"A bar?" Buck asked. "Or maybe a a nightclub? Somethin' like that?"

"The bar closes at one-thirty, sir. It's a quarter of two now."

"Shit."

Buck hung up. It looked like he was going to have to take that walk after all.

In her room across the hall from Buck's, Marcella Mills sat cross-legged on the bed. She was wearing sheer baby-doll pajamas with a neckline so low that the tops of her nipples were clearly visible. In the other room of her suite David Rogers and Julian Keefer were discussing some ideas David had for a TV show. They had been discussing it for hours now, and Marcella was bored. She and David had been "keeping company," as the fan magazines called it, for over a year. The magazines couldn't report that they were actually living together. They weren't married, and that would cause a quite a scandal. Though it might temporarily increase sales for the magazines, they'd be boycotted by the studio for breaking the faith—and in the long run that would be disastrous.

David was a playwright. In 1948 his play *The Summer People* was one of the hottest dramas on Broadway. A number of road companies were still filling theaters across the country with their performances of the play. David's next two plays, *Town Square* and *Afternoon Serenade*, bombed on Broadway and were never picked up by any road company. One Broadway critic said, "David Rogers has proven to be a one-play artist. *The Summer People* was, and remains, a good play. But *Town Square* was predictable and plodding, and *Afternoon Serenade* was so pathetic that it now seems as if his career is dead in the water."

David left Broadway in anger and went to Hollywood to become a screenwriter. The Hollywood crowd accepted him with open arms, aware that someone with a name in legitimate theater would add class to the motion picture industry. He wrote two very successful movies, after which he was regarded as Hollywood's resident literary lion.

David and Marcella had met at a Hollywood party. A romance between them—a bookish, almost foppish playwright and a sex goddess whose naked form decorated the calendars of half the service stations and auto-body shops in the country—seemed very unlikely if not downright ludicrous. But despite the implausibility of such a relationship, one did develop and had been going on now for over a year.

When Marcella got the invitation to appear on *The Demaris Hunter Show,* David came to New York with her. At first she thought it was very sweet of him to come to support her. Then she learned that he was using this as an opportunity to try to interest NBC in an idea to produce several of his plays that he was adapting for television; to that end, he had invited Julian Keefer back to the hotel to discuss his ideas.

Marcella got up from bed and walked over to the door between the bedroom and the sitting room. Opening it, she saw that the two men were deeply involved in conversation, or, to be more accurate, David was intently conversing, with animated gestures, while Julian Keefer was listening. The whiskey bottle on the table, full when they had started talking earlier in the evening, was now nearly empty.

"David," Marcella called, "honey, are you going to come to bed anytime soon?"

"Aren't you asleep yet?" David asked, totally unmindful of the fact that she was nearly naked. Julian wasn't unmindful, though. His eyes nearly bulged out of his head at the sight of Marcella standing in the doorway almost fully revealed, and, as he had in Demaris's dressing room, he looked away in embarrassment.

"Why don't you go to sleep?" David suggested.

"I can't sleep," Marcella pouted. "Not with you still up."

"Well, look, we're busy here. Why don't you take a walk or something?"

"Take a walk? David, do you know what time it is?"

"What difference does that make? We're in New York. 'Time hath no dominion over New York.'"

"Hey, that's pretty good," Julian observed.

"You like that line? I used it in *Afternoon Serenade*," David said.

"All right, David," Marcella snapped. "You want me to take a walk, I'll take a goddamn walk!"

She slammed the bedroom door, then went to the closet. Riffling through her dresses, she pulled one off the hanger and slipped it on over her baby dolls. After shoving her feet into a pair of slippers, she wrenched open the bedroom door again, stomped wordlessly across the sitting room, and pulled open the door to the hall. She closed that door behind her with another resounding bang and stood there for a moment, fuming. She had no idea where she was going or what she was going to do when she got there, but at this point she didn't particularly care.

As she stood there the door to the room diagonally opposite hers opened, and the man who had sung on *The Demaris Hunter Show* earlier came out. She hadn't seen him before he did his number, and, like so many others, she had stopped what she had been doing to watch, mesmerized by his performance.

"Hello," she said throatily.

Buck looked over. "Hello, yourself," he replied.

"You were on the show today," Marcella said. "I saw you. You were pretty good."

"Thanks."

Marcella giggled. "Actually, you were *very* good. My dresser was so taken with you that I almost didn't get ready in time for my own bit."

"Your dresser?"

"The lady who helps me get dressed."

Buck laughed. "From what I could see of your act, you didn't have all that many clothes on in the first place. Don't know why you'd need someone to help you get dressed."

"It does seem silly, doesn't it? I mean, having someone help me get dressed when it's a lot more fun to have someone help me get *undressed*."

"Yeah, I reckon that *would* be more fun—if you had the right person doin' it."

"How about you?" Marcella asked.

Buck ran his hand through his hair and looked at the gorgeous young woman. Like millions of red-blooded American men all across the country, he had seen Marcella's famous calendar pose. He even remembered the stink about it when it was first introduced. The studio had protested loudly and often that though it was indeed a nude photograph of Marcella Mills, the picture had been taken before she was contracted to the studio.

Galaxy Studios disapproved of and abhorred the commercialism behind the selling and publishing of a nude photograph taken of a young actress when she was poor and vulnerable. Of course, the studio's frequent mention of the nude photo—and the two words "nude photo" were always linked—generated a tremendous amount of publicity for Marcella, so much so that the box office draw of her next four pictures was up by nearly seventy percent.

"How about me?" Buck asked, not at all certain he had understood the words.

"Do you think you might be the right person to help me get undressed?"

He grinned. "You're goddamn right I am." He opened the door to his room and motioned for her to enter.

With a smile, Marcella stepped quickly across the hallway and into the room. He closed the door, then turned toward her. "I gotta tell ya, I'm a little surprised—"

Buck was unable to finish whatever he was going to say because she threw her arms around his neck and glued herself to him, opening her lips on his and grinding her breasts and pelvis against his body.

Just as abruptly as she had thrown herself at him, she broke away and went to the other end of the room, casually pulling her dress over her head and dropping it onto the floor. She turned back toward him, her hard nipples making two buttons in the top of her shorty pajamas.

"Tell me, Mr. Buck Campbell, am I interrupting your plans? What were you doing out in the hallway at this hour?"

"I couldn't sleep. I thought I'd go try to find somethin' to drink, maybe relax me a little." His voice was low and gravelly, and his eyes held hers in a steady grip.

"You need to relax?"

"Yeah, well, I thought I did."

"What about fucking?" Marcella asked. "Does fucking relax you?"

Buck laughed. "I reckon it does, darlin'."

Marcella pulled the pajama top over her head, then slipped out of the bottoms. Her naked body was smooth, her breasts full. The soft growth of her pubic hair was so pale that it almost seemed she didn't have any. He found the idea of seeing here in the flesh what he had seen before only in the famous photograph intensely arousing.

At the same time Marcella was undressing, Buck took off his own clothes, finally stepping out of his briefs. He stood there for a long moment, just staring at her.

Marcella walked over to him and reached down to fondle him. "Are you just going to stand there all night?" she asked, her voice husky. "Or are you going to do something?"

"Well, ma'am, I reckon I'll do somethin'," Buck said. He led Marcella over to his bed, then lay down with her.

Marcella, with no foreplay at all, took him into her. She arched her back, mashing her stomach against his, feeling his strong, muscular body meet her rounded, voluptuous one. Her long nails clawed and scratched at his back as she moved with his thrusts, practically exploding around him.

Normally, whenever Marcella made love, especially with David, she was in control. But this time it was different. Buck rode her like an experienced bronc buster, giving her just enough pleasure, then pulling away to make her beg. As Marcella thrashed under him in ecstatic agony he took her right up to the edge. Finally he let out a guttural laugh, then drove deep into her as they climaxed together.

Spent, they lay panting on opposite sides of the bed, trying to catch their breath. Then Marcella giggled.

"What is it?" Buck asked hoarsely.

She rose on one elbow and looked down at him. "I was just thinking how you, Mr. Campbell, are going to be very big." She giggled again. "I mean, beyond being already very big in one regard"—she emphasized her point with a squeeze—"you are going to be a star as well."

Buck reached for her. "That'd suit me just fine, darlin'."

CHAPTER
NINE

JUNE 1955, FROM "TRAILMARKERS,"
EVENTS MAGAZINE:

U.S. ENJOYING GREATEST ECONOMIC
BOOM IN HISTORY

Business is booming, wages are high, and industry is expanding boldly toward broader markets. Though our country has known good times before, we have throughout our history been locked in a "boom and bust" cycle. Now, however, economists are suggesting that we have broken free of that cycle.

Times are good, and Americans everywhere are taking advantage of that fact. Car buyers are letting it be known that they want more horsepower, more chrome, and more gadgets—sometimes even more cars than they need. Housing starts are at an all-time high. People are investing in such things as travel trailers and motorboats, all indications of the strength of our economy.

U.S. businesses are not alone in benefiting from our prolonged period of prosperity. More than 350,000 American tourists traveled to Europe this season, making the American tourist Europe's biggest source of revenue. And, in a statement of the times, more of those tourists flew to Europe than sailed on ocean liners.

The four turbine engines were but a whisper inside the first-class compartment as the World Air Transport Turbo Star, Rockwell-McPheeters's newest airliner, lifted off the runway at Lambert Field in St. Louis. The pilot pulled back on the wheel, and the airplane began a steep, vibrationless climb to cruising altitude.

Willie Canfield, president of WAT, looked out the window of his first-class seat back toward the spinning silver propellers, the pointed engine nacelles, and the razor-thin wing. This was the innaugural flight of WAT's trans-Atlantic turboprop service on one of the thirty Turbo Stars that the company had bought. The remainder of the fleet was still made up of Super Constellations.

"This certainly is a quiet plane," Liesl Canfield remarked to her husband. "Not at all like all the others, where you have to yell to be heard over the motors." She smiled. "Excuse me. Engines," she corrected. "You ought to get more of them."

"We have to go slow," Willie said. "These things are terribly expensive."

"But you said yourself they don't cost as much as the Comet jet the British are flying, and they can carry three times as many people."

"I didn't say the Turbo Star wasn't a bargain, I just said it was expensive. And when we transition into pure jets in a few more years, it will be even more expensive."

"I don't know if I will want to ride on the jets," Liesl said.

Willie smiled. "Sure you will. They'll be faster, smoother, and safer."

"How can they be safer? It would seem to me that anything that goes that fast would be more dangerous."

"Nearly thirty percent of all problems in flight stem from an airplane's propellers," Willie explained. "Runaway props, blades that are thrown, that sort of thing. Eliminate the props, as you do in a jet, and you eliminate those problems."

"Oh, thank you for telling me," Liesl said, looking anxiously through the window at the spinning silver disks. "Now I'll spend the entire flight worrying about the propellers."

Willie laughed. "I don't think you'll have to worry about that. Just relax and enjoy the flight."

Liesl twisted in her seat to look behind her. Her mother, Uta, was pointing something out to her daughter, Tina.

"Mother and and Tina don't seem worried about the propellers," she said. At Willie's insistence, Liesl had raised their daughter to be bilingual, and the girl's English and German were both flawless—unlike Liesl's English, which had retained a slight suggestion of an accent, evident in her pronunciation of such words as "worried."

"Of course not. There's nothing to worry about," Willie said.

"I am so happy that Father has finally agreed to see us," Liesl said. "It's been almost ten years now since he was sent to Spandau Prison. I've never understood why in all that time he would not let us visit."

"He's a proud man. He doesn't want his family to see him this way."

"I suppose you're right." She sighed. "And he didn't want the publicity. For many years the newspapers watched everyone who came to visit, writing stories about them and hounding them. And with Father being the third highest ranking prisoner remaining there—well, they would surely have sought us out."

"I am anxious to meet your father," Willie said.

Liesl looked ruefully at her husband. "We've been married for years, we have a daughter who's nearly six, and yet neither of you has ever met my father. I'm so pleased that you will be meeting him at last."

A stewardess came over to them and leaned across the seat, smiling prettily at Willie. "Mr. Canfield, the captain has just asked if you would care to visit the cockpit."

Willie looked at Liesl, who smiled. "Go ahead. Do you think I believe for one minute that I could keep you out of there?"

"Thanks," Willie said, unbuckling his seat belt and climbing out of his seat and past Liesl. He followed the stewardess to the front of the cabin, where she knocked lightly on the door. It was opened quickly by the second officer.

"Mr. Canfield, welcome aboard, sir," the second officer said. He stepped to one side, and Willie could see past him, between the pilot and copilot, to the huge instrument panel alive with quivering dials, gauges, and winking lights. In the middle of the panel was a small radar set, its beam sweeping back and forth across a glowing green screen.

"This is Captain Bascombe and First Officer Martin," the second officer said.

First Officer Martin left the copilot's seat, then pointed to it with an outstretched arm. "Mr. Canfield, please, take my seat," he offered.

"Thank you," Willie said, slipping into the vacated seat.

The cockpit was a familiar place for him. He had begun flying almost thirty years before and had, in fact, been copilot of the very first commercial airliner to fly the Atlantic. That had been in 1927, just a few weeks after Charles Lindbergh had conquered the Atlantic in his bold solo flight. Lindbergh's accomplishment had captured the imagination of the world, but many insiders in the world of aviation believed that the flight Willie was a part of— crossing the Atlantic in a commercial airliner—was actually more daring and innovative and certainly a more productive feat.

The commercial plane he had flown was a Rockwell-McPheeters Tri-Star, a high-wing, three-engine aircraft

with a corrugated metal skin. It had been the workhorse
of World Air Transport then, and Willie thought it was
huge. But if that Tri-Star and this Turbo Star were placed
side by side, the Tri-Star wouldn't even reach back to the
Turbo Star's wings.

Willie held his hands up to the wheel, which, because the plane was on autopilot, was making tiny move-
ments on its own. He opened and closed his fists a few
times, itching to grab hold.

Captain Bascombe chuckled. "I know what you're
feeling, Mr. Canfield. Just a second. I'll disconnect the
autopilot, and she's all yours."

Bascombe took the plane off autopilot, and Willie
wrapped his hands around the control wheel. He sensed
the old, familiar feel of an airplane communicating with
him in the way that pilots everywhere would understand.
The hydraulics, electrical, and fuel systems of the Turbo
Star were but extensions of his own musculature, blood-
stream, and nerve endings. Man and plane became one
symbiotic being so that it was difficult to tell where one
began and the other left off.

Willie felt it, but he didn't have to explain it. The
other men up here on the flight deck knew without being
told what he was experiencing because, like him, they
were addicted to the thrill of flying.

*World Air seven-one-five, St. Louis ATC, passing you
off to Cleveland ATC. Have a good flight, sir.*

Captain Bascombe picked up his microphone to
speak back to air traffic control. "Thank you, St. Louis.
World Air seven-one-five leaving your frequency now.
Good-bye." He reached down to change frequencies, then
reported into Cleveland ATC, who noted that they had
him on their radar.

"We sure left St. Louis ATC fast," Willie said.

"Yes, sir, that's the way it is when you're clipping off
better than four hundred knots," Bascombe said, pointing
to the airspeed indicator. "We'll be landing at LaGuardia
in less than four hours and in Frankfurt nine hours after
that."

"Wait until we get the jets," Willie said. "That'll cut the time by another third."

"If they ever make these things so fast that you get where you're going before you leave where you are, I'm giving up this business," Bascombe quipped, and the others on the flight deck laughed.

SPANDAU PRISON, NUREMBERG, GERMANY

Karl Tannenhower, once the Reichsleiter of the Nazi Party, Obergrupenführer in the SS, and a member of Adolf Hitler's inner circle, was down on his knees, pulling weeds in the small garden the prison officials had allowed him. His tomato plants were coming along nicely, as were the peppers and cucumbers. Two or three other prisoners also had gardens, though they were raising flowers. Karl appreciated the fact that the flowers did much to improve the drabness of the yard, but he thought vegetables were more practical. And the other prisoners appreciated fresh vegetables with their meals.

"*Guten Morgen, Herr Tannenhower,*" one of the guards, an American, called.

Karl looked up at the guard. "Good morning, Sergeant Kincaid," Karl replied in English.

"You have visitors," the guard said. "Your wife is here. And your daughter and her husband and your granddaughter."

Karl shook his head, then returned to his weeds.

"Herr Tannenhower? Didn't you understand what I said?"

"Yes, I understand. Tell them for me, please, to come back tomorrow. Tell them I am not feeling well." He pulled the weeds vigorously.

Sergeant Kincaid wasn't a war veteran and thus had little of the built-in animosity the earlier guards had. He looked at his prisoner with sympathy, making no effort to carry the message Karl had given him.

"They are your family, Herr Tannenhower," he said. "I think you should see them."

"I do not need you to tell me what I should do," Karl replied sharply.

"I could order you to do it," Kincaid said.

Karl sighed. He looked up at the guard again, his eyes tired and sad. "Sergeant Kincaid, you do not understand."

"Yes, I do understand," Kincaid insisted. "You don't want them to see you like this. But what are you trying to hide from them, Tannenhower? You're a prisoner . . . the whole world knows you're a prisoner. And they came all the way from the States just to see you. You have no right to deny them. And what about your granddaughter? Don't you want to see her?"

Karl stood up and brushed the dirt off his trousers. He was not as tall as the sergeant, though his overall bulk made him appear to be a big man. Karl had been a weightlifter in his youth; then, as a young man in America attending Jefferson University, he had played football. He still followed American football through the American newspapers supplied him by the American guards. Sergeant Kincaid was, and had been for a long time, a fan of the Jefferson University Bears, and when Jefferson U. won the Big Ten championship the previous season, then beat USC in the Rose Bowl on New Year's Day, he brought in a radio so that he and Karl could listen to the game together. When the Bears won, the two men cheered lustily, much to the confusion of the other prisoners and the guards of other nationalities.

"Is she beautiful, my granddaughter?" Karl asked.

Kincaid smiled gently. "Are you kidding? Why, she's as pretty as a little pair of red shoes. Now, there's no way you can just let those good folks cool their heels in there. You've got to see them."

Karl ran his hand through his closely cropped white hair and stared off across the yard. Rudolf Hess and Albert Speer were sitting on a low stone wall, talking quietly. Of all the prisoners in Spandau, Karl was probably closest to Speer. Hess, on the other hand, had been distant and strange from the day they first met, and he was even more distant and stranger now.

Of course, there were those who thought Karl was strange. For the first five years he wrote no letters and refused to accept any. Uta wrote him faithfully, two times a week, as regular as clockwork, but her letters were all returned to her, unopened. Then, four years ago, Karl opened a letter, read it, and answered it. Now he kept up a steady correspondence with his wife and daughter, but he had steadfastly refused to let them come see him until a few weeks ago when, in a very weak moment, he wrote Uta that she could come if she wished, and she could bring Liesl and Liesl's child with her.

Now they were here, and he was having serious second thoughts. He felt panicked over having to face them, and he wished desperately that he had never told them they could come.

"What do you say, Tannenhower? You going to see them?" Kincaid asked.

"Very well, I shall see them," Karl finally said in an expulsion of air that was more than a sigh. "But, please, tell them to give me a few moments to get ready for them. I don't want to see them with dirt on my trousers and on my hands."

Sergeant Kincaid grinned. "I'll tell them. You're doing the right thing, Tannenhower. They'll be very happy."

Uta Tannenhower looked around the room where, in a few moments, she would see her husband again for the first time in ten years. The room was small, roughly nine by fifteen—about the size of just one of the area rugs in her living room back in St. Louis—with a table and chairs in the middle. At one time, Sergeant Kincaid told them, the room had been divided by a half wall topped by a heavy steel-mesh screen.

"But that was in the early days, during and just after all the war trials," he explained. "Back then there was always the fear that someone would smuggle something in to one of the prisoners so that they could commit suicide."

"And you don't worry about that anymore?" Willie asked.

"No, sir, not really. The truth is, the fellas we got here now are all a pretty stable bunch. Except for Hess, and he's just as nutty as a peach-orchard bore, if you get my drift. Anyhow, if they wanted to do themselves in, why, I reckon they've had plenty of opportunities in the last ten years."

"How long have you been a guard here?" Willie asked, making conversation to fill the long, pregnant wait.

"Two years now," Kincaid said. "You know, I was too young to be in the war, but I read about it and about all these Nazis over here. Hitler, Göring, Goebbels, and all the rest. And here I am, talking every day with people like Rudolf Hess, Albert Speer, Karl Tannenhower. Actually, I figured they were all monsters when I used to read about 'em, but the truth is, I kinda like your father-in-law."

"Most of them *were* monsters, Sergeant," Uta said resolutely. She looked at her hands almost as if looking for some stain. "Nearly all of us bear some responsibility for what happened here . . . for what we allowed to happen."

"Well, I don't know much about that," Kincaid said. "Like I said, I was too young. Hell, the war's almost ancient history to me. I know there was some bad things happened to a bunch of Jews or something, but mostly I don't think about that. By the way, your husband once lived in America, you know."

Uta smiled. "Yes, I know."

Sergeant Kincaid laughed sheepishly. "Oh, of course; he is your husband. Anyway, we talk about football and books. We both like football, but we don't like the same kind of books. I like Mickey Spillane, but Herr Tannenhower is a lot more highfalutin. He likes writers like Hemingway and Twainbough."

"Yes, well, his interest in Eric Twainbough is personal," Uta said. "Mr. Twainbough was a guest in our home a few times before the war."

"You don't say? I bet it would have been interesting to sit around and listen in on that conversation. Two famous men getting together like that."

"Yes, it was." Uta's eyes misted over as she remembered the days before the war when she and her husband were gracious hosts not only to Eric Twainbough but to many other well-known people. How exciting everything had seemed then.

The back door to the small meeting room abruptly opened, and Karl Tannenhower stepped inside. Uta looked at him and saw not a white-haired old man dressed in nondescript prison clothes, but a handsome young lieutenant dressed in the World War I uniform of the Imperial Navy. They looked at each other for a long moment, their eyes taking in the years of separation.

"Sergeant, may we . . . embrace?" Uta asked in a choked voice.

"Yes'm, you sure can."

"*Mein Liebchen,*" Uta cried, running toward him. They embraced and kissed and kissed again, then stood there in each other's arms, squeezing each other as tightly as they could, as if trying in some mystical way to become one.

Their eyes filled with tears, and Liesl began crying as well. Willie had never met his father-in-law, but he was so moved by the joy of his wife and mother-in-law, whom he did love, that he, too, was unable to hold back the tears. He couldn't help but smile, though, when he saw that even the sergeant was wiping his eyes.

"Liesl," Karl said to his daughter, when at last he was able to pull himself away from Uta.

"Papa!" Liesl cried, running into his arms.

Tina stood there, quietly watching. Everything had been explained to her. She knew that Karl was her grandfather, that he had been in a war "on the other side" and was now a prisoner of the Allied powers as a result of the war. It had even been explained to her that the meeting between Karl and her mother and grandmother would, in all likelihood, be very emotional. So she was prepared to wait until it was her turn.

Karl looked over Liesl's shoulder and saw the serious-faced child watching and waiting so patiently. He smiled broadly, then squatted down and held out his arm.

"And you are my granddaughter?"

"Yes, Grandfather. My name is Tina, and I am happy at long last to meet you," Tina said, speaking in perfect German.

"What a pleasant surprise," Karl said. "I was afraid for a while she would be chewing gum and listening to American bebop."

"It isn't bebop, Grandfather, it's rock and roll," Tina said. She giggled. "And I like rock and roll very much."

"And this is my son-in-law?" Karl asked, standing up and extending his hand to Willie.

"Yes, Herr Tannenhower," Willie said, shaking Karl's hand.

Karl shook his head in wonder. "Life is strange, is it not? My very good friend when I was in America was your uncle, Billy Canfield—and you have married my daughter and fathered my granddaughter. It is rather like a circle, our families being drawn together in such a fashion."

"Yes," Willie agreed, "it is strange but wonderful."

They spoke of many things over the next several minutes. Karl talked about his garden, and he shared funny stories of things that had happened with the other prisoners or the guards. Then, shortly before they were to leave, Uta took a deep breath to steel her courage, and told him of her plan.

"I am not going back to America, Karl."

"You are not going back? But of course you are. What else would you do?"

"I am going to find a place to live here in Nuremberg. That way I can come see you every visiting day."

Karl shook his head. "No, *Liebchen*, no. I don't think that would be a very good idea."

"Why not?"

"You should stay in America with our daughter."

Liesl laughed. "Papa, I am twenty-nine years old. I have a husband and a daughter. Mama doesn't need to stay in America with me. She should be here, with you."

"But how will you survive?" Karl asked Uta. "Will you take work?"

"Karl, I have plenty of money," she said. "Enough money to find a nice apartment and live comfortably, visiting you whenever it is permitted, until that wonderful day when you will be released so that we can live together."

"But you will be so far apart from one another," Karl said. "What if you get ill, or Liesl or the child?"

"Herr Tannenhower, we have airplanes now that can go from St. Louis to Nuremberg in under fourteen hours," Willie put in. "Within three more years that same trip will take less than ten hours. We've all talked this out and planned for every contingency. It's something that Uta wants to do."

"You call her Uta?" Karl asked in surprise.

Liesl laughed. "Papa, that is the way of it in America," she explained. "It isn't a lack of respect; it's a way of saying we belong together."

Karl nodded slowly. "Yes, I remember this about America." He smiled at Willie. "You will call me Karl."

"All right, Karl," Willie replied. "And what about Uta? She won't stay here if you disapprove. But I think you should know that she very much wishes to."

"*Puffer Torte*," Karl said. "If you ask permission of the prison officials, you can bring pastries. Sometime, will you bring me a Puffer Torte?"

Uta laughed out loud and threw her arms around Karl. "Yes, my love, I will bring you a Puffer Torte. One thousand times I will bring you Puffer Torte."

JEFFERSON UNIVERSITY, ST. LOUIS

Commencement exercises were to be held in the quadrangle in front of Spengeman Hall. A dais had been constructed near Statue Circle, in the shadow of the work of the great sculptor Rodin: a four-times life-size, seated statue of Henry Spengeman, founder and first president of the university.

Also in Statue Circle was a sculpture of William

Bateman, the university's second president and Connie Canfield's father. The life-size statue depicted Bateman standing with his hands resting on a brass rail and looking out over the campus. He was, in the words of the brass placard mounted on the pedestal, "Keeping Watch."

Professor Bateman's statue had, by tradition, become a part of ongoing campus life. It wore a freshman beanie during fraternity initiations, carried pennants during football season, sprouted eyeglasses and textbooks during finals week, and wore a tuxedo jacket and carnation during spring formals. Today the statue was outfitted in a cap and gown for the upcoming graduation ceremonies.

No one but members of the elite Quad Quad could touch Professor Spengeman's statue, and today, as at every formal event, the four new members of the Quad Quad were performing their first ceremonial function by standing guard around it. The foursome would be seniors when school reopened in the fall.

Morgan Canfield was one of the four. He had been elected to the prestigious position, as were the other three, and in achieving that, he carried on the family tradition. His father, John, had also been a member of the Quad Quad, and his grandfather, Robert, had been one of the four founding members, when it was nothing but an informal group with no official sanction. A brass plaque inscribed with the names of the Quad Quad founders was mounted on a small marble pedestal at the top of Statue Circle. The names were: Robert Canfield, as in the Canfield School of Business; Terry Perkins, as in the Perkins Journalism School; J.P. Winthrop, as in Winthrop Hall; and David Gelbman, as in Gelbman Hall.

Prior to the graduation ceremonies, a staff-and-faculty tea was being held in the library—officially the William Canfield Library, though called by everyone, teachers and students alike, Billy Books. John and Faith Canfield were guests at the tea by virtue of the fact that John was a member of the Board of Regents.

Hamilton Twainbough was also present. Ham, a graduate of JU, class of 1943, was now president and chairman of the board of Tannenhower Brewing Company, following in the footsteps of his great-grandfather, the company's founder. However, Ham's invitation to the staff-and-faculty tea came about not because of his position in the community, but because his father, Eric Twainbough, one of America's most famous authors and a Nobel laureate, would be giving the commencement address—that plus the fact that, on behalf of the Tannenhower Brewing Company, Ham had just presented the university with a check for ten million dollars to build a new 85,000-seat football stadium.

Eric Twainbough wandered away from the others to look around the library. He stopped at a glass case displaying a collection of William Canfield memorabilia. There were two dress uniforms, the one he had worn while a member of the Lafayette Escadrille as well as the one he wore serving with the American Expeditionary Force. There were photographs of Billy in each of the uniforms and in the airplanes he flew for each of the services. In addition, there were photos from his college days, including one of him holding a football under one arm, his other arm extended as if stiff-arming a would-be tackler. His leg was drawn up as if he were running, and his face was fixed in a menacing snarl. Sitting in one corner of the case was an old-style football, much fatter than the modern version, which had the names of all the players of the 1914 championship team. One of the names, Eric noticed, was Karl Tannenhower.

From the display case Eric wandered back to the Loomis Booker Section, which consisted of two shelves of the books originally salvaged from the scrap heap by the famed educator. A framed sign alongside a photograph of Dr. Loomis Booker explained the significance of the exhibit. Standing in front of the shelves, holding one of the books and examining the title, was a tall Negro youth. Eric recognized him as Loomis's grandson, Artemus.

"Hi," Eric said, coming up to the youth.

Startled, Artemus turned quickly, then put the book back on the shelf. "I was just looking," he explained.

Eric chuckled and held out his hand. "Artemus, if you don't have the right to look at those books, I'd sure like to know who does."

"You, I guess," Artemus said. "I know my grandfather thought a lot of you."

"He loved me, son. And I loved him," Eric said simply. "He was as much my father as my real father was— maybe more. I just wish he were here to watch you graduate today. He would have been very proud of you."

"I like to think he would be."

"Of course, the fact that you've been drafted by the St. Louis Hawks basketball team would sort of tickle his fancy, too. But, all in all, I think he'd be most proud of you for graduating from Jefferson. He loved this school, for all that it was segregated for his entire lifetime. By the way, where's Deon? Is he here today?"

"No, sir. Deon is in Montgomery, Alabama."

"What's he doing down there?"

"He's going to school at Alabama State."

"Alabama State's a colored institution, isn't it?"

"Yes, sir."

Eric stroked his beard. "I have to say that I'm a little surprised by that. I would've thought that he'd come here with you—or at the very least attend Lincoln University, where your father was a professor for so long."

"Deon is a person who is—how can I best put it?—a person with a restless soul." Artemus smiled. "He's always been a little different."

Eric nodded. "Marching to the beat of a different drum?"

Artemus chuckled. "Yes, sir, you might say that."

"Well, whatever Deon does, I'm sure he'll do well. You two come from damn good stock."

From outside the library someone began blowing a whistle.

"If you'll excuse me, Mr. Twainbough, I have to go," Artemus said. "That whistle is the signal for the graduating class to assemble."

"I guess I'd better be getting ready, too," Eric said.

"Congratulations to you, Artemus. And best of luck to you in the NBA."

"Thank you," Artemus called back over his shoulder. "Maybe we'll see each other again sometime."

Eric returned to the front of the library and found that most of the guests were gone, though Tanner was still there, looking around anxiously.

"Oh, there you are," she said. "A few people were beginning to get worried. They thought you had wandered off and gotten lost."

"You weren't worried, were you?"

Tanner smiled and stuck her arm through his. "Not a bit. Since I got you back, I don't intend to ever lose you again." She held out her hand and looked at her wedding ring. "I knew there was some reason why I hung on to this ring all these years."

"Well, Mrs. Twainbough, shall we go?"

The president of the university, Dr. Robert Stroop, was standing on the sidewalk just outside the library.

"This way, Mr. Twainbough," he instructed. "The other dignitaries are already on the dais."

Eric had one surprise awaiting him. While being introduced as the commencement speaker he learned that he had been awarded an honorary Doctor of Letters degree by the university, and he felt a surge of pride as he slipped into the cap, gown, and hood of the institution. So attired, he stepped up to the podium to give the commencement address.

He spoke for fifteen minutes. At the conclusion of his address he said, "I am not sure if you realize just how significant a place in history you occupy. Your importance is a matter of circumstance—a quirk of time—because, you see, you have come of age in the exact middle of this century. Many men and women alive now can remember the dawn of this century. Many of you will reach its twilight. All of you will have come in contact with representatives of each end of this century's time upon the stage of history.

"You, then, are the bridge, the link between past and future, old and new. The baton has been passed to you, and the rest of the century waits breathlessly on the sidelines to see if you are up to the task of carrying it forward. All we ask of you, my friends, is that you don't drop it."

CHAPTER TEN

DECEMBER 1955, FROM ''TRAILMARKERS,''
EVENTS MAGAZINE:

CULT ASSERTS ACTOR IS STILL ALIVE

Despite police and coroners' reports, a growing cult of teenage fans continues to insist that actor James Dean is still alive.

"We know that he was badly hurt in the car crash," one girl said. "And we know that his face is so scarred that he doesn't want anyone to see him. But we want you to tell him that we love him—whether his face is scarred or not."

Dean was killed instantly when the silver Porsche Spider he was driving swerved into a bridge abutment to avoid hitting another car. He was said to have been driving nearly 100 miles per hour at the time of the accident.

JULIAN KEEFER ANNOUNCES
NEW TV SERIES FOR
PLAYWRIGHT DAVID ROGERS

"The quality of television entertainment is about to rise"—this according to television producer Julian Keefer. "We have just reached an agreement with David Rogers to produce a series of plays written expressly for television.

"There are some who insist that David Rogers is too highbrow for television," Keefer continued, "that his plays are best performed before the more sophisticated audiences of Broadway. But David believes, and the network believes, in the sophistication of the American TV viewer.

"The time has come for Americans to have more to watch than Davy Crockett and Lucille Ball," Keefer concluded, "and with our series, to be called 'David Rogers Presents,' we intend to give them that opportunity."

ARTEMUS BOOKER SCORES 62 POINTS IN
HAWKS WIN OVER PISTONS

Artemus Booker, who last year lit up the boards for Jefferson University, has answered the question everyone was asking: Could he play in the NBA?

"Booker was all over the court," one of the coaches for Detroit complained. "We couldn't box him out, we couldn't stay with him man to man; the only defense we had against him was during the half. He didn't score any points against us during the half."

"WE WILL NEVER INTEGRATE OUR
SCHOOLS," ALABAMA ATTORNEY
GENERAL INSISTS

Despite the Supreme Court ruling banning segregation in the school system, Alabama, along with several other states of the deep South, contin-

ues to ban Negroes from traditionally white class-
rooms.

"The education of our children is the responsibility of the state," the attorney general said.
"Our people do not want a mixing of the races, and
no amount of legislation can change that. Even our
Negroes can clearly see the validity of keeping the
races separate. The Negro child is not as bright as
the white child and would be embarrassed to have
to compete in the classroom."

The attorney general went on to say that any
attempt to force desegregation would be met with
resistance from the highest institutions of learning
down to the one-room schoolhouses.

"We have never had any problem with our
Negroes like they have up north. That's because
we have an understanding that has survived for
hundreds of years. We'd all be better off if the
federal government and the like would tend to
their own business and leave us alone."

MONTGOMERY, ALABAMA

"Mama, do you have to go to work today?" Andrew
Jackson asked.

"Yes, darlin', I do," his mother, Quinisha, replied.

"Sometimes you don't go to work."

"The only time I don't go to work is when the dress
shop is closed."

"Don't we own the dress shop?"

Quinisha chuckled. "Yes, I suppose we do."

She had moved with Andrew from Mississippi to Alabama and bought the dress shop, which had been adver-
tised as an established business "serving the colored
ladies of Montgomery for over thirty years," with money
she and Travis had had in savings plus the settlement from
Travis's G.I. insurance.

Andrew grinned. "Well, if we *own* the store, we can
close it and you don't have to go to work."

"Not a very good idea," Quinisha responded, kissing him on the forehead. "If I close the store, I don't make money, and if I don't make money, we can't eat. Which reminds me, you didn't finish your Corn Toasties."

Andrew took another spoonful of cereal. As he ate he turned the box around. On the back was a big picture of a man in a football uniform, his arm cocked back as if throwing a pass.

"What does the writing say, Mama?" the boy asked.

"You know what it says, Andrew. I've read it to you a dozen times."

"Does it say 'Canfield-Puritex Corn Toasties, Breakfast of Winners. Choo Choo Willis is a winner'?"

"Right."

"He was Daddy's friend, wasn't he?"

"Yes, darlin'. He was your daddy's friend."

The front door opened and a woman's voice called, "Yoo hoo, Mrs. Jackson? It's me, Vela."

Vela Sanders was Quinisha's housekeeper and babysitter. She was very proud of the fact that among her immediate group of friends who worked as maids in Montgomery, she was the only one who worked for someone of her own race.

"We're in the kitchen, Vela," Quinisha called back.

Vela was a short, very stout woman, and as she came into the kitchen she was taking off her coat and scarf, revealing her bulk. "It's cold out there today," she said. "And I thought that bus wasn't never goin' to come. When it finally did, I had to stand up most of the way."

"There were no seats?"

"No, ma'am. Not in the colored section there wasn't. There was two or three empty seats down to the front of the bus, though. You'd think that when there's lots more colored folks than white, the driver would make all the white folks scoot up to the very front to give the colored folks more seats."

"They would never do anything like that," Quinisha said. "That would be too sensible."

Vela laughed. "Yes, ma'am, that be the truth. That would be too sensible."

"Vela, can I have some cinnamon toast?" Andrew asked.

She looked at Quinisha, who nodded. "Well, I 'spect you can," Vela told Andrew, going over to the counter to fix it for him.

Quinisha kissed her son good-bye, then put on her coat and hat, picked up her purse and keys, and went out to the car.

The car was a yellow 1951 Buick Roadmaster. It had been Travis's pride and joy, bought just before he went to Korea. He talked about it in at least half of his letters, and he never tired of getting pictures of it. Quinisha once accused him of enjoying the pictures of the car more than he did the ones of her and Andrew.

The car was nearly five years old and had over eighty thousand miles on it. She occasionally thought about getting a new one, but she was afraid to spend money on a car when she might need the funds for her business. Besides, as long as she held on to the car, she felt that she still had a part of Travis with her.

It took her several tries to get the car started, but finally it kicked over. She let it run for a few minutes to get warmed up, then backed out of her driveway and drove the three miles to her store.

Quinisha's one employee, a young part-time college student named Claudia Baker, was standing outside waiting for her.

"My, you got here early this morning," Quinisha said as she got out of the car.

"Yes, ma'am," Claudia said. "The Women's Political Council at the Dexter Avenue Church is having a meeting today, and I wanted to take some cookies by for them."

"You've got that new man as your preacher, don't you? What's his name?"

"The Reverend Martin Luther King, Jr.," Claudia said.

"He's terribly young, isn't he?"

"He may be young, but he's got fire in his voice— and in his soul. You should come hear that man preach."

Quinisha unlocked the shop door and, once inside,

went around turning on the lights and adjusting the heat. "Maybe I'll come hear him someday," she called over her shoulder. "But the truth is, Sundays are the only days I have to myself, and I like to spend them with Andrew."

"I know what you mean. Deon wants me to spend all day Sunday with him, but I told him he might be my boyfriend, but my world doesn't start and stop with him."

Quinisha laughed. "If I know Deon, he didn't care too much for that answer."

"No, ma'am, he sure didn't." Claudia paused, then asked, "Mrs. Jackson, is it true that you named Andrew after Deon's father?"

"Yes, it's true."

"What was Deon's father like?"

"To tell you the truth, Claudia, I never met him. He was killed in an automobile accident before Travis and I were married. But Travis knew him, and it was Travis who chose the name for our son."

"Deon said his father was a doctor."

"Oh, he was. He was a wonderful doctor. Did you know the white folks of Delta, Mississippi, erected a statue to him? It's right there in the park in the middle of town. They called him 'Brother Doctor.' "

"The white folks did that?"

"They sure did. They credit him with helping to save the town from a big polio epidemic."

"Then I don't understand why Deon hates whites so much."

Quinisha turned and faced the young woman. "It was white people who let Deon's mother and father die," she said softly.

"I thought they were killed in a car wreck."

"They were. It's really quite a tragic story. They were going to Washington so Dr. Booker could accept an award for his work in medicine. He helped develop blood plasma. Blood plasma, of course, has saved lots of lives— especially in the wars. When Dr. Booker was lying there in the hospital, dying, blood plasma could have saved his life. Do you understand what I'm saying, girl? The very thing he invented could have saved his life."

"The hospital didn't have any?"

"Oh, they had it all right. But the plasma they had was reserved for white use only. They ordered some plasma for colored use from another hospital, but it didn't get there in time."

"I didn't know that," Claudia said, looking aghast. "Deon has never told me the story."

"No, I don't suppose it's anything he likes to talk about."

"Did you know he had a full scholarship from Jefferson University?"

"No, I didn't know that."

"Yes, ma'am. He could've gone to the same school his brother went to. And that's a fine school, too."

"Oh, I know. It's right up there with Harvard or Yale. Why didn't he choose to go?"

"His scholarship was in track, and Deon said he didn't want to be like his brother, some 'nigger performing for the white man.'"

"That's what he thinks about Artemus? Why, Artemus Booker is one of the greatest basketball players in America. I'd have thought that Deon would be proud of him."

"Deon says Artemus has sold out."

"I'm sorry he feels that way. My son thinks the sun rises and sets on Artemus Booker." She laughed. "Of course, he feels the same way about Choo Choo Willis and Willie Mays."

"Choo Choo Willis is white, isn't he?"

"Yes. To be truthful, though, it isn't just Choo Choo Willis's football playing that's made him a hero to Andrew. Mr. Willis was a friend of Andrew's father."

"In the Army?"

"The Air Force, child. There's a big difference."

"Do you miss the Air Force, Mrs. Jackson?"

Quinisha blinked several times against the sheen of tears in her eyes.

"I'm sorry," Claudia said quickly. "I shouldn't have brought it up."

"No," Quinisha said, touching Claudia's arm. She

gave a small laugh. "It isn't as if the thought never crosses my mind. Yes, Claudia, I do miss the Air Force. I know, of course, that most of what I miss is Travis, and when I think of the Air Force, I think of him. But there are other things about the Air Force that I miss—the common denominator we all shared that brought everyone, white and colored, closer together. Don't get me wrong. I'm not saying there's no prejudice in the Air Force—it exists there, just like it does here—but it isn't officially sanctioned. We went to the same officers' club, the same PX, the same hospitals; we lived next door to each other in base housing. And I think that that lack of sanctioned prejudice made things better."

"Mrs. Jackson, you need to come to one of our political action meetings," Claudia said.

"Oh, I don't know. I'm not very political."

"But don't you want things to be better? Wouldn't you like for Andrew to grow up in a world where racial prejudice isn't a policy of the government?"

Quinisha was silent for a long moment. "Yes," she finally said. "Yes, I would."

"It won't happen if we just sit around like we have for the last hundred years," Claudia insisted. "People have to *make* it happen. People like us. We could sure use someone like you."

"I'll tell you what I'll do. I'll think about it," Quinisha promised.

The store's first customer came in then, and Quinisha hurried to wait on her. While she was waiting on that one, another customer came in, and Claudia saw to her. From that point on the shop was so busy that the subject of their morning discussion wasn't brought up again.

The day went well—one of the better days Quinisha had had since buying the store. Busy as the shop was, she let Claudia leave early so that she could attend the meeting at the church. Quinisha had a flurry of last-minute customers, so it was dark by the time she locked up, turned off the lights and heat, and closed out the register. She had $207.52, which she put in a night depository envelope and slipped into her purse. She didn't like to carry that much money with her, so she wanted to get it deposited as quickly as possible.

Exiting the store, she locked the door and went over to her car.

It wouldn't start.

She tried again and again until finally the constant turning of the starter drained the battery. Her last attempt to start the car was answered with nothing more than a series of clicking sounds. For just a moment Quinisha felt a quick-building panic; then she looked up and saw three or four people standing on the corner about to board a bus that was just arriving.

Making her decision quickly, Quinisha jumped out of her car, locked it, and ran down to the corner, just a second after the last person had gotten on the bus. By that time, though, the driver had already closed the doors and was starting to pull away.

"Wait!" Quinisha shouted, running alongside the bus.

The driver acted as if he neither saw nor heard her, and he would have driven away if a truck hadn't suddenly backed out of an alley, forcing him to stop. Quinisha didn't wait for the driver to open the doors but reached up and forced them open herself, then stepped on board.

"This isn't an authorized bus stop," the driver growled.

"I was at the authorized bus stop. You didn't pick me up," Quinisha replied, taking a coin from her purse and dropping it into the box.

"All right. You're on now, so I guess no harm's done," the driver said.

Quinisha walked to the back of the bus, found a seat near the window, and sat down. She was surprised at how good it felt to sit, after having been on her feet all day.

The bus lurched through town in a series of jerking stops and starts, letting some passengers off, picking up others. One of the passengers who got on was a woman Quinisha knew, a seamstress named Rosa Parks. Quinisha nodded at her, but Rosa didn't see her. She took a seat in the first row of the colored section.

Within another few stops, every seat on the bus was

filled, and a white man who got on, finding no seat, remained standing, grabbing one of the overhead straps to support himself.

"You four colored folks in that front row there, move on to the back," the driver called.

Nothing happened.

The driver pulled on the brake and got out of his seat, turning to face the passengers.

"Don't give me any trouble, now," he said. "Why don't you just make it light on yourselves? Get up and let me have those seats."

Three of the Negroes got up and moved to the rear of the bus, where they stood stoically holding on to the support straps. Rosa Parks didn't move.

"Didn't you hear what I said?" the driver asked.

"I'm not in the white section," Rosa replied. "I don't think I should have to move."

"Oh, you have to move all right," the driver said menacingly. "The white section is just where I say it is. And I say you're sittin' in it. Now, get up like I told you!"

Rosa remained still, and a murmur of surprise and repressed fear from the others ran through the bus. Quinisha had two thoughts of her own: She was glad that Rosa was defying the driver—and she was glad that it was Rosa and not her.

"I'm not just tellin' you this from some whim," the driver snapped. "The law says you have to move when I tell you to. And that same law gives me the power to arrest you if you don't."

"You do what you have to do," Rosa said calmly. "I'm not moving."

"All right. All right, you are officially under arrest. You just sit right there till I get back."

"Yes, sir, that's just what I intend to do—sit right here," Rosa said.

The driver stopped the engine and left the bus sitting alongside the curb. The passengers were quiet. Rosa Parks remained in her seat, staring straight ahead. A few minutes later the driver returned with a policeman.

"Now, why do you want to cause trouble?" the policeman asked calmly. "Why don't you just get up and move to the back of the bus like you were told?"

Rosa stared straight ahead, silently.

The policeman sighed. "All right, get up," he said, reaching for her and pulling her up from the seat. "We're going down to the station. You're under arrest."

"Thanks for takin' care of it," the driver called almost jovially as the policeman took his prisoner off the bus. He closed the door, started the bus, then pulled out into traffic to continue his route.

"My goodness, where is your car?" Vela asked when Quinisha finally reached her house.

"I couldn't get it started," Quinisha explained. "It's still sitting in front of the shop."

"Oh, honey, you don't want to leave it down there. There's all kinds of things can happen to it if stays all night down there. I'll tell Ralph about it when I get home. He'll go down there and get it fixed up for you and bring it right here to your house."

"Thank you, Vela, that would be wonderful," Quinisha said. She sat down on the sofa and let out a long sigh. "Oh, the most awful thing happened on the bus on the way home."

"What was that?"

Quinisha told her about Rosa Parks refusing to move to the back of the bus and being arrested as a result.

"Oh, that's a shame—and she's such a sweet person, too," Vela said. "I hope they get her out of there before there's any more trouble."

"Mrs. Jackson," Claudia Baker said the next morning, "I'd like you to read this." She held out a mimeographed sheet of paper. "It was written by the Women's Political Action Committee. We're passing them out all over Montgomery."

"Oh? What's it about?"

"It has to do with a colored woman getting arrested

for not moving to the back of the bus. You know her. It was Rosa Parks."

Quinisha's eyes widened. "Yes, I do know her. As a matter of fact, Claudia, I was on that bus. My car wouldn't start last night, and I rode the bus home. I saw everything."

"Then you should stand with us in doing something about it," Claudia said.

"Well, I agree, it was a terrible thing. But what can we do?"

"We're going to boycott the buses, come next Monday. The Women's Political Action Committee is asking everyone not to ride the buses in protest."

"Well, that seems easy enough to do. The question is, will it do any good?"

"I don't know. I guess it depends on whether or not our people stick together. Some of them will have to walk awfully far to get to work if they don't take the bus, and that means they'll have to leave home when it's still dark. And it's awfully cold before the sun comes up."

"I'll do my share," Quinisha promised. "I'll come get you to bring you to work Monday."

"Thank you, but I'll be attending a meeting at church at six-thirty that morning."

"My, so early?"

"Yes, ma'am."

"Well, if I can get Vela to come to work that early, I'll come get you in time for the meeting as well."

Claudia smiled broadly. "And you'll go to the meeting with me?"

Quinisha chuckled. "I don't plan to sit out in the car in the cold and the dark all by myself."

MONDAY, DECEMBER 5, 1955

The meeting room at the church smelled of coffee from a percolating pot. Twenty or thirty women were there, most of them wearing maid's uniforms, having come to the meeting before going to work for their white employers. The atmosphere was upbeat, and they laughed and shared stories of their long walk.

"Will they do it?" someone asked. "Will our people stay off the buses?"

"I don't know. It's cold outside, and most have a long way to go to get to work. I guess you couldn't blame them if they don't."

"But they've got to. If they don't, we'll never get anything done."

"Yeah, and the white folks will be laughin' up their sleeves at us."

"How long until the first bus comes by?"

"It ought to be here any minute now."

"Here it comes!" someone shouted, and all the women, Quinisha included, rushed out of the church to see the bus rolling by, its headlights cutting through the darkness.

"Oh please, Jesus, be empty," someone said fervently.

The well-lighted bus drew even with the church. Quinisha was thrilled to see that it was devoid of passengers.

"There wasn't nobody on the bus! Did you see that? It was empty!" someone shouted. "It's workin'!"

"Maybe it's too early," someone else said. "Maybe that bus don't normally have nobody on it anyway."

"Well, the next one ain't normally empty," one of the other women said. "I know that for a fact. It's the one I ride when I'm goin' to stop by my mama's house before I go to work. It's sometimes so full you can't even get a seat."

"Here it comes," someone said.

The women strained to see the next bus approach, listening to the engine as the driver worked up through the gears from the stoplight at the far end of the street. When it passed, it, too, was empty. The women cheered, and when the next bus and the bus after that were also empty, they cheered again.

"The boycott is workin'!" someone said, her voice catching. "Praise to the Lord, the boycott is workin'!"

Finally the cold and the necessity for many of them to get to work forced the women back inside the church. As they gathered their coats, hats, and bundles, the woman in charge asked anyone who could stay to please do so to prepare for the mass meeting they were planning for that night.

"We've got much to do and not much time to get it done," she reminded them.

"What mass meeting?" Quinisha asked.

"We're asking every Negro man and woman in Montgomery to attend our meeting tonight."

"And Dr. King is going to speak," Claudia put in. "You will come, won't you?"

Quinisha thought about it for a moment, then nodded. "Yes, I'll come. And, Claudia, if you want to stay here and help get things ready, you go ahead. I'll get by without you today."

"Thanks, Mrs. Jackson! Thanks a lot!"

Quinisha made her good-byes to the others, then offered rides to as many as she could fit into her car, silently thanking Vela's husband for having made the repairs the night before.

Throughout the entire day Quinisha could feel an air of excitement from her customers. Everyone knew about the boycott, and nearly everyone knew about the meeting that night. A significant number said they planned to attend.

"I have to confess that I'm amazed at the way the boycott is holding up," Quinisha told one of her regular customers toward the end of the day. "I've made a point of looking out at the passing buses a number of times, and I have yet to see a colored person on one."

"We're calling ourselves Negroes now," the woman, who happened to be a professor at Alabama State, said.

"Why?"

"The word 'colored' has an unfavorable connotation, an Uncle Tom connotation," the professor explained. "It's a white man's word, and we aren't going to use it anymore."

Quinisha laughed. "We're going to confuse them."

The professor laughed as well. "Yes, well, that can't be helped. But you know how white people are. They are simple folk, so easily confused."

Quinisha laughed at the professor's turning around the phrase she had so often heard white people say about Negroes.

Just before closing time Claudia returned to the store, bubbling over with enthusiasm. "Mrs. Jackson, you'd better shut the store early if you want to get a seat at the meeting tonight," she said. "If you come now, I can get you in. If you come any later, there won't be any room left."

"Heavens, are there that many people attending?" Quinisha asked.

"There sure are. The meeting isn't until seven o'clock, but already so many people are there that we're having to put up loudspeakers so folks can listen from outside." Claudia smiled broadly. "And guess what? Dr. King has been elected president of the protest committee."

"Well, good for your Dr. King."

"You should have heard him today. Several of the community leaders were at the church, making plans for the meeting. I was supposed to be helping out in the kitchen, but I snuck into the back of the sanctuary to listen. Oh, it was so exciting!"

"Tell me about it," Quinisha said as she made preparations to close.

"Well, one man wanted to have the meeting in secret, and he wanted to keep secret the names of all the leaders. But Mr. Nixon stood up and asked, 'How do you think you can run a bus boycott in secret?' And then he said, 'People like you preachers have lived off the women-folk for a hundred years, and you ain't never done nothin' for them. Now there's a woman in trouble, and you wantin' to hide behind her skirts like a coward while she goes to court. We've worn aprons all our lives. It's time to take the aprons off and be men.'

"Then Dr. King stood up and said, 'Brother Nixon, I'm not a coward, and I don't want anyone to call me a coward.' Well, they liked what he had to say so much that they elected him president of the whole committee."

"I must confess that I'm looking foward to meeting your Dr. King," Quinisha said as they got into the car.

She had planned to drive to the church, but she soon found that she wouldn't be able to. It was surrounded by so many people that the crowd filled the churchyard and spilled out across the street, pouring into the yards and parking lots of adjacent buildings and blocking off all traffic. Cars were parked everywhere and at all angles, some abandoned smack in the middle of the street. The police had stopped trying to get the cars moved and the crowd dispersed and were now resigned to directing the through traffic to other routes.

"Good heavens, look at this!" Quinisha said. "Who would've thought there would be this many people? How are we ever going to get in?"

"We can get in around back. I've got a key to the basement door," Claudia replied. "And I have two folding chairs hidden in the basement, if no one has found them," she added with a conspiratorial laugh.

They had to leave the car three blocks away and push their way through the crowd to get into the church. They stopped to listen to a policeman speaking frantically into the microphone of his car radio.

"We need more officers down here!" he said.

"*Are the nigras startin' to riot?*" the amplified voice of the dispatcher replied.

"No, nothin' like that. But there's so many of 'em, we can't handle 'em."

"*I understand there's about five thousand of 'em,*" the dispatcher's voice replied again. "*That's no more folks'n come to a high school football game. Surely you can handle that without more officers.*"

"I don't know where you're getting your information," the harried policeman said, "but there's at least fifteen thousand people here . . . maybe more."

"*The captain says do the best you can. If the nigras start riotin', he'll send more officers down.*"

"Ten four," the officer replied in frustration. When

he saw that Quinisha and Claudia were listening to his conversation, he growled at them, "Move on."

The two women obliged.

"Did you hear that, Mrs. Jackson? More than fifteen thousand people are here!" Claudia said.

"I'm beginning to worry about whether or not you can get us in."

"Don't worry. Just stay close, and don't get lost in the crowd."

It took a few minutes of pushing and shoving, but they finally managed to get around to the back of the church, then down a dank set of concrete steps, where Claudia unlocked the door, then quickly locked it again behind them. The basement was very dimly lit, the only illumination coming from a single dangling yellowish bulb that lit the stairs at the far end of the room. Claudia ducked behind the furnace, where she found the two folding chairs. Smiling, she handed one to Quinisha.

"This way," she said.

When they got upstairs, they saw that the sanctuary was filled to capacity, with those who had been unable to get in peering in through the windows from outside. People were packed in the balconies and aisles and sitting on the floor anywhere there was enough space for a body. Over by the piano some of Claudia's friends had spread themselves out to hold a space for her and, seeing her, rearranged themselves enough to allow Claudia and Quinisha room. Quinisha nodded her thanks as she opened her chair, then sat and looked up at Dr. King, who had already come to the pulpit and was just beginning his talk.

"We are here this evening for serious business," King began quietly.

"*Yes, Lord,*" a few in the crowd responded in counterpoint.

"We are here in a general sense, because first and foremost we are American citizens . . ."

"*Yes, sir. Amen.*"

". . . and we are determined to apply our citizenship . . ."

"Yes, Jesus."

". . . to the fullest of its means." He stretched out the word "fullest." "But we are here in a specific sense . . ."

"Amen."

". . . because of the bus situation in Montgomery."

"Yes, Lord."

"The situation is not at all new."

"It ain't new, Lord."

"The problem has existed over endless years. Just the other day . . ."

"Just the other day, Lord . . ."

"Just last . . . Thursday . . . to be exact . . ."

"Uh-huh. Thursday . . ."

". . . one of the finest citizens in Montgomery . . ."

"One of the finest, Lord . . ."

". . . not one of the finest Negro citizens . . . but one of the finest citizens in Montgomery . . ."

"You got that right."

". . . was taken from a bus."

"They took her off the bus."

". . . and carried to jail and arrested . . ."

"Took her to jail."

". . . because she refused to give up . . . to give her seat to a white man."

"Amen. Yes, Lord."

"If such a thing had to happen, then I'm happy it happened to a person like Mrs. Parks, for nobody can doubt the boundless outreach of her integrity!"

King's eyes were flashing now, and he gripped the podium with both hands and leaned forward.

"Nobody can doubt the height of her character!"

"Nobody, Lord."

"Nobody can doubt the depth of her Christian commitment!"

"You got that right."

"But because this good, Christian woman refused to get up to give her seat to a white man . . ."

"She wouldn't get up, Lord."

"She was arrested."

"Took her to jail."

"And you know my friends, there comes a time"—King paused and held up his finger for emphasis, then shouted out the next few words—*"there comes a time when people get tired of being trampled over by the iron feet of oppression!"*

This time, instead of a few individual responses, there was a sudden explosion of noise, instant pandemonium to answer King's exhortation. Before, they had listened to him politely; now they were with him emotionally, and they yelled and stomped on the wooden floor until Quinisha, who was also caught up in the excitement of it, could feel every nerve in her body vibrating in harmony.

"There comes a *time,* my friends, when people get tired of being thrown across the abyss of humiliation, where they experience the bleakness of nagging despair.

"There comes a *time* when people get tired of being pushed from the glittering sunlight of life's July and are left standing amidst the piercing chill of an Alpine November."

That brought about another thunderous roar from the crowd.

"We are here because we are tired now. But we are not advocating violence. In the words of the old spiritual, We shall overcome . . . and we have overcome violence. I want it to be known throughout Montgomery, and throughout this nation, from sea to shining sea, that we are a Christian people. And the only weapon that we have in our hands this evening is the weapon of protest."

"Amen. Yes, Lord."

"If we were incarcerated behind the iron curtains of a communistic nation, we couldn't do this."

"No, Lord."

"If we were trapped in the dungeon of a totalitarian country, we couldn't do this. But the great glory of American democracy is the right to protest for right."

Again, the crowd exploded in applause.

"There will be no crosses burned at any bus stops in

Montgomery. There will be no white persons, men or women, boys or girls, pulled out of their homes and taken out on some distant road and murdered. There will be nobody among us who will stand up and defy the constitution of this nation."

"No, Lord, we ain't gonna do that."

"My friends," King went on, "I want it to be known that we're going to work with grim and bold determination to gain justice on the buses in this city."

"Justice."

"And we are not wrong. We are not wrong in what we are doing. For if we are wrong . . . the Supreme Court of this nation is wrong. If we are wrong . . . God Almighty is wrong."

Thunderclap after thunderclap exploded over the audience, rising to a higher and higher pitch until King had to lean into the microphone to cut through it. "If we are wrong . . . Jesus of Nazareth was merely a utopian dream and never came down to earth! If we are wrong . . . *justice is a lie!"*

Again, thunder exploded inside and outside the church. King, holding on to both sides of the podium as if the noise might sweep him away, looked at the audience with eyes that seemed to shoot the very lightning bolts from which the thunder was born. Finally, when the crowd was quiet enough to hear him, he finished his speech.

"And we are determined here in Montgomery to work and fight until justice runs down like water and righteousness like a mighty stream!"

The audience stood as one and applauded wildly as Dr. King made his way out through the crowd. From all over the church people strained and reached out to touch him. Quinisha, who had joined in the applause with the others, felt physically and emotionally spent.

LOS ANGELES

The door to the locker-room slammed open, and the players lumbered through like a herd of angry elephants. Huge, padded men, their faces dirty, their uniforms grass-stained, their cleats clattering on the concrete floor, moved sullenly around the room, settling on benches and banging open locker doors.

"Fuck! We gave up ten points in the last quarter!" someone said disgustedly. "Ten points! I mean, we just stood around with our thumbs up our asses and watched 'em run over us. Son of a bitch! It was embarrassing!"

The game was the Pro Bowl, professional football's equivalent of baseball's annual All-Star Game, with the players representing their teams and the division their team played in. These East Division players were losing to the West by a score of 29 to 19.

One of the players for the East was the quarterback for the New York Giants, Choo Choo Willis. He had gone down hard in the first quarter and had to sit out the second quarter with a painfully throbbing knee. Now he limped over to one of the training tables. Like the players, the trainers came from different teams. The trainer for the Giants wasn't here, and to Train Willis, it was a little like getting sick away from home and having to go to a strange doctor.

"Say, Doc," Train said, "see what you can do about this, will you?" He dropped his pants, then hopped up on the table with his bare legs hanging over the side.

The trainer didn't even have to ask what was wrong. He could see it. The right knee was swollen to half again its normal size, and it was already turning blue.

"Choo Choo, you can't go back out on this knee after the halftime," he said. "If you do, you'll be risking your entire career."

Train reached down to massage the knee and winced with pain.

"You want to know the truth, Doc?" he said. "I think my career is about over anyway."

"No, I wouldn't say so. You've still got a few good

years left." He laughed. "I don't know why I'm trying to talk you into staying, though. You're with New York, and I'm with Baltimore."

"Yeah, and so is Art Donovan. He and people like him are why I'm ready to hang it up. You think it's fun to stand out there and get beat up on, play after play, game after game, year after year?"

"Yeah, well, you backs get all the glory and all the money," a big tackle said. "We guys in the line have to get some fun, so we get it by beating up on you. And it is fun, ain't it guys?"

"Almost as good as sex," one answered, and they all laughed.

"Listen," Train said, "do you know why they use people like you as down linemen?"

"I'll bite. Why?" a big tackle responded.

"Because you haven't evolved far enough from the ape to walk erect."

Although all the linemen growled, the other backs laughed.

"Well, we can fix you so you can't walk period," one of the linemen joked, and a couple of them started toward him.

"Looks like you've already done that," Train said, pointing to his knee. He held out his hands. "Kings X," he laughed.

"Look at me, fellas, I'm a lineman. *Oooh, oooh, oooh,*" one of the backs said, hopping around the dressing room and grunting like an ape.

"Get 'im, Lou!" one of the linemen shouted, and two of them grabbed the back, then turned him upside down. Each one took a leg. "Make a wish," one of them said.

"All right, you guys, settle down," one of the coaches shouted. "You want to take a chance on endin' someone's career by just fuckin' around?"

"Hey, Coach, I don't care if he gets hurt or not. He don't play on *my* team," one of the linemen said.

"Wait a minute," the other lineman said. "He plays on *my* team! Let him go, you big, dumb bastard!"

"Bubba's not a bastard," one of other backs said.

"Yeah," Bubba replied.

"He's just big and dumb."

The locker-room dissolved in laughter.

The trainer put an ice pack on Train's knee, then began wrapping an ace bandage around it. "So you're going to quit," he said. "Well, the truth is, I don't understand why any of you do it. Remember, I get to see the end result, and I see more broken bones, torn cartilage, separated shoulders, and smashed knees than a good-sized hospital. So if you really are serious about quitting, you'll get no argument from me. What will you do?"

"You're looking at the new public relations director for the Canfield-Puritex Corporation," Train said.

"What, cereal?"

"Yes. Among other things. I'll start working for them after the first of the year. I'll have my own office, my own desk, my own secretary . . ." He looked across the room and saw Big Art Donovan heading for the shower. "And, best of all, there won't be anyone like that beating the shit out of me."

"You'll miss the game, Choo Choo," one of the other players said.

Train grinned. "Yeah, well, if I ever get to missing it too much, I can always go stand in the street and let a cab run over me."

CHAPTER ELEVEN

Valentina Golitsyn took the thermometer from Kiril Barshay's mouth and read the mercury.

"What is it, Comrade Golitsyn?" Barshay asked.

"Thirty-seven point seven degrees," Valentina answered. "A slight temperature. You have a minor cold, that is all."

"Then I can go to the Christmas party?"

Valentina looked at Barshay and smiled. "Christmas party, Comrade? You, a good Communist, wish to celebrate Christmas?"

"Are you not going to the party?"

"Yes, but for me it is not a Christmas party, even though it comes on the eve of the Orthodox Christmas."

"It is not a Christmas party for me, either. At least, not in the religious sense," Barshay said. "But there is

222

something to be said for history and tradition, don't you think? I should think you of all people would—" Barshay stopped in midsentence, then cleared his throat in embarrassment.

"You are referring to my mother?" Valentina asked.

"I'm sorry, Comrade. I had no right. You are a good party member—no matter what your mother was."

"I am a good party member, that is true," Valentina said. "And my mother was a minor Romanov princess, that is also true. She was also a Christian right up until the day she died, so Christmas was always very meaningful for her. I can remember tales she told me of the gala Christmas parties she attended in her youth—parties with food and wine and music and dancing; parties held in great castles lighted by enormous crystal chandeliers and furnished with expensive carpets and furniture and magnificent paintings and decorated with fabulous Christmas decorations, the cost of any one enough to sustain a family of four for a year. And while these parties were going on, outside in the ice-clogged streets of what was then Petrograd, people were freezing to death or dying of starvation."

Valentina abruptly shook her head. "But I was not yet born and so I have no such memories. For that I am grateful, for who would want to remember such a time?"

"No one, I am sure. Things are much better for us all now than they were before the Revolution." Barshay smiled. "So, we agree: It is not a Christmas party. It is a party to celebrate the wonderful life of the Soviet citizen."

"They will have to celebrate without you," Valentina said. "I can't allow you to go. I can't allow you to mingle with the others. You might infect them as well."

"But you said it was only a little cold. A little cold can't hurt."

"And if your little cold spreads? The work being done here would suffer because of it. We could lose many man hours. Do you wish to be responsible for that, Comrade Barshay?"

Barshay looked out the window. "No, I wouldn't

want to be the cause of anything like that. I want our work here to continue. It *must* continue."

"I am glad you understand, Comrade," Valentina said, giving him an envelope with a few pills. "Take these and get some bed rest."

"These pills will cure the cold?"

Valentina laughed. "I'm afraid not. Not even the superior medical technology of the Soviet system has been able to develop a cure for the common cold. I have given you aspirin."

Barshay opened the small envelope, dumping the aspirins into his hand. He swallowed them, then said glumly, "Bed rest. What will I do in bed?"

"Perhaps you can read a book," Valentina suggested.

"Yes, I could do that. I'll study the effects of thermodynamics on vehicles reentering the earth's atmosphere."

"Heavens! Such ponderous reading might well prolong your illness. Read a novel."

"I don't read fiction," Barshay admitted. "I don't believe I could even tell you the name of one novel—except perhaps *Doctor Zhivago,* and, of course, I would never read that book, for it is clearly subversive."

"I have a book you might enjoy," Valentina said. "Stop by my house later, and I will lend it to you. It is called *The Edge of Infinity,* written by an American author named Eric Twainbough."

"Eric Twainbough? Yes, I have actually heard of him," Barshay said. "I read about him when I was in school. He was an American journalist who believed in the Revolution. The stories he wrote about the proletariat helped win recognition for the government that replaced the Czar's government. And you say he has written a novel?"

Valentina laughed. "He has written many, many novels. In fact, he is much better known for his novels than for the newspaper stories he wrote of the 1917 Revolution. This book won the Nobel Prize for literature."

Barshay took the book. "Well, I will be interested to see what he has written. What is the story about?"

"It is about an American movie director who is disgraced because he wouldn't answer the questions of the U.S. government when they accused him of being a Communist."

"Is it critical of the American government?"

"It is critical of the fervor of the government's anti-Communist program."

"Very well. I will read the book. I feel we should support him since he is, no doubt, disgraced in his homeland."

"On the contrary," Valentina replied. "He is much honored in his country."

"He is critical of the government, yet the Americans honor him?" Barshay asked, taken aback.

"Yes."

Barshay shook his head. "The Americans are a strange race."

As he opened the door to leave the one-story medical building, a frigid blast of air rushed in, immediately cooling the small room by several degrees, even though the door was only open for a few seconds. Valentina bustled over to the red-hot kerosene stove. Warming herself, she looked out the window at the gantry tower from which the test rockets were launched.

Tyuratam-Baykonur was the most secret base in all Russia. Here the military had designed and was now testing intercontinental ballistic missiles, huge rockets capable of lifting an atomic bomb off the launch pad in the Soviet Union and delivering it to any spot in the United States.

The door opened and closed again, and Valentina turned to see who had entered. It was her husband, Dr. Yuri Golitsyn. He joined Valentina at the stove.

"I believe it may snow," he said, holding his hands out to catch the warmth.

"Will the snow work a hardship on you?" Valentina asked.

"No," Yuri said. "We will be working inside for many more days." He smiled. "Besides, Tamara enjoys the snow. Perhaps I will make her a snowman tomorrow."

"She would enjoy that," Valentina agreed.

Yuri was Valentina's second husband. Her first, a medical doctor, had been killed almost twenty years earlier in Spain, during that country's revolution. A nurse herself, Valentina, too, had served as a Soviet volunteer to the Spanish Loyalists during the Spanish Revolution, returning home when the Loyalists lost to Francisco Franco's Nationalists.

Shortly after she had returned home, World War II started, and Valentina again volunteered her services as a nurse on the front lines. Her dedication to duty, coupled with an acute shortage of men brought on by the terrible loss of life during the war, prevented Valentina from remarrying for many years. She was prepared for a life of spinsterhood when, in 1950, at the age of thirty-three, she met Dr. Yuri Golitsyn.

Yuri was a doctor of physics, a scientist employed by the Soviet rocket program. When he was transferred to the secret base at Tyuratam-Baykonur, he arranged for Valentina to take a position in the medical department so that she could go with him. Their family was increased with the birth of their daughter in 1952.

"I just saw Barshay leaving," Yuri said. "Is he ill? I will need him for the tests we are to run next week."

"He should be fine by then. He has only a slight cold. He is upset because I wouldn't let him attend the party. I gave him some aspirin—and a book to read."

"One of your father's?"

Valentina looked over at the several Russian translations of Eric Twainbough's books. "Yes," she replied. "I gave him one of my father's books."

"Why don't you write him?" Yuri asked. "I would think he'd be very interested to learn that he has a Russian daughter whom he has never even heard about. Not to mention a granddaughter."

"Yuri, we have been through all this before."

"Yes, yes, I know. As a child you were hurt and angry because your father didn't come for you and your mother after the Revolution."

"No, you still don't understand. I wasn't hurt and angry because he didn't come for us. And I wouldn't have wanted to go with him even if he had. I am a citizen of the Soviet, and I am proud of that fact. I don't want to be an American. But my mother looked for him every day, and she died a little each day that he didn't come.

"He didn't come, he didn't send word that he was alive, he didn't know nor did he care if my mother was still alive, and he didn't know nor did he care if I even existed. And he never tried to find out. It is for these things that I can't forgive him."

"Times were different then," Yuri said. "Perhaps your father made inquiries that you knew nothing about. Besides, you saw him in Spain, didn't you? You even gave blood for him when he was wounded."

"Yes, I did," she said, her tone testy. "I have told you all this before. We have talked about all this before."

Yuri ignored her comments. "You saw him and you knew that he was your father, but you said nothing that would let him know that you were his daughter."

"No. I said nothing."

"Then you must bear as much blame for the continued estrangement as does your American father."

"Yes."

"Valentina, if you hate your father so much, why do you keep copies of all his books?" Yuri asked.

"Please, Yuri, you don't understand, and I can't explain it to you," Valentina said. "Can't we find other things to talk about?"

"All right. Let's talk about the dinner party tonight. Have you made arrangements for someone to stay with Tamara?"

"Yes. Anna will stay with her."

"Good. I am definitely looking forward to tonight," Yuri said. "I am told that the commissar of supplies has drawn rations by a factor of three for the dinner."

"That is a foolish waste of food," Valentina grumbled.

Yuri laughed. "You are far too serious."

Valentina stayed at the clinic until the time she was authorized to close. Then she bundled up for the walk to the tiny house that served as family quarters for her, Yuri, and their three-year-old daughter, Tamara.

The house was nearly half a kilometer from the clinic, and it was so cold that by the time Valentina got there a ring of ice had collected in the fur of her parka hood. Entering the house, she took off the parka, then stood at the outer edge of the circle of heat emanating from the roaring kerosene stove because it was too painful to warm too quickly.

"Mama!" Tamara said, running to meet her. "See what I can do!" The child scampered over to a small tumbling pad that had been laid out on the floor and did a series of forward somersaults. When she reached the other end of the mat, she turned toward her mother with a big smile on her face. "Did you see?"

"Yes, dear. You were wonderful."

"Papa is going to make a snowman tomorrow," Tamara said excitedly.

"Only if we get a fresh snow," Valentina replied. "The snow that's on the ground now is no good. It's too frozen."

"I hope it snows," Tamara said, going to the window and wiping away the frost to look outside.

A short, stout, middle-aged woman wearing an apron and smelling of spices came into the room. Anna Mironovna was the Golitsyns' housekeeper, and tonight she would be looking after Tamara while Valentina and Yuri attended the huge party being given at the community dining room.

"Come, my little one," she said to the child. "I have some hot soup for you." Looking at Valentina, she added, "I hope you and Comrade Golitsyn have a most enjoyable time tonight."

Valentina smiled warmly at the grandmotherly woman. "Thank you, Anna. And since you can't attend, I will bring back a wonderful pastry for you."

The personnel at the rocket base were divided into four groups. There were the people who worked on the rockets, the people who worked on the engines, the military personnel, and the administrative personnel, made up primarily of political officers.

Administration had decided it was advantageous to keep the work groups compartmentalized. Therefore, the rocket people tended to work, live, and play together, while the engine people and the military people did the same. On a few rare occasions there would be an event that drew them all together. This party was just such an event. As a result, Yuri Golitsyn, who was a member of V.P. Glushko's engine team, was seated at a table with Sergei Pavlovich Korolev, who headed the rocket design team.

"How is work coming on the new engine?" Korolev asked Yuri.

"Work is going well," Yuri replied. "Have you not seen the reports?"

Korolev spread caviar on a small cracker, then popped it in his mouth. He smiled with satisfaction as the tiny, flavor-filled eggs burst open. A few little black balls were on his fingers, and he sucked them off before he spoke.

"Oh, yes, Comrade Golitsyn, I read the reports. I read all the reports. But there are reports and there are reports. I want to hear from the lips of one of the project engineers himself that the engines will be ready to fit to the new rocket when the new rocket is ready to launch. Tell me—and it is very important that I know—are there any problems that have not shown up on the reports?"

"One slight problem with the fuel induction nozzle," Yuri admitted, wondering even as he spoke why he was confessing this to someone from a different team. "But," he added quickly, "the problem is not insurmountable. I am confident that we will be ready to marry the engine to the new rocket design when the time comes."

"Good, good," Korolev said. He smiled. "I think now is the time to share my idea with the others."

"Your idea, Comrade? What idea?"

"Listen to me, all of you," Korolev shouted above the din, getting the attention of the others in the dining room.

Because Korolev had been working on rockets since before World War II, and because he was now the highest-ranking scientist on the rocket base, his call for attention garnered immediate response. At all the other tables in the dining room conversations stopped and laughter halted as everyone looked at him to see what he had to say.

Korolev took his knife and stood it on end beside his plate.

"Imagine that this is my new rocket design, with Glushko's new engine," he said. "We will call this the booster."

"I beg your pardon?" someone asked. "What will we call it?"

"The booster," Korolev repeated. "Like so much of the world's technical terminology, it is an American word. It is a term the Americans use for giving something a lift, and it fits our purposes beautifully."

Korolev picked up a fork and held it against the knife about halfway up the shank so that the tines of the fork were higher than the point of the knife.

"And this is the existing, smaller rocket with the existing, smaller engine. We will attach it to the first rocket, and this we will call the second stage."

He then took an olive from the condiment bowl and stuck it on the fork tines. "And this is the payload."

"A nuclear bomb," someone suggested.

Korolev shook his head. "No, it isn't a nuclear bomb. But when launched it will have more power than a hundred nuclear bombs."

"A new type of explosive? I didn't even know we were working on such a device."

Korolev shook his head again. "It isn't an explosive device—at least, not the type you are thinking about. The explosion this device produces will be psychological, a propaganda blast that will spread all the way around the world. We will launch the rocket thusly," he added, lifting the knife and fork from the table.

"Now, at this point," he continued, "only one rocket engine will be functioning. That will be the booster, made up of the new rocket design and the new engine. Then, when the booster engine has expended all its fuel, the first stage will fall away." He demonstrated by pulling the knife away as if it were falling back to earth. "After the separation of the booster rocket, the second stage will ignite," he said, demonstrating by thrusting the fork up higher. "The second stage will then proceed out of the earth's atmosphere and into space. At that point the payload will be separated"—he pulled the olive from the fork—"where it will remain perfectly balanced between the pull of space and the earth's gravitational pull, which will keep it in place. As a result it will become an artificial moon, orbiting the earth once every one and one-half hours."

Korolev finished his demonstration by holding a grapefruit to represent earth and describing circles around it with the olive.

"Comrade Korolev, in order to achieve orbit in the way that you describe, we would have to attain a velocity of twenty-four thousand kilometers per hour. Do you think we can do that?"

"I have computed the weight and the atmospheric resistance parameters of my new rocket in the two-stage configuration. If the new engine will produce the thrust Glushko claims for it, we can, with a small payload, achieve orbit."

"What sort of payload?"

"Right now nothing more than a small radio transmitter, I'm afraid," Korolev said. "But think of the impact such a thing would have on the rest of the world. It would pass over international territory, yet far above international airspace. It would be a great testimony to our rocket program."

"How soon will we do this wonderful thing?" Yuri asked.

The smile left Korolev's face, and he sat back down. "Ah, my friends, that is the rub. I have already suggested the idea—only to be turned down."

"Why would you be turned down?" Yuri asked in a disbelieving voice.

"I can answer that for you," Commissar Yeselin said, wiping his mouth with a napkin, "as I am the one who turned him down. Comrade Korolev's new rocket design, Comrade Glushko's new engine, all the electronics—in fact, everything that was, is, and will be created at this place—is part of the military program. Therefore, everything we do must have a military application. I can see no military application from a small radio transmitter that circles the globe every ninety minutes."

"Yes, but as Comrade Korolev explained, there would be a tremendous psychological advantage to such a program," Yuri said. "Everyone would look up to Soviet scientists and technology. We would be the envy of the world."

"The world need not envy us," Yeselin said. "They need only fear us."

"Comrade Yeselin, there is another reason for adopting Comrade Korolev's plan to launch an earth-circling satellite," Valentina suggested.

"And what would that be?"

"Something very important to all of us who work here. Let me try to explain." She paused a moment, collecting her thoughts. "You see, all of us are very aware of the potential for death and destruction should one of these rockets be launched in anger against America. Our technology, and the technology of the Americans, has reached the point to where, with the mere press of a button, millions of people could be incinerated."

"Better that we kill millions of them than they kill millions of us," Yeselin replied.

"Perhaps. But would it not be better if neither Soviet nor American citizens were killed by the rockets our two countries are building?"

"You talk of utopia. We live in the real world," Yeselin scoffed.

"I don't think it's utopian talk not to want to kill millions of other human beings. The thought of our being an instrument in such a genocide is so horrible that we all have nightmares. I know this is true because I treat men and women who come to the clinic for some potion that will make the nightmares go away."

"Who are these cowards?"

"I am one," Yuri said.

"And I," Korolev added.

"And I," declared another voice.

"And I," said still another, until an entire concert of voices had spoken up.

"The point is," Valentina continued before Yeselin could react to the sudden and unexpected outpouring of admission to her comment, "there is nothing *I* can give them—no potion to still the bad dreams. But there is something *we* could do." She pointed out the window of the community dining room, in the direction of the launching gantry. "If those of us who work here could believe that part of our efforts was being directed not only toward machines that could kill so massively but also toward machines that would represent a victory for Soviet technology and a triumph of the human spirit to be shared by all mankind, then I believe the nightmares would go away."

Valentina's statement was followed by thunderous applause.

"Comrade Yeselin," Korolev said then, "if we do not build the satellite, you may rest assured that the Americans will. And if the Americans build it, they will get the glory and the prestige. And when that time comes, everyone of us here at Tyuratam-Baykonur will write a letter to the Secretariat in which we will explain that the prestige of such an accomplishment could have belonged to the USSR, had you not refused to carry our recommendations on for further consideration."

The others agreed with Korolev's threat.

Yeselin eyed his workers, contemplating the minirevolution taking place in his command. The last thing he wanted was trouble; he had risen to his position because he had managed to avoid trouble. But avoiding trouble meant eschewing initiative, and the truth was, he was now at a point where he could go no higher unless he managed to show some initiative.

The risk would be great—initiative that resulted in negative results was dealt with instantly and harshly. On the other hand, the rewards were equally great if the initiative showed positive results. If, as Korolev claimed, such an endeavor would elevate the prestige of Soviet technology around the world, then he, Yeselin, stood to reap most of the reward. He smiled and held out his hands to quiet the crowd of scientists and technocrats.

"Very well. I will carry your request forward. And," he added portentously, "I will give it my personal endorsement."

JANUARY 1956, MONTGOMERY, ALABAMA

At precisely seven o'clock P.M., Claudia Baker walked to the front of the meeting room of the Dexter Avenue Church and picked up the gavel. She rapped it on the table a few times, trying to still the laughter and the talking. Approximately one hundred young men and women were seated in the room, all between the ages of eighteen and twenty-four. The faces were overwhelmingly black, though there were a couple of conspicuously white faces in the audience.

"May I have your attention please?" Claudia said. "May I have your attention?"

When her polite efforts produced no results, Deon Booker shouted, *"Shut up!"*

The unexpected harshness of his shout brought about an immediate, tense silence. Then someone laughed, and the tension was broken.

"Thank you for your loud, but polite, call to order," Claudia said, and again everyone laughed. "We are here today," she continued, "to organize the Montgomery Students' Coalition, a car pool to carry our people to and from work during the bus boycott. Now, first of all, how many of you have cars?"

Three fourths of the hands in the room went up, including the hands of the three white students, two males and one female.

"We don't need any white folks' cars," someone growled.

"Yeah!" another said.

"Yes, we do!" someone else shouted, and the meeting broke into arguing factions. Claudia pounded on the table several times before she was able to restore order.

"Our white friends asked to attend this meeting," she said, "because they don't like what's going on, and they want to work with us to bring about a change."

"Yeah? Well, we don't need them."

"Yes, we do," Claudia insisted. "Think about it. We will never improve our lot until some of these Jim Crow laws are changed, and there aren't enough of us to change them. We need support from the white community."

"Yeah, well, this is *our* movement! We don't need any whitey comin' along to tell us what to do!"

One of the white youths raised his hand, and Claudia acknowledged him. Hesitantly, he stood up and looked around at the group.

"My name is Jimmy Wales," he said. "I don't want to suggest anything or participate in any decision-making process. Neither do my two friends here—nor do any of the other white people who aren't here today but who support your cause. All I want to do is help you in whatever way I can. If it helps to offer my car to carry riders, I'll do that. If it helps to speak out on behalf of your cause to other whites, I'll do that. And if you feel that it would help more by staying out of the picture entirely, offering you only my prayerful support . . . then I'll do that. I am not your enemy." He pointed to the other white youths. "He is not your enemy, nor is she."

Someone started clapping at the back of the room, and everyone turned to see who it was. Dr. Martin Luther King was standing there.

"It's Dr. King!" a young woman said, and a ripple of excitement passed through the room.

He walked through the crowd to the front of the room, then looked at Claudia. "With your permission, Madam Chairman, I would like to say a few words to your group."

"Yes, Dr. King, of course," Claudia said.

King turned to the group. "Although I am the pastor of this church, this is your organization, and I will stay out of it so that you may run it any way you please. I will say only that I, as well as the Dexter Avenue Church and the Negro community of Montgomery, am grateful for your concern and your help. I would, however, like to address the issue that was just being discussed as to whether or not we want or need the assistance of our white brothers and sisters."

He focused on their individual faces, one by one in turn as he continued.

"What you have to keep in mind here is that our struggle is not a struggle of Negro against white. This is a struggle of righteousness against evil. The racial policies that discriminate against our people are mean-spirited and evil.

"Evil does not like to come out into the sunlight . . . evil does not like to fight fair . . . evil does not like to see the powers of good and the powers of righteousnes united for one common purpose. No, my friends, evil enjoys seeing good-hearted men and women of color and good-hearted men and women of the white race suspicious and frightened and separated from each other, for evil understands that it is easier to break one twig than it is to break a bundle.

"And so, if you would serve the forces of evil, then you will turn your back on our white brothers and sisters when they say they want to join us. If you would serve the forces of evil, you'll be a tiny drop of water on a hot skillet to cook away in an instant. If, on the other hand, you would serve the force of righteousness, you will join that one tiny drop of water with hundreds and thousands of other drops of water, black and white, old and young, man and woman, boy and girl, until you become a mighty, gushing torrent, not to be cooked away in an instant, but enough to put out the fires of hatred forever."

As one, everyone in the room stood and broke into applause and cheering.

"And now, my friends, if you will excuse me," King

said. "I must return to my study and give time to the preparation of my sermon this Sunday." He smiled. "Many of you will, no doubt, be bringing people to church in your car pool this Sunday. What better way to wait to take them home than to stay for the services?"

"Dr. King, you'll do anything to get folks to come to church, won't you?" someone shouted.

King left amidst laughter, more cheering, and calls of good-bye. Then Claudia gaveled the meeting back to order.

"Let's now have a vote on whether we will accept the assistance of our white brothers and sisters," she suggested.

"I move that we accept the assistance of our white brothers and sisters," someone called.

"Second the motion."

"Madam Chairman?" Deon said.

"The chair recognizes Deon Booker."

"I would like to amend the proposal."

"In what way?"

"I would like to the proposal to say, 'Whereas the assistance of our white brothers and sisters is gratefully accepted, all leadership positions of the Montgomery Students' Coalition are, and shall continue to be, the exclusive franchise of the Negro.'"

"I would like to second that motion," Jimmy Wales said quickly.

"All right. All in favor of the proposal as amended, signify by saying aye."

"*Aye!*" came the overwhelming response.

"The ayes have it; the motion is carried. Now, let's get down to the business at hand: that of establishing passenger pickup routes and schedules and allocating driver assignments."

"What about money?" someone asked.

"This isn't a job, Leroy. This is volunteer work," somone said.

"I'm volunteering me, and I'm volunteering my car," Leroy replied. "But I'm not volunteering my gas. If we're going to be driving around all day long, then we ought to get paid for the gasoline. I mean, the people we're hauling would be paying to ride on the bus, wouldn't they?"

"Leroy's got a point there."

"We can't take money directly," Deon said. "If we do, we can be arrested for running a taxi service without a license."

"Maybe the riders could pay the money into a central car pool fund, and we could get gasoline expenses from that fund," someone suggested.

"That's a good idea," Deon replied. "We can look into that."

Many other suggestions and ideas, some valid, some not, had to be addressed, and the meeting lasted for another couple of hours. Finally, at around ten o'clock, the meeting broke up, and all the students left carrying copies of their schedules. Deon watched them leave, then came back into the room, where Claudia was emptying ashtrays, picking up paper coffee cups, and straightening chairs.

"I'll give you a hand," he said.

"Thank you. You know, that was really exciting having Dr. King come talk to us, wasn't it?"

"Oh, it was all right," Deon replied, folding up the chairs and carrying them to the closet.

Claudia looked at him in surprise. "What do you mean, 'all right'?"

"I mean it was all right."

"Don't you like Dr. King?"

Deon was silent, making the snapping noise as he folded the wooden chairs seem even louder.

"Deon?"

He sighed. "He reminds me of my grandfather."

"He does? Well, that's wonderful! Your grandfather was a very great man. Everyone has heard of Loomis Booker."

"Oh, yes, everyone has heard of him," Deon agreed. "George Washington Carver, Booker T. Washington, and Loomis Booker. Those are the three names mentioned in all the schoolbooks for all the white children. Uncle Toms, all three of them."

"Deon!" Claudia gasped. "How can you say that about your own grandfather? I thought you loved him."

"I did love him," Deon said. "But I loved him as my grandfather, not as the great savior of the Negro race—colored race, he called us."

"Well, everyone used the word 'colored' then. That doesn't mean anything. Even the NAACP means National Association for the Advancement of Colored People."

"When I was a boy, I thought my grandfather was a great man," Deon admitted. "I saw the way the other Negroes treated him, approaching him with their hat in hand, almost as if they were frightened of him. . . . 'Yes, Professor Booker.' 'No, Professor Booker.' Most of the time they came to see him when they were having some problems with the white establishment, and they wanted my grandfather to intercede for them."

"And did he?"

"Oh, yes. My grandfather would put on his jacket and his hat and go down to the courthouse or the city hall or the hospital or the municipal utilities office—wherever he was needed—and he would negotiate with some white son of a bitch who didn't have one fourth of my grandfather's education or one eighth of his intelligence . . . and he would treat them like they were rulers of the roost."

"Did he accomplish what he wanted?" Claudia asked.

"Most of the time, yes. You see, everyone knew that my grandfather was welcome in the governor's office, in the office of the richest man in the state, or even in the President's office, so they wanted to stay on his good side."

"Then I don't understand," Claudia said. "Why do you call him an Uncle Tom?"

"He was an Uncle Tom because he had the power, and he was afraid to use it."

"But you just said that he *did* use it."

"No. He pleaded, he bargained, he cajoled. He never once *demanded*. King is like that. The way he speaks, the way he can stir up emotion in people . . . He's got the power, but does he demand? No, he doesn't demand. He says, 'Don't do anything to make the white man mad. Don't do anything violent. Just don't ride the buses . . . be very passive . . . if you are struck, turn the other cheek.'"

"And you don't go along with that?"

"I think we should put our requests for fair treatment in the form of demands."

"Deon, you aren't talking about a revolution, are you?" Claudia asked. "Because that would be very stupid. In the first place, there would be a lot of folks killed. And in the second place, we would lose. There are just too many of them and too few of us."

"No, I'm not talking about a revolution—at least, not in the sense of taking up arms and going to war. But there are things we could do that would make our demands more forceful. The Supreme Court has ruled that school desegregation is unconstitutional, but do you see any Negroes going to Auburn or the University of Alabama? For that matter, do you see any in Sidney Lanier High School right here in Montgomery? The answer is no. What we should do is go down to that high school, about ten thousand strong, and so disrupt the classes that if no Negroes can learn there, then neither should any white kids. We—"

A blinding white light suddenly filled the room. Shards of glass flew in from the window, concurrent with a thunderous explosion. The ceiling caved in, and the floor rippled and rolled like a wave on the ocean, then splintered apart. A thick cloud of dust filled the air, and the smell of cordite burned the nostrils. Then all the lights went out and it was dark, except for a wavering orange glow from a fire somewhere, started by the explosion.

"*Claudia! Claudia!*" Deon shouted.

"I'm over here," Claudia replied.

"Are you all right?"

"I . . . I think so," she answered. Her voice was strained. "I've been cut. Oh, Deon, I'm bleeding. I'm bleeding bad."

Deon pulled himself out from beneath a pile of broken timbers and fallen ceiling tiles. His ears were ringing, and his nose and throat were burning, but he was pretty sure he wasn't hurt.

"Claudia, where are you?" he yelled.

There was no answer.

"Claudia!" he screamed. He started throwing things aside, working his way through the wreckage. He saw a smoke-filled flashlight beam cutting through the darkness.

"Is anyone in here?" a voice called.

"Yes!" Deon shouted. "Me and Claudia! She's hurt! We've got to find her!"

Another flashlight beam joined the first, then a third and then a fourth. They swung back and forth through the smoke-filled room.

"Get some water on that fire over there," someone ordered.

"Don't worry 'bout the fire; it ain't very big. We got to find Claudia," another said.

"It may not be very big, but we don't want it to get any bigger."

"Here she is!" someone shouted.

"How is she?" Deon asked anxiously, going toward the voice. Behind him, he could hear water being poured on the small fire from buckets that were being passed from parishioner to parishioner.

"Looks like she'll be all right. She's cut up pretty bad and she's bleedin' some, but she'll be all right."

Deon reached her and knelt beside her. She was illuminated by the flashlights, and he put his hand to her face. She winced in pain. Her cheeks felt rough, like sandpaper, and he realized that there were tiny pieces of glass imbedded in the skin.

"Are you all right, baby?" he asked.

"I'm fine, Deon. How are you?"

"Fine. I'm not even hurt." Deon looked up at the others. "What was it?" he asked. "What the hell happened?"

"It was a bomb," someone said.

"A bomb? You mean someone's bombing Montgomery? They're dropping bombs on us from planes?" That was the only thing Deon could think of.

"No. A homemade bomb. Leroy saw it."

Deon glared at the speaker, then said, "Where is Leroy? Leroy, you in here?"

"Yeah, I'm here," Leroy answered.

"Tell me what you saw," Deon demanded.

"There was a car drove up," Leroy explained. "It stopped just outside the church. At first I thought it was some folks comin' to the meetin' late, so I started over to tell 'em it was all over. Then I saw that it was four white men. One of 'em stuck his arms out the window holdin' somethin' in his right hand. Then he lit it with a cigarette lighter and threw it toward the church—just right outside here, where we'd been meetin'. I seen sparks comin' from it, and I thought it must've been a whoppin' big firecracker. Then it went off with an awful explosion. And the car drove off with the tires screamin'."

"Those motherfuckers," Deon swore.

"Son, you're in a church," someone reminded him.

"I don't care if I'm standing outside St. Peter's pearly gates. If I ever find out who the motherfuckers are who did this, I'm goin' to rip them a new asshole!"

"Deon?" Claudia asked suddenly.

Deon looked down at her. "Yes, baby?"

"Why am I still lying here? Help me up." She started to rise, but one of the rescuers put his hand on her shoulder to hold her down.

"No, no," he said. "You'd better stay right where you are, Claudia. We've called an ambulance for you."

"An ambulance? I'm not hurt that bad. I just got a few cuts and scratches, that's all."

"Maybe so, but it'd still be better if you let the doctors look at you."

Deon could hear the sound of approaching sirens; whether it was a fire truck, an ambulance, or the police, he didn't know. He could also hear angry and confused shouts from the growing crowd.

The first emergency vehicle to arrive was the fire

truck. Three raincoat-clad, helmeted firemen came rushing in, carrying axes and a fire hose.

"Is there anyone hurt?" the fire chief asked.

"A girl over here."

"Is she trapped under anything?"

"No, but she's cut up pretty bad."

"Anyone else injured?"

"Not that we know of."

"You two men, start searching the premises. Make certain there's no one else in here," the fire chief ordered. He knelt beside Claudia. "How are you feeling, miss?"

"Woozy," Claudia answered.

"The ambulance is on the way."

Almost on top of the fireman's words was another siren, then another, and another still, as the ambulance and two police cars arrived at virtually the same time.

The ambulance attendants came into the wreckage carrying a stretcher, and they carefully picked Claudia up, put her on the stretcher, then carried her outside.

"I'm coming with her," Deon said.

"Not in the ambulance you ain't," the driver said.

"Fine, but I'm still coming down to the hospital."

"Suit yourself."

Deon walked outside with them, holding Claudia's hand until they loaded her into the back of the Cadillac ambulance.

"How about that?" Claudia asked with a small laugh. "I'm getting a ride in a Cadillac."

The faces of the crowd, the wall of the bombed church, and the adjacent shrubbery were painted in alternating washes of red and white as the emergency lights on the fire truck, ambulance, and police cars flashed. The rear door of the ambulance was shut, the driver hurried to the front door and climbed in, and then the siren started, a low growl that quickly accelerated to a high-pitched wail. The crowd parted to let the ambulance through.

Deon sprinted toward his car.

"Hold it!" one of the police officers shouted. "Where do you think you're goin', boy?"

"To the hospital!" Deon shouted.

"You're not goin' nowhere, boy," the policeman said. He was a sergeant and evidently in charge of the officers who had responded to the call. "At least, not until I say you can. You are a suspect in a felony."

"I'm a *what*?"

"There's been a bombin' here, and you are our prime suspect."

"You're crazy! You think *I* did this?"

"He didn't do it!" Leroy shouted.

"No, no!" others in the crowd cried. "He didn't do it."

"How do you know he didn't do it?"

"Because I seen who it was," Leroy said.

"Who was it?"

"It was four white men."

"Four white men? That's all you can tell me? It was four white men?"

"Yes. They stopped their car right over there," Leroy said, pointing to the spot. "Then one of them leaned out the window and threw the bomb. After that they drove away."

"You got any evidence to back up your story?"

"What the hell kind of evidence do you want?" Deon asked angrily. He pointed to the wrecked church. "You got a building that was bombed. Isn't that evidence enough?"

The police sergeant pointed at Deon with his night stick. "Boy, you'd better watch that mouth of yours," he said. "I'm talkin' to this boy right here, not to you."

Deon tensed, but two or three of the Negro men reached out to restrain him—not roughly, but firmly enough to make the point.

"Easy, Deon," one of them said quietly.

"Now, you, boy," the police sergeant said to Leroy, "can you describe these men you said you saw?"

"They were white."

"Beyond that, I mean. Were they old, young, tall, short, skinny, fat?"

"I don't know. The one who threw the bomb was average."

"An average white man," the police sergeant said. He sighed.

"Yes."

"Now, that don't give me a hell of a lot to go on, does it?" the sergeant said. "All right, we're goin' to have to take both of you down to the police station."

"What do you mean, you're going to take us down to the station? Are you arresting us?" Deon asked.

"No, you're not a suspect anymore. But you are a material witness. Both of you are. So we have to take you into custody. Put the cuffs on 'em," he ordered.

"No! No!" the crowd shouted.

"Wait a minute!" Deon protested. "If we're just witnesses, why are you cuffing us?"

"It's just routine," the police sergeant said. "It don't mean nothin'."

It wasn't until one of the other policemen slipped the handcuffs on that Deon realized he had broken a wrist from the blast. He winced in pain as the cuffs were snapped closed.

"You ain't takin' them two nowhere!" a man shouted. "Not without a fight you ain't!"

"Don't you people start causin' no trouble here," the police sergeant warned. "I told you, they aren't under arrest." At that moment several more sirens could be heard, and the sergeant smiled broadly. "You hear them sirens? We've got backup on the way here. If you start somethin', there's goin' to be some serious trouble."

"Here's Dr. King!" someone shouted.

"Here's the preacher."

"He'll take care of things."

King had finished working on his sermon and gone home before the meeting of the Montgomery Students' Coalition had concluded. But he had been called about the bombing of his church and hurried back. It was evident as soon as he got out of his car how angry the crowd was, and he raised his hands to pacify them.

"Please, my friends, don't panic," he said, making a great effort to keep his voice calm. "Everything is going to be all right."

"You better believe everything's going to be all right, soon as I get my Smith & Wesson and put a bullet in that white man's ass," someone shouted.

"No, don't do that. Don't do anything to provoke the policemen. Don't get any weapons. If you have any weapons on your person now, take them home. He who lives by the sword will perish by the sword. Remember, that is what Jesus said. We aren't advocating violence. We want to love our enemies. I want you to love our enemies. Be good to them. This is what we must live by. We must meet violence with peace, hate with love, bigotry with understanding."

"Listen to what the man's sayin'," the police sergeant said as nearly a dozen more armed policemen hurried up to join their fellow officers. "He's the only one out here makin' any sense."

"I want you people to remember that I did not start the bus boycott," King told the crowd. "I was asked by you to serve as your spokesman, and I was elected president of the protest committee. I will do this willingly, and with pride, as long as I can do it with dignity, honor, and love. But I want it to be known throughout the length and breadth of this land that if I am stopped, our work will not stop. For what we are doing is right. What we are doing is just. And God is with us."

"Amen," a dozen or more voices said.

The police sergeant tried to speak then, but he was booed, and when he tried to shout the crowd down, they booed more vociferously.

King raised his arms to quiet his people.

"Remember," he said calmly, "we will meet hate with love. Give the policeman a chance to speak."

The police sergeant waited a moment, then said, "I want you to know that none of us here condones this bombin'. And we will do our best to find out who it was. Now, go home and go to bed. Stay calm, stay off the streets, and let us do our job."

"And now, Sergeant, if you would do something for us?" King asked.

"What is it?"

"These two young men," King said, pointing to Deon and Leroy. "By your own admission, they are not under arrest. If all you want is their testimony, I'm certain they would agree to show up and give a sworn statement. Tomorrow."

"I don't know . . ." the police sergeant said, scratching his neck. He looked at Deon and Leroy. "What are your names?"

"I'm Leroy Cain."

"Deon Booker."

"Booker? Booker. Where've I heard that name? You been in trouble with the law before?"

"He's Artemus Booker's brother," someone said.

"The basketball player? Oh, yeah, I heard of him. I don't care much for basketball. Football's my game."

"Maybe you've heard of this young man's grandfather," King suggested. "Loomis Booker?"

"Loomis Booker, yeah, sure, I heard of him," the sergeant said, grinning. "Everyone's heard of him. He had somethin' to do with the peanut, didn't he?"

"Yeah, the peanut," Deon mumbled.

The sergeant sighed. "All right." He nodded to one of the other officers to release the handcuffs. "All right, I'll let these two boys go. But I'm goin' to need them downtown tomorrow to sign a statement 'bout what they seen here tonight."

By the time Deon reached the hospital where Claudia had been taken, he could barely move his left wrist. He was holding it in his right hand when he went into the "Colored Emergency Ward." There was no one around.

"Hello?" Deon called. "Anyone here?"

No answer.

Deon opened a door that led down a long corridor. The corridor, too, was deserted. He started down it and had gone about thirty feet when a white nurse coming from a side corridor confronted him.

"What are you doing back here, boy?" she demanded.

"I'm looking for a young woman who was brought in here a little while ago," Deon said.

"We've had five colored women brought in," the nurse replied. "That's why I'm over here on the colored side."

"Yes, ma'am. The person I'm looking for is named Claudia Baker. She's about nineteen, pretty—she was in a church that was bombed tonight."

"Oh, yes, I know the one. She's fine."

"Can I see her?"

"I suppose so. Go through this door, third room on the right. There's a colored doctor in with her now. If he says it's all right, you can see her."

"Thanks," Deon said.

"Listen . . ." the nurse called out to him. Deon looked back at her. "I want you to know that most of us don't go along with anything like bombing a church," she said in a sympathetic voice. "It's only the lowest kind of a person who would do something like that."

Deon nodded. "Yes, ma'am, you're right."

He pushed through the door, then followed the nurse's directions to Claudia's room. Looking in, he saw her on a paper-covered table, lying on her stomach. She was nude, and a doctor and a nurse, both black, were hovering over her. The doctor was using a pair of tweezers to pluck shards of glass from Claudia's back while the nurse was going along behind him, applying antiseptic to the wounds and bandaging those that required it.

"Excuse me," Deon said.

The doctor turned in surprise.

"You want to get out of here and leave this girl some modesty?" he snapped.

"It's all right, Doctor," Claudia said. "I'd like him to stay, if you don't mind."

The doctor sighed, then shrugged. "All right. I don't mind if she doesn't."

"Thanks," Deon said. He stepped into the room. "How are you feeling?" he asked Claudia.

Claudia gave a small laugh. "You ever see those red

pincushions that Mrs. Jackson has down at the shop?
That's how I feel."

"Were you there, too?" the doctor asked Deon.

"Yeah, I was in the room with her."

The doctor looked up. "You're lucky you weren't cut
up like she was. Say, what's wrong with your arm?"

"I'm not sure," Deon said, glancing at the arm he
was supporting gingerly. "I think I may have broken my
wrist."

"I'd better have a look at it."

"No, no, take care of Claudia."

"I'm about done with her," the doctor said. He gave
the tweezers to the nurse. "She can finish up. Come on,
let's get it X-rayed."

The doctor came back, holding up a large negative
plate. "It's broken, all right," he said. "Let me set it and
get a splint on it." He pulled out a brown envelope for the
X-ray picture, then looked at Deon. "What's your name?"

"Deon Booker."

"Booker? You know, there was a great colored doctor
by the name of Booker."

"Andrew Booker," Deon said.

The doctor smiled. "That's the one. I'm surprised
you've heard of him, but I'm pleased, too. I think more of
our young people should hear about colored men who've
accomplished something more than winning boxing
matches or hitting a baseball. How did you happen to
hear about Andrew Booker? His name isn't in any of the
school textbooks, I know."

"He was my father," Deon said matter-of-factly.

The doctor's eyes widened in surprise. "He was?
Then . . . Loomis Booker is your grandfather?"

"Yes. Aren't you going to mention my brother,
Artemus?"

"My God, I'm in the presence of royalty!"

Deon chuckled. "No, you aren't. Every family has to
have a black sheep, and I'm the black sheep in my family."

"Oh, I wouldn't say that. I am curious, though. What are you doing in Montgomery, Alabama, of all places?"

"I'm attending school at Alabama State, boycotting buses, dodging bombs, and trying to get into the pants of the girl you have stretched out on the table in there." Deon laughed. "Seeing her naked a few moments ago was the closest I've come."

CHAPTER
TWELVE

Bobby Parker, now a nineteen-year-old private first class in the Army, parked his black '49 Chevy under the trees at the heliport—actually a twenty-acre field, mostly concrete, known as "Tac Able." His blocked fatigue hat had a bright orange band around the crown, signifying his status as a maintenance instructor in the U.S. Army Aviation School.

Being a PFC in the Army wasn't exactly where Bobby had planned to be at this point in his life. While still a senior in high school, he had learned that the newly created United States Air Force Academy was giving exams for appointments. The idea of being a member of the academy's first graduating class appealed to him, so he took the exam. He passed the first exam, which was given at the U.S. Post Office in Sikeston, Missouri, then advanced to the final selection phase, which was conducted at Scott Air Force Base in Illinois.

He stayed at Scott for one week, taking a battery of academic, psychological, and physical exams. Finally he was sent back home and told to wait for further notification. One month later he was told that he had been selected as a first alternate from the state of Missouri. A short time after that he received another letter thanking him for his participation in the Air Force Academy selection process. He was also told that since all the principals had elected to accept their appointments, his appointment as alternate was rescinded. That meant he was free to pursue his education at the school of his choice.

Then there was the second obstacle in Bobby's post-school plans. He had developed a real love for writing while in high school, so he decided that if he couldn't attend the Air Force Academy, he'd study journalism at Jefferson University. Bobby's father, however, was convinced that his son's future lay in engineering, and he had insisted that Bobby attend the Missouri School of Mines and Metallurgy in Rolla.

"But I don't like math, and I'm not interested in physics or chemistry," Bobby had declared. "I enjoy English, history, and social studies. I made very good grades in those classes, whereas I barely passed math and science. In fact, if I'd been stronger in those subjects, I might have made principal instead of alternate to the Air Force Academy."

"Well, now, that's just my point," Richard Parker had said. "You need more study in math and science. If I'm going to pay for it, you're going to school at Rolla."

Bobby lasted one semester at Rolla. At the semester break he went down to the post office, stepped into the room shared by the Army, Navy, Air Force, and Marine recruiters, then held out his arms.

"Whoever wants me can have me."

"Gotcha," the Army sergeant had replied, reaching across his desk to grab Bobby by the wrist.

After basic training Bob, as he now preferred to be called, was posted to Fort Rucker, Alabama, where he attended the Single-Rotor Helicopter Maintenance Course, MOS 672, Class 56-12. Graduating in the top five

percent of his class earned him a position on the Aviation
School faculty, so while most of the other graduates of his
class were sent on assignments throughout the world, Bob
was posted to permanent duty at Fort Rucker. It was
there that he learned he was eligible to apply for admission to the United States Military Academy at West Point
as a member of the active duty armed forces.

"You won't even have to take tests again," the personnel officer had told him. "The tests you took to enter
the Air Force Academy are still valid, and because you can
be appointed either from your home state's quota or the
quota allocated to the active duty armed forces, you'll
double your chances of selection."

Bob had filled out the application forms, then gone
out and bought a set of gold bars. Someday, he often told
himself, he would put them on.

Until then, he'd continue to serve as an instructor in
the Army Aviation School. The class he'd be teaching that
afternoon was 1811-4, Procedures of Connecting and Dis-
connecting External Loads. In this case, external loads
meant those carried by sling beneath the helicopter, and
the class would be taught in the form of a practical exercise. This entailed having a helicopter approach the load
—for purposes of the exercise, an old, nonfunctioning
jeep—then lower its hook to where a student on the
ground, working in conjuction with a student in the
"box," or cargo compartment of the aircraft, would make
the connection. The helicopter would take off, make a
pass around the field, come back, and set the jeep down
gently.

This was generally a class that everyone, instructor
and students, enjoyed because it got them out of the classroom and gave them the opportunity to fly.

The students weren't there yet, but Bob's assistant
instructor was, and he was standing near the empty student bleachers listening to the radio. The song was Elvis
Presley's "Don't Be Cruel," and the AI, PFC Charles
Briskie, was singing along, using a spanner wrench as a
microphone and throwing in all of Presley's moves.

"Charley, did you lay on the helicopter?" Bob asked.

". . . to a love that's true," Charley sang, pointing to the east.

Bob saw an H-34 approaching. "Does the pilot know we need him for the rest of the afternoon?"

". . . want no other love . . ." Charley sang, nodding his head affirmatively.

"And you have the jeep ready?"

" . . . the jeep is re-a-dy." Charley sang the words to the tune of the song on the radio.

"Here comes the bus," Bob said. "Turn off the radio."

Reluctantly, Charley turned it off. "You don't like Presley, do you?"

"He's all right. I like Campbell better."

"Buck Campbell? He's a hillbilly."

"Yeah, he does hillbilly every now and then. But so does Presley. Anyhow, Buck Campbell has some real good stuff out."

"You just like him 'cause you met him."

"Well, I didn't actually meet him. But I did see him do a show in my hometown once, before he got famous."

"He's real famous now," Charley said. "Shit, he's so famous he's dickin' Marcella Mills. Course, ol' Buck's just like Elvis. He could dick anyone he wants. But if he can have Marcella Mills, why would he want anyone else?"

Bob laughed. "Yeah, I hear you."

The bus ground to a halt outside, and the students started filing off.

"Here comes the class," Charley said. "You figured out yet how we're goin' to do this?"

"Four in the aircraft, four on the ground, and the rest waiting in the bleachers," Bob replied.

The class went on for the rest of the afternoon, with Bob instructing the students in the helicopter and Charley staying with the ones on the ground. It was a pleasant day, with still, cool air so that the short flights, even though they were up and down, were not all that uncomfortable. Sometimes if it was really hot, the flights could

be brutal, and the instructors had to switch people around
to keep them from getting airsick.

The next four students hopped excitedly into the box.
Bob sat three of them on the canvas bench seat across
from the door and put the other one on the seat next to
him.

"*Parker,*" the pilot's voice said in Bob's headset. The
pilot was Mister Easterman, a warrant officer who had
himself just recently graduated from the Warrant Officer
Candidate's Course.

"Yes, sir?"

"*How many more are there?*"

"Eight more after this group."

"*That's what, three more times, counting this?*"

"Yes, sir. Do we have enough fuel?"

"*We'll be all right if we don't take too long getting
hooked up. You and Briskie sort of take charge of things,
okay?*"

"Yes, sir, I'll tell Charley."

Bob passed the pilot's instructions on to Charley to
be certain that the initial connection to the jeep was made
very quickly. As soon as the connection was made, Charley gave Bob the thumbs-up signal.

"Go, sir; we've got a good hook," Bob told the pilot,
and the helicopter took off, dangling the jeep beneath it.

As they climbed out of Tac Able, Bob looked out
through the open door on the side of the helicopter at the
blocks of long, two-story, green-roofed wooden barracks
that housed his company. They were called "temporary
barracks," even though they'd been built in World War II
and were still in service. As the helicopter rose higher,
Bob could see all the way across the post to the headquarters building, where the general's white helicopter sat in
front of the flagpole, awaiting his bidding. Beyond that
was the officers' club—off-limits to Bob now but in his
future if his application to West Point was accepted.

Easterman banked the helicopter around, and they
started back across the wide open area that was Tac Able.

"Evans," Bob said to one of the students, shouting to

be heard above the helicopter's noise, "get in position. When I tell you to cut the load, you cut it."

"Okay."

"Do you know what to do?"

"Yeah, when you say cut the load, I just move this," the student said, putting his hand on the quick load release mechanism.

"No, don't touch it!" Bob screamed, but it was too late. Evans had already moved the lever, and the jeep was cut loose, starting a thousand-foot plummet.

"What the hell happened?" Easterman shouted in Bob's headset when the helicopter suddenly grew lighter.

"Jesus, Mr. Easterman, we dropped our load!" Bob replied.

"Oh, shit!"

Easterman put the helicopter into an immediate and stomach-churning autorotation.

Bob leaned over to look out through the door and saw the jeep getting smaller and smaller as it hurtled downward. Charley and the students on the ground had evidently seen what had happened, because they were all running as fast as they could to get out of the way.

When the jeep hit, it flew apart, throwing wheels, body parts, and engine components in all directions. It was like watching a movie with the sound track out of sync, because it hit in absolute silence, though a second later Bob heard the crash, even from this distance and above the whine of the helicopter's transmission and the pop of rotor blades.

"Anybody hurt?" Easterman asked.

Bob didn't think so, but he wanted to be very sure, so he leaned out for a closer look.

"Goddammit! Is anybody hurt?" Easterman shouted desperately.

"No, sir!" Bob replied. "Nobody hurt, sir."

By now the helicopter had reached the bottom of its autorotative descent, and the nose pitched up sharply as Easterman flared out for the landing. They landed on the far side of the field, almost a mile from where the jeep had hit and even farther away from the bleachers where the other students had regrouped. Bob looked across the field and saw that in addition to his students, other people were gathering—other classes, other instructors, and a few passersby.

"*Parker?*" Easterman said.

"Yes, sir?"

"*Get the fuck out of my helicopter.*"

"Sir, we're way the hell away from our point. Can't you put us down over—"

"*GET THE FUCK OUT OF MY HELICOPTER!*"

"Yes, sir," Bob mumbled, motioning for the students to get out. As soon as they were clear, Easterman pulled pitch, and the H-34 took off, its rotor wash dusting them painfully with sand and loose gravel.

His head slumped, Bob started back for the bleachers. That day when he would put on his set of gold bars suddenly seemed a lot farther away.

PANAMA CITY, FLORIDA

Panama City was only ninety miles from Fort Rucker, close enough to make it a popular weekend destination for those on the base. Bob, Charley, Logan Pounders, and Tom MacMurtry had taken advantage of that fact for a weekend pass a few days after the disastrous helicopter class. They had gone down in Pounders's '51 Ford convertible and were driving along the beach road with the top down, whistling and yelling at all the girls in bathing suits walking by.

"Come on, girls, don't you want a ride?" Charley called. "There's plenty of room in here."

The girls laughed and flirted back, but none of them took the offer.

"I wonder why none of 'em wants a ride?" Tom asked.

"They probably have to wash their hair," Bob said wryly.

"What?"

"Nothing."

"Hey, guys, why don't we stop there and get something to eat?" Charley suggested, pointing to a restaurant across the street.

"You're always thinking of your stomach," Tom said.

"Not always. I think of my cock, too, but I can't do anything about that. I *can* eat."

"Yeah, well, you guys are crampin' my style," Logan insisted.

"What do you mean?"

"I mean, I've never had any trouble with the girls before. But you guys, you're scarin' 'em all away."

"Listen to the ladies' man."

"No, I'm serious. If I was by myself, I'd already be gettin' laid."

"Uh-huh. Well, we could always put you out of the car."

"Yeah, thanks. It's my fuckin' car, remember? 'Sides, how would I get back?"

"You're such a ladies' man, maybe you could talk one of 'em into taking you back to camp."

"Aw, hell, never mind. I'll tough it out. Who knows? Maybe I'll bring you guys luck."

They stopped at the Surf 'n' Turf. The parking lot was full of cars, and the restaurant, which featured hamburgers and beer, was full of young people, all half naked and tanned.

"God, look at us," Bob said when they had climbed out of the car. "We stand out like sore thumbs."

"Why? We aren't in uniform," Tom said.

"Are you kidding? We're all wearing khaki trousers, sports shirts, GI haircuts, and dog tags. We might as well be in uniform."

"Hut, two, three, four," one of the boys standing just outside the restaurant said under his breath as the four soldiers walked by. The others around him laughed.

"See what I mean?"

"I ought to go back and clean that son of a bitch's plow," Logan said, though he made no motion to do so.

"Not a good idea," Tom said. "There are about fifteen of them. There are only four of us."

"Three," Charley corrected. "I'm not getting into any fight any of you guys start."

"Me neither," Bob said. "I'm trying to get into West Point. All I need is to get picked up for some barroom brawl."

"This ain't a barroom, it's a restaurant. 'Sides, who said I was goin' to start a fight?" Logan growled. "I just said I should, that's all."

They slid into a booth, and when the waitress came over, they ordered hamburgers and two pitchers of beer.

"Damn, we're lucky. She didn't even card us," Bob said as the waitress walked away.

"Are you kidding? We're America's fighting men. She wouldn't card us."

"Hey, look at that, over there," Bob said, nodding toward a booth where four girls were seated. "Four of them and four of us. What do you say?"

"I say you'd better let me handle it," Logan said.

"How're you gonna do it?" Tom asked.

"They're sittin' next to the pinball machine. I'll go start a game. When I get that old board lit up and it starts ringin', they'll look up. That's when I'll bring 'em all over here."

"That's stupid. Why don't we just all go over there and introduce ourselves?" Tom suggested.

"'Cause first we got to get 'em interested in us," Logan said.

"All right, lover boy," Tom agreed. "You do it. But don't screw up."

"Hey, don't worry, I got you covered."

Logan walked over to the pinball machine and made a big deal out of examining it very closely. He walked around and looked underneath it from one side; then he walked around to the other side to look underneath. He squatted down and eyed it across the top, holding his hand flat over it as if checking to see how level it was. Then he came to the front and tested the spring strength of the plunger, pulling it out and letting it snap back several times. He operated the flippers, one at a time, then together. He put his hand on each side of the machine and shook it, gently at first, then harder.

"Hey, look!" Charley said. "The girls are watching him."

"Hell, everyone in the place is watching him," Tom said. "He's making a damn fool of himself, is what he's doing."

"Have you ever seen him play, though? He's pretty damn good," Charley said.

"Maybe so," Bob said. "But playing pinball isn't exactly like playing football or anything. I mean, I can see all the girls flocking around a quarterback. I can't see 'em climbing over each other to reach a pinball champion."

"Maybe in hick towns like Sikeston it's that way," Charley said. "But in the big cities, girls get turned on by men who can play the machines."

"The machines? That's what you call them in the big city of Pine Bluff?" Tom teased.

"Yeah, just machines, not pinball machines."

"We'll have to remember that, Bob, if we ever want to make time with any girls in the big city of . . . *Pine Bluff.*"

When Logan was finished checking out the machine, he put his hands in his pockets, first one, then the other, and came up empty both times. Then, with a sigh of disgust, he came back over to the booth.

"Somebody give me a nickel," he said.

Eagerly, Charley gave him a nickel. "Go get 'em, Logan. I already got mine picked out."

Logan returned to the pinball machine to play for glory and sex. He put the nickel in, and the machine lit up. He pumped up the first ball, hit it, then tried to shake it. The machine read TILT.

"*Tilt?*" Logan said loud that everyone in the restaurant looked over at him. He hit the side of the machine hard. "Why, you cheatin' son of a bitch!"

"Hey!" one of the men behind the counter shouted. "You hit that machine again, bud, and I'll have the cops out here."

"It tilted," Logan answered.

"Of course it tilted, the way you were treating it. If you don't know how to play, don't start on this one. This one isn't for amateurs."

The four girls laughed, and Logan, his face flaming red with embarrassment, slunk back to the booth just as the hamburgers and beer arrived.

"They weren't so much anyway," he told the others. "When you got a real close look at 'em, I mean. They were too young. Jailbait, all of 'em."

"Well, I don't know about you fellas, but if I don't get some tail while we're down here, I'm going to be cranky and out of sorts for the whole weekend," Charley said.

"Me, too," Tom added. "I haven't had any since I came to Fort Rucker. I haven't been without that long since I was twelve years old."

"Since I was nine," Logan said.

"Yeah, it's been a long dry spell for me, too," Bob put in. He didn't tell them exactly how long his dry spell had been. He was eighteen, and he was a virgin.

"If worse comes to worst, I know what we could do," Logan said. "I mean, it's not somethin' I'd ordinarily do if I was by myself, but with you guys along to cramp my style, it might be the only way we're goin' to get any."

"What are you talking about?" Tom asked.

"We could get us a whore."

"A whore? Are you serious?"

"Yeah. I mean, I don't normally pay for it, you understand. But I know how bad you guys are wantin' to get laid."

"I don't normally pay for it either," Charley said.

"I *never* had to pay for it," Tom said. "What about you, Bob? You ever had to pay for it?"

"No," Bob answered truthfully. "I never have."

"Ah, what the hell," Tom muttered. "I do want to get laid. Let's do it."

With Tom breaking the ice, the others went along as well.

"How do we do it?" Bob asked.

Logan laughed. "What do you mean, how do we do it? Don't you know how to do it? You just . . ." He made a circle with the thumb and forefinger of his left hand, then pushed the middle finger of his right hand in and out. The others joined him in laughter.

"I know how to do *that*," Bob rejoined. "I mean, how do we find a whorehouse?"

"Oh, hell, that's easy. We'll just go to the cab stand and ask one of the drivers to take us there," Logan suggested.

The prospect of finally losing his virginity made Bob so excited that he couldn't finish his hamburger. The others didn't seem to have that problem, though, and they talked animatedly of the women they had known while wolfing down their food. Bob listened and laughed, but added nothing to the conversation.

They left the restaurant and drove downtown, then parked the car and walked over to the taxi stand. Four yellow cabs were parked along the curb, the drivers standing on the sidewalk, chatting among themselves.

"Better let me do the talkin'," Logan suggested, and, as before, the others acquiesced leadership to him.

"Excuse me," he said when they reached the cab drivers.

One of the drivers took the cigar he was smoking out of his mouth, spitting the piece of tobacco that clung to his lip, and asked, "Yeah, whaddya want?"

"I was wonderin' if you could help us."

"You wanna go somewhere?"

"Yes."

"Where?"

"Uh, well, that depends on you," Logan said.

The cab driver stuck the cigar back in his mouth and took a puff, then squinted through the smoke. "Boy, you want to spit out what it is you're gettin' at? You ain't makin' a hell of a lot of sense here."

Logan rubbed his hands together nervously, then stepped away. "Uh, you tell him, Tom."

Tom stepped forward, clearing his throat. "What my friend is trying to say is that we are . . . uh . . . desirous of a little feminine . . . uh . . . companionship."

"Huh?"

"Girls?" Charley suggested.

The driver pulled the cigar from his mouth and spit again. "Girls?"

"Yeah, you know, a, uh, special kind of girl?"

The driver's face spread in a wide grin. "Shit! You boys're wantin' some poontang, ain't you? Hell, why didn't you come right out and say it?"

"Poontang, yes," Tom said, nodding eagerly. "Yes, that's what we want."

"Well, hell, get in the car. I'll take you boys there. I know where you can get rode hard and put away wet." He laughed. "Poontang. Goddammit, why didn't you just come out and ask for it in the first place?"

Bob sat in the backseat with Tom and Charley. Logan sat in the front with the driver.

"I don't normally pay for it," Logan told the burly cabbie, "but my friends here— Well, they're wantin' some real bad, and I figure this is one sure way."

"What's the place like?" Bob asked the driver.

"Whaddya mean, what's it like?"

"Is it clean?"

"Boy, I'm not tryin' to sell you the goddamn house, I'm just takin' you to where you can get a little pussy, is all."

"Sorry," Bob mumbled.

The cab driver drove west out of town, then turned down a long dirt road that ran alongside a weapons-storage area for the U.S. Navy.

"Is it out here, by the Navy storage area?" Logan asked.

"Yep."

Logan laughed. "I bet the sailors that work out here like that."

The driver turned off the dirt road, then went down a narrow, twisting lane. The headlights bounced off the palmetto trees and scared up a rabbit that bounded along in front of the car for several yards before finally veering off.

"What kind of whorehouse would be way out here?" Charley asked in a leery voice.

"The kind that don't want no trouble with the Panama City police," the driver answered.

"Oh, yeah," Charley said. "Well, I guess that makes sense."

Finally the car passed through a very heavy growth of shrubbery, then stopped. The lights played on a small frame house that was up on pilings and leaned to one side. A rickety porch, half of its roof caved in, ran along the front of it, and an old car seat sat on the porch. It was dark inside the house except for a wavering blue light.

"This is it?" Logan asked.

"This is it. I'll go in and tell her she's got company."

"Wait a minute," Bob said. "You mean there's just one girl?"

"Goddamn, son, how many can you fuck in one night?"

"Well, I mean, don't we each get one?"

The driver laughed. "Now, don't you worry none. You boys ain't gonna wear it out." He got out of the car and walked around the back. The air was alive with a thousand voices of frogs and other night creatures.

"What do you think?" Logan asked, twisting around in the seat to talk to the others.

"I don't know," Charley said dubiously. "This sure isn't like any whorehouse I've ever seen."

"I thought . . ." Bob started, then stopped.

"You thought what?"

"I thought there'd be a lot of girls, and we could go in and maybe look around, then take our pick."

"Yeah, well, most of 'em is like that," Logan said. "Only what I think we got here is just one woman in business for herself. Hell, it might be better this way."

"Why would it be better?"

" 'Cause she's probably not as professional as the others. This'll be just like screwin' a regular girl. I say we give it a try."

"Yeah, well, we've come this far, and from what I figure, the cab driver's goin' to get his part whether we go on in or not. So we may as well go all the way," Charley said.

"Yeah, I agree," Tom said.

"That's three of us who are goin'. What about you, Bob?"

"Hell, yeah, I'm goin'," Bob said. He wanted to shout out in excitement. This would be his first time. There was no way he wasn't going to go.

The driver came back to the car. "Okay, boys, she said she'll take you one at a time. It'll cost you five dollars apiece for her, and five dollars apiece for me."

"You get five dollars from each of us?" Charley asked.

"Unless you want me to go back into town and leave you boys out here."

"No, don't do that!"

"Well, if I· wait, I'm gonna be losin' fares. I gotta have somethin' to make up for it."

"All right," Logan said. "Cough it up, guys."

With shaking fingers, Bob extracted five dollars from his wallet and handed it to the driver.

"Okay, who's first?" the driver said.

"I'll go first," Tom replied.

Bob was glad Tom had volunteered. He wanted to do it, but he sure didn't want to be first.

The other three waited in the car while Tom went around to the back of the house.

They were silent for a few moments, watching the house as if Tom might reappear for some reason. Then Charley turned to Bob and said, "I been thinkin' about you droppin' that jeep yesterday. Man, you were one lucky son of a bitch, you know that? I mean, if that'd hit someone . . . man! It would've squashed 'em flatter'n shit. Yep, you're one lucky son of a bitch."

"I wished I'd seen that," Logan said. He made a spiraling motion with his right hand. "*Bam!*" he said loudly. "I'll bet that son-of-a-bitchin' jeep scattered into a million parts."

"What are you fellas talkin' about?" the driver asked.

Charley told the driver of the incident the day before, embellishing the story with anecdotes about how he and the students couldn't tell exactly where the jeep was going to fall and how they had to run harder than they'd ever run in their lives to escape unscathed. "All I can say, Bob, is you're one lucky son of a bitch," he repeated.

"I don't want to talk about it anymore," Bob said.

"Yeah, I don't blame you. I mean, you would've really been in some deep shit if that had hit anyone, you know? You are one lucky son of a bitch."

"You keep saying that, but *you're* the one who was on the ground, Charley," Bob said. "Seems to me like *you're* the one that's the lucky son of a bitch. You could've been the one squashed."

"Son of a bitch!" Charley exclaimed. "Son of a bitch! I never thought of that! You're right! I'm the one that's the lucky son of a bitch!"

They all fell silent again. After a while Logan mused, "Wonder what's takin' Tom so long?"

"Hey, don't rush the man," Charley replied. "He's probably in there humpin' up a storm."

A few minutes later Tom emerged from the back of the house and walked hurriedly toward the car.

"How was it?" Charley asked.

"I've got to pee, man," he answered.

"Go over there," the driver suggested, pointing to a yucca plant.

"How was it?" Charley asked again.

"It was great," Tom called back over his shoulder, talking over the sound of splashing water. "Best piece of ass I ever had."

"Son of a bitch, I'm next!" Charley said, opening the door quickly before anyone could stop him.

When Charley finally returned, he also reported that it was the best he'd ever had. "You go now, Bob."

"You want to go next?" Bob asked Logan.

"No, man. If I go, I'll ruin it for you," Logan replied. "After I get through with her, there won't be anyone else can satisfy her tonight."

"Logan Pounders, you're as full of shit as a Christmas turkey," Tom suggested.

"When do you, uh . . . ?" Bob started.

"When do you what?"

"When do you give her the money?"

"What I did was, I had the five dollars in my hand and I just give it to her the moment she opened the door."

Bob nodded. With fingers trembling more now than when he paid the cabbie, Bob took out another five-dollar bill. Then he took a deep breath to try to calm down. This was his moment of truth. He opened the door of the cab and walked around to the back of the house. The door was closed. He didn't know whether he should just open it or knock. He decided to knock.

The door opened, and a woman stood there looking at him. She was wearing a thin housecoat held together by one button at the waist. It gaped open at the top, showing her bra, and at the bottom, showing her panties. The only light on in the house was the flickering blue light of the television set. By that light he could see that the woman was much older than he had thought she would be. In her thirties at least—maybe even forties. Her face was sort of sharp-featured, and she had a prominent nose and a weak chin. She couldn't, by any stretch of the imagination, be called pretty. But she was a woman . . . and Bob was about to lose his virginity.

"Here," he said, handing her the money. From within the darkened shadows of the house came some sort of creaking sound, but he couldn't make out what was making it.

Creak, creak, creak.

"You the last one?" the woman asked in a flat voice. She stuck the bill down into the pocket of her housecoat.

"No, ma'am. There's one more," Bob replied.

The woman raised a cigarette to her lips and took a puff. It glowed red in the dark. She exhaled audibly. "Well, come on in," she said. "You ain't gettin' nothin' done standin' out there on the back stoop."

"Yes, ma'am," Bob said, stepping into the house.

The house had only one room, which was divided into two halves by a wire with a quilt thrown over it. That was Bob's first surprise. The second surprise was seeing a man rocking in a chair, watching TV. That was the source of the creaking sound.

"Good evening, sir," Bob said.

Creak, creak, creak.

"You like *Gunsmoke*?" the man asked, not turning his gaze from the TV set. Bob looked beyond him and saw Matt Dillon and Chester standing in front of the U.S. marshal's office in Dodge.

"Yes, sir."

Creak, creak, creak.

"You think Matt's gettin' any pussy from Miss Kitty?"

"I . . . I don't know."

"You know what I think?"

"No, sir."

"I think Chester's gettin' some on the side." The man laughed a loud, wheezing laugh. "Yessir, I figure ever' time ol' Matt leaves Dodge, Chester limps his skinny little ass over to the Long Branch and dicks Miss Kitty." He laughed again.

Creak, creak, creak.

"You go on and do what you have to do, Marshal. I'll take care of things with Miss Kitty for you," Chester said just then.

"Do you see? Do you see what I mean?" the man asked with a wheezing cackle.

Creak, creak, creak.

The woman neither laughed nor joined the conversation. With an expressionless face she pulled the quilt to one side, revealing an old cast-iron bedstead, its covers badly mussed, that filled most of the other half of the quilt-divided room.

"In here," she said in a flat voice.

"Yes, ma'am," Bob said, stepping behind the quilt.

The woman took off her dressing gown and hung it on the bedstead, then stepped out of her panties. She didn't take off her bra.

Bob looked at her in fascination.

"You plannin' on doing this with your clothes on?" the woman asked.

"Oh, uh, no, ma'am." Ignoring her sarcasm, Bob quickly removed his clothes. From the other side of the curtain he could hear the voices coming from the TV and the steady *creak, creak, creak* of the rocking chair.

The woman lay on her back, half propped up on her elbows with her legs spread. She took one final puff of her cigarette, then ground it out in a fruit-jar lid. It joined at least a dozen other cigarette butts.

"I'm ready," she said.

"What about your bra?"

"What?"

Bob cleared his throat. "Your bra," he said. "Aren't you going to take off your bra?"

"Jesus," the woman muttered. She sighed, then reached around and unhooked the bra and slipped it off. Her breasts were very small . . . not at all like the breasts of the women whose pictures Bob had ogled in magazines.

"Well, well, well. If it isn't Marshal Dillon. What are you doing over here, Dillon? You're a little out of your territory, aren't you?"

"I'm a United States marshal, Simmons. My territory is anywhere I want to be."

Creak, creak, creak.

Bob crawled in bed, then got on top of her. His dog tags dangled down; he shoved them around so that they were on his back.

"You boys can come along peaceable, or you can come along belly-down over your saddle. It really doesn't matter to me."

Creak, creak, creak.

Bob was having difficulty making the connection, so the woman reached down and put his penis in her for him.

"There, is that better?"

"Yes, ma'am. Thank you."

Bob began thrusting, and the bedsprings squeaked loudly. He stopped.

"What is it? What's wrong?" the woman demanded.

"He'll hear us," Bob whispered.

"You think he don't know what's going on in here? Either do it or get off."

"Yes, ma'am."

Bob started again.

Squeak, squeak, squeak went the bedsprings.

Creak, creak, creak went the rocking chair.

"Marshal, look out, on the balcony!"

Bang! Bang! Bang!

Squeak, squeak, squeak.

Creak, creak, creak.

Bob's dog tags slipped around and dangled in the woman's face. She slapped at them in irritation.

"What the hell?" she said. "What is that?"

"My dog tags, ma'am."

"Well, take 'em off."

"No, ma'am, I can't do that. I'm supposed to wear them all the time. When I take a shower . . . when I sleep, even."

"Well, get 'em out of my face."

"Yes, ma'am."

Creak, creak, creak.

Squeak, squeak, squeak.

"You shot . . . me, Dillon. I thought I was faster. I really . . . thought . . ."

Bob felt a cramp starting in the sole of his foot and he lurched up, then held himself still for a moment until it went away.

"Uh, honey, that was good," the woman said, thinking he was finished. She put her hands on his shoulders and pushed him off. "If there's someone else out there, tell him to hurry, will you? I want to watch *The Demaris Hunter Show.*"

Bob started to tell her that he wasn't finished, but he decided not to. Instead, he sat up on the bed and began reaching for his clothes. "Yes, ma'am. I'll send him right in."

When he was dressed, he stepped around the quilt.

"Gunsmoke! Brought to you by . . ."

"Pretty damn good, wasn't it, boy?" the man in the rocking chair asked, not turning around.

"Yes, sir."

"She knows what that pussy's for, all right."

Bob stepped outside and just stood for a long moment in the cool, dark air, listening to the croaking frogs.

He was dizzy, frustrated, and disappointed. Did he do something wrong? Why didn't he finish? Why didn't he enjoy it? *Is this what everyone is always talking about?* he asked himself. *If so, it sure isn't what it's made out to be.*

He took a few deep breaths, then walked back around to the front of the house.

"Okay, it's my turn now," Logan said, getting out of the car.

"How was it?" Charley and Tom asked in unison.

Bob pasted a big grin on his face. "About the best I ever had."

AUGUST 1956, CHICAGO, DEMOCRATIC NATIONAL CONVENTION

When Morgan Canfield returned to the hotel suite with a sackful of hamburgers, his father was on the telephone and his mother and sister were in the sitting room, watching the convention. Not content to follow the events on only one network, John Canfield had arranged for two additional TV sets to be brought in, and all three were turned on, showing ABC, CBS, and NBC. The sound on the CBS coverage was the only one turned up so that Walter Cronkite's voice alone filled the room.

"I've got food," Morgan said, putting the hamburgers down on a coffee table.

"I swear, if I eat another hamburger I'm going to turn into one," Alicia complained as she pulled one out and·unwrapped it, then opened the bun and took off the onions.

"I thought you liked onions," Morgan said to his sister, his tone sarcastic. "What's the matter?"

"I just don't feel like onions," Alicia replied.

Morgan laughed as he took a big bite. "You think Senator Kennedy won't kiss you if you have onion breath?"

"Here," Alicia said. "If you want onions so much you can have mine." She threw her onions at her older brother.

"Will you two behave yourselves?" Faith Canfield said to her children. "I swear, no one would ever know you're twenty-one and nineteen. You're both acting more like two-year-olds."

John hung up the phone then and came over to take out a hamburger for himself.

"What's happening with the delegation?" Alicia asked her father.

John unwrapped the burger and took a bite. He shook his head. "Missouri is still officially committed to Hubert Humphrey for vice president."

"I don't understand Adlai," Faith said. "He promised Jack Kennedy that *he* would be his choice for vice president."

"I think Jack *is* his choice," John said. "But he decided to throw it open to let the convention decide."

"Why would he do that? Surely he doesn't really want Kefauver—not after the dog-and-cat fight they had during the campaigning."

"It's all politics, Faith. Stevenson's advisers have convinced him he can't win with a New England Catholic on the ticket. You've been around this business your entire life—first with your father and then with me when I worked for Roosevelt. You know how this game is played."

"Yes, I know how it's played, but that doesn't mean I approve. I hate politics."

"Really?" Alicia asked. "Are you telling me you don't think Chicago is the most exciting place to be in the world right now? I just wish I was a delegate."

"How could you be a delegate? You can't even vote," Morgan pointed out.

"I know, I haven't yet reached the age of majority," Alicia said. Then she added caustically, "You, on the other hand, have instantly become a savant merely by having turned twenty-one."

"That is the way our forefathers, in their infinite wisdom, made the law," Morgan intoned.

"Maybe someday nineteen-year-olds will be able to

vote. Laws can be changed, after all. Grandmother got the law changed so women could vote."

"So what? Even if it gets changed, it wouldn't happen in time to do you any good in this election."

"Do you think I'm concerned with injustice only as it applies to me?" Alicia asked. "I want the law changed because it's wrong. It's like the speech Dr. Martin Luther King made to the convention the other day. I applaud his work, even though the injustice done to the Negroes doesn't affect me personally. And I think Governor Stevenson is wrong by not including a civil rights plank in the platform."

"There you go again. Donna Quixote, jousting with windmills," Morgan teased.

"What's wrong with that?" Alicia said sharply. "Daddy says if it weren't for the Don Quixotes of the world, we'd all be up to our asses in windmills."

"Alicia!" Faith said. "That is very unsuitable."

"Well, that *is* what Daddy says," Alicia defended.

John chuckled. "She's got you there, Faith."

"No, she has *you* there. And I don't care who says it, it is still a very unsuitable statement."

There was a knock on the door, and Alicia opened it to see Senator John Kennedy. He smiled and brushed back the hair falling onto his forehead.

"Hello, Alicia," he said in his broad Boston accent. "Uh, is your father in?"

"Yes! Yes, he is," Alicia said, blushing slightly. She stepped back from the doorway. "Come in."

"Jack," John said, getting up from the sofa and extending his hand in greeting. "It's good to see you. Want a hamburger?" He pointed to the sack.

"Thank you, no," Kennedy replied. "Bobby brought in a big bucket of popcorn, and I've been munching on that all day." Kennedy ran his hand through his hair again. "I guess you know why I'm here."

John sighed and made a motion for Kennedy to sit down. Kennedy chose the footstool, then pulled one knee up and wrapped his arm around it.

"Is your back hurting you?" Alicia asked. She knew

about his back, how he had injured it during the war and how the pain was often excruciating. She knew, also, that this position alleviated it somewhat.

Kennedy smiled. "A little," he admitted. "But only because I've been on my feet a lot."

"Jack, I'm afraid it doesn't look good in the Missouri delegation," John said. "The best I can promise you is that we won't be supporting Kefauver."

"I see," Kennedy said, his disappointment clearly audible.

"I want you to know that I tried," John went on. "I tried very hard. I explained that if Missouri would switch its vote to you, we could be the ones to put you over the top. But as you know, our delegation is loyal to President Truman—and Truman is loyal to Humphrey."

"Did you, uh, explain to them that if I don't go over the top now, I'll lose the momentum? And if I lose the momentum, do they know where the momentum will go?"

"Yes, they know that. I told them it was a distinct possibility that if we didn't get behind your candidacy now, a steamroller effect could start building for Kefauver. I thought that piece of information might bring them around, seeing as how President Truman has such little regard for Kefauver. It didn't work. I'm afraid Missouri is going to stick with Humphrey to the very end. It's going to be a bitter floor fight."

Kennedy was silent for a long moment. "No," he finally said, shaking his head. "It's not going to be a bitter fight."

"I don't know how we're going to avoid it."

"I'm going to withdraw my name and throw my support behind Kefauver."

"Why would you do that?"

"To avoid the bitter fight you're talking about. I want to come out of here with a united Democratic party, not a bunch of special-interest groups who just happen to be thrown together in one convention hall."

"But you're leading in the delegates race right now. If anyone is going to capitulate—"

Kennedy held up a finger. "I didn't say capitulate, I said withdraw."

"All right, withdraw. If anyone should withdraw, it should be Kefauver."

Kennedy shook his head. "No, John, I appreciate your support, I really do. But Bobby has been polling all the delegations that are currently supporting someone other than Kefauver or myself. They're going to stay with their man for one more ballot, and then they're going to switch to Kefauver. And when they do, my candidacy will be over."

"I'm sorry," John said.

"So am I." Kennedy flashed a grin. "On the other hand, four years from now, I'll be remembered for my statesmanlike generosity."

John returned Kennedy's grin. "You're going for the top spot in '60, aren't you, Jack?"

"It's much too early to announce," Kennedy said dryly.

"I'll vote for you," Alicia put in. "I'll be old enough then."

"Thank you," Kennedy said. "And what about you, Morgan? Will I have your vote as well?"

"You'll have more than my vote, Senator," Morgan said. "If you can find room for me in your campaign, I'll work for you."

"Well, your father helped get Roosevelt elected in '32. So I'd say you come from pretty good stock. If you want to work for me, Morgan, I will personally see to it that there's room for you." He stood up and took John's hand. "And I thank you for your efforts on my behalf this year. Now, it's time for me to show my magnanimous statesmanship. I am going to the floor to withdraw my name and offer my support to Kefauver."

"Jack, I'm awfully sorry I couldn't do more," John said, taking Kennedy's hand.

Kennedy shook hands with Morgan, then with Alica, whose eyes filled with tears, and finally with Faith. "I appreciate your help—all of you," he said as he left the room.

"Do you think he really will run in 1960?" Alicia asked her father when the door had closed.

"I think you can take it to the bank."

"But surely he wouldn't challenge Governor Stevenson if he is president?" Faith asked.

"Let's be realistic," John said. "Eisenhower's approval rating is as high right now as it was on the day he was first elected. There is no way Stevenson will be elected. In fact, not getting on a losing ballot is probably the best thing that ever happened to Kennedy."

CHAPTER THIRTEEN

OCTOBER 1956, OZARK, ALABAMA

The Ozark High School colors were the same as the Sikeston High School colors, so for Bob Parker, watching the War Eagles play football that Friday night was almost like watching the Bulldogs. There was, he was quick to point out to his friends, one major difference: Sikeston had lost only one game since 1947, whereas Ozark was barely able to put together a winning season.

It was now nearly halftime, and the score was Ozark 14, Enterprise High School 7.

The gun sounded, ending the first half.

"Want some popcorn or somethin'?" Logan Pounders asked.

"Not yet," Bob replied. "I want to watch the band."

"The band?" Logan laughed. "Are you kiddin'? Who the hell watches the band?"

"I do. I was in the band."

"That doesn't mean you have to watch it now, does

it? I'm goin' to get some popcorn." He got up and started to leave.

"I like the twirlers," Bob said.

"The twirlers?" Logan looked at the band forming up for the halftime show. Six twirlers stood in front of the band, all wearing very short, very tight, one-piece red uniforms, with white tasseled boots that accented shapely legs. "Yeah," Logan said. "Yeah, the twirlers. Listen, maybe I'll watch 'em, too." He sat back down.

The band marched out onto the field and formed a big circle.

"And now, ladies and gentlemen, the Ozark High School Marching Band performs for you their version of 'Rock Around the Clock'!" the field announcer said into the PA system, his voice echoing back from all the speakers.

The twirling line formed the hands of a clock. As the band played the number, they "rocked" around the clock, wriggling and prancing to the delight of the crowd.

When that number was over, the band re-formed, and the twirlers moved to the front, marching with high, prancing steps until they were in position. Standing directly in front of Bob and Logan was a pretty, shapely blonde. Like the others, she threw her arms high over her head, then brought them back down to her waist. An errant tendril of golden hair fell across her forehead, and she jutted out her lower lip, trying to blow it out of the way.

"Holy shit," Logan said. "Have you ever seen anyone any sexier than that little blonde?"

Bob knew her. He didn't know her well, but he did know her. He had met her at an open house at the First Baptist Church of Ozark held for the soldiers the month before. He hadn't seen her since then, but he did remember her name. It was Marilou Pepperdine.

"I've been out with her," Bob lied.

Logan looked at him in surprise. "What? You're shittin' me!"

"No," Bob said. "I met her a few weeks ago."

"And you took her out?"

"Yeah, sure."

"Where'd you go?"

"The Fan Drive-in."

"No shit? You took her to the drive-in movie?"

"Yeah."

"How is she? Did'ja get any?"

"She's a nice girl."

"Even nice girls like it."

"We didn't do anythin'."

"You didn't even cop a feel?"

"Well, yeah, I mean, we made out a little. Just a little. We didn't go all the way."

"Tell you what, if you can get that far with her, I can go all the way. I'm goin' to ask her out for tomorrow night."

"You can't do that. You don't even know her."

"Maybe not, but you do. All I need is for you to introduce me. I'll take care of the rest."

"I don't think that'd work out very well."

"Why not? You afraid I'll beat your time?"

"No, that's not it," Bob said. "I've got a date with her tomorrow night."

"Bullshit."

"No, I do."

"Twenty dollars says you don't."

"All right, you wait right here. As soon as the band gets off the field, I'll go get her and bring her here."

"All right. It's a bet."

Bob hadn't gone out with Marilou, of course, and had no date with her for the next night. Angry with himself for getting himself into this situation, he wondered how he'd get out of it. Then he decided that at this point it couldn't get any worse, so, taking a deep breath, he walked down to the end of the bleachers where the band always sat and waited for them to return from their halftime show. They soon concluded the program with the Ozark High School "Alma Mater," and then the drum majorette released them, and they started coming back, disassembling their instruments, taking off their hats and jackets, laughing and talking. A group of the twirlers was together.

"Marilou?" Bob called.

She looked over, and from the expression on her face Bob knew that she was confused as to who he was. Then she smiled.

"I know you," she said. "Your name is Bob Parker. You came to the open house at our church last month. But you never have come back," she scolded.

"I've been working Sundays," Bob lied. "I'm surprised you remember me."

"Sure, I remember you. Are you enjoying the game?"

"Yes," Bob said. "I've never seen a team that still runs the single-wing attack. It's sort of interesting to watch."

"I don't know what that means," Marilou said. "I just hope we beat Enterprise, that's all. Are you going to the dance afterward?"

"The dance? What dance?"

"Tonight after the game. There's a dance in the gym."

"I didn't know about it. Am I allowed to go? I mean, being in the Army."

"Sure. You can go if you're with me," Marilou said easily.

"Really?"

"Unless you don't want to."

"I'd love to go," Bob said, grinning broadly. "Listen, would you like to go somewhere with me tomorrow night? Maybe a movie or something?"

"Are you asking me for a date?"

"Yes, I guess I am," Bob answered. "Oh, uh, that is, unless you have to wash your hair or something."

Marilou laughed. "Whatever makes you think I'd have to do that?" She touched it. "Is it dirty?"

"No, no, it's beautiful!" Bob said. "In fact, I've never seen prettier hair. It's just that girls seem to have to wash their hair a lot when they're around me."

Marilou laughed again. "You're funny."

"Funny ha, ha? Or funny weird?"

"Funny," Marilou repeated without explanation. "Do you have a car?"

"Yes."

"Elvis Presley made a movie, did you know that? It's called *Love Me Tender*, and it's playing over in Dothan tomorrow. Would you like to go see it?"

"Great!" Bob said. "Oh, uh, would you do me a favor?"

"What's that?"

"I have a friend with me here. I told him I knew you, but he didn't believe me. In fact, he bet me twenty dollars that I didn't know you. Would you come with me and meet him?"

Marilou laughed. "Sure, as long as you spend some of the twenty dollars on me."

Bob took Logan aside, and as Logan paid off his bet, Bob told him that he had promised to take Marilou to the dance that evening. "That means you'll have to get your own way home," he added.

"No problem," Logan said. "I saw some of the other guys here. I'll get a ride back with them. But when you get back to the barracks, I want a full report."

"On what?"

"You know," Logan said. He pointed at Bob. "And don't let me down!"

Bob spent the second half of the game sitting in the Ozark band section beside Marilou. After the game they started toward the gym. Emboldened by his success so far, Bob reached for Marilou's hand. She didn't resist him.

"Listen, is this homecoming or something?" Bob asked.

"Homecoming? No, why?"

"Why the dance?"

"We have a dance after every game with Enterprise. And they have a dance after every game with us. They're always fun, but they're more fun when we win, like to-night."

"Wait till you see it, everybody!" someone shouted as they ran out of the gym. "We've got the bug! We've got the bug! It's in there on the stage!"

"Oh!" Marilou exclaimed. She laughed uproariously. "Can you imagine that? We've got the bug! Those crazy boys! They must've sneaked over there and done it during the game."

"The bug?"

"The boll weevil," Marilou explained. "Several years ago, the boll weevil wiped out all the cotton in this part of the state. The farmers were looking for something else to get into, so they started raising peanuts. Now that's the number one crop, and it makes more money than cotton ever did. So the people in Enterprise got this brilliant idea of erecting a statue to honor the boll weevil. They think it makes them famous for having the only statue in the world that honors a pest. I think it makes them crazy."

"Oh, yeah," Bob said. "I've seen the boll weevil." He pointed toward the gym. "And you're saying it's in here?"

"Yes. We stole it two years ago, too, so the town fathers welded it down. I don't know how those boys got it this time."

They entered the gym and found a crowd clustered around the stage where, sitting on a chair smack in the center of the stage, was Enterprise, Alabama's famous boll weevil. A lot of teasing and taunting was going on between the kids from Enterprise and the kids from Ozark; then someone blew a whistle, and everyone looked toward the door.

"It's the sheriff," someone said.

The crowd parted as the sheriff, a smallish man with a thin face and a neatly trimmed blond mustache, came in. He stood there with his hands on his hips and a half smile on his face, staring at the boll weevil. Then he looked out over the crowd and shook his head.

"Now, boys, I'm not even goin' to ask who went over there and stole this bug," he said, pointing at the statue.

Everyone laughed.

"But the chief of police over in Enterprise called me and asked me to bring it back to him, and I've got to do that."

"Come on, Sheriff, let us keep it till after the dance," someone asked. Several others added their pleas.

"I can't do that," the sheriff said. He pointed to a

couple of Ozark boys. "How about you two boys puttin'
that damn bug in the back of my car?"

Glumly, the two he appointed picked up the cast-
iron statue and carried it back through the crowd amidst
catcalls and whistles until finally they were outside. The
sheriff paused at the door.

"Okay," he called back, "now you folks can enjoy the
dance."

"Killjoy!"

"Spoilsport!"

With the boll weevil gone, the tension that had been
building up between Enterprise and Ozark dissipated.
"Unchained Melody" began playing over the loudspeaker,
and within moments the gym floor was filled with dancers, including Bob and Marilou.

"Leave it to my father to spoil the fun," Marilou said.

"Your father?"

"The sheriff. You mean, you didn't know he was my
father?"

Bob grinned. "No, I didn't. I guess that means I'd
better behave myself, huh?"

"Well, not *that* much," Marilou replied, pressing herself surprisingly close to him as they danced.

During the course of the evening Marilou introduced
Bob to all of her girlfriends, concluding with, "You can
look, but hands off. I saw him first . . . he's mine."

No one had ever actually spoken to him or about him
in such a way, and Bob found it extremely flattering.

"Oops, there it is," Marilou said. " 'Stars Fell on
Alabama.' That's always the last song."

If anything, they danced even closer for that song,
and Bob believed that dancing close to this Alabama girl
to that song might have been the most romantic thing he
had ever done.

It was even better the next night when they went to
the movie in Dothan. Marilou cried when Elvis was
killed, and when she leaned her head on Bob's shoulder,
he put his arm around her. After the movie they came

back to Ozark and stopped at Hambone's Drive-in for hamburgers and Cokes. Marilou introduced him to everyone there as "my Yankee boyfriend." Bob was surprised on both counts. He had never particularly considered himself a Yankee, and he didn't know that Marilou considered him her boyfriend.

He didn't see her during the following week, but he did phone her. On Monday and Tuesday nights he went down to the telephone center to make the calls. On Wednesday night he drew guard duty, and he made a point of being first to report to guard mount so that he could have his choice of posts. He took Post Number Five.

Post Number Five was the ammunition dump. Such duty had an element of risk because ammo dumps had been known to explode—a lightning strike or a smoldering cigarette butt could set off an explosion of enormous proportions—almost always killing whoever was close by. To minimize the damage of an explosion, should one occur, the ammo storage facility was located about four miles away from the main base, in a totally isolated area.

The isolation was what made Post Number Five attractive to Bob, for there was no way the sergeant of the guard or the officer of the guard could approach without him knowing. The guard vehicle was a three-quarter-ton truck, and the high-pitched whine of the differential on a three-quarter-ton truck could be heard from two miles away. So if Bob chose to sit out his two-hour guard stint rather than walk, he'd be warned in plenty of time to get up and "walk his post in a military manner" long before the truck got there. Even more advantageous, Post Number Five had a class-A telephone mounted on a pole just inside the gate. A class-A telephone allowed the caller to phone off post—and Bob availed himself of that as soon as the guard truck was out of sight. He talked to Marilou for nearly an hour, and before hanging up, he made a date with her for the following Saturday night.

After the phone call he sat on the side of one of the storage bunkers, LOOKING up at the moon and the stars and listening to the whippoorwills and the strange *boing*

boing sound the skunks made. He found himself fantasiz-
ing about what it would be like to be an officer, after he
graduated from West Point: He'd come back to Fort
Rucker and go to flight school.

As an officer, of course, he'd live in the BOQ, which
was a lot nicer than the barracks. And with his officer's
pay he could buy a new car. He liked the Chevrolets a lot.
Maybe a two-door Bel Air hardtop . . . two-tone black
and white. He had seen a new '57 model in front of the
PX the other day. Some sergeant was driving it. God, it
was beautiful. Of course, by the time he graduated from
the Point, the '62's would be out. That'd be even better.
He pictured himself in his officer's uniform, driving his
new car, with Marilou by his side.

"Am I driving too fast for you, honey?" he would ask.

Marilou would be sitting close to him, and his right
arm would be around her, his hand just over her breast
. . . maybe even stuck down inside her shirt and under
the bra, cupping the breast.

"No, darling, you aren't driving too fast," Marilou
would answer. "I feel very safe with you."

Friday morning, while Bob was working on lesson
plans, he got a telephone call from the company clerk
informing him to report to personnel before ten hundred
hours.

"What's it about?" Bob asked.

*"Why are you asking me? I'm just a Spec-four. They
don't tell me these things,"* the clerk replied.

"Am I being shipped overseas?"

"You're not going to know until you go down there."

Bob hung up the phone with a queasy feeling in his
stomach. Why now? he wondered. If he had gotten orders
to go overseas when he graduated from crew chief school,
he would've gone gladly. But he was settled in here now.
He had friends, a car, and he was waiting to hear about
his application to West Point. He also had a girl. He'd
never had a girl before. He didn't want to leave Fort
Rucker now that he did.

"Hey, don't worry about it," Logan Pounders said to
him when Bob relayed his fears. "You'll have a great time

in Germany. They say those frauleins love havin' sex with Americans."

"Logan, is that all the hell you ever think about?"

"What, you mean there's somethin' else?"

"Anyway, it might not be Germany. It might be Korea."

"Whoa, that's even better. I hear you can get whatever you want from Korean whores for a quarter."

Scowling, Bob closed his books. Fifteen minutes later he was parking his car in front of base personnel. Going inside, he checked at the desk and was told to see the administrative officer.

"You are PFC Parker, Richard R., RA27520287?" the administrative officer, a chief warrant officer, asked.

"Yes, sir," Bob said apprehensively.

The CWO studied a letter for a moment. "Did you apply for West Point?"

"Yes, sir," Bob answered. "Is there something wrong with the application?

"You haven't gotten married since then, have you?"

"No, sir."

"Have you ever been married?"

"No, sir. Sir, is there something wrong?" Bob asked. "If there is, tell me what so I can get it straightened out."

"According to Department of Army, they don't have a statement declaring that you are not married or have never been married."

"I don't know what happened to it. I did sign it," Bob said.

"Here's another one," the CWO said, shoving a form across the desk. "Sign here."

"Will it get there in time? I mean, can they still consider me?"

The warrent officer chuckled. "Don't worry, Parker. You sign this statement, and by noon I'll have orders cut, appointing you to the U.S. Military Academy Preparatory Course."

"What? You mean to tell me the application's already been approved?"

"Subject to you signing this statement it has."

"*West Point!* Wow! I can't believe it! I'm going to West Point!"

"Congratulations, Cadet Parker. You are about to be a ring knocker."

When Bob went into town the following Saturday night, he was brimming over with excitement and couldn't wait to tell Marilou the news about his appointment. But when he rang the bell it was her father who came to the door.

"Yes?" he said.

"Oh, uh, hello, Sheriff Pepperdine. Is Marilou here?"

The sheriff stepped away from the door. "Yes, she's here," he said. "Come on in."

"Thanks."

Bob went inside and sat down.

"I don't believe we've met," the sheriff said. "I'm Hence Pepperdine."

"Yes, sir. I mean, we haven't met, but I know who you are. I'm Bob Parker."

"You a soldier boy?"

"Yes, sir."

"Well, I don't have nothin' against soldier boys. Long as they stay outta trouble. It's when they bring liquor into my county that I have trouble with 'em. Dale County is dry, you know."

"Yes, sir."

"Where you from?"

"Sikeston, Missouri."

"Never been to Missouri. What's your father do?"

"He's in the trucking business."

"Truck driver?"

"Yes, sir, but he owns two trucks, so he drives one and he has a driver who drives the other one."

"How old are you?"

"Eighteen, sir."

"That's pretty young. Did you drop out of school to join the Army?"

"No, sir. I graduated from high school. I even went to college for one semester."

"Where'd you go?"

"Missouri School of Mines," Bob said. "But I'm going to go to—" Bob was about to tell him of his West Point appointment when Marilou came into the room.

"For heaven's sake, Daddy, will you stop giving him the third degree?" Marilou scolded. She was still putting on one of her earrings.

Bob stood quickly. "You look nice."

"Thank you. Are you ready to go?"

"Yes."

"Wait a minute," Hence said. "Go where?"

"We're going to the movies," Marilou told him.

"No, you're not. You're goin' to the governor's dinner with your mother and me."

"I'm not going to any old governor's dinner," Marilou said, pouting.

"Yes, you are."

"No, I'm not. Come on, Bob." Marilou started for the door.

"Now, you just hold on there, young lady!" Hence said, raising his voice sharply. "I said you're goin' to the governor's dinner with your mother and me, and that's final. Now, if you want me to, I'll call and make arrangements for your friend to go, too."

"No, what you can do is call them and tell them I'm not going," Marilou said. She started toward the door again, and Bob, who was beginning to get very nervous, stepped out of the way.

Hence grabbed Marilou by the shoulder and pulled her back. "You listen to me, young lady!"

"I don't have to listen to you," Marilou said sharply. "I'm not a prisoner on one of your chain gangs. And I wish I wasn't your daughter. You've never been a father to me! I hate you, you son of a bitch!"

Bob felt his stomach churning. This had very rapidly gotten completely out of hand. He'd have given anything in the world to be somewhere else—anywhere else—right now.

"You watch your mouth!" Hence said, cuffing her face with a quick, short slap.

"*Oww!*" Marilou screamed. She careened across the

room and hit the wall, then slid down to the floor. She put her hand to her mouth, and when she pulled it away, blood covered her palm.

"*Bob!*" she shrieked. "Did you see that? Are you going to just stand there and let him beat me like this? He's always beating me!"

"What's that you said?" Hence asked, starting toward her.

"*No! No! Stay away from me, you bastard!*" Marilou crossed her arms in front of her face and ducked her head as if getting ready for a pummeling.

"Leave her alone!" Bob heard himself shout.

Hence stopped and looked over at Bob. His face was contorted with rage, and his eyes flashed with anger. He pointed at Bob, looking for a moment like an Uncle Sam recruiting poster.

"Boy, you stay the hell out of this!" He turned back toward Marilou.

"I said leave her alone!" Bob shouted again, louder this time. He grabbed Hence by the shoulder and spun him around. Hence tried to put his arm up, but it was too late. Bob hit him with a hard roundhouse right, knocking him into the television set. The screen broke with a loud pop, filling the room with sparks and smoke.

"My God! What's going on in here?" Marilou's mother screamed, rushing into the room, still in the process of dressing for the governor's dinner.

Hence, who was sitting on the floor, rubbed his chin with his hand and looked up at Bob. "Virginia Mae, you go back into the bedroom," he said, addressing his wife without taking his eyes off the young soldier. "And as for you, you son of a bitch, you're about to face my gun!" he told Bob menacingly.

"Hence, no!" Virginia Mae screeched. "Don't shoot him!"

"I'm gettin' the hell out of here!" Bob said, rushing out the door. Marilou picked herself off the floor and went with him.

"Come on, we'll go next door to the Taylors'," she said.

They ran across the lawn, through a hedge of honey-suckle bushes, up a driveway, and onto the front porch of the house next door. Bob began pounding on the door, looking back anxiously over his shoulder, positive that at any moment Sheriff Pepperdine would come crashing through the honeysuckle with his gun blazing.

"Howard! Howard! Let us in!" Marilou shouted.

The door opened, and a short, heavyset man with glasses stood there.

"For heaven's sake, Marilou, what is it?" the neigh-bor asked. "What's wrong?"

"Daddy's going to kill Bob," Marilou blurted.

"Do you have a gun, sir?" Bob asked desperately. "Give me a gun . . . anything . . . a twenty-two rifle, a shotgun . . . *something*! Her father's goin' to kill me!"

"Hence isn't going to kill anybody," Howard Taylor said. "You two come on in."

"Close the door! Lock it!" Bob said.

An attractive woman in her thirties appeared. "How-ard, what is it? What's going on?"

"I'm not sure, exactly, Linda. There's been some sort of trouble."

"Over at the Pepperdines'?"

"Yes, ma'am," Bob answered for her husband. "Marilou's daddy is goin' to kill me!"

"Why, that isn't like Hence at all. Why on earth would he want to do something like that?"

"Because I knocked him through the television set," Bob said. "But I don't want you to get the wrong idea. I mean, Marilou's not pregnant or anything like that."

"Of course I'm not pregnant!"

"Well, I didn't think you were," Linda Taylor said. "I know you aren't that kind of girl."

"I think I'll go talk to Hence," Howard said.

"If you're going over there, you'd better take a gun!" Bob warned. "The sheriff is really mad."

"Young man, why don't you come into the living room and sit down?" Linda offered. "You'll be all right in there."

"Yes," Marilou said, taking his hand. "Don't worry,

Bob, I'll protect you. I won't let Daddy do anything to you."

"Son of a bitch!" Bob exclaimed suddenly. "Son of a bitch, how did I get myself into this mess?" He glanced at Linda Taylor. "Oh, excuse me, ma'am, for the language."

"That's quite all right," she replied dryly.

Bob and Marilou sat on the couch, Marilou holding his hand in hers, rubbing it with her other hand.

"I should've minded my own business back there," Bob said.

"How can you say that?" Marilou asked. "My father is a brute. You were right to stand up to him the way you did. You were right, and you were brave. Why, I was never so proud of anyone in my life as I was of you when you hit him."

"I don't know," Bob said. "I think it was the dumbest thing I ever did."

Howard came back into the house then, with Virginia Mae Pepperdine by his side.

"Oh, honey, are you all right?" Virginia Mae asked Marilou.

"I'm fine, thank you. But I'm not going back to that house," Marilou said.

"What about you?" Virginia Mae asked Bob. "Are you all right?"

"Yes, ma'am."

"Well, Hence wants to see you."

Bob shook his head. "No, ma'am. I don't want to see him."

"It's all right. He's calmed down now. He's not going to kill you."

"Does he have his gun?"

"No. I took it," she said.

"You're sure he doesn't have a gun?"

"I'm sure. He's out in the car. He's going to go to the governor's dinner by himself. He said he's sorry he told you he was going to kill you. I think you should go talk to him."

"You're sure it'll be all right?"

"I'm sure."

Bob sighed, then got up from the sofa. "Okay. I'll go see him."

With trepidation he went outside and walked back through the honeysuckle bushes and across the lawn to the driveway of the Pepperdine home. Hence was sitting in his car with the engine running and the window down on the driver's side. He had the parking lights on.

"Sheriff?" Bob said hesitantly. "You wanted to see me?"

"Yeah. Come around here and talk to me," Hence answered.

Bob halted. "I'd rather you got out of the car, sir," he said.

Hence chuckled. "You aren't going to attack me again, are you?"

"No, sir!"

Hence got out and held both his hands out toward Bob, showing him that he was unarmed. "Listen, boy, I'm sorry I said I was goin' to kill you. I didn't really mean it."

"And I'm sorry I hit you," Bob replied.

"That's all right. I admire you for wantin' to protect my daughter."

Marilou appeared and stepped beside Bob, who put his arm around her.

"I wish none of this had happened," he said.

"Well, it did, and we can't turn back the clock," Hence said. "But if you two want to go to the movies, go ahead. I'll tell the governor you couldn't make it tonight."

"That's not good enough," Marilou said.

"What? What's not good enough?"

"Going to the movies. You think we can just go to the movies now and forget all about this?"

"Well, what do you want?"

"We want to get married."

"Married!" came a squeal from behind them. Virginia Mae was standing there, her face filled with surprise.

Bob figured his face looked even more surprised.

"Is that a fact?" Hence asked. "Well, you're a senior in high school. You'll graduate in seven more months . . .

if you still want to get married then, I won't have any objections."

"No," Marilou said.

"No, what?"

"We want to get married now. Tonight."

"That right, boy? You want to marry my daughter tonight?"

Marilou leaned into Bob, and he gave her a squeeze. He had never felt anyone or anything as vulnerable as she seemed to be then, and he felt extremely protective of her. But they had never even mentioned marriage, and he didn't really want to get married. Not yet, anyway. What could he say? He couldn't just turn around and walk away. It would really hurt her feelings. And if he deserted her now, when she really needed him, she'd probably never have anything to do with him again. He felt that he had no choice. He had to stand by her.

"Yes," he said.

"Well, it can't be done. It takes three days to get married in Alabama."

Bob let out a slow sigh of relief.

"That's all right. We'll go to Mississippi," Marilou said. "We can get married right away in Mississippi."

Hence shook his head. "I'm an Alabama sheriff. I'm on a half dozen of the governor's committees. Now, how's it goin' to look if my daughter goes to Mississippi to get married? No, ma'am. If you're goin' to get married, you're goin' to get married in Alabama."

"Well, we're going to get married tonight," Marilou insisted. "So you'd better do something to get it fixed up."

Hence sighed. "All right, I'll go back inside and call the governor again."

"What dress are you going to wear?" Virginia Mae asked, her eyes sparkling. She had clearly warmed to the idea.

"I thought I'd wear the blue one that Grandmother gave me," Marilou answered.

"Oh, yes, that's real pretty."

"And I'll have Melissa as my maid of honor," Marilou continued.

"Yes! And her father can marry you. You know, he's a part-time preacher," Virginia Mae said, caught up in the excitement.

Like a sleepwalker, Bob Parker went over to the front steps and sat on the bottom one. He shook his head in bewilderment and dismay. Why was Virginia Mae Pepperdine helping her daughter plan a wedding? Why didn't she try to talk her out of it? It looked like this crazy thing was actually going to happen! He was going to be married to a girl he barely knew, and there was no way out of it.

Hence came back outside a few moments later. "All right, I've got it all fixed up," he announced. "Go on over to the county health clinic. Governor Folsom said he'd have someone there to process your blood tests. Then you'll have to stop by Judge Sing's house and get your license. After that, come on back here. You can get married in the livin' room."

"I want some flowers!" Marilou called over her shoulder.

"Honey, it's eight o'clock Saturday night," her mother answered. "Where in the world do you think we can get flowers?"

"Daddy can do it," Marilou insisted. "He can do anything."

They got to the clinic before the doctor did, then sat in the car, in the dark, waiting for him. Bob briefly wondered what they would talk about under the circumstances, but he needn't have worried. They didn't talk. Instead, Marilou kissed him eagerly, excitedly, and Bob returned her passion. By the time the doctor arrived, they were breathing heavily.

Marilou straightened her blouse; Bob wiped the lipstick off his face. Then the couple got out of the car and hurried up the front walk, catching up with the doctor on the porch as he stood fumbling with his keys. The doctor, wearing blue jeans and a pullover shirt, commented, "You young folks must really be in a hurry to get married. The governor himself called me out of my house."

"We *are* in a hurry," Marilou replied.

"I don't normally open the door myself," the physician explained as he tried various keys. "It's going to take me a while to find the right key. Ah, there it is," he finally said.

Once inside, he was all business. He took blood samples from each of them, then sent them to wait in the dimly lit waiting room, while he disappeared down a long, dark corridor. It was almost forty-five minutes before he returned, holding two small pieces of paper.

"Here you go," he said.

"Is it all right?" Marilou asked. "Can we get married? Do we both have the same kind of blood?"

"Marilou, that's not why you have to—" The doctor stopped, then sighed. "Yes," he said, smiling, "you both have the same kind of blood. You can get married."

"Oh, goodie!" Marilou said excitedly.

They hurried back outside, and Marilou directed Bob to Judge Sing's house. He lived in a huge old turn-of-the-century wood-frame house with a wide, wraparound porch. It had multiple cupolas and was trimmed with yards of gingerbread decoration, much of which was broken and all of which needed paint. Only one light was on, and it glowed dimly from downstairs. Marilou didn't bother to knock; she just opened the door and shouted.

"Uncle Vernon? Uncle Vernon, it's me, Marilou."

"Is the judge your uncle?" Bob whispered.

"Well, actually, he's my cousin twice removed," Marilou said. "But he's so much older than I am that I couldn't call him cousin, so I've always called him uncle."

A tall, thin, old white-haired man shuffled into the foyer from one of the side rooms. He was wearing a faded robe that might have been red at one time and well-worn carpet slippers that flopped loudly as he walked.

"Hello, sweetheart," the judge said in a surprisingly firm voice. "Your daddy called me and said you were going to get married tonight. It's kind of sudden, isn't it?"

"Yes, sir, I guess it is," Marilou agreed. "This is my

fiancé." She giggled. "You know, I've always wanted to introduce someone as my fiancé, so I'd better do it now because he won't be that for very long."

"Well, come on in here, and I'll make out the license for you two lovebirds."

"Lovebirds," Bob murmured. *Funny*, he thought. *That's the first time the word "love" has been mentioned.*

Bob and Marilou followed Judge Sing into what had been a dining room. Indeed, a very long dining-room table, with no fewer than fourteen soiled-cushioned chairs arrayed around it, sat in the middle of the room. But it was obvious that it had been a long time since the table had been used for its original purpose, for it was piled from one end to the other with a mountain of papers, folders, books, and magazines. Dangling from the ceiling over the table was an electric cord and a chain that at one time probably supported a chandelier. Now there was only a single bare sixty-watt light bulb so covered with dust that the light struggling to get through looked yellow.

"Hmm, I believe I had a blank marriage license here someplace," the judge said, sifting through one pile of paper. At last he said triumphantly, "Ah! Here it is!"

He pulled out a wrinkled, printed form, then tried smoothing it out with his hand. Taking a pen from his robe pocket, he unscrewed the cap and tested the ink. Then he took out a pair of wire-rim glasses from the other pocket and put them on, fitting the earpieces over his large ears very carefully, one at a time. That done, he leaned down over the table and studied the form for a moment.

"I don't normally do this part of it, you know," he said. "So I'm goin' to have to read up a bit on the directions. Let's see here . . . Marilou, honey, how old are you?"

"I'm seventeen."

"You're eighteen, darlin'," he announced, filling in the blank.

"No, I'm seventeen, Uncle Vernon. I just had my birthday a couple of weeks ago."

"That may be, but the law says you have to be eighteen—so, you're eighteen."

"Oh."

"How old are you, boy?"

"Eighteen," Bob said. He grinned. "Guess I'm in the clear."

"The law says you're twenty-one."

"Oh."

"What's your name?"

"Richard R. Parker."

"Richard?" Marilou said, looking around in surprise. "Your name is Richard?"

"Yes."

"Well, that doesn't make any sense. Why are you called Bob?"

"Actually, it's Richard Robert Parker," Bob explained. "My dad's called Richard—some people call him Dick—so they call me Bob."

"Okay, Marilou, Bob, here it is," Judge Sing said, blowing the ink dry, then handing over the completed form. "Just have the preacher sign this when he's done, and you'll be all legally married."

"Thank you, Uncle Vernon."

"Do I owe you anything, sir?" Bob asked.

"No, it's my wedding present."

"Thanks."

Leaving the judge's residence, Bob and Marilou returned to her house. It was now close to midnight, and Bob was astounded at the number of cars parked around the place. The curbs on both sides of the street were completely lined, the driveway was full, and there were even cars parked in the yard. The young couple had to park almost a full block away.

"Where'd all the people come from at this hour of the night?" Bob asked as they walked up to the house, which was now ablaze with lights.

"Most of them will be either people who owe Daddy for political favors or people who want something from him," Marilou said, a touch of cynicism in her voice.

They hurried up the front steps and into the house.

Standing in the doorway to the living room, Bob surveyed the room. Every chair, sofa, and inch of the wall was filled with humanity, and he didn't recognize one person there. The impression he got was that the room was a vast sea of teeth, flashing eyeglasses, and clanking coffee cups. And there were masses of flowers . . . flowers everywhere. He had never seen so many flowers, and he marveled that anyone could get so many together at this hour on a Saturday night. Marilou was right. Apparently her father *could* do anything.

"Well, Preacher, here they are," Hence Pepperdine said to a corpulent man with thinning blond hair. "You about ready to marry these kids?"

"Soon as I finish this cup of coffee, Hence," the man replied.

Bob peered into the preacher's cup. There appeared to be about one swallow of coffee left. One swallow was all that stood between him and getting married. Then the preacher lifted the cup, and the swallow was gone.

"Let's do it," he said.

Bob and Marilou took their places in the big arched doorway between the living room and the dining room. The preacher stepped in front of them, cleared his throat, then began to read. After all the customary questions and responses, he finally reached the operative phrase:

"I now pronounce you man and wife. You may kiss the bride."

As the guests cheered the kiss, the full impact hit Bob that the high school girl he was holding in his arms—the girl whom he had dated only twice (counting the postgame dance last week) was now his wife. *He was married!*

When Bob opened his eyes the next morning, the sun was streaming in through the windows of Marilou's bedroom. She was still asleep, with the covers up to her neck and her blond hair spread out on the pillow. Her parents had spent the night with Marilou's grandmother so that the newlyweds could have the house all to themselves for their wedding night. At first it had been awk-

ward in bed—painful for her, frightening for him. The
second try was a little better.

This was the first time Bob had seen Marilou's bedroom. Actually, he wasn't sure that it wasn't the first time
he had ever seen *any* girl's bedroom, and while his bride
snored softly on the pillow beside him, he made a slow,
curious examination.

A big rag doll sat on the dresser, leaning back against
the mirror. The doll's hair was made from bright yellow
yarn. A three-by-five card taped to the mirror beside it
said: THIS BLONDE HAS MORE FUN THAN MARILOU! ICKY!

Stuck in the mirror frame was a photograph of Billy
Scott, one of the Ozark football players, in uniform.
"Love, Billy," was scrawled across the bottom of the pic-
ture.

Countless jars, bottles, and containers of various
types of makeup were spread across the top of the
dresser.

A Japanese fan was tacked to the wall, along with a
white, red-trimmed block letter O. The programme from
last year's junior play was also tacked to the wall, along
with pictures of Elvis Presley.

A bulletin board held a color photo of Marilou in her
twirler's uniform and pictures of her in various clowning
poses with her friends. There was also a newspaper head-
line declaring: HENCE PEPPERDINE WINS SHERIFF'S SPOT IN
LANDSLIDE VICTORY!

Suddenly, from just on the other side of the door,
Bob heard someone singing.

> "Brighten the corner where you are.
> Brighten the corner where you are. . . ."

The door to Marilou's room opened, and a large
black woman came in. She was wearing an apron and
carrying a feather duster. Bob pulled the cover up to his
chin.

"Good morning," he said.

"Oh! My!" the woman gasped.

Marilou abruptly opened her eyes, then smiled. She

sat up and stretched, and when she did the bedcovers fell down, exposing her nude body from the waist up. Quickly, Bob reached down and pulled the cover back up, draping it over her shoulders.

"Miss Marilou!" the maid squealed.

"Hi, Sarah," Marilou said. "Oh, it's all right. We got married last night."

Sarah shook her head slowly. "Lord, child, I hope so," she said.

"Are you decent?" another woman's voice called from the front of the house.

"Just a minute!" Marilou answered. She got out of bed and padded naked over to a pile of clothes to find a robe.

"Child, it ain't right you paradin' aroun' nekkid like that," Sarah said.

"Oh, Sarah, you've seen me naked ever since you used to change my diapers," Marilou scoffed.

"I ain' never seen you nekkid with a *man* in the room."

"But I told you. This is my husband."

Despite Marilou's reassurances, Sarah left the room. A few minutes later, Bob and Marilou went into the living room, Marilou in her frilly robe, Bob wearing the same clothes he'd had on last night—the only clothes he had with him. Marilou's mother and father were there.

"Come on out to the car, boy," Hence said. "We're goin' for a ride."

"We'll fix some breakfast while you're gone," Virginia Mae offered.

Hesitantly, Bob followed his new father-in-law outside and got into his car, emblazoned with the sheriff's seal.

They drove all over Ozark without speaking, though the drive wasn't made in silence since Hence hummed a tuneless melody the entire time. Once or twice Bob asked a question, but Hence just looked at him without replying, continuing his tuneless humming. Finally they left town and drove down a long dirt road, through an expanse of forest.

"Where are we going?" Bob asked.

Hence looked over at him, still humming. Finally he spoke for the first time since leaving the house. "Up here just a little ways."

They drove for another few minutes; then Hence turned off the road, and Bob saw that they were at the county dump. Flies swarmed around mountains of reeking garbage and an acre or more of old refrigerators, rusting bed frames, discarded bicycles, springs, buckets, tubs, and every other kind of detritus known to modern man. Hence turned off the car engine, then pulled out his gun.

"Get out of the car, boy," he ordered.

"*What?*" Bob gasped.

"I said get out of the car."

Oh, my God! Bob thought. *He's going to kill me! He's going to kill me and bury me under all this garbage, and no one will ever find my body! And he's got so much political influence that he can convince everyone who was at the wedding last night that it never even took place!*

"Well, boy, are you goin' to just sit there?" Hence asked.

Reluctantly Bob got out, but he stayed on the opposite side of the car from the sheriff. He watched as Hence walked over to the edge of one of the excavations, then pointed his pistol across the wide hole. The gun popped loudly, and on the other side of the hole, a bottle burst. Hence shot again, hitting another bottle.

"See that can?" he said, pointing to a soup can sitting on top of a discarded metal counter of some sort. He shot, and the can spun off the counter.

Two more shots produced two more hits. Then he emptied the cylinder and reloaded. He walked back to Bob and handed him the pistol.

"Let's see what you can do."

Bob was actually a pretty good marksman. This morning, however, his heart was pounding, his palms were sweating, and his hands were shaking. He hit only two bottles out of six shots.

"Ha!" Hence barked. "I guess it's a good thing for you we didn't shoot it out last night, ain't it?"

*   *   *

When Bob and Hence returned to the house, Virginia Mae was on the telephone. She covered the mouthpiece and spoke to Bob as he came in.

"It's Alice," she said.

"Alice? You mean, my *mother*? How would she know to call here?" Bob asked.

Virginia Mae shook her head. "I called her. I got the number from information." She handed the phone to Bob. "I think you'd better talk to her."

Bob felt his stomach churning as he took the phone.

"Hello, Mother."

"I've been talking to Virginia Mae, Bobby," his mother said. "She sounds like a nice lady."

"Yes, ma'am, she is."

"And Marilou sounds like a nice young girl."

"Yes, ma'am."

There was a beat of silence for a moment, then Alice continued. "Bobby, Virginia Mae said that you were going to have something important to tell me. Please don't tell me that you're engaged. I'm sure Marilou is a very sweet girl, but Virginia Mae tells me she's still in high school. And you're so young yourself. I hope you haven't done anything foolish, like get engaged."

"We're not engaged, Mother."

Alice breathed an audible sigh of relief. "Well, thank goodness for that. I was afraid for a moment there that—"

"We're married," Bob interrupted.

There was another beat of silence.

"What?"

"We're married. We got married last night."

"I . . . I . . . here. You'd better talk to your father."

Bob could hear some muffled words from the other end of the phone; clearly his mother was talking to his father with her hand over the receiver. A few moments later Richard Parker was on the phone.

"What's going on down there?" he asked.

"I got married last night, Dad."

There was no reply.

"Dad?"

"What?"

"Did you hear what I said? I said I got married."

"I heard."

"Well, you didn't say anything."

"Is she pregnant?"

"No."

"Then that seems to me like a hell of a thing to do, just to get into a girl's britches," Richard finally said.

"It's not like that, Dad. Really it isn't."

"Well, there's nothing to be said about it now. What's done is done. Here's your mother."

"We're coming down there," Alice Parker said.

"You don't need to do that."

"We're coming down there," she said again. "I ought to at least get to meet her. After all, she is my daughter-in-law."

"Well, you always wanted a daughter," Bob said lightly.

"Yes, but not this way. Not so soon. I . . . I can't talk anymore." It wasn't until then that Bob realized his mother was crying. "I hope you're both very happy," she managed to say, sniffling.

"We will be," Bob said.

"Oh, Bob," Alice suddenly asked, "what about your application to go to West Point? Have you considered that?"

Bob felt all the blood drain from his head, and his heart lurched. He had received his appointment last week. Now, he knew, that appointment would be invalid. This was the first time he had thought of it since the whole crazy mess began last night.

"It doesn't matter," he said quietly.

"It doesn't matter? What do you mean, it doesn't matter? Of course it matters! They aren't going to approve your application if you're married."

"I got the answer last week," Bob said. "It was"—he paused for a moment; he couldn't face them with the truth —"it was disapproved," he finally said.

"Oh, I'm sorry. I didn't know that. I thought it was still being considered."

"Yeah, well, I couldn't bring myself to tell you yet," Bob said. "I was too disappointed."

"Under the circumstances, it's probably just as well that it was disapproved," Alice said. "I mean, it would be awful to finally get your appointment, then not get to use it, wouldn't it?"

"Yes, ma'am," Bob said.

"Well, all right. You give your new wife—" Alice paused with a catch in her voice. "It seems so funny to be saying that," she went on, "but you give your new wife a hug and kiss for us, and we'll see you soon."

Bob hung the phone up and looked at Marilou.

"What did she say?" Marilou asked.

"She said you sounded like a very nice girl, and she was sure we would be very happy. She also wanted me to give you a hug and kiss from them."

Marilou's smile verged on the triumphant, and she linked her arm with Bob's. "Oh, how sweet!" she said. "I just know that your mother and I are going to get along splendidly."

CHAPTER FOURTEEN

Valentina Golitsyn was taking inventory of the medicines on hand when her husband burst into the small medical services building.

"Valentina! Valentina, the test of the new fuel induction valve was a success! We are back on schedule!"

"*Your* valve?" Valentina asked.

"Yes! Sergei Korolev himself congratulated me," Yuri Golitsyn said.

Valentina laughed with delight and embraced her husband. "Oh, Yuri, I am so proud of you!"

"Come," he said. "They are about to load the Sputnik into the rocket. We have been invited to witness it."

"What an honor!" Valentina replied. Picking up medicine bottles and putting them on the shelves, she said, "Just let me close up here, and I will be with you."

305

*   *   *

The huge assembly building loomed high against the bright blue autumn sky as Valentina and Yuri approached. Some distance away from the assembly building was the launch site, and Valentina thought that the four steel arms of the service tower, pulled back as they were, resembled the petals of an opening flower. When a rocket was ready for launching, the four arms would come together, forming a collar that clutched the rocket securely in its steel grip.

For the time being the rocket was still in the assembly building. At the foot of the rocket, on a small dolly, sat the silver sphere that would be launched into space. The sphere had been officially named Sputnik—Russian for "traveling companion."

"There it is," Yuri said, pointing to the small globe, even smaller-looking when viewed against the rocket that would send it out of the atmosphere. "That's Sputnik. Look closely, Valentina. Tomorrow it will be in outer space."

Valentina grabbed Yuri's arm. "Oh, it's so exciting!"

"Yuri, Valentina, come!" Sergei Korolov called to them from the doorway of the assembly building. "Come into the control room with me. We are about to load Sputnik into the nose cone. After that we will test its radios."

Valentina followed the men into the giant control room. Here, Yeselin, Korolev, Glushko, and a dozen more scientists and engineers stood looking through the big windows out onto the floor of the assembly room. They all watched as a crane lowered its grappling hook to grasp the silvery sphere. The ball, with its four whip antennas sticking out, was lifted up toward the nose section of the rocket, then placed in the cone, antennas folded back. The cone was closed, and the grappling hook was pulled away.

"It's loaded," someone said.

Everyone looked over at Korolev. Though all the engineers and scientists involved in the project were here—including the rocket designers, the engine designers, and those who worked on the guidance systems and the other basic components of the rocket—it would become Korolev's exclusive responsibility once it all came together.

"Well, my friends," he said, "let's see if our little traveler will be able to speak to us." He nodded at one of the men sitting by a control panel. The engineer flipped a couple of switches.

For a moment there was silence; then a collective gasp said what everyone was thinking: The radios had failed. But suddenly the engineer smiled sheepishly.

"I don't have the speakers turned on," he confessed. He made another adjustment, and over the loudspeakers came a clear, distinct signal from Sputnik's radio: *"Beep, beep, beep."*

"Listen carefully to that sound, friends," Korolev said, smiling broadly. "In a very few days the entire world will hear it."

In the predawn darkness of October 3, 1957, the rocket was loaded onto a flatcar inside the assembly building, then drawn slowly along tracks laid into the floor, clacking over each rail joint. The huge doors of the assembly building opened wide to allow the rocket to pass outside, where the polished nozzles of its engines glittered softly under the starry sky.

By the time the rocket was halfway along its half-mile journey to the launch site, the sun was rising over the flat steppe, bringing first warmth and then heat. As it grew hotter, the scientists became concerned. The rocket's transit was halted while scientists and engineers conferred as to whether Sputnik might suffer some harm from the increasing heat.

"We could put a white cloth over the nose cone," one of the engineers suggested.

The others agreed, and a white canvas was spread over the top of the rocket, but when they monitored the temperature a few moments later, they saw that the white cloth wasn't going to be enough.

"Maybe we could pack it in ice."

"No, if water gets inside, it could short out the radios."

"Dry ice?" another suggested.

"That would be too cold. Some of the components might become brittle and break."

"We don't have to cool it too much. If we just had some air moving, that would be enough."

"All you're needing is air?" one of the maintenance men asked, peering through the group at the rocket. He was not a scientist or even an engineer, just one of the many support personnel.

"Excuse me, Comrade," Yeselin said, "but can't you see these scientists are contemplating a problem? Please tend to your own business, and let these gentlemen attend to theirs."

"I was just going to make a suggestion, that's all."

"I'm sure we don't need any suggestions from a laborer."

"Wait a minute, Comrade Yeselin," Korolev said, holding up his hand. "All of us who work here at the Cosmodrome are a team—scientist and worker. If this gentleman has a suggestion as to how we can cool Sputnik, I would like to hear it. Please, Comrade, what is your idea?"

"I work in the paint shop," the maintenance man said. "I have a very fine air compressor in my shop that will put out a good, strong stream of air. Why don't we put that compressor on the flatcar, then tape a long hose along the side of the rocket, with the nozzle pointing to the nose? That would cause air to move across the Sputnik."

"Do you think you could rig up such a device?" Korolev asked.

"Yes, I'm sure I could."

Korolev nodded. "Then do so."

The mechanic's quick-fix method proved effective, and when the telemetry readings showed the temperature dropping a few degrees in the nose, he beamed proudly under the congratulations of the others. Again the flatcar was put into motion, and the rocket continued its trip out to the launch pad. Once it was in place, giant cranes raised the rocket to the vertical position; then the four arms of the gantry tower began slowly moving toward it, like the closing petals of a Venus's flytrap, until at last the four parts of the collar came together. Now the rocket was ready and held securely in place.

Korolev and the others went up to the top deck of the service tower and inspected the rocket, making certain that it had not been damaged in the erection. Then, smiling, he turned to the others.

"Gentlemen, I must fly to Moscow and report that all is ready." He looked at his watch. "It is now launch, minus twenty hours. Begin the countdown."

OCTOBER 4, 1957

Special bleachers had been erected near enough to the site to afford an excellent view of the launch. It was here in the predawn darkness that the scientists and engineers, whose work was now done, gathered with their families to watch the fruition of their months of work.

Yuri Golitsyn, whose improved fuel induction nozzle had allowed Glushko's new engine design to produce enough power, was there with Valentina and their young daughter. It was still dark, and Tamara, who had been awakened from a sound sleep, rubbed her eyes sleepily. Yuri and Valentina had considered letting her stay in bed, watched over by their housekeeper, but they decided that this was too important a moment in history to let her miss.

"Many years from now—perhaps when colonies on other planets are a reality—Tamara can tell her grandchildren that she was present on the day mankind launched its first space vehicle," Yuri said.

Tamara, of course, was far too young to understand the significance of what she was about to see, but though she was still quite sleepy, the fact that she was outside in the middle of the night was exciting, and she could also see the excitement in her parents and in the other adults.

She sat on her father's lap with her arms around his neck, watching, wide-eyed, the strange and exhilarating show that was going on around her.

Finally a bugler made his appearance at the launch pad, now illuminated by floodlights. The clear tones of his instrument were heard above the sounds of the gasoline-powered compressors and generators that were running on the pad. Then, as the bugle was lowered, a blinding flame licked down from the rocket engines. That was followed by a deep, rolling thunder, and then the rocket was totally enveloped in clouds of flame, smoke, and vapor.

"Oooh!"

"Aaah!"

"Look!"

For a second Valentina was afraid that the rocket had exploded, though she had seen launches before and knew this was normal. Then the long, silver, slender body of the rocket began to emerge slowly from the cloud. At almost the same moment a brilliant splash of light lit up the entire sky, pushing back the predawn darkness. So bright was the light that the launching tower, the assembly building, all the support machines, vehicles, bleachers, and assembled people were illuminated as clearly as if it were midday. Now the sound was upon them, a steady, rushing roar louder than the passing of a hundred trains.

The rocket rose smoothly and rapidly, increasing speed as it climbed, shooting a long, wavering flame behind it. As it got higher the ambient light grew dimmer until, finally, it was dark again, seemingly darker even than before because the brilliance of the exhaust flame had so dilated everyone's eyes. By now the rocket could be followed only by the light of its escaping fire, and even that grew smaller and smaller as it raced up into the night sky. Soon only the sharpest eyes could pick it out among all the stars above the steppe.

Cheers exploded from everyone watching as the crowd was overcome with elation. People embraced, kissed, waved their arms excitedly, and sang. A few even began to dance.

"Come, Valentina, let's get to a radio receiver!" Yuri said. "I want to hear Sputnik's signals."

He wasn't the only one with that idea; by the time they reached the control room, scores of people were gathered around the speakers. The tiny *beep, beep, beep* could clearly be heard. Then the satellite passed out of radio range.

"In ninety-five minutes," Yuri said, "we'll know if it was entirely successful."

"How?" Valentina asked.

"If we achieved orbit, it will pass all the way around the world, then come back again."

"Is there no way we can find out before that? I shall go mad with nervousness."

Yuri laughed. "In that case, we shall all go mad together. Look around the room."

Valentina glanced at the others. Some were pacing nervously about; others were chewing their fingernails. Many were smoking, and many of those would light a new cigarette from the butt of the old.

"I see what you mean," she said. She nodded at a large coffeepot. "Coffee?" she asked her husband.

"Yes, please." Yuri felt Tamara's relaxed weight in his arms, and he smiled. "I think I'll find a place to put our little adventurer," he said softly. "She seems to have had about all the excitement she can handle."

He walked over to a vacant green sofa by the far wall. Tamara didn't wake when he laid her down. Valentina came over holding two cups of coffee.

"Do you think it's still up there?" she asked.

"Yes, I'm sure it is. It was a perfect launch. If the engine developed its optimum thrust, orbit should have been achieved."

"What could keep the engine from developing optimum thrust?"

Yuri took a swallow of coffee, sucking it through extended lips to cool it. He stared over the rim of the cup for a moment, his mind looking out into space.

"If the fuel induction valve doesn't perform as it

should, it will be unable to reach maximum velocity," he finally replied.

"Yuri! You mean the success or failure of the entire project now depends upon your valve?"

"Yes."

Valentina grinned and put her hand on her husband's. "Then we have nothing to worry about. I have every confidence that the valve will work properly."

"It's time!" someone shouted, and everyone in the room fell silent as the radio receiver was turned up. A steady rush of sideband noise came over the loudspeakers for several seconds; then, breaking through the static, loud and clear, was the signal: *Beep, beep, beep* . . .

"Yuri! Yuri!" Glushko shouted. "Your valve did it!"

"It was your engine, Comrade Glushko!" Yuri shouted back.

"What about our guidance system?" another man shouted.

"And our rocket design," still another insisted.

"Don't forget, comrades, I painted the numbers on the rocket," a woman declared, and everyone laughed.

Then Sergei Korolev climbed up onto a table and held his arms out for silence. His eyes were shining with tears of joy, and when the crowd grew quiet, he told them, "This is a victory for all of us." He looked at Yuri. "Comrade Golitsyn's fuel induction valve, Comrade Glushko's engine, those who worked on the guidance system, the electronics, the rocket design"—he laughed— "yes, and even those who painted the rocket . . .

"Today we have witnessed the realization of the dream of mankind: that we would not forever be bound to this earth. Many have predicted that man would conquer space someday, and Sputnik is the first confirmation of this prophecy. The conquering of space has begun. We can be proud that it was begun by the Soviet Union. A hearty thanks to all of you!"

OCTOBER 1957, FRENCHMAN'S FLAT,
NEVADA

Bob Parker, now a specialist third class, sat on the
edge of the canvas bench, looking through the door of the
H-34 as it approached the helipad at the Army Composite
Test Group. The ACTG was composed of soldiers on temporary duty from bases all over the country. Bob was TDY
from Fort Rucker. He and the others were there to take
part in an atomic bomb test. After the blast tomorrow,
members of the ACTG would get as close to the atomic
cloud as they could, testing the limits of battlefield operations after a tactical nuclear blast.

For now, that was all Bob knew about the situation,
though there was supposed to be a meeting in the mess
tent at 1900 hours.

"Parker?" the pilot, Captain Kilby, said into Bob's
headset.

"Yes, sir?"

*"Where do you want me to set down? Do you need to
do anything to the ship before tomorrow?"*

"No, sir, it's all ready," Bob replied. "You can set her
down out on the flight line."

*"What about fuel? I don't see anyone out here to meet
us."*

"I'll get the truck out, sir."

"Good," the pilot said.

The blades popped loudly as the helicopter descended through its own rotor wash until, about five feet
off the ground, just high enough to keep from kicking up
too much dust and sand, the pilot stopped the descent.
He then hovered slowly over to one of the square pads
made from perforated steel planking. As the aircraft was
gently set down, Bob watched the silver Oleo struts on
the landing gear compress. When they were fully com-
pressed, indicating that the aircraft was solidly down, he
jumped from the box and ran around to the front of the
'copter so the pilot could see him. When he was satisfied
that the ship wouldn't have to be repositioned, he drew
his finger across his throat as a signal for the pilot to cut

his engine. As the blades began freewheeling down, Bob shoved the yellow chocks against the wheels. Pulling out the blade-tie-down straps, he waited until the blades stopped whirling, then secured one and tied it to the tail cone.

The pilot climbed down from the cockpit, carrying the small green, plastic-covered flight logbook.

"Any new write-ups in the dash twenty, sir?" Bob asked.

"Nothing new," Kilby said. "But I wish you'd get that fresh-air vent fixed. It's driving me nuts, spinning around like that."

"Tell you what. Seven-one-five is on EDP for rod-end bearings," Bob said. "There's no way those bearings are going to get here before the shot tomorrow. I'll take the air vent from it. That is, if you'll clear it with Mr. Brandywine for me. He doesn't like for us to take parts off Red-X aircraft."

"He's right," Kilby said. "That's how hangar queens are born. You take one part, then another, then another, and the next thing you know, all you have left is a hulk. But this is a special case—we need to have as many aircraft up as possible tomorrow. You go ahead and do it. I'll clear it with the maintenance officer."

"Thank you, sir," Bob said. "I'll get right on it."

Thirty minutes later, with the helicopter fueled and serviced, Bob was just finishing replacing the fresh air vent when Logan Pounders drove up in a jeep.

"Colonel Metzger wants everyone in the mess tent," he said.

Bob looked at his watch. "Why does he want us now? I thought the briefing was at seven. It's just after five."

"Somethin's come up," Logan said.

"Okay, I'm finished anyway," Bob said. "Close up my toolbox while I write up the dash twenty, will you?"

"Okay," Logan said agreeably.

On the DISCREPANCY line of the maintenance record, Bob found the red diagonal entry: Fresh-air vent broken, pilot's side. He put his initials over the red diagonal, then in the ACTION TAKEN section wrote: *Replaced with fresh-air vent taken from A/C 715.*

Moments later he was riding in the jeep's passenger seat as Logan drove back across the airfield toward the row of tents that served as living quarters, administrative offices, and mess hall.

"So exactly what is this something that's come up that the colonel moved the meeting up?" Bob asked. "Has he got a hot date in Reno?"

"You got me," Logan said. "All I know is it's somethin' big."

"Something big. What do you mean, something big?"

"I don't know. Somethin' to do with the Russians. I think maybe they're gettin' ready to move into West Germany or somethin'."

"Bullshit."

"I'm not shittin' you," Logan said. "I'm tellin' you, somethin' is up with the Russians, man."

When they reached the mess tent, several others were already there. The supper meal was ready. Bob could tell by the aroma that they were having pork chops, and it made him hungry. But the chow line wasn't open yet and wouldn't be until after the mysterious meeting.

"Did you hear about the Russians?" someone asked Bob as he got out of the jeep.

"Wait a minute, you mean Logan is telling the truth? The Russians *did* do something?"

"I'll say they did. They launched a missile," the soldier said.

"A missile? Where?"

"Toward us, man. Toward the United States."

"*WHAT?!* Where did it hit?"

"It hasn't hit anywhere yet."

"When did they launch it?"

"I don't know, man. All I know is, they launched it."

"Shit, that can't be true. If so, we'd be at war now."

"Yeah, well, maybe we are. I heard we're not even goin' home," Logan said. "I heard we aren't even goin' to drop the bomb here tomorrow; we're just goin' to load it up and take it with us."

Bob thought of Marilou back in Ozark. Ironically, she probably knew more about what was happening than he did, because she would've been watching it all on television. He had been out there in the field for two weeks, and in that two weeks he hadn't watched one TV program, listened to one radio, or seen one newspaper. He wished there was some way he could call her—not only to tell her that he might not be coming back home, but also to find out what she knew about the situation.

On second thought, it was probably just as well that he not call her. They had been married for a year, and they had fought almost the entire time. The temper Marilou had shown on their wedding night had quickly manifested itself in their marriage. He thought of the fight they had the night before he left for this TDY. It had started because she was angry with him for volunteering to go on temporary duty with the composite unit that would be testing the bomb. Bob thought it would be an interesting experience and good for his career. She told him it was selfish of him to leave her alone for two weeks —and besides, she had said snidely, what career was he talking about?

"You're just an enlisted man! Who would've ever thought that Marilou Pepperdine would marry an enlisted man? When I was in high school, I was the president of the class, the head twirler, and the president of the Twentieth Century Sorority," she said. *"I was going to attend school at Auburn, where I would have pledged Tri Delt—just like all my friends. But no! What am I now? I am nothing! I am the wife of a private!"*

"I'm a specialist third class; that's an E-four," Bob rejoined.

"Private, E-four, sergeant . . . what difference does it make? Like I said, you're an enlisted man. I can't believe that I wound up marrying an enlisted man."

"I could have been an officer," Bob reminded her.

"Oh, so now you're going to bring up how I stopped you from getting your appointment to West Point, are you? If you knew you had the appointment, why didn't you say something?"

"I don't know—you seemed determined to get married."

"And you sure took advantage of it, didn't you?" Marilou retorted. *"You knew I wasn't thinking straight that night. My God, who could think straight, watching you and my father brawling like a couple of common hoodlums?"*

"Marilou, do you want a divorce?"

"And be even more of a laughingstock among my friends? Heavens no! No, my dear husband, we're stuck together, you and I, so we may as well make the best of it. All I can say is, thank God we don't have any children. It's bad enough being Mrs. Housewife. I couldn't take a bunch of screaming brats and messy diapers."

"At ease!" someone yelled, jerking Bob out of his painful memory. All conversation in the mess hall stopped as Colonel Metzger and his staff came in. Metzger was carrying a small swagger stick, and he slapped it nervously against the side of his leg as he faced his men. Bob tried to read the expression on the colonel's face, but he couldn't.

"Men," Metzger said, "I have heard some of the wild rumors circulating through the group, and I thought it was time I came down here and gave you the straight scoop. Some of you may have heard that the Russians launched a missile this morning and that it's heading for the U.S." He paused to let that sink in. "Well," he continued, "in a way, that's true."

"What?"

"There's a missile coming here?"

"Are we at war, sir?"

The colonel held up his hands to signal everyone to be quiet.

"At ease!" the first sergeant shouted.

"It isn't exactly a missile," Colonel Metzger continued. "What it is, is a satellite. The Russians are calling it Sputnik. I'm told that means something like 'little traveler.'"

"Colonel, just what is this . . . satellite?"

Metzger made a fist with his left hand. With the index finger of his right he began circling his fist. "The moon is a satellite," he explained. "Some scientists believe the moon was once a piece of earth that broke away billions of years ago. Others believe it was just a body moving through space that came close enough to earth to be caught in the earth's gravitational pull. Whatever it is, gravity holds it locked in an orbit around earth. Now, from what I understand, the Russians have put up a small artificial moon, a device fired into space by a rocket, that, like the moon, is orbiting around the earth."

"Sir, is this thing passing over the United States?" someone asked.

Metzger nodded. "Every hour and a half," he answered.

"Colonel, does this-here artificial moon have an atomic bomb on it?" someone else asked.

Metzger sighed. "I wish I could tell you with absolute certainty that it doesn't, but the truth is, we don't know for sure. The Russians have told the world that it contains only a few 'scientific instruments,' whatever that means."

"If it does have a bomb, can they bring it down on us, anywhere they want to?"

"We don't really know the answer to that, either," the colonel admitted.

"Sir, why don't we just send up a couple of our missiles and shoot the son of a bitch down?"

Metzger shook his head. "We can't do that. Russia has announced that Sputnik is part of the International Geophysical Year. They claim that the launch is for the benefit of all mankind. If we shot it down, we'd be the bad guys. And the truth is, I'm not sure we could shoot it down anyway."

"Shit."

"Colonel, are we on alert? Are we going overseas?" someone asked.

Metzger smiled and shook his head again. "No, we aren't on alert. But in light of what has just happened, I think that tomorrow's exercise is more important than ever. God help us if it should ever come to that, but if the situation arises where tactical nuclear weapons are used, then we'll need men who can operate as near the blast as quickly as possible. We'll be testing those limits tomorrow. The Russians may have a rocket that can put a satellite in orbit—but we have the finest fighting men in the world."

"Damn right!" someone shouted, and everyone else cheered.

"Gentlemen, I will see you tomorrow."

The helicopters were dark shapes silhouetted against the red dawn sky when Bob walked out to the flight line the next morning. Several other crew chiefs were already there in various stages of their daily inspections. Bob untied the blade, took off the pitot-tube cover, and wiped away the overnight condensation from the windshield. Though he had fueled and serviced the helicopter just last night, he opened the fuel caps and looked inside, then checked the dipsticks for both engine and transmission oil. He then drained the moisture away from the tank and waited for his pilot to show up.

The H-34 was capable of carrying a crew of three plus a fully equipped infantry squad. According to their action plan, the soldiers and the aircrews would witness the blast from specially prepared trenches around the edge of the airfield. The helicopters would wait until after the blast, and then an entire infantry battalion would be lifted and flown as close to ground zero as the radiation sensors would let them go. The purpose of the exercise was to provide psychological training for soldiers who might be asked to go into battle immediately after a battlefield tactical nuclear blast.

A jeep with a red flag tied to its whip radio antenna

came driving quickly along the flight line. The jeep was equipped with a loudspeaker.

"Attention on the flight line! It is now T minus five minutes. All personnel proceed to the trenches!"

The men had been issued very dark glasses, which they now put on—though as they were too dark to see through under ordinary circumstances, they were left flipped up just above the eyes. They were told to look away from the blast area until after the initial flash.

"You ever seen one of these things go off before, Captain Kilby?" Bob asked.

"Never have," Kilby replied.

"Me neither. Are you nervous?"

"Not really. Why? Are you?"

"Well, not about the blast, exactly," Bob said. "I'm wondering, though, if we're going to get any unusual turbulence when we fly through it."

"We shouldn't," Captain Kilby said. "The shock wave will have already passed by then."

"One minute!" the loudspeaker blared. *"Everyone put on their dark glasses! Face away from ground zero!"*

Turning around, Bob flipped the glasses down. They were so dark that it had the same effect as blindfolding himself.

"Five, four, three, two, one!"

Although by now it was already a bright day, the light of the blast was so intense that even through the dark glasses Bob could see in vivid detail every vehicle, stick, rock, and grain of sand. The illumination lasted for several seconds, then faded, and Bob turned to look at the blast site, remembering to keep the glasses on.

The sight that greeted him was unbelievable. A huge bubble of fire—not flames, but a pure white light—was forming on the distant horizon. It continued to grow, larger and larger, so that for a second Bob had the irrational thought that it wasn't going to quit growing, but would eventually engulf them all.

The fireball lasted for about thirty seconds, bright at first, then gradually diminishing. Then, about thirty seconds later, the shock wave reached them with a loud bang and crack. Since this was the first time Bob had witnessed an atomic bomb blast, he was surprised that there was something familiar about the sound. Then he realized what it was. He had once been very close to a lightning strike, and this was exactly the same kind of sound.

The shock wave arrived concurrently with the sound, a huge wall of pressure that made Bob's skin tingle. Carried along with the shock wave was a wall of debris, as if blown before a strange sort of wind, unlike any wind he had ever experienced before.

Then there was silence—a long, long, eerie silence. A huge, rolling black cloud of smoke and vaporized residue began rising, climbing higher and higher where it rushed out to form a big cap, and Bob realized then with a little thrill that he was seeing the famous mushroom cloud that was the signature of all nuclear blasts.

After that a hot wind came up, rushing from behind them back toward the blast, as if the bomb were sucking up all the oxygen.

"Okay, let's go!" someone shouted. "Into the aircraft!"

All up and down the line, men crawled out of the trench and headed for the helicopters. Captain Kilby and Warrant Officer Downing were the pilots of Bob's helicopter, and they clambered up the side of the aircraft and into their seats. The infantry squad got on board as Bob took the fire extinguisher out front to stand guard while the engine was started. A moment later, with the rotors spinning overhead, Bob hopped into the helicopter and slipped on his headset.

"Up!" he said, letting the pilot know that he was ready.

The helicopter lifted up from the pad, turned the nose toward the mushroom cloud that now looked so solid that it appeared to be a permanent part of the landscape, then took off. It joined other helicopters already in the air.

As Bob looked down through the open door at the desert floor rolling below, he could see another network of trenches, much closer to ground zero than he had been.

And several hundred yards ahead of these trenches were hundreds of soldiers marching toward the cloud.

Bob looked at the radiation badges he and the others were wearing and was reassured. They were still reading "safe."

CHAPTER

FIFTEEN

The succulent smell of baking ham permeated Della Booker's house. Artemus Booker leaned his large frame forward on the sofa and looked through the door toward the kitchen.

"Grandmother, how much longer?" he asked. "I'm starving to death in here."

Della, wearing an apron and carrying a wooden mixing spoon, stepped into the living room. She shook her head and chuckled, "I swear, Artemus, you haven't changed one bit since the day you and your brother came to live with Loomis and me. You always could eat more than any two men I ever knew."

"You always said growing boys had to eat," Artemus countered.

"Yes, and look what happened. You started growing and you didn't stop. You're a giant."

"I'm only six five. I wish you could see some of the

really big fellows in the NBA," Artemus said. "I'm almost a dwarf beside them."

"That's the way I am beside *you*," Deon complained, putting down the paper he was reading in his favorite chair.

"Well, I *am* your big brother, after all," Artemus said, grinning.

Deon groaned. "That was a cheap laugh. Anyway, now I know what happened. Grandmother took food off *my* plate to feed *you*."

"Deon!" Della said with an exasperated gasp. "I did no such thing!"

He laughed. "That's all right. You can make it up to me by letting me have just a little piece of that ham now —just to hold me over until dinner."

"No," Della replied. "This is the first time we've managed to have an Easter together in I don't know how long, and I'm not going to spoil it by letting you boys get into the ham before I'm ready. You just sit there and watch TV. Dinner will be ready soon." She turned and went back to the kitchen.

"It was nice, you buying this house for Grand- mother," Deon said softly to his brother.

"I was glad I could do it for her," Artemus answered. "Besides, I'm making really good money, and I couldn't think of anything better to do with it."

"Uh-huh, I read about your new contract," Deon said. "Sixty thousand a year, the paper said." He tented his fingers, then held them against his pursed lips for a long moment as he looked at his brother.

"What is it, Deon?" Artemus asked. "Why are you looking at me like that?"

"Artemus, do you have any idea how much money Dr. Martin Luther King makes a year?"

"No, not really."

"I mean, he's pretty well-known, isn't he? He's met with world leaders, he's given speeches in churches and colleges all across America, he's been on television and in newsreels and newspapers and magazines. . . . He's as well-known as you are."

Artemus laughed. "I'd say he's better known. You'd be surprised at how many people there are out there who don't like basketball. And the ones who don't have never heard of me."

"Dr. King makes five thousand dollars a year," Deon said.

"Five thousand! Man, I would've thought he made more."

"Where would he get it from?"

"I don't know. Maybe from speaking fees or something."

"The money he gets for speaking goes back to pay the expenses for all he does."

"And you're trying to tell me there's not just a little left over for King?"

"No."

Artemus smiled. "Then he's missing the boat somewhere."

"You don't really know anything about him, do you?" Deon asked. "I mean, to suggest something like that."

"Come on, Deon, I was just teasing."

"Do you know anything about what men like King and Rustin and, for that matter, what *I* am trying to do?"

"I guess not."

"You guess not. Of course you don't. Why should you? Why should you even care? You're well taken care of —what difference does it make to you if others of our race are being oppressed? You just go right on jumping through the hoop."

"Deon, just what are you trying to say to me?" Artemus asked testily. "Are you telling me you think I'm wasting my time playing basketball? It's an honest profession."

"You don't have to justify it to me. If you want to play the white man's game, it's up to you," Deon said, shrugging.

Artemus hooted. "A white man's game? You're calling *basketball* a white man's game? My God, have you ever been to a game? Sometimes twenty or thirty minutes will go by with not one white face on the floor."

"But who's in the stands, my brother? Answer me that," Deon challenged.

"Basketball fans."

"*White* basketball fans. Oh, yes, there are a few Negroes in the stands, too, but for the most part they're filled with white fans who've come to see the trained monkeys."

"And that's what you think we are? Trained monkeys?"

"When you do something that has no earthly purpose other than entertaining the white man, yes, you are a trained monkey."

"And you are full of shit," Artemus rejoined. "I suppose next you'll be telling me not to take the white man's money."

Deon smiled. "No, that's the only good thing about it."

"Well, I'm glad we at least agree on that point."

"But while we're on the subject of money, have you stopped to think that here you are, twenty-three years old, and you make in one year what it takes Dr. King twelve years to earn? And that Grandfather and our father didn't make that much money together in their entire lives?"

"Times have changed," Artemus said, uncomfortable with the discussion.

"Can you live with that?"

Artemus sighed. "What is it, Deon? Do you need some money? If so, just ask. I told you a long time ago, anytime you wanted—"

"No!" Deon said sharply, holding up his hand. "I don't want your money. I don't *need* your money."

"Then what the hell is it?" Artemus snapped. "What is all this about?"

"Artemus, there isn't a Negro child in America who doesn't look up to you," Deon said. "And I wouldn't be surprised if most of the white children didn't also think you're a hero. Can't you see what a platform that gives you?"

"A platform?"

"Yes, a platform. You could take a stand against racial discrimination."

"Take a stand against racial discrimination? Do you think I'm in favor of it?"

"You may as well be, for all you've done for those of us who are fighting the battles."

"Deon, have you forgotten that I gave a check for ten thousand dollars to the Montgomery Students' Coalition?"

"You gave it anonymously," Deon said.

"Yes, I did, but I've also given to other charitable organizations anonymously. I've always been suspect of people who make a big thing about their charity."

"Goddammit, Artemus, that's just what I'm talking about!" Deon sputtered. "You're talking about this like it's some charity! It's not, don't you understand that?"

"Then what is it?"

"It's war!" Deon sighed, then stroked his cheek. "You remember me telling you about Claudia Baker, don't you? How she was one of the original members?"

"Yes. She was the one who got hurt in the church bombing," Artemus said.

"She was a beautiful girl, full of life and vitality. She made you feel good to be around her, and when the movement started, she was right up front."

"You're talking about her in the past tense. I thought she recovered from the bombing."

"Physically, yes. But she's been permanently scarred, and she's very self-conscious about those scars, convinced that they're disfiguring. She does have disfiguring scars, but the disfigurement doesn't come from the scars on her face; the disfiguring scars are the ones on her soul. She has never been the same since that day. Oh, she still works for the movement—operating the mimeograph machine, stuffing envelopes, making telephone calls, things that keep her in the background. But she's lost the spark she once had."

"I'm sorry to hear that," Artemus said.

"Me, too," Deon replied. "Because our movement can't afford to lose people like Claudia—people who have leadership and vitality. Dr. King has it, but he's known as a civil rights leader. What we need now are a few well-known leaders from outside the civil rights field. Movie stars, singers, sports figures. People like you."

"All right," Artemus said. "I'll donate another ten thousand dollars."

"Goddammit! We don't want your goddamn money, we want *you*! Don't you understand me, you white man's nigger?" Deon shouted.

Artemus stood up quickly and made a fist. Defiantly, Deon stood up to him.

"For heaven's sake, boys, what is going on in here?" Della asked, coming in from the kitchen, her face and voice fearful.

Artemus and Deon glared at each other for a long moment; then, abruptly, Artemus laughed.

"You stubborn little shit. You would try to stand up to me, wouldn't you?" he said to his brother.

Deon smiled back. "It wouldn't be the first time you ever whipped my ass."

"Boys, please, whatever it is, put it behind you," Della begged. "Come to dinner now. This is Easter Sunday. This is the Lord's day."

There was no further discussion of the subject that had nearly brought the two brothers to blows—neither during dinner nor later, when they were visiting in the living room. Artemus entertained his grandmother and Deon with funny tales of life on the road with the basketball team, and Deon shared anecdotes of the civil rights struggle going on in Alabama, some amusing, some tragic.

Artemus leaned forward on the sofa. "Deon, does your Martin Luther King—"

"He's *everyone's* Martin Luther King, Artemus," Deon interrupted.

"Deon, you talk about him like he is Lord Jesus Christ himself," Della said.

"He is."

"Watch your mouth, boy! That's blasphemy!"

"I don't mean it in a blasphemous way, Grandmother," Deon said. "I mean that Mike is—"

"Mike?" It was Artemus's turn to interrupt.

Deon smiled. "That's Dr. King's birth name. There aren't too many people who know that and fewer yet who call him that."

"Is that what *you* call him?" Della asked.

Deon laughed sheepishly. "No, Grandmother. I call him Dr. King."

"Uh-huh. Well, now that you've tried impressing us with how familiar you are with him, tell us why you think he's the Christ," she said.

"Well, not the Christ himself, but he is the personification of all that Christ taught. And think about it. If Jesus were to come to earth today, he would surely come as a Negro. But, Artemus, you were about to ask a question about him, weren't you?"

"Yes, I was wondering if your Martin Luther King really believes that the passage of civil rights legislation will suddenly make everyone love Negroes. You can't do that with law."

"You sound like Eisenhower when he said you can't legislate morality. So I'll give you the same answer Dr. King gave *him*. He said, 'Mr. President, I don't want a law passed where the white man will love me. I only want a law passed that will keep the white man from lynching me.'"

"That sounds reasonable enough," Artemus said dryly.

"Yes, I suppose it does sound reasonable, here in Grandmother's living room in St. Louis, Missouri. But try it out on a bus in Montgomery."

Later that evening, long after Della had gone to bed and Deon was sitting in the living room watching Jack Paar on *The Tonight Show*, Artemus stepped out onto the front porch. The dark lawns, shrubs, and trees around him were filled with the sounds of cicadas and frogs. From the sky overhead came the sound of an airliner climbing out of Lambert Field, and when he looked up, he saw its red and green lights blinking against the vault of stars. Behind him the screen door opened and then closed; Deon had come out to stand on the porch with him.

"It's peaceful out here," Artemus said, not looking around.

"Yes."

"I was lucky to be able to get this house for her. There aren't that many on the market in this neighborhood, and when they do come available, they're grabbed up pretty fast."

"By this neighborhood, you mean upper-class Negro neighborhood?"

"Yes, of course."

"Right."

"What are you suggesting, Deon? That I buy a house in a white neighborhood and move Grandmother in there?"

"Of course not. That's not possible, is it?"

"No. But I wouldn't do it even if it were. What would Grandmother do there? Make friends with all her white neighbors? Could you see her going to afternoon bridge with the Canfields or the Danforths?"

Deon laughed. "Not really."

They were silent for a moment; then Artemus spoke again.

"I know what you were saying before. And I confess that I feel guilty because I haven't spoken up more about racial injustices. I mean, even in my own sport—dominated as it is by Negro players—discrimination exists. Do you know how many Negro referees there are? How many Negro scorekeepers? How many Negro trainers? Or statisticians?"

"I have no idea."

"Well, there aren't very many. And when you get into the coaching area, the answer is really simple. There are none."

"And you go along with that?" Deon asked.

"No, I don't go along with it. I—" Artemus paused, then sighed. "Yes," he admitted. "Yes, I do go along with it, because I have no choice. I don't like it . . . but I do go along with it."

"Artemus, don't you see? You could start there," Deon said. "You don't have to come down to Montgomery and take part in one of Dr. King's prayer vigils to do your part. You could speak out against the racism in the NBA. And if you could draw everyone's attention to that—it's at least something."

"Do you know what would happen to me if I called the NBA racist?"

"I'm sure you wouldn't be very popular with the powers that be."

"I'd be dropped like a hot potato."

"What if you went to all the other players and asked them to stand by you? What if you organized them and—"

"They would never do it," Artemus said firmly.

"How do you know they won't until you try?"

"Deon, you pointed out that I'm making sixty thousand dollars a year. And I'm not the highest paid player in the league—not even on my team. That means there are an awful lot of Negroes making an awful lot of money. Do you think they could make that kind of money anywhere else?"

"I wouldn't think so."

"Suppose I did get a couple of the others to stand by me. Suppose I got several others. It's a cinch I wouldn't get them all—not with the kind of money they're making by doing something they love to do. And if I didn't get them all, little brother, the ones who supported me would be out on their collective asses, and the ones who didn't support me would take up the slack. The games would go on, and the average white man in the stands would never even notice the difference."

"But oppressed Negroes all over America would know," Deon said. "And they would applaud you for it."

"Deon, even if I did make this one bold statement, what then? Scuttling my career would be a flash in the pan. But when that flash dimmed, what further use would I be to anyone—to Grandmother or to you or to myself? I don't have the eloquence of a Dr. Martin Luther King. I couldn't sustain my importance to the cause. Where would I go? How would I make a living? I couldn't work in the white man's world; they'd view me as an agitator. And believe me, those Negro players who would remain in the NBA would *not* benefit from my futile gesture. If anything, it would make their lot worse. What you're asking me to do is throw away everything I've worked for, for no good reason. Well, that's asking a hell of a lot, Deon. And I won't do it."

"Artemus, I never thought I would say this about my own brother," Deon said quietly, "but you are a coward."

Artemus stared into the night without answering. After a moment he heard the door open and shut as Deon went back inside.

Then, alone in the night, Artemus wept.

FORT WOLTERS, TEXAS

When Sergeant E-5 Parker reported to the admissions office for Warrant Officer Candidate School at Fort Wolters, he was met by a tactical training NCO.

"Is there something I can help you with, Sergeant?" the noncom asked pleasantly. His name tag identified him as Weathers.

"Yes," Bob said. He held up a manila envelope that contained his 201 File and his orders. "I'm reporting in to Warrant Officer Candidate School. Is this where I go?"

Bob didn't really have to ask. He knew this was where he was supposed to be, not only by the signs but also because scattered around on the lawn and in the parking area were a dozen or more soldiers, all being braced and yelled at by the tactical NCOs. However, SFC Weathers had spoken to him, and he felt obligated to reply.

"You've come to the right place," Weathers answered. "It's right inside that door. Just sign in and hand your orders to the processing clerk. After that, why don't you come on back out here, and I'll show you where to go?"

"Gee, thanks, Sergeant," Bob said. "That's very nice

of you." He was a little confused as to why the sergeant was being so kind to *him* when everyone else was being harassed.

"Are those guys new candidates?" Bob asked, nodding toward them.

"I do believe they are," Weathers answered.

Bob laughed. "They must've screwed up really bad."

"Yes," SFC Weathers said, smiling pleasantly. "Well, they were all privates, fresh out of basic training, you see, and this is a difficult course. But, you being a sergeant, I'm sure you won't have any trouble." He pointed toward the administration building. "Just go on in," he invited.

"Thanks."

Bob handed his orders to the clerk, then signed in. "What building will I be assigned to?" he asked the clerk.

"Don't worry about that, Candidate," the clerk answered. "That unpleasant NCO standing just outside the door will help you with that."

"Unpleasant? He wasn't unpleasant to me," Bob replied.

"Maybe he just likes you." The clerk chuckled. "Aren't you the lucky one?"

Bob picked up his duffel bag and started back outside where, as the clerk had pointed out, SFC Weathers was standing patiently, waiting for him.

"Did you get signed in?" Weathers asked, still smiling congenially.

"Yes, thank you."

The smile fell away instantly, and Weathers's face contorted into an expression halfway between a sneer and a snarl.

"CANDIDATE PARKER! EVERY TIME YOU OPEN YOUR MOUTH YOU WILL SAY, 'SIR, CANDIDATE PARKER!' AND ONLY THEN WILL YOU UTTER WHATEVER INANE, UNIMPORTANT LITTLE PIECE OF SHIT YOU FEEL COMPELLED TO UTTER! DO YOU UNDERSTAND THAT?" Weathers screamed at the top of his voice.

"I'm sorry, I didn't know I was supposed to say 'sir' to a sergeant," Bob replied.

In a slightly lower but still-piercing voice, the non-com replied, "You are a warrant officer candidate, Candidate. You will say sir to everyone and everything! You are the lowest thing in the universe, Candidate! You are lower than whale shit, which resides on the ocean floor. Now, how low are you?"

"Sir, I am—"

"You are a dumb asshole, aren't you Candidate? How long does it take you to learn?"

"Sir, Candidate Parker! I am lower than whale shit, sir!"

"And where does that whale shit reside, Candidate Parker?"

"Sir, Candidate Parker! Whale shit resides on the bottom of the ocean, sir!"

"No, that is not where it resides. You are a dumb asshole! Where does it reside?"

"At the bottom—"

"What did you say to me, Do-screw?"

"Sir, Candidate Parker! Whale shit resides"—Bob stopped for a second to recall the exact wording—"on the ocean floor, sir!"

"See, it is not impossible for you to learn," Weathers said. "Improbable, but not impossible. Do you think you will survive this course, Candidate?"

"Sir, Candidate Parker. Yes, sir!"

"Then get those stripes off your arm, Candidate. You are no longer a sergeant. You are a lowly Warrant Officer Candidate. You are disgracing the rank of sergeant by wearing those stripes."

"Sir, Candidate Parker! Yes, sir," Bob said, reaching up and ripping the stripes off his sleeves.

After nearly fifteen minutes of harassment, not only by Weathers but by sometimes as many as a half-dozen others, Bob was finally allowed to proceed to his barracks. It was nearly midnight before all the activity calmed down and he was allowed to go to bed.

Some of the other candidates were already beginning to wonder if they had made a mistake in choosing to come to Warrant Officer Candidate School—but there was no question in Bob's mind. When he got married he had thrown away forever any chance of going to West Point. Now, however, by attending the flight-training program, he could win his wings and an appointment to the rank of warrant officer, W-1.

Before he entered the Army, Bob hadn't even known what a warrant officer was. Now he knew there were four grades of warrant officers: W-1, CW-2, CW-3, and CW-4. He knew also that warrant officers generally served as technicians rather than commanders, and throughout the Army they could be found in such fields as missiles, electronics, communications, supply, personnel, and aviation. The four grades of warrant were somewhat equivalent in pay and respect to the first four commissioned grades. Warrants were addressed as "mister," treated as officers in all respects, and rated salutes from enlisted men. The rank and prestige of a warrant officer appealed to Bob almost as much as the flying.

"Warrant officers can never make general," Mr. Easterman had told Bob before he left Fort Rucker for Warrant Officer Candidate School. "But they have *made* a lot of generals."

Preflight was designed to weed out as many candidates as possible, and over the next four weeks the WOCs had to run everywhere they went. In the mess hall they could sit for their meals only when every chair at their table was full—and then only on the first four inches of the chair. They had to eat a square meal by bringing their forks straight up to the level of their mouth, making a right-angle turn to bring the fork straight across to their mouth, then returning the fork to the tray in the same way before the food could be chewed. They spit-shined floors and shoes and made their bunks so tightly that a quarter would flip over when dropped on the blanket.

After four weeks of almost twenty-four-hour-per-day harassment, preflight was over. By now nearly one fourth of the class had been eliminated. It was possible for a candidate to drop out of the course merely by going to the orderly room and requesting dismissal, and many of those who couldn't take the constant harassment had taken that

option. Others had been eliminated by "board action."
Those who remained—and Bob breathed a sigh of relief
because he was one of them—were told the preflight part
of their course was over. They were about to begin primary flight training.

Bob had an advantage over many of the other candidates. He had been a helicopter crew chief for nearly two
years, most of that time as an instructor in the maintenance school that produced crew chiefs. Crew chiefs not
only maintained helicopters, they flew with them. Because of that, Bob was already oriented toward helicopter
flight; thus, the sensation of being in a box that did not
itself fly, but rather was supported in the air by hanging
from a spinning disk that *did* fly, was not new to him.

When at last it was Bob's turn to take his first in-
structional ride, he hurried anxiously from the bleachers
to the "flying classroom." The helicopter they were using
for instruction was a Hiller H-23, the kind of craft whose
front was a large plastic bubble. It was sitting on the
ground in front of them with its engine running and the
main-rotor and tail-rotor blades spinning. Bob ducked under the whirling blades, then sat in the seat, feeling the
vibrations and listening to the clack, clatter, roar, and pop
of the engine, transmission, and rotor system.

"Strap yourself in," the instructor pilot said. The IP
was a civilian.

"Yes, sir," Bob said. When the IP started to show him
what to do, Bob said, "That's all right, I've been a crew
chief for two years."

"Good. Then I don't have to point out which is the
collective and which is the cyclic, do I?"

"No, sir."

"Point them out to me."

"This is the collective," Bob said, pointing to the little stick under his left hand.

"What does it do?"

"When you pull up on the collective it adds pitch or
bite to the rotor blades, so the helicopter goes up."

"Wrong."

"Wrong?"

"The helicopter goes up only if you add power at the same time," the IP said. He pointed to the throttle, which, like a motorcycle throttle, was a twist type. "When you pull up on the collective, you must roll in power. When you go down, you back off on the power. Do you understand that?"

"Yes, sir."

"Show me the cyclic."

Bob pointed to the stick that came up from the floor between his legs.

"And what does it do?"

"It changes the pitch in only one blade at a time in a cyclical fashion, thus tilting the rotor disk and providing directional control."

"Very good," the IP said. "You do know the controls, don't you?"

"Yes, sir."

"And the antitorque pedals?"

Bob pointed them out, explaining that they put pitch into the tail rotor, thereby keeping the helicopter straight by overcoming the torque created by the engine. "You push the left pedal as you add power and the right pedal as you decrease power," Bob said, remembering that from his crew chief training.

"Excellent," the IP said. "We aren't going to have any trouble at all, are we?" He lifted the helicopter smoothly and easily, then flew over to a large field. He lowered to about a five-foot hover and pointed the helicopter toward a small maintenance shack painted in red-and-white checkerboard squares. "Now," he said, "I'll keep control of the cyclic and collective, you take the pedals. All I want you to do is keep us pointed toward that building."

"Yes, sir." Bob put his feet on the pedals and could feel the tremor and vibration of the whole ship.

"You've got it," the IP said.

The building started slipping off to the right, and Bob pushed on the right pedal. He pushed too far, and the building whipped by to the left.

"You *do* see the building I'm talking about, don't you?" the IP said dryly. "I believe it's red and white."

"Yes, sir. I see it," Bob said.

"Ah, then you're doing better than I am, because I seem to have lost it."

"It's way over here to my left," Bob said sheepishly.

"I've got it," the IP said, putting his feet back on the pedals. Instantly, the building popped back into the center of the glass bubble. "Perhaps you didn't understand. I want you to keep the building right there in front of us."

"Yes, sir."

"Okay, you've got it."

The building began drifting away again.

"What's the matter? You don't like the colors?"

"I'm sorry," Bob said. As he pressed first one pedal then the other, trying to peg the building in the middle, the helicopter began to swing back and forth. Finally the aircraft turned so much that the building was no longer in sight.

"Do you know where the building is now?"

"Uh, I think it's behind us. Yes, sir, it must be behind us."

"Good thinking. Do you believe you can find it?"

"Yes, sir."

"Please, do so."

Bob pushed one pedal hard and the helicopter suddenly spun all the way around. The building flashed in front, going by so fast that it was a blur.

"Was that it?" the IP asked calmly.

"Yes, sir, I believe it was."

"I've got it," the IP said.

The helicopter stopped its spinning, and the building was pegged in front of them as still as if it had been painted on the bubble.

"Okay, you've got that mastered. Let's go on to the collective," the IP suggested.

Bob's collective and cyclic techniques proved to be about as smooth as his technique with the antitorque pedals. When he was given all three controls at the same time, he was certain he would have killed them both had the IP not taken over at several crucial points. By the time they returned to the staging area, he was red-faced and too embarrassed to talk to any of the others. He ducked under the spinning rotor blades and ran toward the bleachers as the next man hurried out to take his turn. He was almost certain he would not be allowed back in a helicopter ever again.

To Bob's pleasant surprise they did let him back in the helicopter, and he gradually learned how to keep, in the words of his IP, "all these vibrating, agitating, clattering parts in the air, moving in roughly the same direction at roughly the same time."

Finally the day came when, after successfully demonstrating that he could autorotate all the way to the ground without killing himself and the trainer, the IP stepped out of the cockpit.

"It's all yours, Parker," he said. "Don't bend it up." He gave Bob a wave as he ducked under the rotors and ran off, leaving Bob all alone.

Bob sat there for a moment, feeling the tremors the small H-23 fed back through the collective and cyclic sticks in his hands and the pedals at his feet. He looked out through the bubble, then up, where he could see the little black line of the leading edge of the rotor disk spinning just overhead. He moved the cyclic back and forth and watched the line dip and climb. When he glanced back at the panel he could see the quivering needles of the many dials, including the two needles joined together in the tachometer dial, one showing engine RPM, the other showing rotor RPM.

Bob was about to fly solo, and this was the most thrilling moment of his life. He smiled. He wasn't frightened, just excited. He squeezed the mike button on the cyclic.

"Three-three-one, lane six for takeoff," he said.

"Three-three-one, winds zero-eight-nine at fifteen, altimeter two niner-niner-eight, clear to takeoff."

"Three-three-one," Bob answered. He took a deep breath, rolled in power, raised the collective, and pressed in the left pedal. He turned into the wind, pushed the cyclic forward to generate forward motion, then felt the helicopter beginning to move. When he reached translational lift, the helicopter started climbing, and the ground dropped away under the chin of the bubble. He held a one-thousand-foot-per-minute climb until he was at twelve hundred feet; then he turned left and looked back at the airfield he had just departed. From that aspect, the other helicopters, the cars and trucks, the people, and the buildings looked miniscule. He felt a tremendous sense of detachment as if there were actually two worlds, the one he was seeing below and the world of the H-23 helicopter of which he was the only inhabitant.

Bob had never felt a more exhilarating sense of freedom than he was feeling at this very moment. He wanted to shout and laugh and scream with the thrill of it, but he held back. Then he realized that there was no need to restrain himself: He was up here all alone, the emperor of this little world.

He opened his mouth and shouted as loud as he could.

FORT RUCKER, ALABAMA

Bob parked his green, two-door, 1959 Ford Custom 300 on the side of the road by the stage field, then got out and looked at the long row of H-19 helicopters. After the small H-23's he'd been flying, the Sikorsky H-19 seemed enormous. He was particularly looking forward to this phase of his flight training, because as a crew chief he had spent many hours in the H-19.

But beginning Monday, Bob would be flying the H-19 as a pilot. He was not yet a full-fledged, earned-his-wings pilot. But he already had eighty-five hours in the H-23 and was now ready to move, along with the remaining members of his class (now fewer than fifty percent of the starting number) on to advanced training.

The H-19 looked somewhat like a giant tadpole on wheels. It was powered by a huge radial engine that sat at an angle in the nose just below the pilot and copilot's

compartment. It had seats enough in the cargo compartment to carry ten passengers, though Bob knew from experience that it could do so only on cool days, only if all
the passengers were of slightly below normal weight, and
only if the helicopter made a running takeoff.

The lot of the candidates improved somewhat once
they reached Fort Rucker, for here Bob and the other
married candidates were authorized to live off post. Most
of those taking advantage of that privilege had to move
their wives down to Fort Rucker from wherever they had
been during the difficult days of preflight and primary.
Bob had no such problem since Ozark, Alabama, which
billed itself as the "Home of Fort Rucker," was where he
and Marilou had been living. In fact, Bob just returned to
the same house he'd been living in when he left for Fort
Wolters.

Marilou was excited that her husband would soon be
an officer and she could "join all my friends who married
officers at the officers' club." She was about to get a taste
of the social life that would now be hers, for at that very
moment she and Bob were on their way to a special reception for the married candidates and their wives being
given by the commanding officer of the WOC School and
his wife.

Though it was early fall, the Third Army Command
hadn't yet authorized the change into Army greens, so
Bob was still dressed in summer khakis, complete with
long-sleeve shirt and tie. On his left pocket was an orange
patch embroidered with a black silhouette of a helicopter
—the selfsame H-19 Bob was now standing by the side of
the road and looking at.

Marilou, wearing a light-blue silk dress, long white
gloves, and a white hat with a small veil, was impatiently
waiting in the car. When she decided that Bob had been
out of the car too long, she leaned out the window and
asked tartly, "Are you just going to stand there and look at
those things? I don't want to sit here in the car getting all
sweaty."

Bob got back into the car but continued to eye the
helicopters. "Aren't they beautiful, Marilou?"

"They're the same thing you've been flying in all along."

"Yes, but before I was a crew chief. Now I'll be the pilot."

"I liked it better when you were the crew chief."

He turned to look at her. "Why?"

"I don't mind you riding when someone else is flying. Then I don't worry so much."

"Thanks a lot for the vote of confidence," Bob said dryly. "Anyway, I thought you wanted me to be an officer."

"An officer, yes. But why do you have to be a pilot? Couldn't you just get your commission without having to fly?"

"Warrant officers aren't commissioned. They're appointed."

"Commissioned, appointed . . . It doesn't make any difference to me as long as you're an officer."

Marilou had been in her element at the reception: helpful to the other wives—most of whom had absolutely no experience in social activities—charming to the commanding officer, and gracious to his wife.

"You are a lucky young man, Candidate Parker," the CO had told Bob as he had stood nursing his drink and watching Marilou dazzle and charm all the guests. "Your wife seems to know all the social graces. Someone like that is very good for an officer's career."

And she was. The other candidates' wives elected Marilou president of the PHT, or Pushing Hubby Through, Club. They held teas and weekend barbecues and even planned study sessions in which the men would get together and review their classroom work while the wives left them alone except to furnish coffee and sandwiches.

It was all great fun until the last week of the course. One of the candidates was on a solo flight, practicing for his final check ride, when he lost an engine shortly after takeoff. He set up his autorotation, turning the helicopter into the wind, not realizing that his new heading took him right toward the power wires that stretched across the end of the field. The H-19, which was otherwise descending in a perfect autorotation, hit them, then flipped over and crashed upside down. One of the blades swept through the cockpit, killing the pilot instantly.

Anytime a fatal helicopter accident occurred at Fort Rucker, word spread quickly through the base—and because Fort Rucker was an aviation training school, accidents happened with alarming frequency. In fact, even the commanding general had been killed when his helicopter crashed. General Bogardus Cairns had been a very popular general, and the Army had honored his memory by changing the name of Ozark Army Airfield to Cairns Field.

Though everyone learned of any accident quickly, the specifics as to what happened, and more importantly as to who was killed, were normally kept quiet to allow the next of kin to be properly notified. That was supposed to be the humane thing to do, but during such times of uncertainty, everyone on the base, from the general's lady on down to the candidates' wives, were equal in their fear. It could be anyone lying out there in the burning helicopter, and people on the base and in the towns around the base sweated and hoped and prayed while they waited for the news.

Knowing what their wives were going through, the other fliers one by one made phone calls home, assuring their loved ones that they were safe and passing on messages as to who else was safe. Then, because everyone gradually learned who *hadn't* been killed, the process of elimination told them who *had*. So when the olive-green Army staff car stopped in front of number 7 Anne Street in Ozark and three officers got out, Linda Branchfield, who was holding her two-year-old daughter tightly to her, knew exactly why they had come to her house.

After the notification team left, the other wives of the PHT Club came over to offer their help and comfort to the bereaved woman. Marilou Parker was conspicuous by her absence. Several of the wives repeatedly tried to call her but got no answer. Had they been on the other end of the call, they would have seen a house in shadows, darkened by the closure of all the blinds. In the bedroom farthest away from the constantly ringing phone, they would have found Marilou lying in her bed with the sheet pulled up to her chin. As an organizer of parties, as a sparkling hostess and scintillating guest, she was a whiz. But she had just discovered that she was totally unable to deal with this kind of death.

However, by the time the class graduated that Friday afternoon at one, Marilou was fully recovered. She explained to the other wives that she had been in Montgomery on the day of the accident and didn't learn of poor Mrs. Branchfield's plight until it was too late. She did, of course, send a beautiful spray of flowers to the funeral up in Ohio.

The graduating class wore tropical worsteds for the ceremony. The wings were already in place, but the bars were pinned on by wives, girlfriends, or mothers. Bob had Marilou pin one bar on his left shoulder, while his mother pinned the other bar on his right. When he left the graduation hall and stepped out into the bright sunlight, several enlisted men were waiting just outside the door to be the first to salute. Traditionally, the first enlisted man to salute would earn a dollar, which was why so many of them were here. But there was one man, in civilian clothes, whom Bob was particularly happy to see.

"Congratulations, *Mister* Parker, sir!"

"Logan!" Bob said, grinning at his friend. "What are you doing here? I recall you telling me that once you got out of the Army, nothing would bring you back."

"Yeah, well, that's what I intended," Logan Pounders said. "But when I heard you were graduatin' from flight school, I just had to come down here and see if it was true." He laughed. "I guess they'll let just anyone be a warrant officer these days."

"What about you?" Bob asked. "What are you doing now?"

"Nothin' much. I had a job out at the airport for a while, but when the cancer got worse, I had to give it up."

The smile left Bob's face. "How are you doing?"

"Ahh, better some days than others," Logan replied. "I guess you heard about Captain Kilby."

"Yeah, I heard he died last month."

"That's somethin', ain't it?" Logan asked. "I mean Kilby and me both gettin' cancer like that. We were in the same unit." He shrugged. "Hell, maybe there was somethin' in the food at the mess hall or in the water or somethin'."

"Well, I ate the same food and drank the same water as you. And so did a lot of other guys," Bob said.

"I know." Logan sighed. "I guess it's just a coincidence, both of us gettin' cancer and both of us workin' in the same section. I've just been turnin' it over in my mind, is all, tryin' to figure out where it come from. I mean, as far as I know, there ain't no one in my family ever had it before." He chuckled. "It's like winnin' a drawin', ain't it? Only I ain't never won nothin' before. And to tell the truth, I could've passed this by, too."

"Yeah, it's a shame," Bob said self-consciously.

"Hey, but what the hell. I didn't come here to talk about cancer," Logan said, breaking into a big smile. "I came here to help you celebrate your graduation. You are goin' to celebrate, aren't you?"

"You better pluck your magic twanger, Froggie," Bob replied. "We're going to have one hell of a party out at Lake Tholoco. Come along. You'll be my guest."

"I don't know if I can stand bein' around that many officers all at the same time," Logan joked. "But what the hell, I'll give it a try. After all, it ain't likely to make me feel any lousier. . . ."

CHAPTER
SIXTEEN

SUMMER, 1959, FROM "TRAILMARKERS,"
EVENTS MAGAZINE:

MONKEYS IN SPACE

The United States came closer to its goal of putting a man into outer space last Thursday when it launched a rocket carrying two monkeys to a height of 360 miles. The little space travelers were reported to be none the worse for their epic flight.

The simian "crew" was composed of Able, a seven-pound rhesus monkey, and Baker, a one-pound squirrel monkey. They were both heavily wired during their suborbital space flight, thus providing information about the rigors of space flight and their effect on living things.

The National Aeronautics and Space Administration (NASA) said that it will continue to launch such test flights right up until the time the first of

346

its seven "astronauts" flies a mission, now said to be some two years in the future.

FALLOUT SHELTERS ARE BIG BUSINESS

Selling for just over a thousand dollars, fallout shelters are sweeping the country. The shelters are designed to be buried in the backyard, where a family would live for weeks following a nuclear attack.

"These are not blast-proof bomb shelters," a spokesman for the industry explained. "But they will help people survive the radiation carried by wind and fallout after any nuclear attack."

Many have called the fallout shelters exercises in futility, explaining that few people would actually survive an atomic war. However, a spokesman for the State Department disagrees, saying, "Several millions of our citizens will survive the initial explosions of any nuclear attack. It is only prudent then that they have some means of shelter to help them fend off the second wave of nuclear destruction—that of radiation poisoning. These fallout shelters will allow our citizens to exist for many weeks until the immediate danger is passed.

"Contrary to the doom-and-gloom predictions of some people," the spokesman went on, "a nuclear war can be survived if the people are adequately prepared and do what they are told."

MARCELLA MILLS AND BUCK CAMPBELL TO STAR IN NEW MOVIE

Marcella Mills, long regarded as one of Hollywood's biggest sex symbols, and Buck Campbell, heartthrob of millions of female music fans, will soon be working together as well as living together. Shooting is scheduled to begin on their new film about Nashville, Tennessee, called *Music City*, a name by which Nashville is often referred to.

Though married for two years, this will be the

first time the actress and the singer have joined forces professionally. "It's a natural," producer Emmett Avery said. "The only unusual thing about it is that it hasn't happened before now."

Marcella Mills and Buck Campbell have had some rocky times in their marriage, and their stormy relationship has often been the subject of gossip columnists' speculations. Many are now questioning whether their marriage can hold together long enough for *Music City* to be completed.

Producer Avery scoffs at the doubters. "Marcella and Buck are both creative and dynamic people," he said. "Anytime two people with such strong personalities are thrown together, there will be difficulties. However, there is a lot of love between those two—certainly enough to weather the hard times. No one need worry as to whether the picture will be made. It will be made; I personally guarantee it."

BEVERLY HILLS, CALIFORNIA

Leaning forward on the expansive white couch in the living room of the expansive Avery mansion, Marcella scooped some caviar onto a triangle of toast and popped it into her mouth. It had taken her a while to develop a taste for the expensive delicacy, but now she loved it.

"It's very good, isn't it?" a tall, dark, and well-groomed young man in his midtwenties asked.

"Yes," Marcella answered. A few of the tiny black eggs had slipped off the toast onto her finger, and she sucked them off. "I should have eaten lunch. It's ridiculous to try to make a meal of caviar."

The young man smiled. "Why not? You're a movie star, aren't you? If you wanted to, I would think you could eat champagne and caviar for every meal."

"I suppose I could," Marcella agreed. "But if I did

I'd get damn tired of it. And I would hate to tire of champagne and caviar."

"I know what you mean," the young man said. He looked around the crowded room. "I thought this was supposed to be a party for you and Buck. Where is he?"

"Who knows?" Marcella chuckled. "Sometimes I don't even know where he is when he's standing right in front of me."

"Well, I'm glad *you* came, at least. Would you like another glass of champagne?"

Marcella brushed back a lock of pale blond hair with one hand while she held her glass out with the other. "Who are you?" she asked.

"I'm Zach Manley."

"Zach Manley? Should I know you, Zach Manley?"

"There's no reason you should, Miss Mills. So far I've only done a few small roles. But I do have ambition."

"Yes, I'm sure. Everyone out here has ambition." Marcella made a shooing motion with her hand. "Run along, Zach Manley, and get that champagne for me. Or were you only leading me on?"

"No, no, I meant it. Don't go away. I'll be right back."

Marcella watched the darkly handsome young man work his way through the crowd. Then she walked over to look through the enormous picture window at the enormous swimming pool beyond the flagstone patio. Besides the bar in the house, there was another by the pool, and at least three dozen more partygoers were outside. She sensed someone coming toward her, and when she looked around, she saw her producer, Emmett Avery. With his thin, nervous body and beady-eyed, narrow face, he reminded her of a weasel. His reputation corresponded with his appearance.

"Goddammit, where the hell is Buck?" Avery asked, snapping open a gold cigarette case and offering one to Marcella before he took one for himself.

"Who knows?" Marcella replied, giving Avery the same answer she had given the young actor. She put the cigarette in her mouth, then leaned over for a light. "Who ever knows?"

Avery lit Marcella's cigarette, then his own, and he blew out a long puff of smoke before he spoke again. "I thought he was going to be here tonight. The whole idea of the party was to show everyone there were no problems. I don't want our investors worrying about their money. You said you would get him here."

Marcella shook her head. "Uh-uh," she retorted. "I said I would *ask* him to come. More than that I cannot do."

"If that redneck cracker bastard fucks up this deal, I'll run his ass back to Arkansas or Tennessee or wherever the hell he's from, and he'll never work in this town again," Avery growled.

Marcella laughed.

"What's so goddamned funny?"

"You said that like that'd be threatening to him," she replied. "Don't you know there's nothing in the world he'd rather do than go back to where he was four years ago?"

"All right, so he doesn't like the fame. A lot of people don't. But he likes the money, doesn't he?"

Marcella took another puff of the expensive imported cigarette, letting the smoke out audibly before replying, "Not particularly."

"We're bound to have *some* hold on him, some way of making him toe the line. Maybe you can—"

Marcella laughed again. "I'm afraid I can't help you there, either. Half the nights he doesn't even bother to come home, and most of the time when he does, I don't even know it because he doesn't come up to the bedroom. The only way I know he spent the night at our house at all is if I find him down in the living room or the den asleep in front of the TV."

"I thought you two were Hollywood's most sensuous couple," Avery said.

"I'm afraid you've been reading the shit put out by your own publicity department. We haven't slept together in over a year."

"How do you stand it, living like that?"

Spotting Zach returning with her champagne, Marcella smiled provocatively. "I have my little diversions," she answered.

Avery followed Marcella's gaze and frowned. Then he raised his finger in warning. "You be very careful, do you hear me? I don't want this picture scuttled by some scandal."

"Oh, don't you worry about me, darling. I'll be good," Marcella purred. "I've always been . . . good."

FLAGSTAFF, ARIZONA

The ten-year-old Ford pickup truck had been red at one time, though the sun had long ago faded it to a rather dingy brown. It was grimy and dust-covered, and the windshield was so dirty that only the swaths made by the wipers allowed Buck Campbell to see out.

The fact that the truck was old and dirty belied what was under the hood. Buck had put in a souped-up '57 Cadillac V-8 engine, making the truck capable of doing 120 miles per hour—a shock to anyone who, impatient at being behind an old truck, would try to pass.

Buck had bought the pickup for two reasons. The first was that he liked it, liked the feeling of driving around in an old truck. It helped put a wall between himself and all the phony people he came in contact with in Hollywood. They were the ones who drove Cadillacs, Lincolns, Imperials, Mercedes-Benzes, and even Rolls-Royces. They wore flashy jewelry and expensive suits and ten-dollar haircuts. They spouted words like "fabulous" and "marvelous" and "wonderful" and didn't mean any of them.

The other reason he drove the truck was for the anonymity it bestowed. By now Buck's face had been in hundreds of magazines, and he had been a guest star on dozens of TV variety shows. He had even made one movie and was about to make another one—with his equally famous wife—but because no one would ever expect to see someone like him driving an old truck, no one ever recognized him.

Occasionally he'd stick a rifle behind the seat, throw camping gear in the bed, and drive off on an impromptu hunting trip, sometimes being gone for up to a week without contacting anyone. At other times he'd drive off with no particular destination in mind. Like now.

Buck knew that Emmett Avery was hosting a gala party tonight, and he knew, too, that he was expected to be there, smiling and shaking hands and talking to people as if he really cared what any of them said. But there was no way he could go through all that, so the day before he had stuffed a couple of extra jeans, shirts, and undershorts into a canvas bag, then tossed that and a bedroll into the back of the truck and taken off.

He had spent last night in the desert, under the stars. Tonight, he decided, he'd get himself a motel room, and as he came into Flagstaff on Route 66, he figured this town would be as good a place to stay as any. Before he got a room, though, he decided that he might as well eat, maybe even get a beer or two. He pulled into the parking lot in front of a roadhouse, then got out. When he slammed the door, a solid sheet of dirt slid off, and when he patted himself down, he raised a cloud of dust.

It was cold—not frigid, but cold enough that the denim jacket he was wearing felt good. He walked across the gravel parking lot, then up on the porch. Music was coming from inside, and he knew instantly that it was live music. He pulled open the door, and the music seemed to rush up to meet him.

The good-sized room was lighted only by the spotlights on the stage. A hundred or more customers were sitting at tables in the dark, some drinking, many smoking, a few talking quietly, but most listening to the music. Buck didn't know the artists—but he sure knew the art. He had done this same thing for years, and he felt a strange, emotional pull toward the stage. He found himself wishing he could trade places with the lead singer. Let the lead singer be Buck Campbell, and he, Buck would be— Well, he didn't know who the singer was.

He grabbed an empty table near the stage and sat down. "Excuse me, miss," he said to a passing waitress, "who's that fella singin'?"

"That's Tommy Lomax. He's real good, ain't he?" the waitress answered.

"Yes, he is."

"Can I get you somethin'?"

"A beer," Buck said. "And can I get anythin' to eat?"

"Sure, what do you want?"

"Bacon and scrambled eggs, I guess. And some fried potatoes would be good." He grinned. "Hope your cook don't mind whippin' up breakfast at night."

She grinned back. "Comin' right up."

Buck ate his supper and drank the beer. In fact, he drank five more beers as he sat there in the dark, listening to the band play. Finally the lights came on again, and the customers began filing out of the place. Buck stayed at his table, watching as the band put their instruments away.

"Good set," he said to them.

"Thanks," Tommy Lomax replied. He looked at Buck curiously. "Do I know you, mister?"

Buck shook his head. "Don't think so."

"Are you a musician?"

"I pick a little."

"Are you any good?"

"Not bad."

"I need another guitarist. Our lead guitarist up and quit on us last night. We got by tonight with a few chords, but we won't be able to get away with that long."

"Now't you mention it, I did notice you was a mite thin in a few places," Buck said, smiling.

Tommy picked up a guitar and took it out to Buck's table. "Let me hear somethin'," he said, holding out the instrument.

Buck took the guitar and for a few moments just ran his fingers lightly across the strings. He was actually an accomplished guitarist, though, of course, what he was known for was his rumbling voice and his distinctive singing style.

His fingers suddenly exploded across the strings. The

guitar that had produced simple accompaniment for country-and-western music suddenly rang with a Spanish classical-style chord progression and an intricate melody. It filled the room with its power and drive, and the waitresses who were bussing tables stopped to listen. The doors to the kitchen opened, and the kitchen employees came out to hear as well. Even the jaded-looking bartender whose face declared that he had heard it all stopped wiping off the counter and listened intently. From a hall that led to back-room offices, the owner of the roadhouse, a half-smoked cigar protruding from the corner of his mouth, also came to explore the source of the music. Finally Buck brought the piece to a fiery crescendo, but even after the strings were silent, the last chord seemed to echo and reecho from the far corners of the room. He handed the guitar back.

"Yeah!" Tommy Lomax said in quiet awe. "I guess you can play the guitar. Would you like a job?"

Buck stared at Tommy for a long time before he finally sighed and shook his head. "Mr. Lomax, you have no idea how tempting your generous offer is. But I guess I'll decline. Thanks, anyway."

Spotting a phone booth over against the wall, he walked over to it and dialed the operator. When she came on, he put through a collect call to his home.

Bells! I'm hearing bells! Marcella thought. Zach's lovemaking had lifted her to the heights of ecstasy, and she was not only feeling orgasmic explosions all through her body, she was also hearing bells.

Goddammit, I really am *hearing bells!*

"Oh, shit!" she muttered, when she realized that the telephone beside the bed was ringing. She reached for it, knocked it onto the floor with a clatter, then picked it up again. "This had better be damned important!" she snarled.

A woman's voice came over the line. "I have a collect call for anyone at this number from Buck. Will you accept the charges?"

"For anyone at this number?" Marcella asked.

"Yes, ma'am. Will you accept the charges?"

Marcella looked over at Zach, who, when she reached for the phone, had rolled off her. He was lying on his back now, still breathing heavily, as he coasted down from his own completion. She chuckled. For a moment, she considered handing the phone to her young lover. But she resisted the urge.

"Yes," she finally said. "Yes, I'll accept the charges."

"Go ahead, sir," the operator said.

"Well, don't do me any goddamn favors by acceptin' the goddamn call," Buck's voice growled.

"Where the hell are you?"

"Flagstaff. It's in Arizona."

"I know where the fuck it is. The question is, why are you there? You know Emmett had a party for us tonight."

"Then you just answered your own question," Buck said. "That's why I'm here."

Marcella sighed. "You're impossible, do you know that?"

"Listen, you tell Emmett his movie is safe. That's why I'm callin'. To tell you I'm not runnin' out or nothin'. It's just that—well, hell, you know how I am about bein' around all them phony-assed people. I don't like that partyin' shit, is all. I'll work my ass off for him, but I won't go to any parties."

"I don't know if that will do any good or not," Marcella said. "He may decide that he can't depend on you. He may decide to drop the whole project."

"Whatever," Buck said. "It don't make a shit o' difference to me."

"No, I guess it *don't*," Marcella said, purposely repeating his grammatical error—even though she knew it would be lost on him. "Are you coming back home anytime soon?"

"Not tonight, for sure." Buck chuckled. "Guess that means that you won't have to send whoever you got with you home."

"Do you really think you being here would make any difference about that?" Marcella asked coldly.

"No, I don't reckon it would," Buck admitted.

"Good night, Buck. I hope you're enjoying yourself." She reached over and let her hand slide down Zach's naked body until it rested on his inert penis. When she began playing with it, she felt its reawakening tremors. "I know I am."

Buck hung the phone up, then started back to his table. The waitress who had waited on him was watching him. He had flirted with her a few times during the night, and she had seemed receptive. He had noticed also that she was the most rapturously attentive member of his audience during his impromptu guitar playing.

"Tell me, darlin'," he said in his rumblin' voice, standing closer to her than convention would dictate, "do you have any idea where a fella could sleep warm tonight?"

"Has anyone ever told you you look and sound just like Buck Campbell?" the girl asked.

"I *am* Buck Campbell."

"Of course you are. And I'm Marilyn Monroe."

"If I was Buck Campbell, could I find a place to sleep warm tonight?"

"Depends on what you mean by sleepin' warm," the girl replied, closing the small gap between them even more. "A blanket and a feather bed will keep you warm."

"Uh-huh," Buck said. "And so will a woman."

"You ain't really Buck Campbell," the woman said.

"How do you know?"

"I looked out in the parkin' lot. There ain't but three cars and a couple of pickup trucks left out there now. There sure ain't no Cadillacs or nothin' like Buck Campbell would be drivin'."

"All right, so you learned my secret. Sometimes I just pretend."

"Still, you look and sound just like him." The girl

brushed back her long brown hair. "I ain't never done nothin' like this before, you know."

"No, I don't reckon you have," Buck said easily. "I mean, hell, I can look at you and see you ain't that kind of girl."

"I can't believe I'm doin' it now. It's just that you look so much like him. And you sound so much like him."

"Darlin', you ain't said yet what you're plannin' on doin'," Buck rumbled.

The girl grinned coquettishly. "Why, I plan to sleep with you, if you want me."

"When?"

"I get off in fifteen more minutes."

"What's your name, darlin'?"

"Rodale."

"Rodale, if you don't feel right about this, why, I reckon I could go on."

"No!" she said sharply. "No, you just wait right here for me." She laughed and brushed her body against his. "This may be the closest I'll ever come to sleepin' with Buck Campbell. If you turn me down now after gettin' me all worked up, why, I'd just die."

Buck smiled. "Well, now, we can't be lettin' you die, can we, darlin'?"

IN TENNESSEE, NEAR FORT CAMPBELL, KENTUCKY

The dials on the instrument panel glowed a soft red, providing enough illumination to be read but not enough to disturb Bob Parker's night vision. Though it was cold outside, the exhaust heater circulated sufficient warm air in the cockpit and down into the box to keep the H-34 warm. Still, the flight jacket did feel good.

Bob was in the left seat. The right seat, that of the pilot-in-command, was occupied by CW-2 Jim White. They had flown to Nashville and were now returning to Fort Campbell.

White was doing the actual flying, leaving Bob to

spend most of his time enjoying the view. Twenty-five hundred feet below, the Cumberland River gleamed a soft gold in the moonlight. Here and there on the dark horizon twinkled lights from farmhouses, and on the highways cars seemed to be crawling slowly behind their tiny swaths of light.

White was a country music fan, and he had the DF station tuned to WSM in Nashville. The song they were listening to was "Gone" by Ferlin Husky, which was enough of a crossover song that even Bob could enjoy it.

"I wish they'd quit playing all this popular horseshit and get back to the real shit-kicking music," White grumbled.

"You don't like this?"

"Hell, no. I like music about cheatin' women, trains, whiskey, and cigarettes. Things shit-kicking music is supposed to be about."

Bob laughed.

"You flown the Huey yet?" White asked.

"I got an orientation ride in one down at Rucker."

"How'd you like it?"

"Fantastic. Thirteen hundred horsepower from a five-hundred-pound engine. You can't overload the damn thing. If you tied it down, the engine and transmission would just pull itself out of the ship."

"We're supposed to be getting them this summer," White said. "I can hardly wait."

"Yeah, I'm looking forward to it, too. But the H-34 is a good ship."

"Yeah, it is," White said. "It's a hell of a lot better than the H-19. As a matter of fact, I heard that the Marines are sticking with the H-34. They aren't even going to the Huey."

"Yeah, that's what I heard, too."

They fell silent again for a while, then White asked, "How's your writing coming along?"

Bob smiled. It was no secret among his friends that he wanted to write a book, and he spent at least a couple of hours every evening, plus the entire weekend, at his typewriter.

"I haven't sold anything yet," he replied. "But I have received a couple of good rejection letters."

White laughed. "How can a rejection letter be good?"

"Well, it's good if they actually take the time to comment on your book, not just send a preprinted rejection form. And if you get a real editor's name at the bottom of the letter, not just 'The Editors.' "

"What are you working on now?"

"A story about a guy who flies helicopters for an off-shore oil-drilling company in Louisiana."

"Is the pilot in your book getting a lot of pussy?" White asked.

"It's not that kind of book."

"Why not? Don't you want it to sell?" White abruptly pointed to the radio. "Give 'em a call."

Bob looked down to see that they were now passing over the officers' quarters area of Fort Campbell. He keyed the microphone, and when he did, the music was automatically cut out.

"Campbell Army Airfield, this is Army five-one-five, one mile east for landing."

Army five-one-five, winds are calm, clear to land on runway twenty-seven.

"Request hover approach directly to the One Hundred First Battalion apron."

Request approved.

"Army five-one-five."

White descended to the designated area, hovered over to the pad, then set the H-34 down and waited for their crew chief to position them. The crew chief signaled, White cut the engine, and Bob flipped off all the switches. Bob took off his helmet and listened to the sound of the rotor coasting down and the descending hum of the gyros.

"You want to stop by the Pill Box for a couple of beers?" White invited as he began filling out the flight log.

The Pill Box was a small officers' club annex in the hospital area, frequented by pilots because it was so handy to the airfield. The main officers' club, on the other hand, was all the way across the base.

"No, thanks," Bob said. "I'm going to try and get a few pages written tonight."

White chuckled. "Remember what I said: If you want to sell the book, you'd better let your hero get some pussy. Lots of it."

It was nearly nine o'clock when Bob reached his house on Werner Drive. So many cars were there that he couldn't park in his own driveway and had to park down the street. As he walked up to his house he could hear music from the show *No Strings* blasting from the hi-fi inside. Except for candles, it was dark, and the house smelled of incense.

A small, pale man was heading from the kitchen to the living room, carrying a tray of freshly baked brownies. "Hi," he said. "Welcome to the lair. Everyone else is in the living room. Come on in."

Bob, who was wearing a flight jacket over his one-piece gray flight suit, took off the jacket and hung it in the closet just inside the door. When he stepped into the living room, he saw nearly a dozen young men sitting on the floor or leaning against the walls or furniture. As usual, no one was bothering to sit in a chair or on the sofa.

Marilou, who was wearing a bulky sweater and tights, was sitting cross-legged in the middle of the floor, arms folded across her chest, eyes closed, cheeks puffed out.

"Marilou, Bob is here," one of the young men said. Though Bob didn't know many of them, he knew this one. Paul Rosen was a specialist-five who worked in the post library. He was also president of the Fort Campbell Little Theater Group. Most of the men here were members of the Little Theater Group.

Marilou opened her eyes, then held up a finger, telling Bob to wait for a moment.

"What the hell is going on?" he asked Paul.

"Marilou is trying to establish contact with her spirit guide," Paul explained.

"How, by holding her breath until she dies?"

A few of the others laughed nervously.

Bob turned the record player down and the lights up.

"Hey, don't do that!" someone yelled.

"You want to listen to loud music in the dark, go back to the barracks," Bob said. "In my house, when I come home, I like to see what's going on, and I like to hear myself think."

Marilou opened her eyes, then let her breath out in one expulsive gasp. "Bob!" she chastised. "You're frightening them."

"I'm frightening them? What, a bunch of purple goddamn vapors? What the hell have they got to be scared of?"

"What's the matter, didn't your flight go well?" Paul asked. He looked at the others, some of whom really did look frightened, and assured them, "Never mind him, fellows, his bark is much worse than his bite."

In fact, Bob did rather like Paul. He had a biting sense of humor that Bob found funny.

"There wasn't much flying," Bob said. "It was mostly riding. Mr. White was the pilot."

"Ah, so that's the trouble. He wouldn't let you drive. Well, never mind. Why don't you just go back into your closet and write your great American novel? Have you eaten yet? I'll bring your supper."

"Paul made a nice quiche," Marilou said.

"Quiche?"

"You'll love it," Paul insisted.

"Uh, Paul," one of the others said nervously. "There isn't any left."

"Yes, there is; I made sure there was one piece left."

"I didn't know we were saving it. I gave it to Tony. He had to leave to go on guard duty, and he hadn't eaten yet."

"Oh, dear me," Paul said. He put his finger on his chin. "I guess we don't have any quiche after all."

"That's all right," Bob said, actually glad there wasn't

any. It sounded suspect. "We have any bologna? I'll make myself a sandwich."

"No, no," Paul said quickly, "you need to get started writing. I'll make your sandwich. How do you want it?"

"Fry the bologna. Mustard and onion."

"And a cold beer," Paul added. "I'll bring it right to you."

"Okay, you're on," Bob said and headed up the hall.

When Paul told Bob to go to his closet and write, he wasn't being facetious. Bob really did write in what was supposed to be a walk-in closet at the end of the hall. Here he could shut the door, turn on the overhead light, and retreat into his own world.

Entering his tiny "studio" and pulling the door closed, he turned on the small electric Smith-Corona, then rolled two sheets of white paper into it. To the right of the typewriter stood a stack of typed manuscript, 112 pages high. On page 111 Bob had left one of his characters trapped under a pile of logs in a backwater bay. When the tide came in, the water would go over the character's head unless the hero, a helicopter pilot named Jim, could get him out of the jam. At the bottom of page 112 Jim had just decided to hook up his sling attachment to the logs and, using the water to help him, pull them away. Bob had purposely stopped at this point yesterday to pick up the thread of the story today.

> Running back to the helicopter, Jim started it and was quickly hovering over the pier. Burt had already wrapped the cable around the main group of logs and now stood on top of the dam, waiting to engage the cable with the lifting hook of the helicopter.
>
> Jim brought the ship down directly above Burt, who signaled through Laura which way the ship had to move so that contact could be made. Finally the cable was hooked up, and he gave the signal for the chopper to start back. Laura pointed into the air, and Jim increased the power until the torque was near the maximum.

*The RPM started bleeding off, but Jim stayed
with it until the ship developed a severe wobble
and he could feel that he was about to lose it.*

"He's going to crash!" Laura screamed.

*Jim dropped the cable. The load on the rotor
system relaxed, and the ship shot straight up about
150 feet. Stabilizing the controls, Jim made a circle
around the area and moved back into position over
the logjam. He hooked up again and began the process all over, staying with it this time until one of
the logs loosened, then another, and another still.*

Hugh was free.

It was nearly midnight when Bob took the last page
from the typewriter and laid it on top of the growing pile.
He was now 120 pages into the story and felt that it was
going pretty well. He reached around to rub the back of
his neck, and it wasn't until then that he realized that the
music and the talking and the laughter had all stopped. At
almost the same moment the closet door opened and
Marilou stood there. She was naked.

"They're gone," she said.

"I would hope so."

"Are you ready to go to bed?"

Bob smiled. "Is that an invitation?"

"About as blatant as I can get."

"Yeah, I'm ready."

Bob worked his way out of his cramped writing
closet and followed Marilou into their bedroom. They still
had no children, though it wasn't for lack of trying.

"Did you rehearse your parts or plan your play or do
whatever it is you do when they're all over here?" Bob
asked.

"They were just over here to relax and have a good
time," Marilou said.

"Marilou, I don't mean to cast aspersions on your
friends, but if I didn't know better, I'd think they were
fruits."

Marilou giggled. "Silly."

"No, I'm serious. Haven't you ever noticed how they

just sort of float around? And none of them has a girl-friend—at least, not that I've ever seen."

"You're serious, aren't you?"

"You're damned right, I'm serious."

"No, I mean, you're serious that you don't know."

"Don't know what?"

"Of course they're homosexual," Marilou said. "Every one of them."

"They can't be queer, Marilou, or they wouldn't be in the Army."

"Bob, I swear, sometimes you are so naive."

Bob stopped in his tracks. "Wait a minute. You mean all of them? Paul, too?"

"Paul is the queen bee of the whole bunch. The others just adore him."

"Why do they hang out over here all the time?"

"Paul explained it to me. For some reason there are some women to whom homosexuals are attracted. Judy Garland, for example."

"Queers like Judy Garland?"

"Of course they do. Why do you think we had such a crowd to watch *The Wizard of Oz*? Anyway, don't call them queers. Call them—"

"Purple vapors."

Marilou laughed. "They actually got quite a kick out of that. They talked about it after you left."

"You were about to tell me why they all congregate over here," he reminded her.

"Paul said I'm one of those kind of women who attract homosexuals," Marilou said. "I'm really quite flattered."

"Yeah? Well, tell them to get their own damned women."

"Bob, you're jealous!" Marilou laughed. "I can't believe you're really jealous of homosexuals."

"It's not that I'm jealous; it's just that I don't like having a houseful all the time. Anyway, what do you get out of it?"

Marilou pressed her naked body against Bob, then stuck her hand down inside his trousers.

"Darling, it's not what I get out of it. It's what *you* get out of it," she said, kissing and fondling him at the same time.

"What I—uhmm." When he could talk again, he said, "What do you mean, what I get out of it?"

"Well, when I see all those nice-looking young men I can have all sorts of thoughts about them—and it's safe because I know they aren't interested in me sexually. And the more I think about it, the more sexually aroused I become, until by the time they leave I'm ready to climb the walls. And, my dear husband, you are the only man around who can actually do anything about it. Do you understand?"

"It's convoluted logic, but I suppose I do."

"Well, are we going to bed? Or are we going to do it standing right here in the doorway?" Marilou asked, lifting one leg and wrapping it around him.

Afterward, as Marilou smoked a cigarette, Bob told her about the pages he had written. "I think it was a really good scene." He laughed. "But Jim White thinks that if I want to sell it, I'm going to have to let my hero get a lot of pussy."

"Well, why not? *You* just did," Marilou snickered. "Oh, that reminds me, I almost forgot. You got a letter from Saber Books today."

"A letter?"

"Yes."

Bob sat up in bed. "Wait a minute, Marilou. Are you saying a letter and not a package?"

"No, it was a letter."

"Damn! They normally send the rejection letter with the manuscript."

"Maybe you didn't send the return postage," Marilou suggested.

"I always send return postage. Where is it?"

"In the living room on the TV."

Bob went to get the letter, but he didn't open it until he returned to bed. Switching on the lamp on the night table, he held the envelope in his hands for a long time, looking at the elegant typeface of his name and address. Then he ran a finger over the raised black lettering of the return address, almost caressing it. The envelope was buff-colored and had a luxurious feel to it. He was quite sure he had never received a nicer piece of mail.

"Well, aren't you going to open it?" Marilou asked.

"Yeah," Bob said. He tore the end off, then took out the page.

Dear Mr. Parker:

We have read your ms *Lilies Are for Dying* and feel that we would like to publish it, providing you agree to our terms. We would like to change the title to *Nude, Ready, and Willing.*

We admit that your title is more thematic than ours, but we must consider the marketability of the product, and our title, we feel, will have a broader appeal.

There are also a few changes that we would like to suggest—perhaps strengthening the eroticism of a few scenes and adding a few additional erotic scenes. On the whole, however, we feel that your book will fit our needs perfectly.

We are prepared to offer you an advance of R250 for your book, against a royalty of one cent per copy sold. If these terms are agreeable, please notify us of your acceptance at the earliest, and we will send you the contract.

Congratulations.

Sincerely,
Marie Adams, Editor

"Marilou!" Bob shouted excitedly. "I sold a book!"

FALL 1959, ABOARD THE KENNEDY AIRPLANE

Although the campaign for president had not yet officially begun, Senator John Fitzgerald Kennedy was crisscrossing the nation, accepting invitations to speak "anywhere," John Canfield had said almost blasphemously, "where two or three are gathered in his name."

This evening he had spoken at a farmers' recognition banquet in Iowa, having in fact manipulated the invitation because his handlers had convinced him that he would need to reach out to farmers. John Canfield had also attended the recognition dinner, at Kennedy's invitation, and was flying back to Hyannisport, Massachusetts, with him.

It was dark outside, and as the twin-engined Martin slipped through the night sky, the stewardess moved down the aisle, pushing a cart bearing a large, steaming tureen of tomato soup.

"Thank you," Kennedy said as she ladled some into a bowl for him. "And would we, uh, happen to have any sour cream?"

Bobby Kennedy turned in his seat. "Oh, do you mean it was *supposed* to be sour?" he joked. "I threw it out."

The others laughed.

"Senator, how long have I been a part of this crew?" the stewardess asked. "Do you think I would attempt to serve you tomato soup without sour cream?" She reached under the cart and brought out a small container, which she handed to the senator.

"Ah, thank you, Susan," Kennedy said. "Thank you very much."

She served the others, and for several minutes everyone was quiet as they ate. The only sound was the subdued roar of the plane's two large engines. Through the black windows a lightning storm flashed across the distant sky, lighting up the horizon in bursts of brilliance that lasted for a millisecond and then disappeared. The airplane dipped and rolled as it plowed through the sea of turbulent air. Everyone finished their soup in a hurry.

Kennedy turned his chair away from the window so that he was facing toward the aisle. John Canfield was just across the aisle from him.

"So," Kennedy asked, "how do you think it went tonight?"

"It went well," John replied.

"You certainly were a big hit. With your agriculture background, they all respected you."

John chuckled. "I just represent a large market for their product. Canfield-Puritex is the largest single buyer of corn products in the U.S."

"I'm glad you don't have presidential fever," Kennedy said, flashing a grin. "I'd hate to take you on in the Corn Belt."

"Who are you kidding, Jack? I have a feeling you'd be willing to take on anyone, anytime, anywhere."

Kennedy laughed. "I do like a good fight," he admitted. The plane bounced again, and he lifted his knee up under his chin, put his heel on the edge of his seat, and wrapped his arms around his leg to brace himself. "What about Stuart? Is he going to fight me? Turn around here, Bobby, and get in on this," he added.

The airplane had been designed to allow the seats to swivel, affording conversational groups, and Bobby now took advantage of that capability.

"Our people tell us that Stu Symington is going to get into the race," he said.

"In the primaries?" John asked. He shook his head. "No, I don't think so. Your fight in the primaries is going to come principally from Humphrey."

"I don't think Hubert can raise enough money to fight us in every primary," Bobby suggested.

"No, but he'll fight you in a couple of key states and at least one that he can win. He'll take you on in one where you're sure to win but in which he'll hope to scar you and one that could go either way."

"We have to give him credit," Jack Kennedy said. "If

he can't contest them all, that's the best way to go. Of course, there's Lyndon to worry about, too."

"How formidable is Johnson?" Bobby asked.

"He's going to be tough," John replied. "Johnson has twenty years of political debts owed to him, and he'll be calling in every one."

"And what will Stuart do?"

"Well, Senator Symington has Missouri, of course."

"*Et tu?*" Senator Kennedy asked.

John chuckled. "No, he doesn't have me. Don't get me wrong, Jack, Symington is a good man, and, if it came to it, I think he'd be a good president. He has been very good for Missouri. And, of course, he has Truman solidly in his camp."

"And Clark Clifford," Kennedy added.

"Yes, and Clark Clifford. And Clifford is no lightweight. But I don't think Symington has enough national appeal to get the nomination, and if he *did* get it, I don't think he'd win in the general election. That would just give the election to Nixon, and that I am not prepared to do. You've got my support, Jack."

"I appreciate that, John," Kennedy said. "I just hope it doesn't put you in too bad with your home state crowd."

"That brings up a point," Bobby said. "That is, if you don't take offense at my asking."

"Ask."

"Suppose the Symington forces put up a big battle, and you come down solidly in our camp. Won't that be detrimental for you in Missouri? What I'm saying is, even if we win, how much help could you be for us in Missouri if you're ostracized for not supporting the favorite son?"

"That's a good question," John said. "But the truth is, I would be of some value to the Symington campaign precisely because I *am* in your camp."

"I don't understand," Jack said.

"Look at it this way. There's you, Humphrey, and Johnson—not to mention Stevenson still hoping for a shot. Every one of you has a broader national base than Senator Symington, so there's no way he could take any of you on head-to-head. His only hope is to be a compromise candidate."

"You mean let us all knock each other off, then come in and pick up the pieces?" Bobby asked.

"Well, I think they'd rather use the term 'patch things up' than 'pick up the pieces,'" John said. "In order for that to work, he's going to have to be the second choice of everyone. Humphrey's people will want Humphrey first, Symington second. Your people will want you first, Symington second. Johnson and Stevenson the same thing. Therefore, he can't afford to make any of you angry —and so he won't be upset that I'm in your camp. And, again, if your campaign loses momentum, he would hope to be the beneficiary of the fallout. Then my being here would be an asset to him."

"Would you support him?" Bobby asked.

"Yes," John answered. "I believe I would." He smiled. "But I really think that's a moot point. We aren't going to have to go to our second choice. Jack will be the Democratic nominee."

"And then the fight will really begin," Bobby said.

"Which means I need my rest," Kennedy said. "So if you gentlemen will excuse me?" He reached up and flipped off the overhead light, then turned his seat back around.

Someone came up to Bobby with a question, and, excusing himself, Bobby turned his attention to the questioner.

Like Jack Kennedy, John turned off his overhead light, then leaned back in his chair and looked out the window. The thunderstorm the plane had skirted a short while earlier was now so far behind them that the lightning was little more than beautiful rose-colored flashes flickering on and off in the distance.

John's thoughts segued from the distance of space to the distance of time and how, almost thirty years earlier, when just twenty-five, he had helped Franklin Roosevelt win the office of president of the United States. He had been extremely active in that campaign, moving to Washington to devote full time to the effort. Now his business and obligations made that kind of commitment no longer feasible, though he would offer Kennedy whatever help he could within those restrictions. He had a feeling, though, that Kennedy wouldn't need too much outside help. Jack Kennedy had youth, vitality, money, and family.

John looked at the senator's reflection superimposed on his own window. There was no doubt in his mind: In every way, John Fitzgerald Kennedy would be the man of the sixties.

ABOUT THE AUTHOR

Writing under his own name and 25 pen names, ROBERT VAUGHAN has authored over 200 books in every genre but Science Fiction. He won the 1977 Porgie Award (Best Paperback Original) for *The Power and the Pride*. In 1973 *The Valkyrie Mandate* was nominated by its publisher, Simon & Schuster, for the Pulitzer Prize.

Vaughan is a retired Army Warrant Officer (CW-3) with three tours in Vietnam, where he was awarded the Distinguished Flying Cross, the Air Medal with the V for valor, the Bronze Star, the Distinguished Service Medal, and the Purple Heart. During his military career, Vaughan was a participant in many of the 20th century's most significant events. For example, he served in Korea immediately after the armistice, he was involved in the Nevada Atomic Bomb tests, he was part of the operation which ensured that James Meredith could attend the University of Mississippi, he was alerted for the Cuban Missile Crisis, and he served three years in Europe.

THE AMERICAN CHRONICLES
by Robert Vaughan

In this magnificent saga, award-winning author Robert Vaughan tells the riveting story of America's golden age: a century of achievement and adventure in which a young nation ascends to world power.

From the author of *The North and South Trilogy*—a
magnificent story as only John Jakes can tell it—and
an unforgettable new family to stand beside the
Kents, the Mains, and the Hazards....

John Jakes

HOMELAND

First of a new series!

As America hurtles through the final explosive events of the
nineteenth century, a young German immigrant named
Pauli Kroner is about to realize his dream: He will taste a life
of privilege in the Chicago mansion of his uncle, Joe Crown,
head of a brewery dynasty. Here he will become Paul Crown,
a bold, ambitious man driven by a powerful vision. His rise
from penniless newcomer to pioneer newsreel cameraman
will span a tumultuous decade of strikes, war, family scandal, and heartbreak in the country he has chosen as his...

"Pick up *Homeland* and read a couple of chapters and
you'll very soon discover why John Jakes sells a lot of
books. He is, quite simply, a master of the ancient art of
storytelling."—*The New York Times Book Review*